tioner and Her Way of Life

ORIGINAL STORY: Mato Sato
ART: Ryo Mitsuya
CHARACTER DESIGN: nilitsu

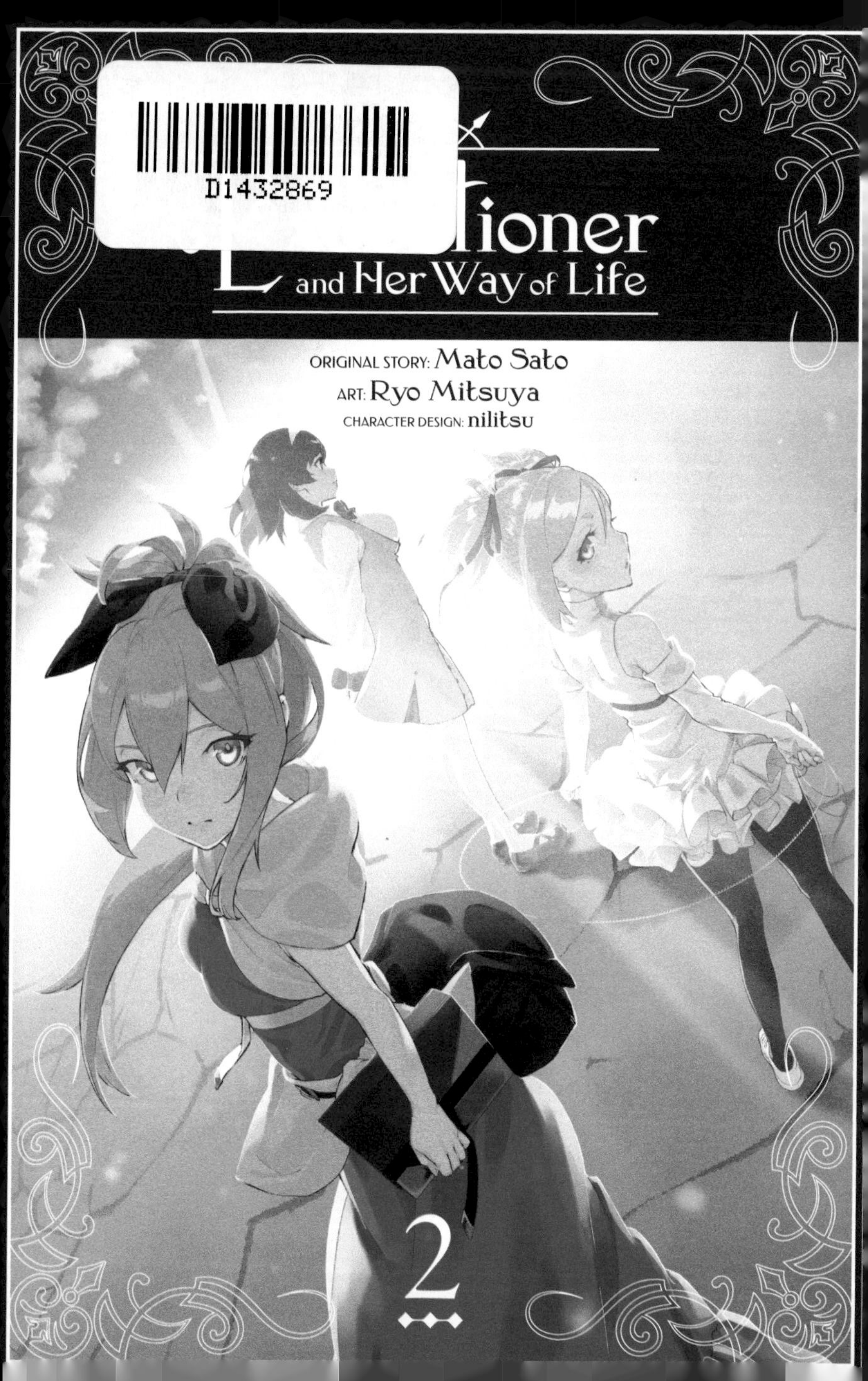

2

The
Executioner
and Her Way of Life

◆◆◆ — CHAPTER 7: Berserker ——————————— 003

◆◆◆ — CHAPTER 8: Final Strike ——————————— 025

◆◆◆ — CHAPTER 9: Pure Trust ——————————— 047

◆◆◆ — CHAPTER 10: The Will to Walk On ——————— 069

◆◆◆ — CHAPTER 11: Ancient Capital Garm ————— 097

◆◆◆ — CHAPTER 12: Guiding Figure ——————————— 119

◆◆◆ — CHAPTER 13: Cries for Help ——————————— 143

◆◆◆ — INTERLUDE: Prelude to a Journey ——————— 186

CONTENTS

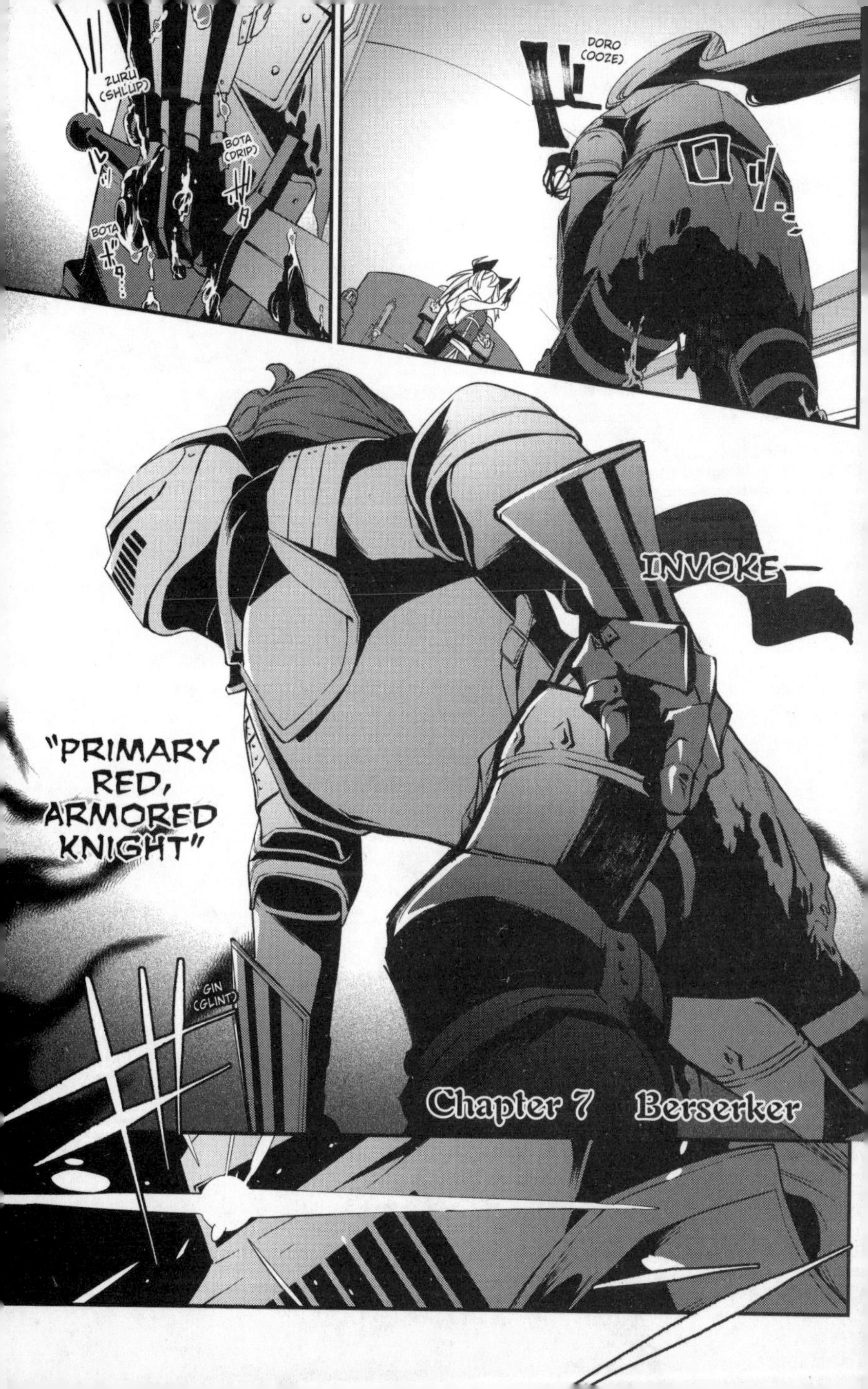
DORO (OOZE)
ZURU (SHLUP)
BOTA (DRIP)
BOTA
INVOKE—
"PRIMARY RED, ARMORED KNIGHT"
GIN (GLINT)
Chapter 7 Berserker

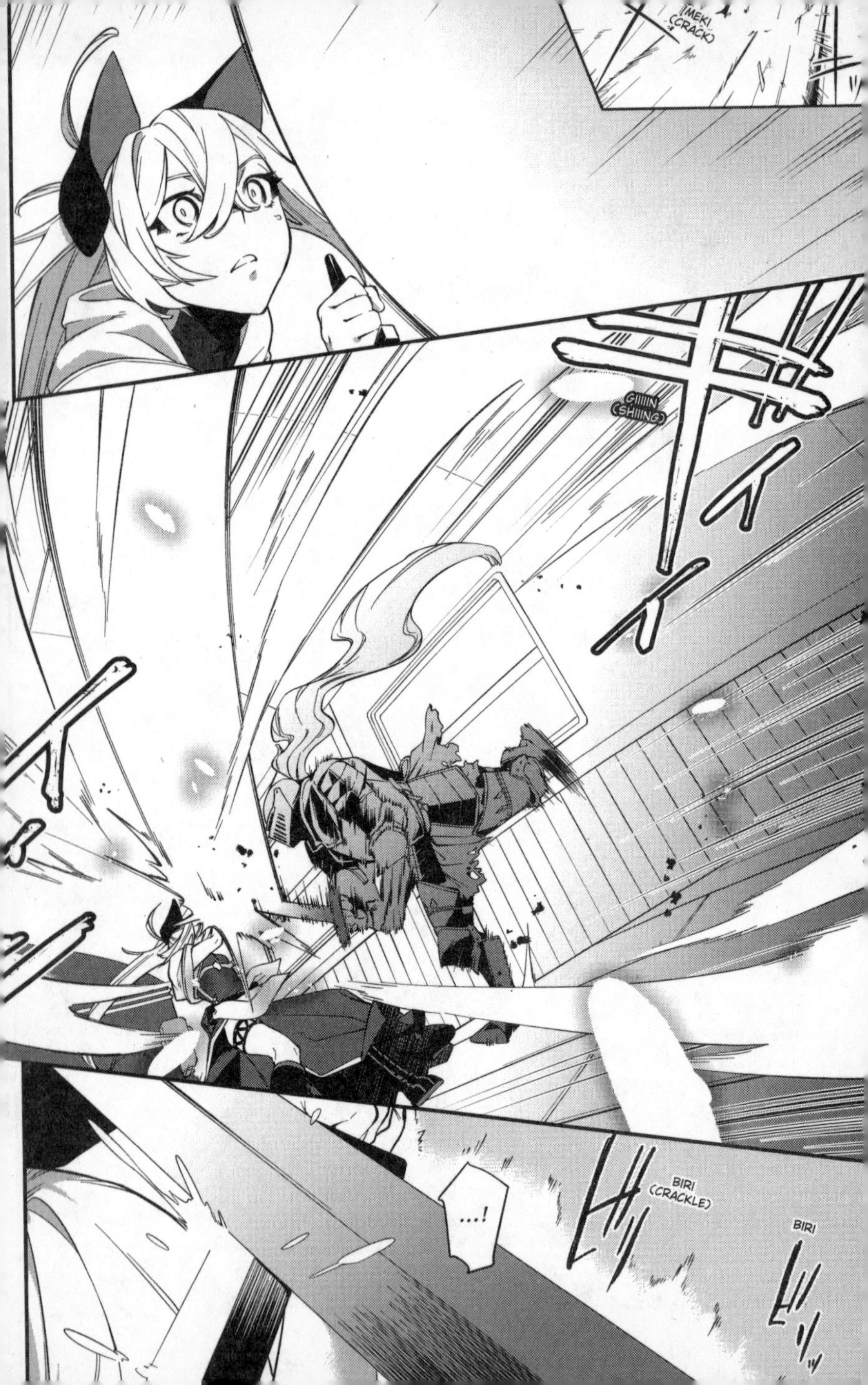
MEKI (CRACK)
GIIIIN (SHIIING)
BIRI (CRACKLE)
BIRI
...!

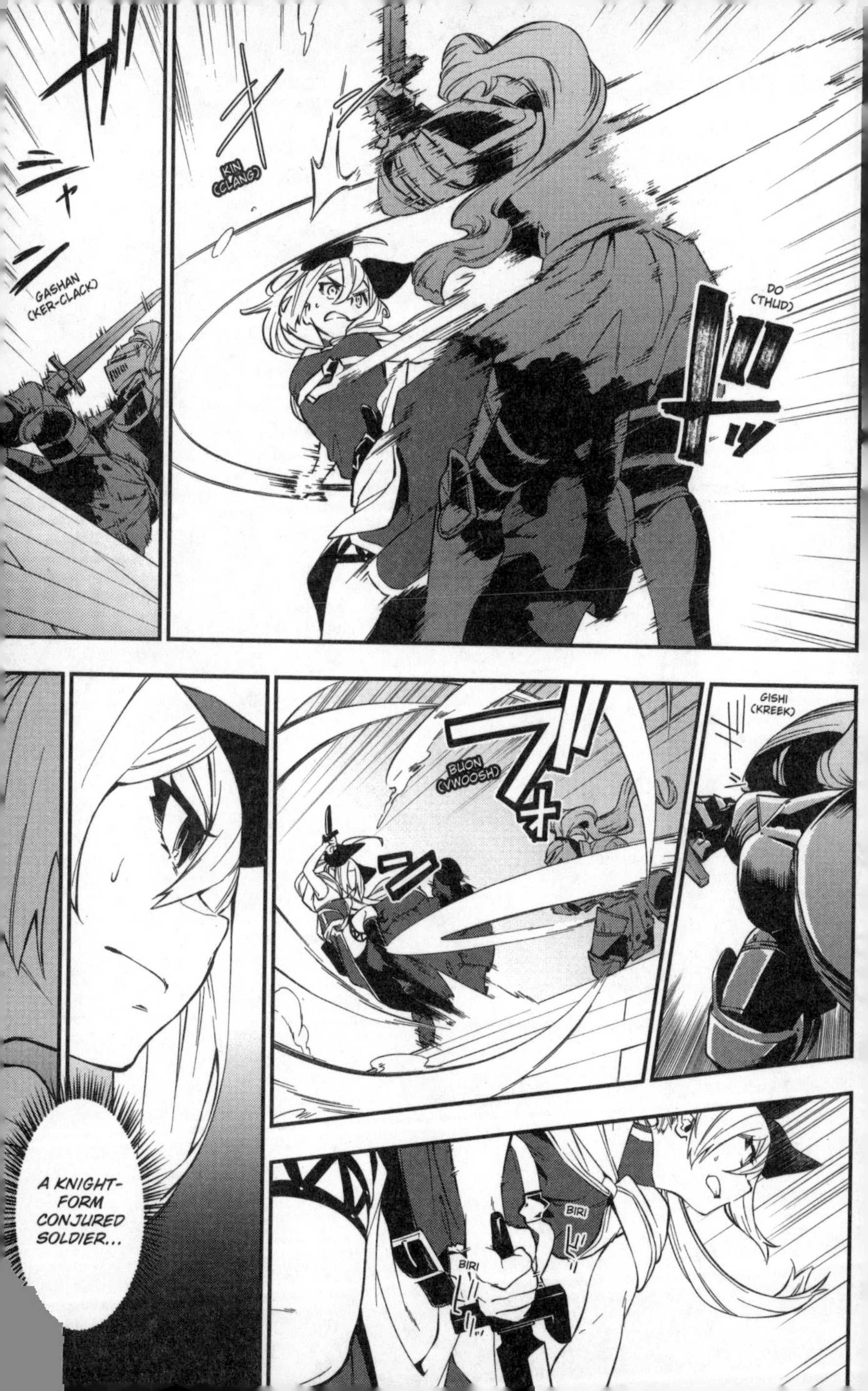
DO (THUD)
KIN (CLANG)
GASHAN (KER-CLACK)
GISHI (KREEK)
BUON (VWOOSH)
BIRI
BIRI
A KNIGHT-FORM CONJURED SOLDIER...

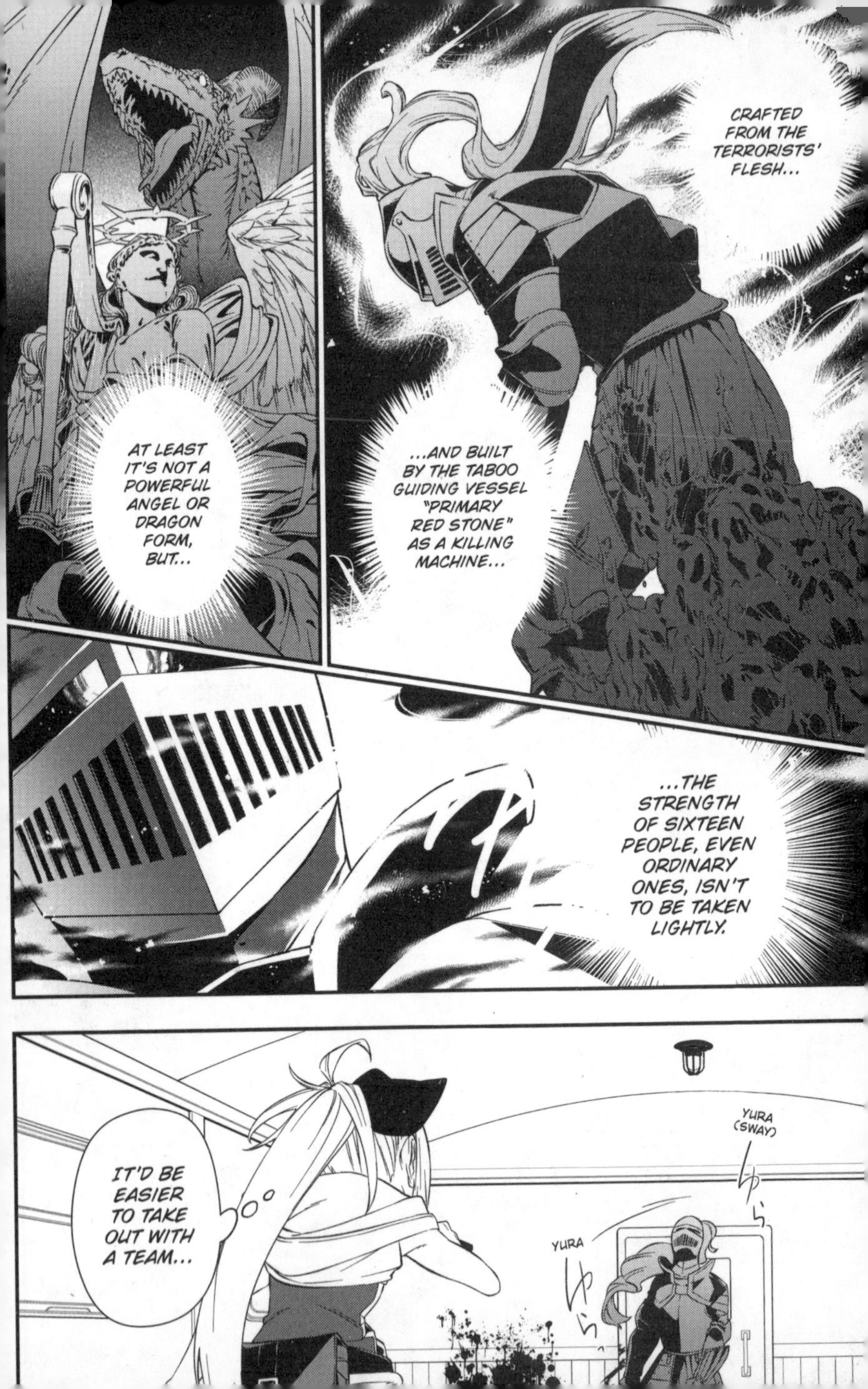

CRAFTED FROM THE TERRORISTS' FLESH...
...AND BUILT BY THE TABOO GUIDING VESSEL "PRIMARY RED STONE" AS A KILLING MACHINE...
AT LEAST IT'S NOT A POWERFUL ANGEL OR DRAGON FORM, BUT...
...THE STRENGTH OF SIXTEEN PEOPLE, EVEN ORDINARY ONES, ISN'T TO BE TAKEN LIGHTLY.
YURA (SWAY)
ゆら
YURA
ゆら
IT'D BE EASIER TO TAKE OUT WITH A TEAM...

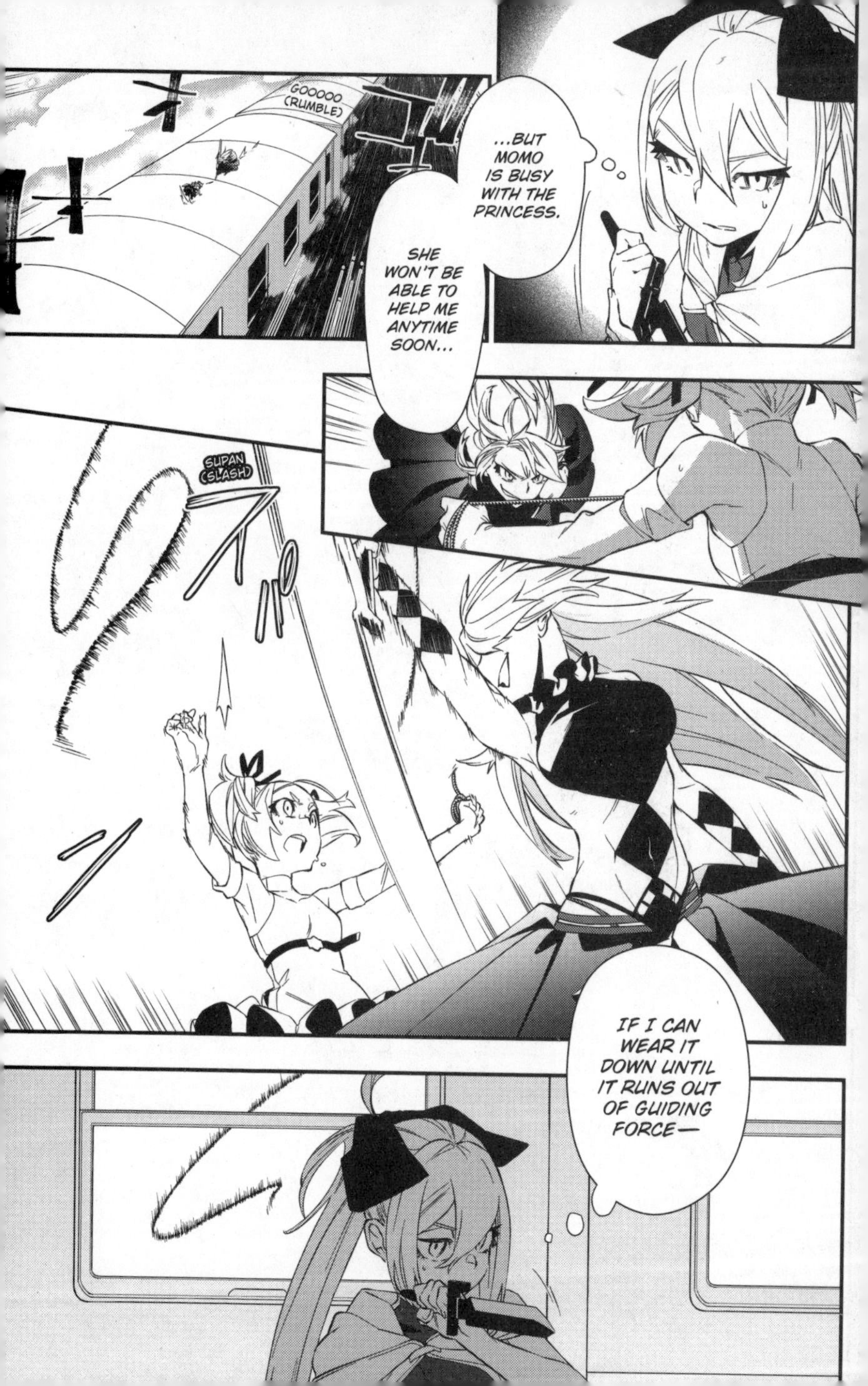
...BUT MOMO IS BUSY WITH THE PRINCESS.
SHE WON'T BE ABLE TO HELP ME ANYTIME SOON...
GOOOOO (RUMBLE)
SUPAN (SLASH)
IF I CAN WEAR IT DOWN UNTIL IT RUNS OUT OF GUIDING FORCE—

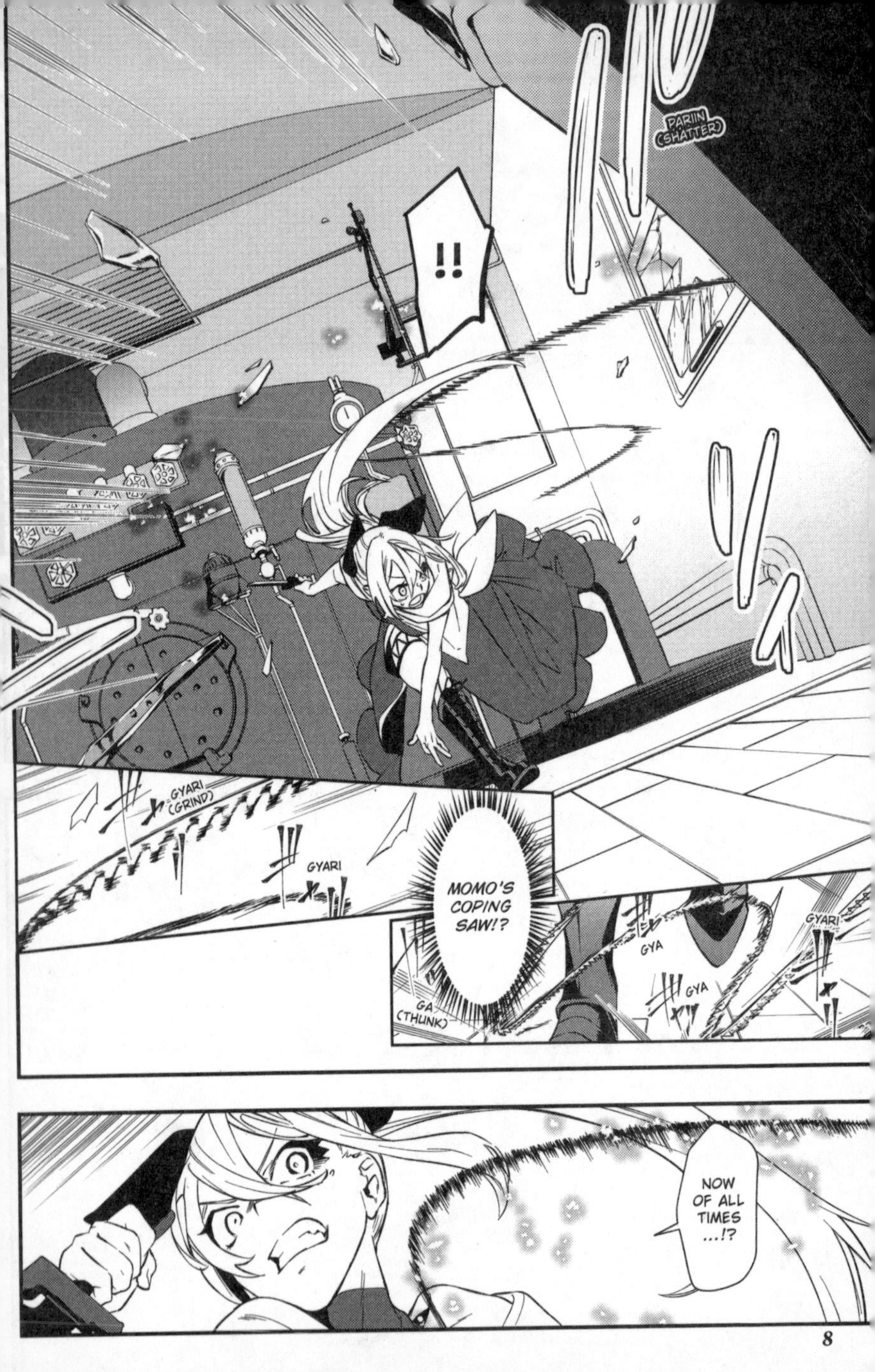
PARIIN (SHATTER)
!!
GYARI (GRIND)
GYARI
MOMO'S COPING SAW!?
GYARI
GYA
GYA
GA (THUNK)
NOW OF ALL TIMES ...!?

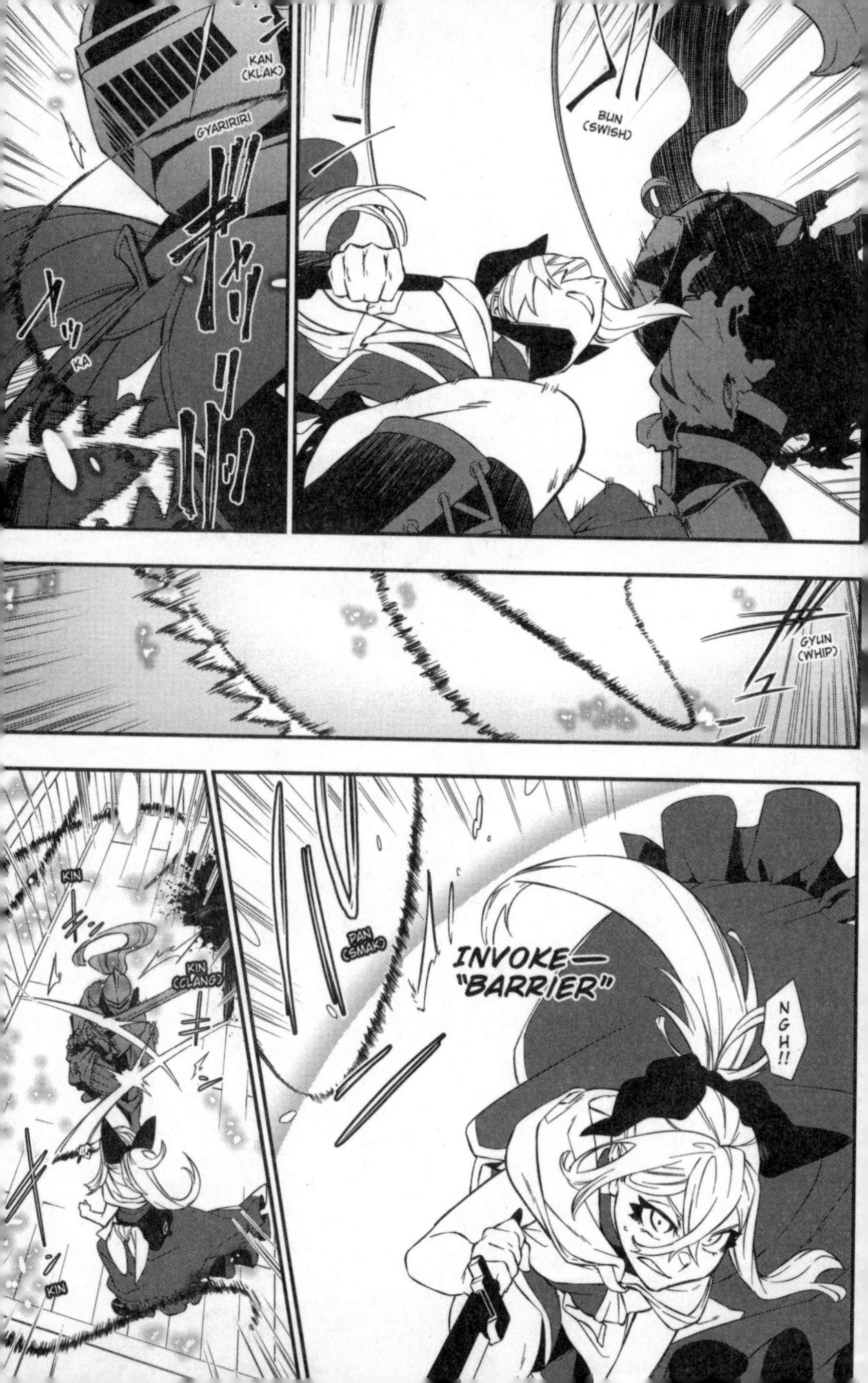
BUN (SWISH)
KAN (KLAK)
GYARIRIRI
KA
GYUN (WHIP)
NGH!!
INVOKE—"BARRIER"
PAN (SMAK)
KIN
KIN (CLANG)
KIN

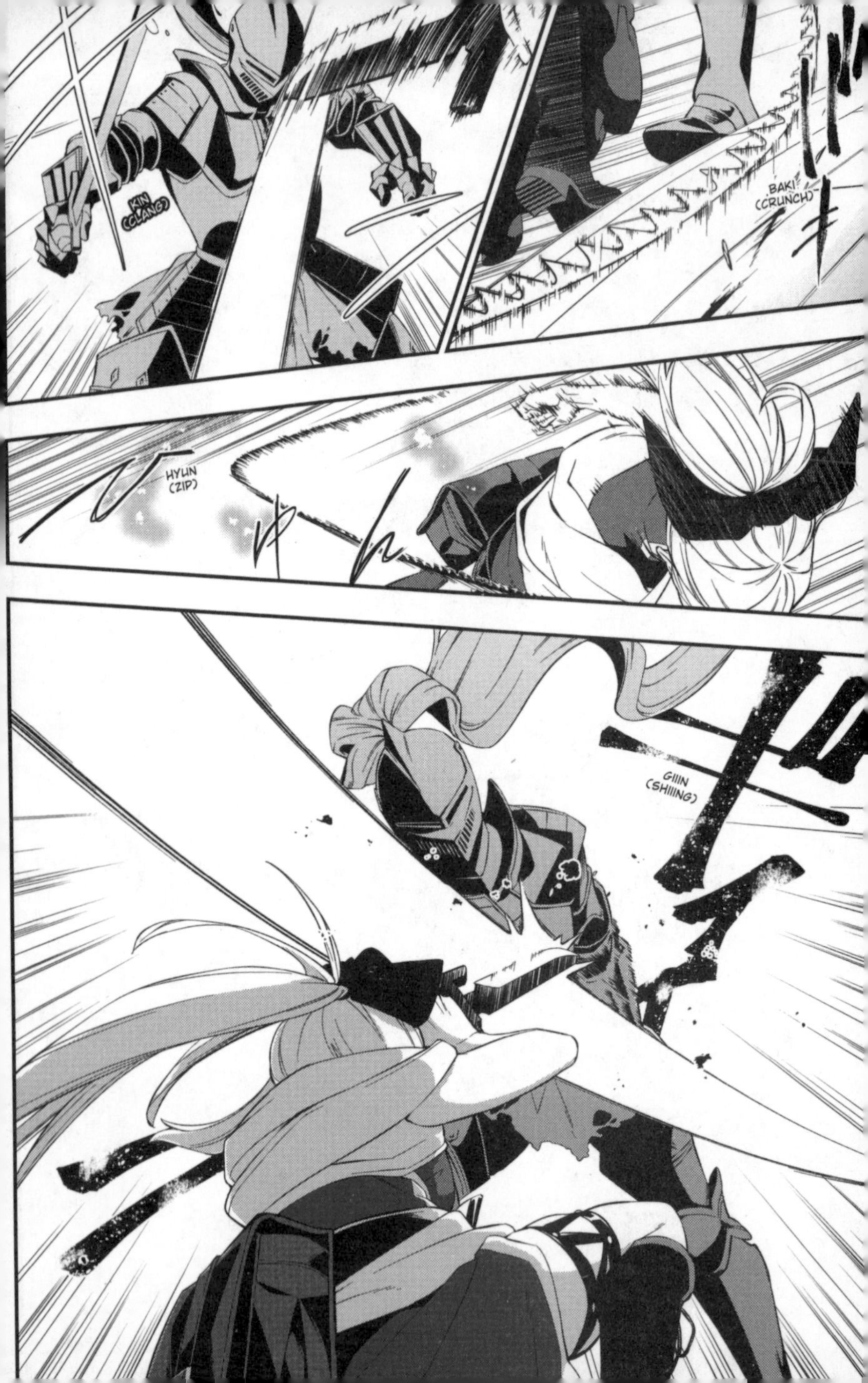
BAKI (CRUNCH)
KIN (CLANG)
HYUN (ZIP)
GIIIN (SHIIING)

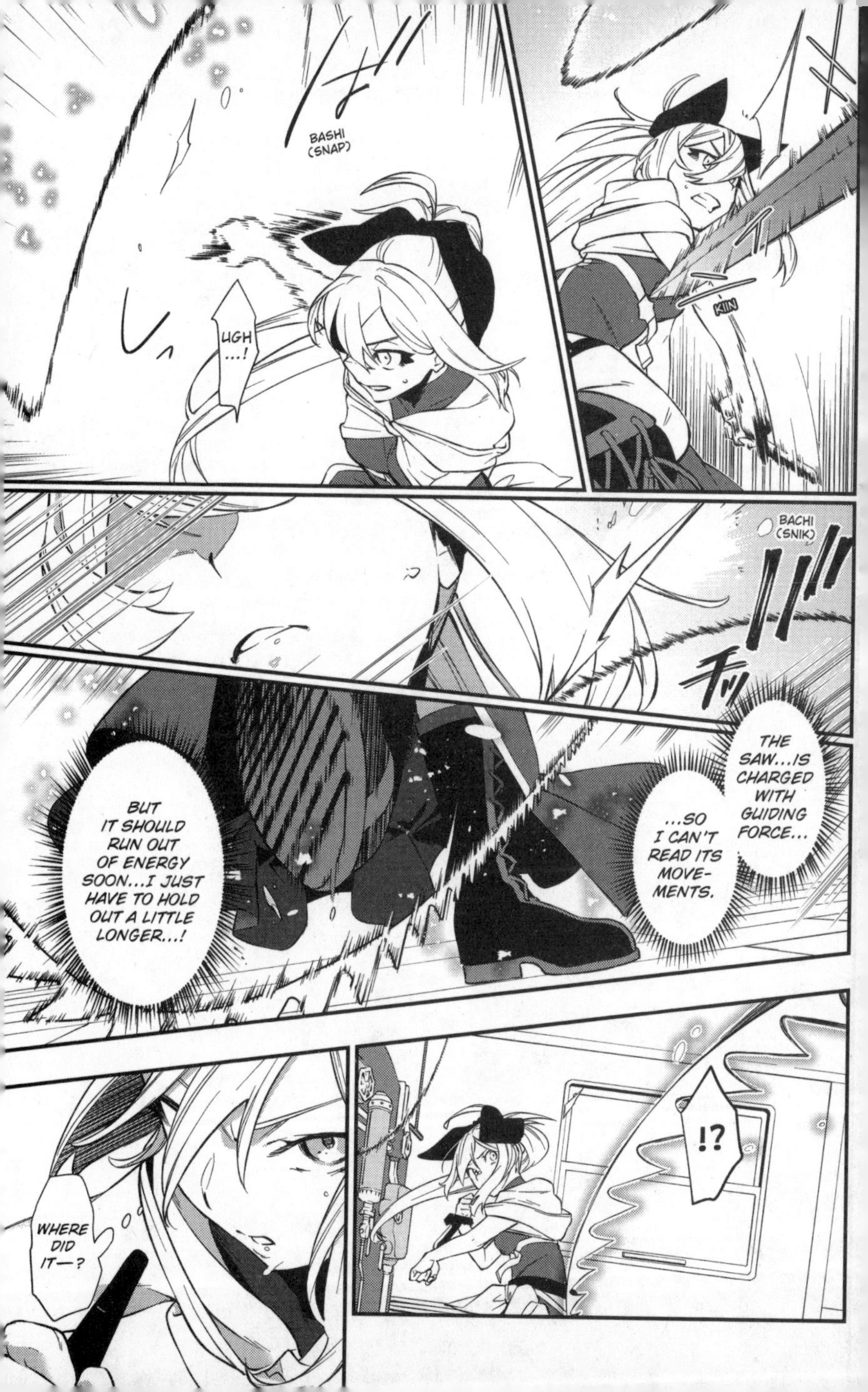
KIN
BASHI (SNAP)
UGH ...!
BACHI (SNIK)
THE SAW...IS CHARGED WITH GUIDING FORCE...
...SO I CAN'T READ ITS MOVEMENTS.
BUT IT SHOULD RUN OUT OF ENERGY SOON...I JUST HAVE TO HOLD OUT A LITTLE LONGER...!
!?
WHERE DID IT—?

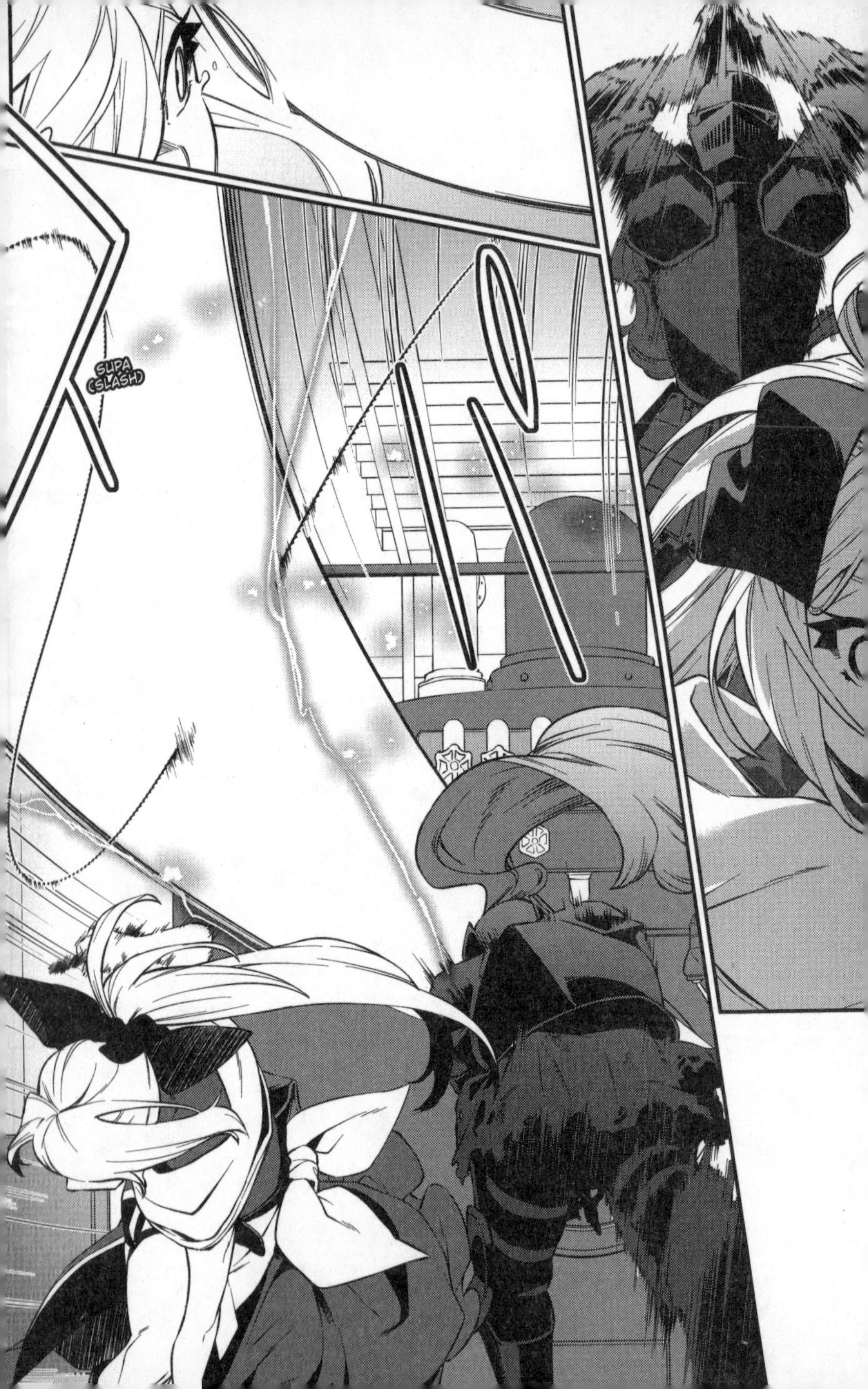
SUPA (SLASH)

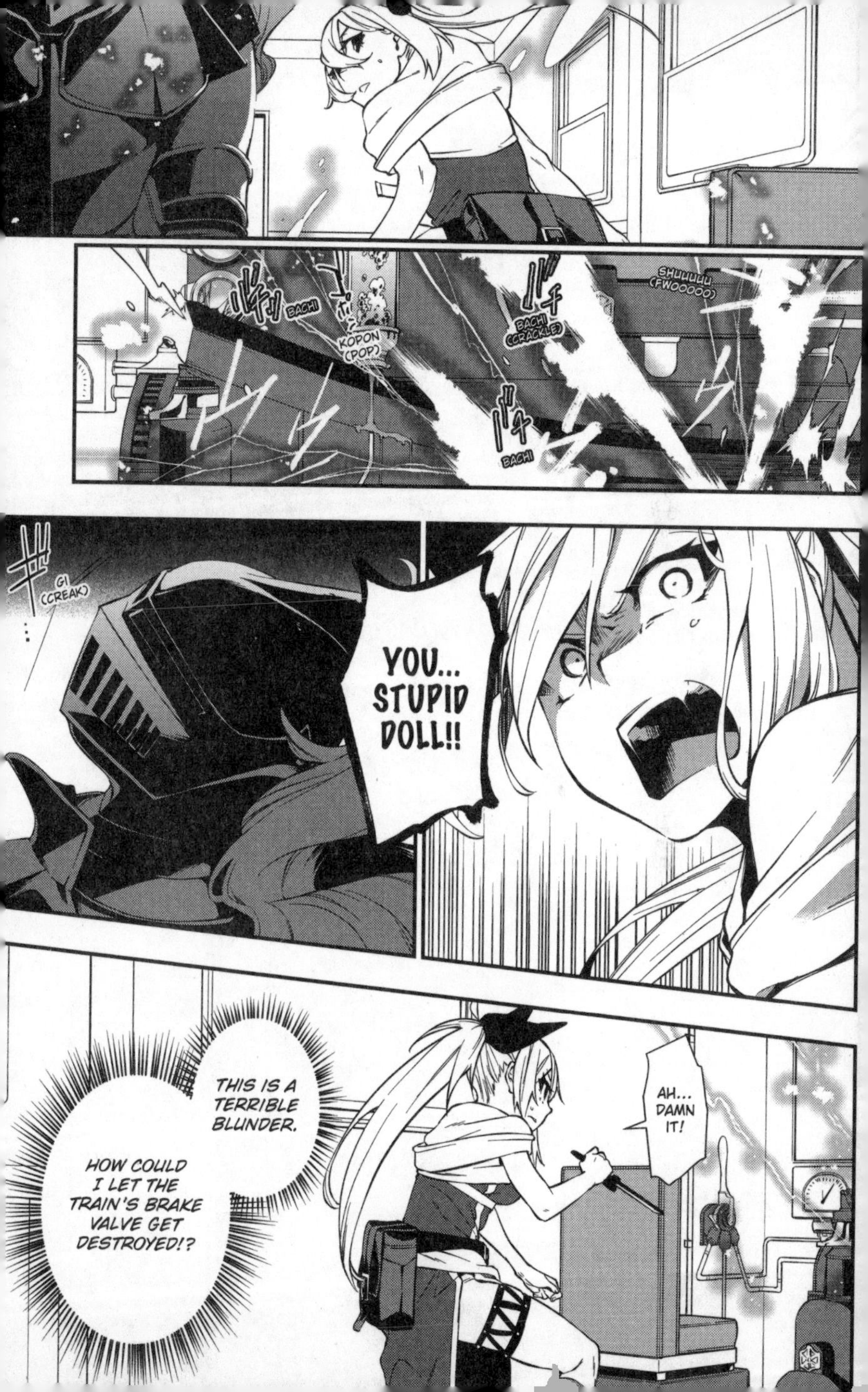
SHUUUUUU (FWOOOOO)
BACHI (CRACKLE)
BACHI
KOPON (POP)
BACHI
YOU... STUPID DOLL!!
GI (CREAK)
...
AH... DAMN IT!
THIS IS A TERRIBLE BLUNDER.
HOW COULD I LET THE TRAIN'S BRAKE VALVE GET DESTROYED!?

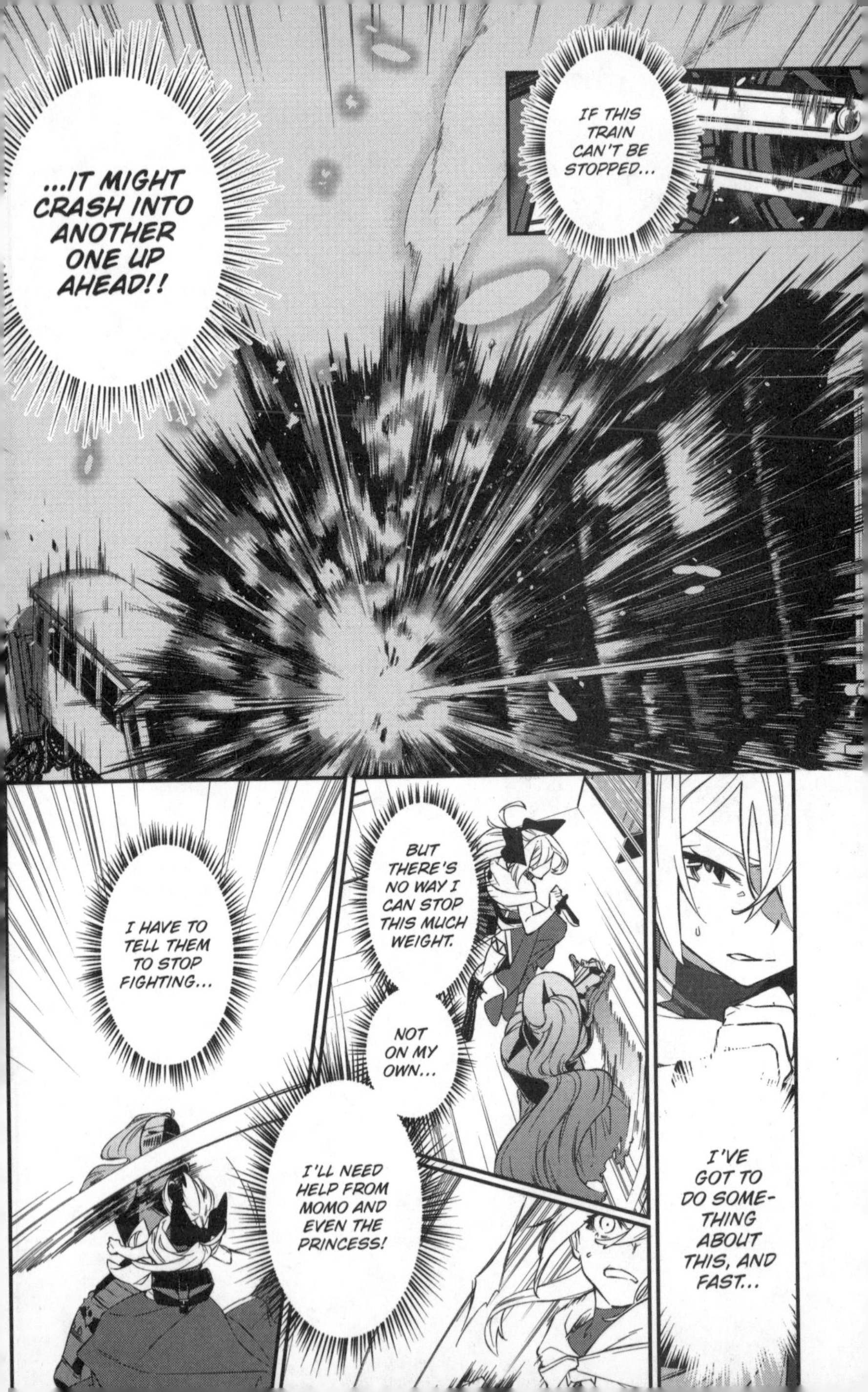
IF THIS TRAIN CAN'T BE STOPPED...
...IT MIGHT CRASH INTO ANOTHER ONE UP AHEAD!!
I'VE GOT TO DO SOME-THING ABOUT THIS, AND FAST...
BUT THERE'S NO WAY I CAN STOP THIS MUCH WEIGHT.
NOT ON MY OWN...
I'LL NEED HELP FROM MOMO AND EVEN THE PRINCESS!
I HAVE TO TELL THEM TO STOP FIGHTING...

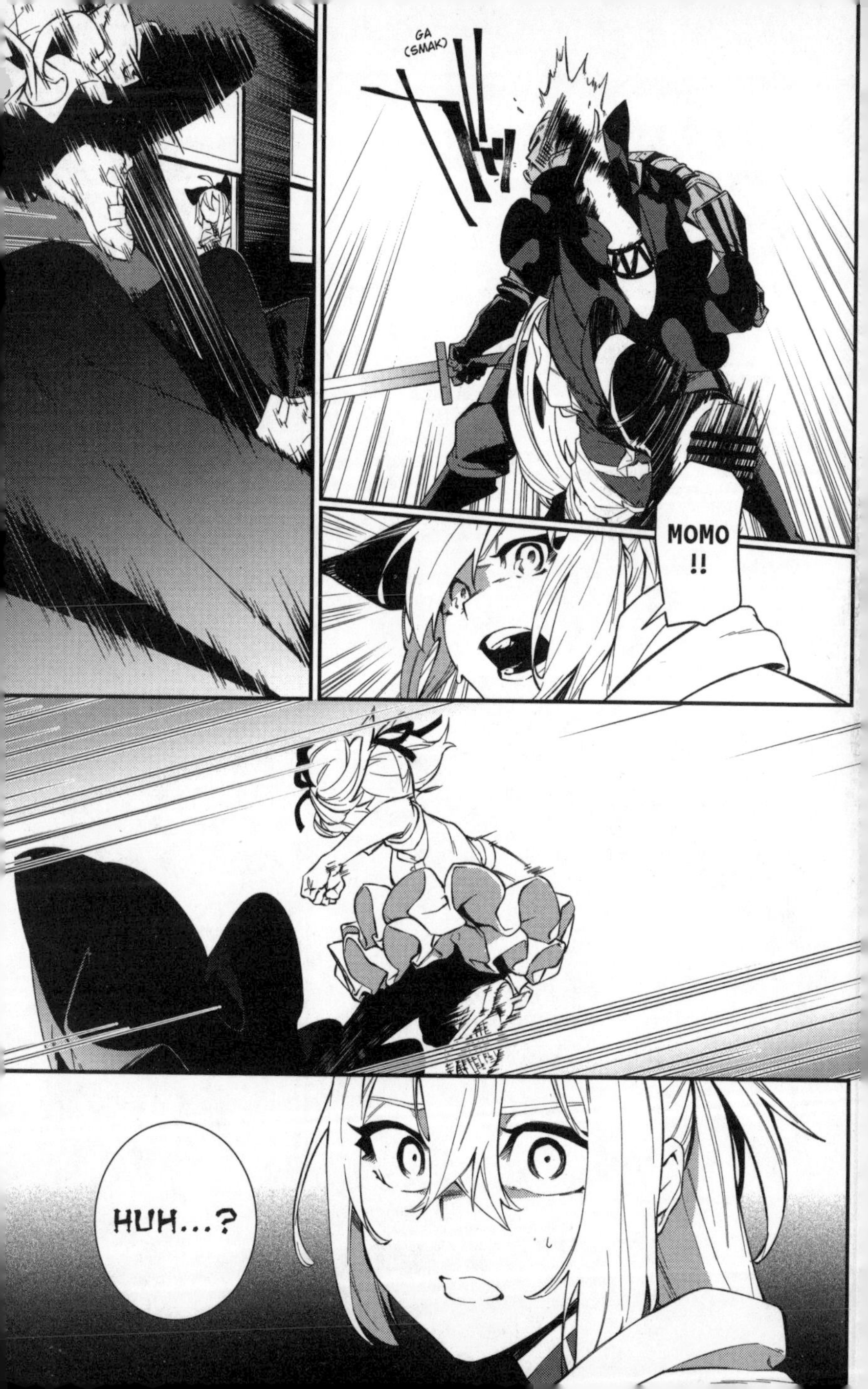
GA
(SMAK)
MOMO !!
HUH...?

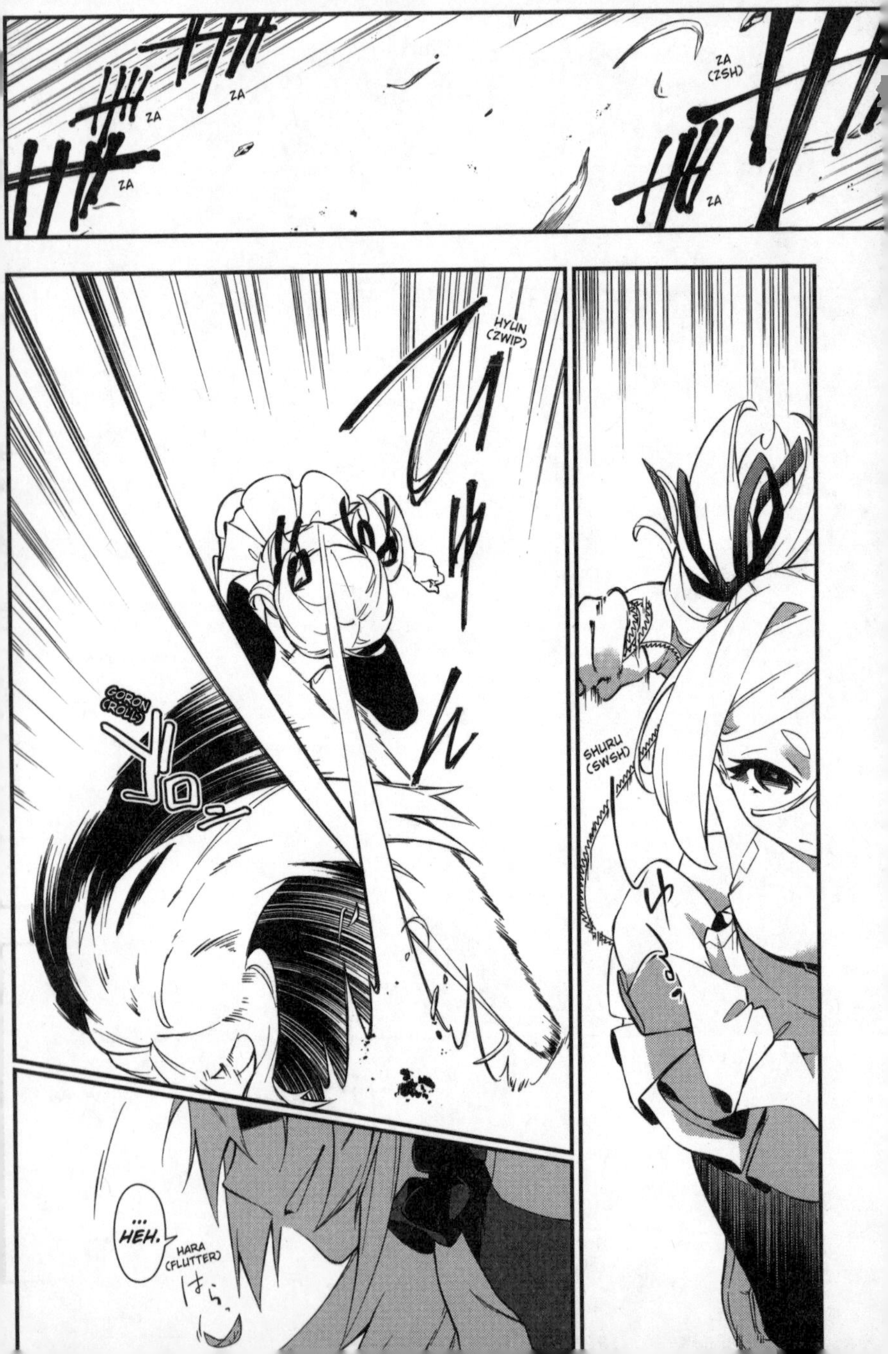
ZA (ZSH)
ZA
ZA
ZA
ZA
SHURU (SWSH)
HYUN (ZWIP)
GORON (ROLL)
... HEH.
HARA (FLUTTER)

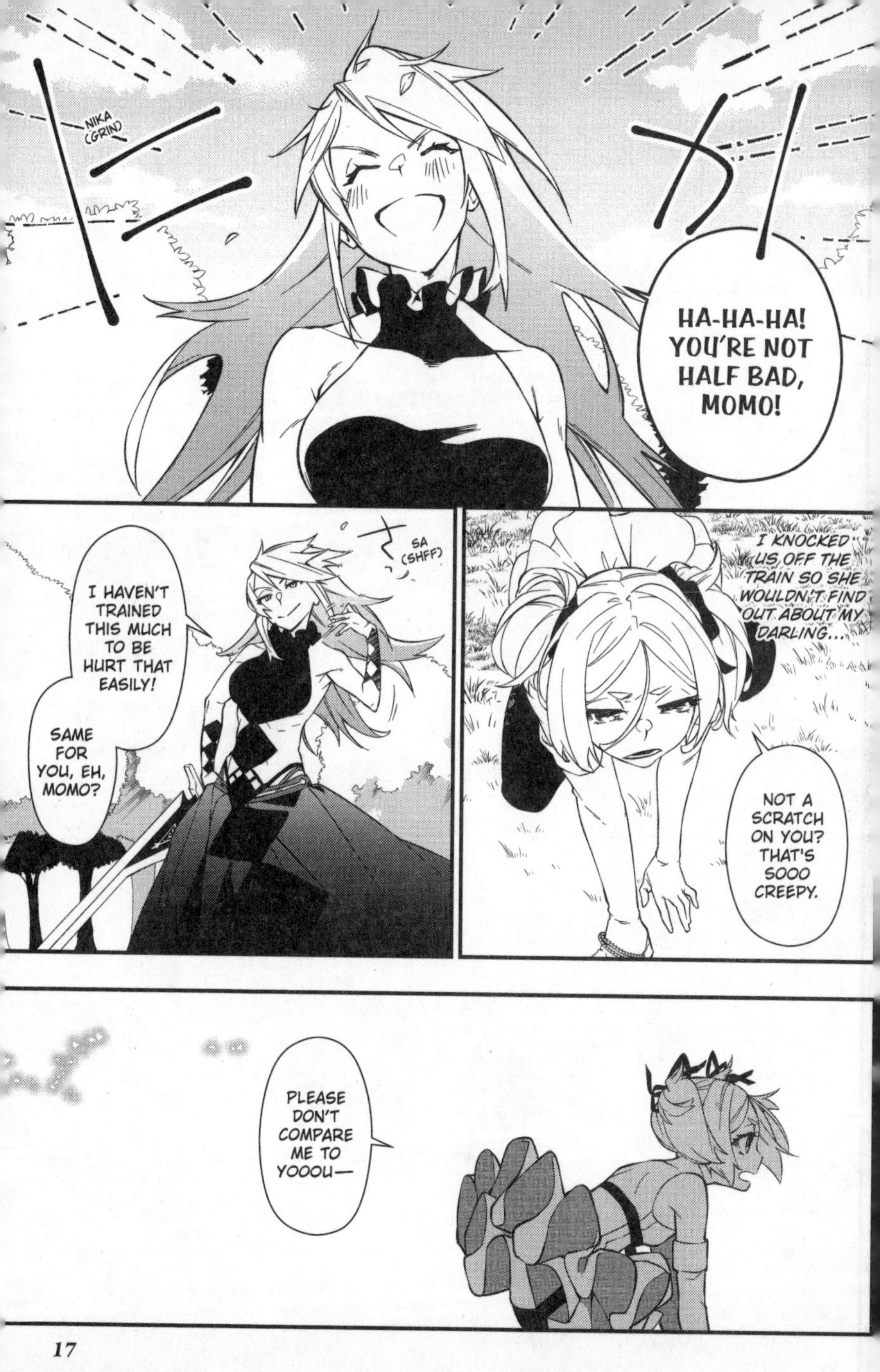
NIKA (GRIN)
HA-HA-HA! YOU'RE NOT HALF BAD, MOMO!
I KNOCKED US OFF THE TRAIN SO SHE WOULDN'T FIND OUT ABOUT MY DARLING...
NOT A SCRATCH ON YOU? THAT'S SOOO CREEPY.
SA (SHFF)
I HAVEN'T TRAINED THIS MUCH TO BE HURT THAT EASILY!
SAME FOR YOU, EH, MOMO?
PLEASE DON'T COMPARE ME TO YOOOU—

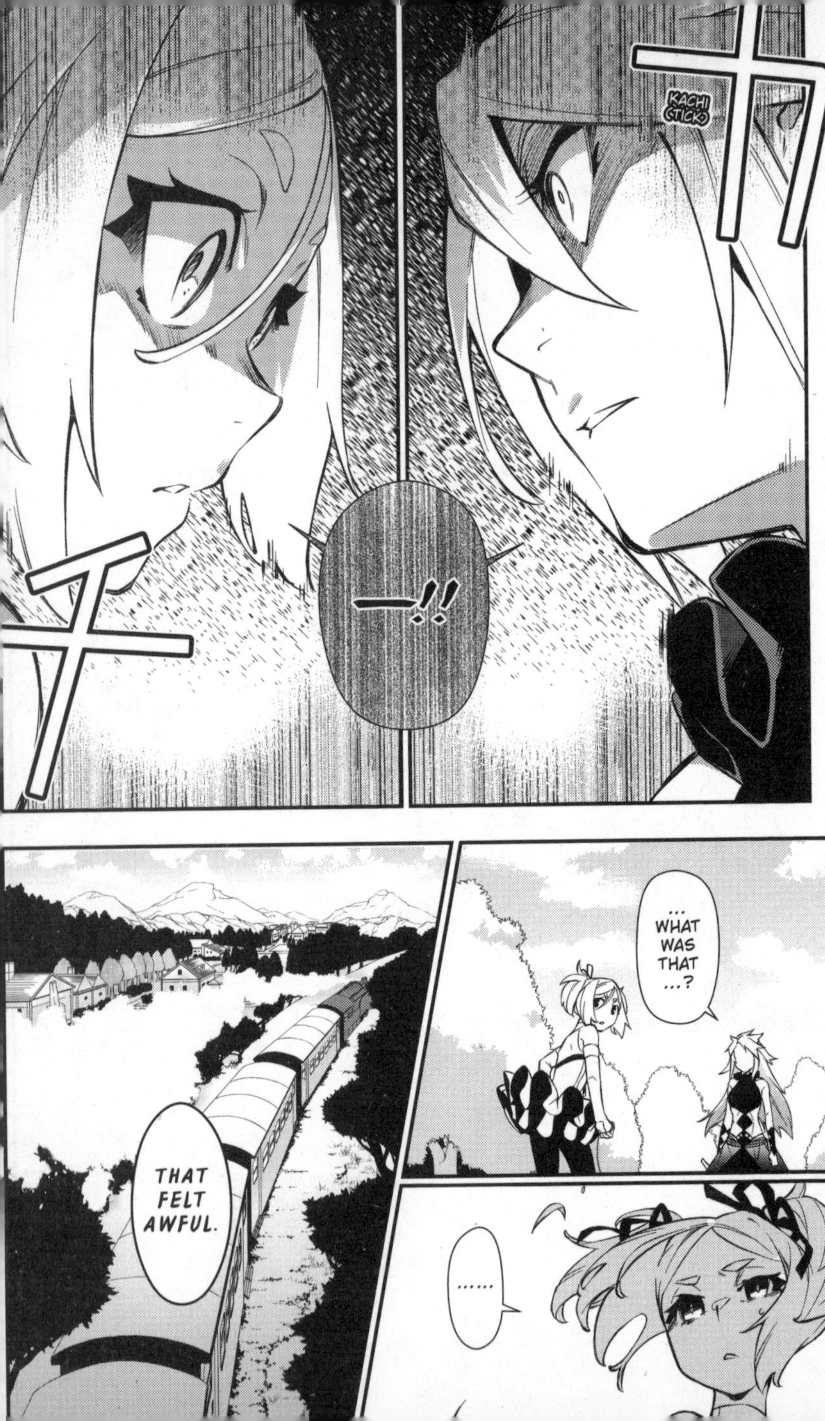
カ
KACHI (TICK)
—!!
チ
...WHAT WAS THAT ...?
......
THAT FELT AWFUL.

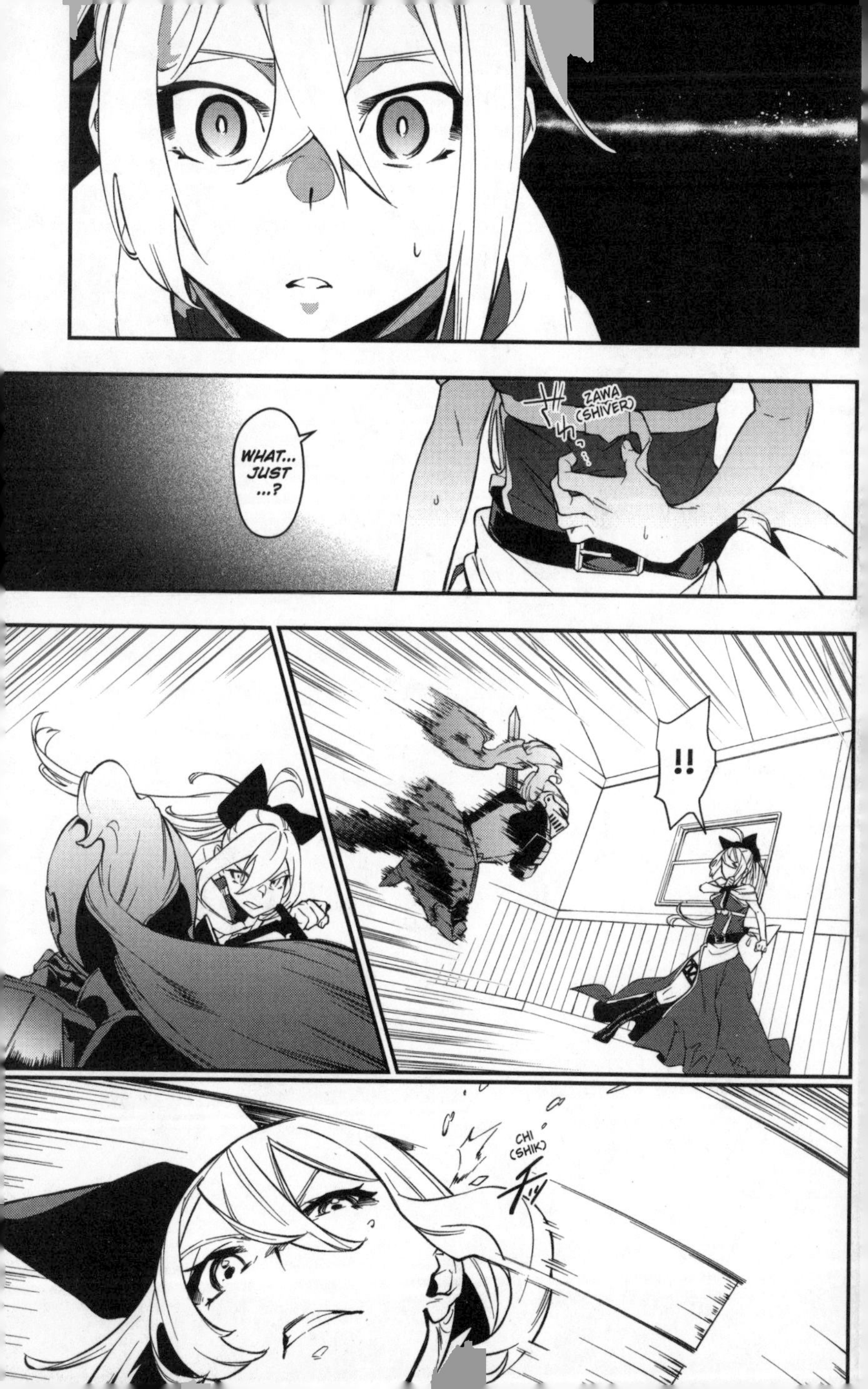

ZAWA (SHIVER)
WHAT... JUST ...?
!!
CHI (SHIK)

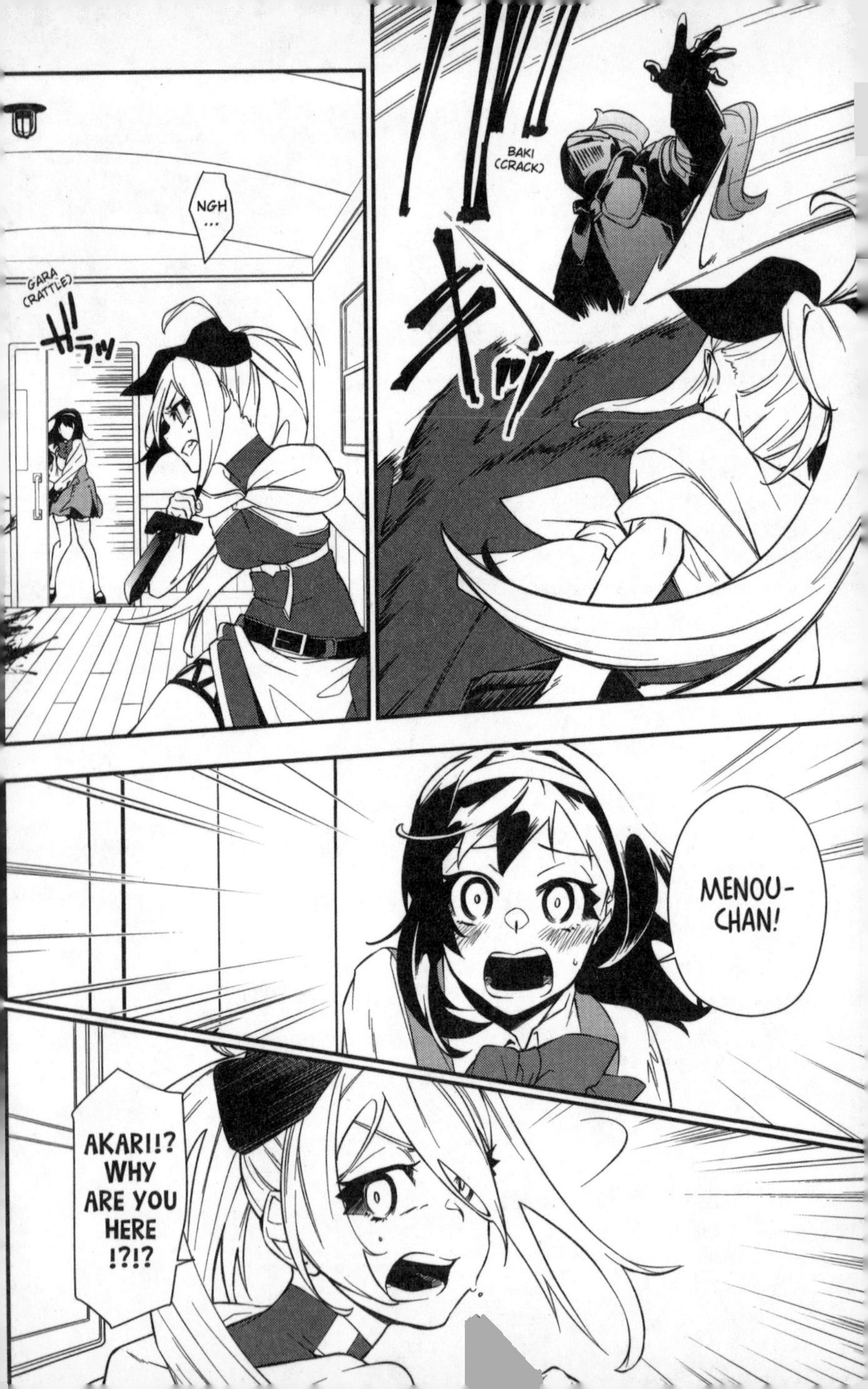
BAKI (CRACK)
NGH...
GARA (RATTLE)
MENOU-CHAN!
AKARI!? WHY ARE YOU HERE !?!?

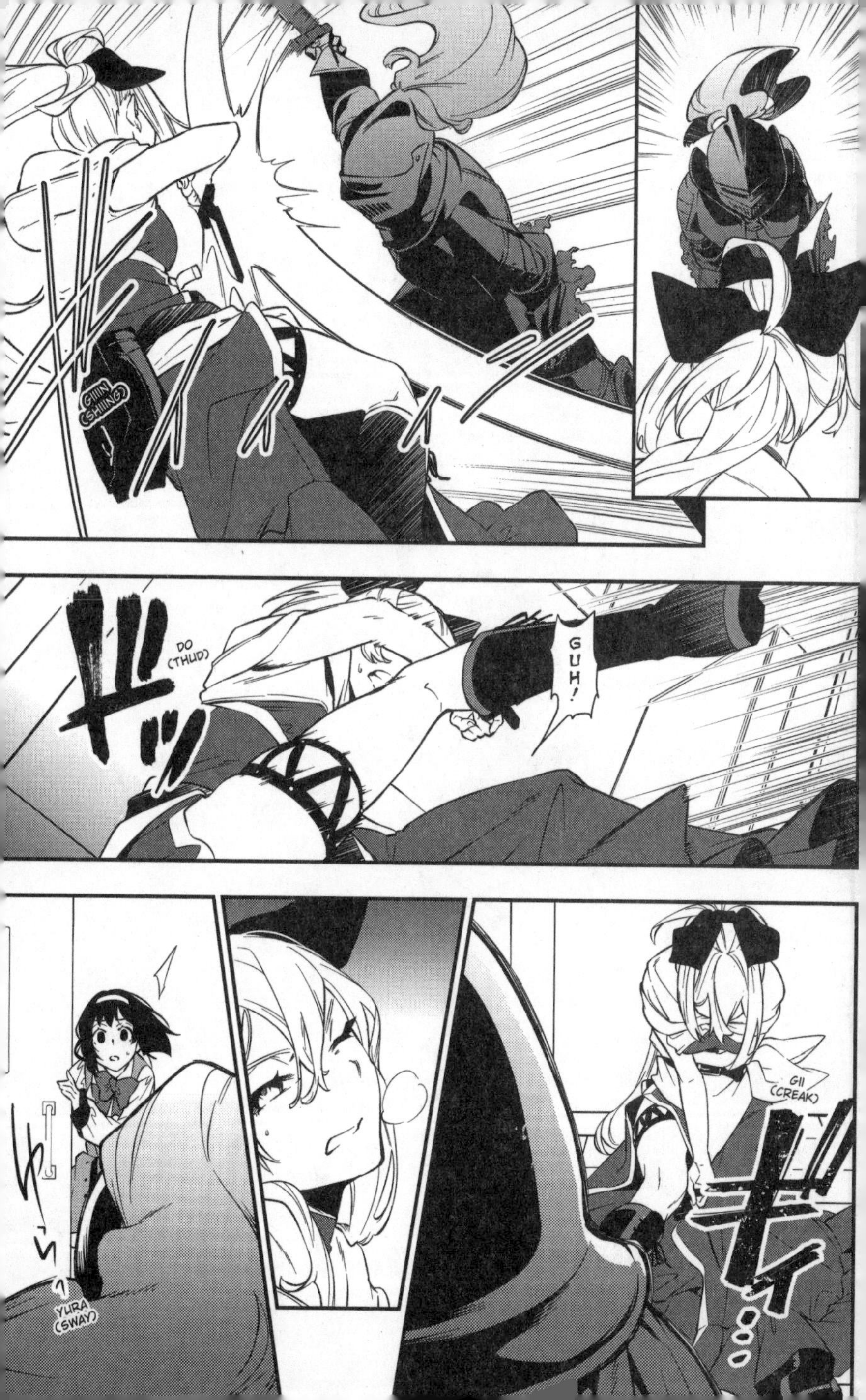
GIIIN (SHIIING)
GUH!
DO (THUD)
GII (CREAK)
YURA (SWAY)

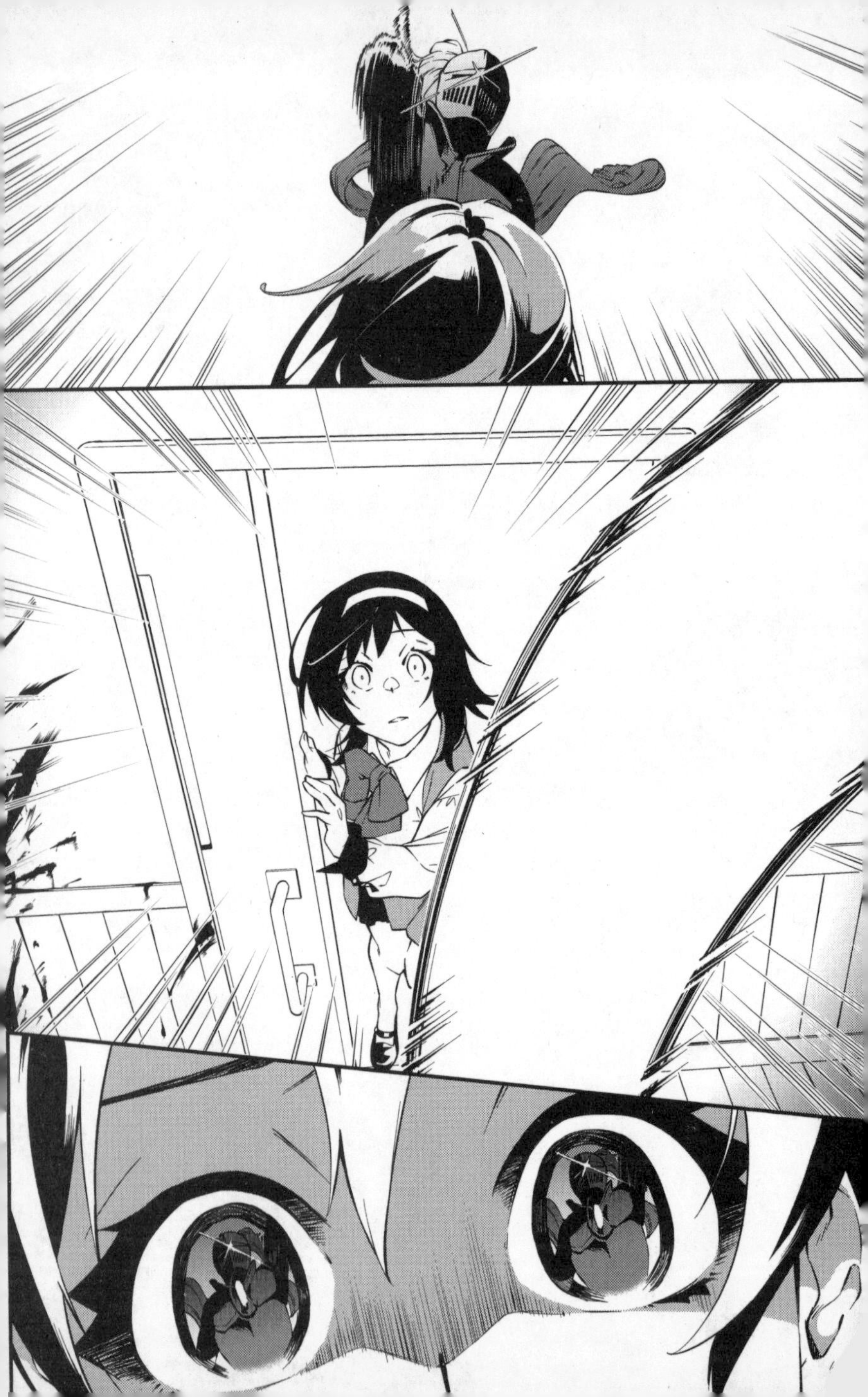

The Executioner
and Her Way of Life

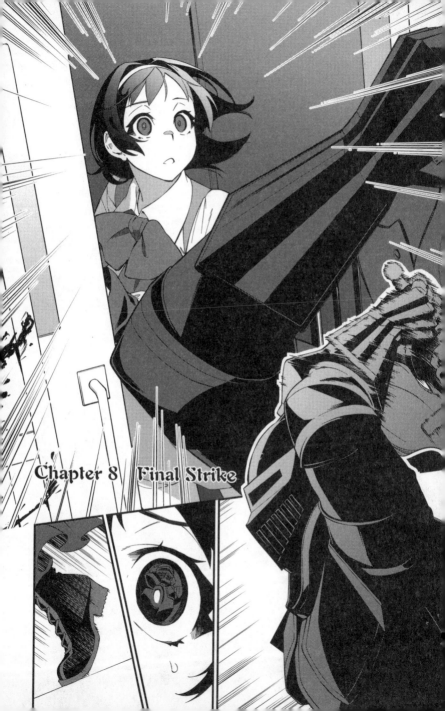

Chapter 8 Final Strike

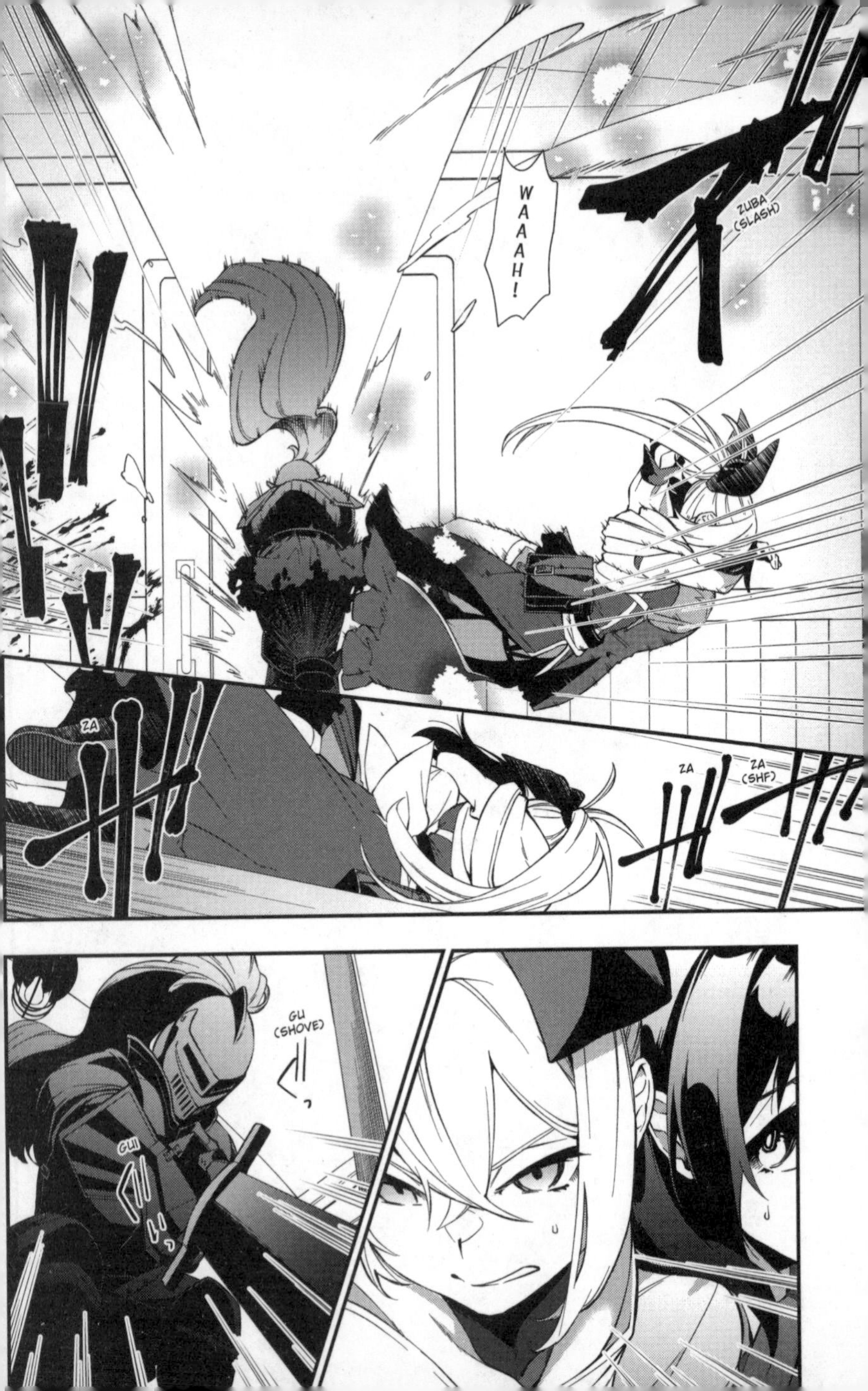
ZUBA (SLASH)
WAAAAH!
ZA (SHF)
ZA
ZA
GU (SHOVE)
GUI

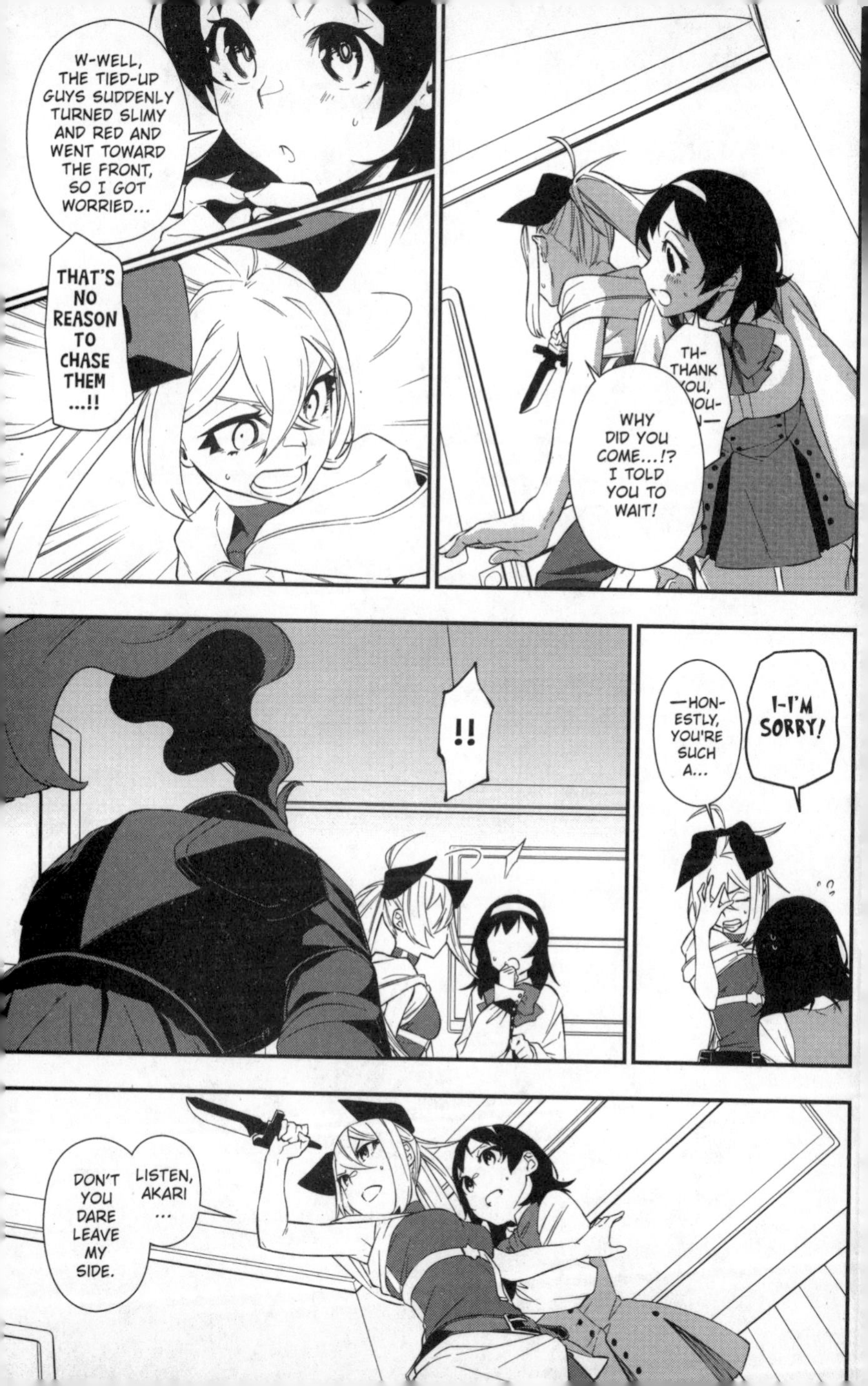
TH-THANK YOU, YOU-N—
WHY DID YOU COME...!? I TOLD YOU TO WAIT!
W-WELL, THE TIED-UP GUYS SUDDENLY TURNED SLIMY AND RED AND WENT TOWARD THE FRONT, SO I GOT WORRIED...
THAT'S NO REASON TO CHASE THEM ...!!
I-I'M SORRY!
—HONESTLY, YOU'RE SUCH A...
!!
LISTEN, AKARI ...
DON'T YOU DARE LEAVE MY SIDE.

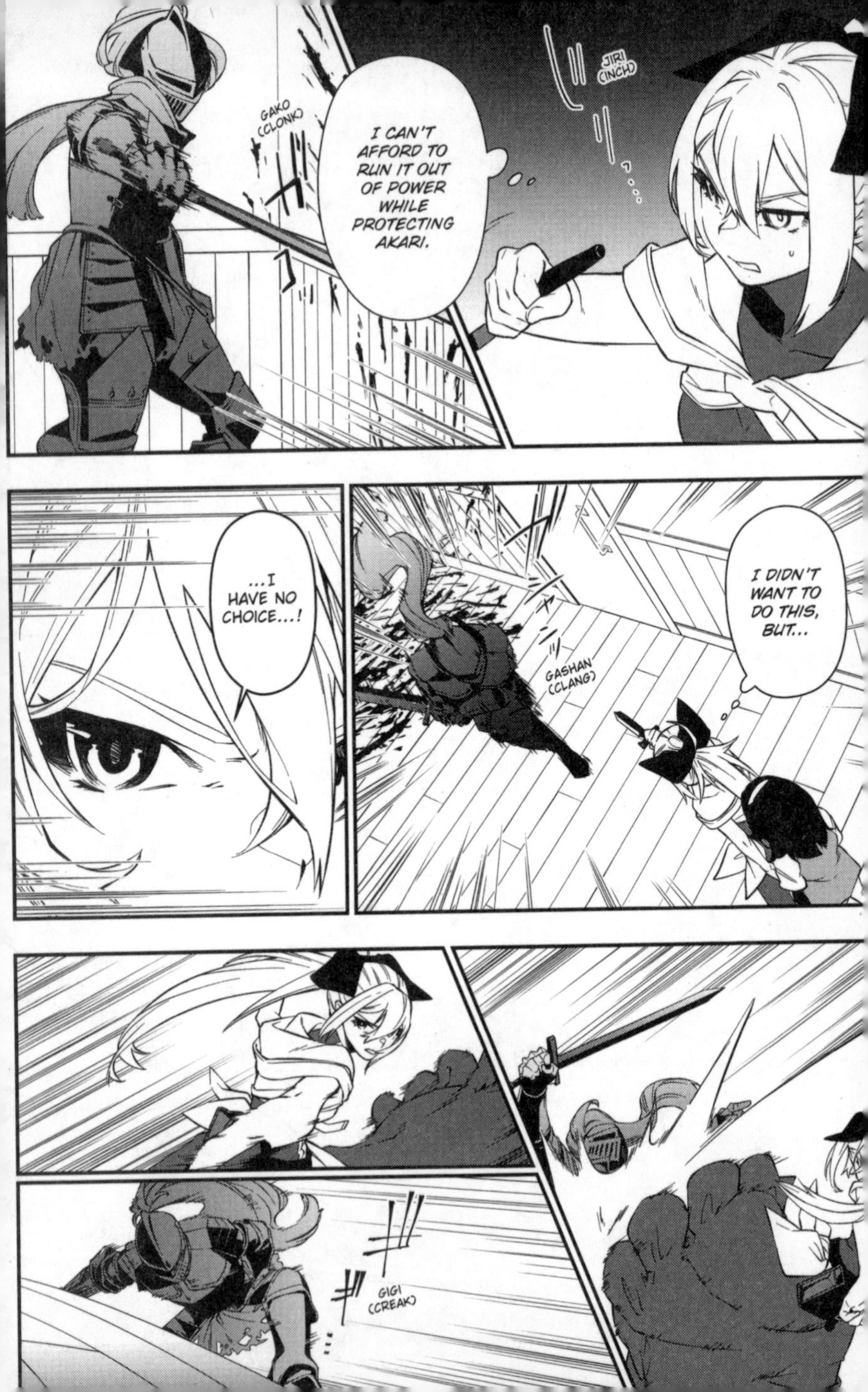
JIRI (INCH)
I CAN'T AFFORD TO RUN IT OUT OF POWER WHILE PROTECTING AKARI.
GAKO (CLONK)
I DIDN'T WANT TO DO THIS, BUT...
GASHAN (CLANG)
...I HAVE NO CHOICE...!
GIGI (CREAK)

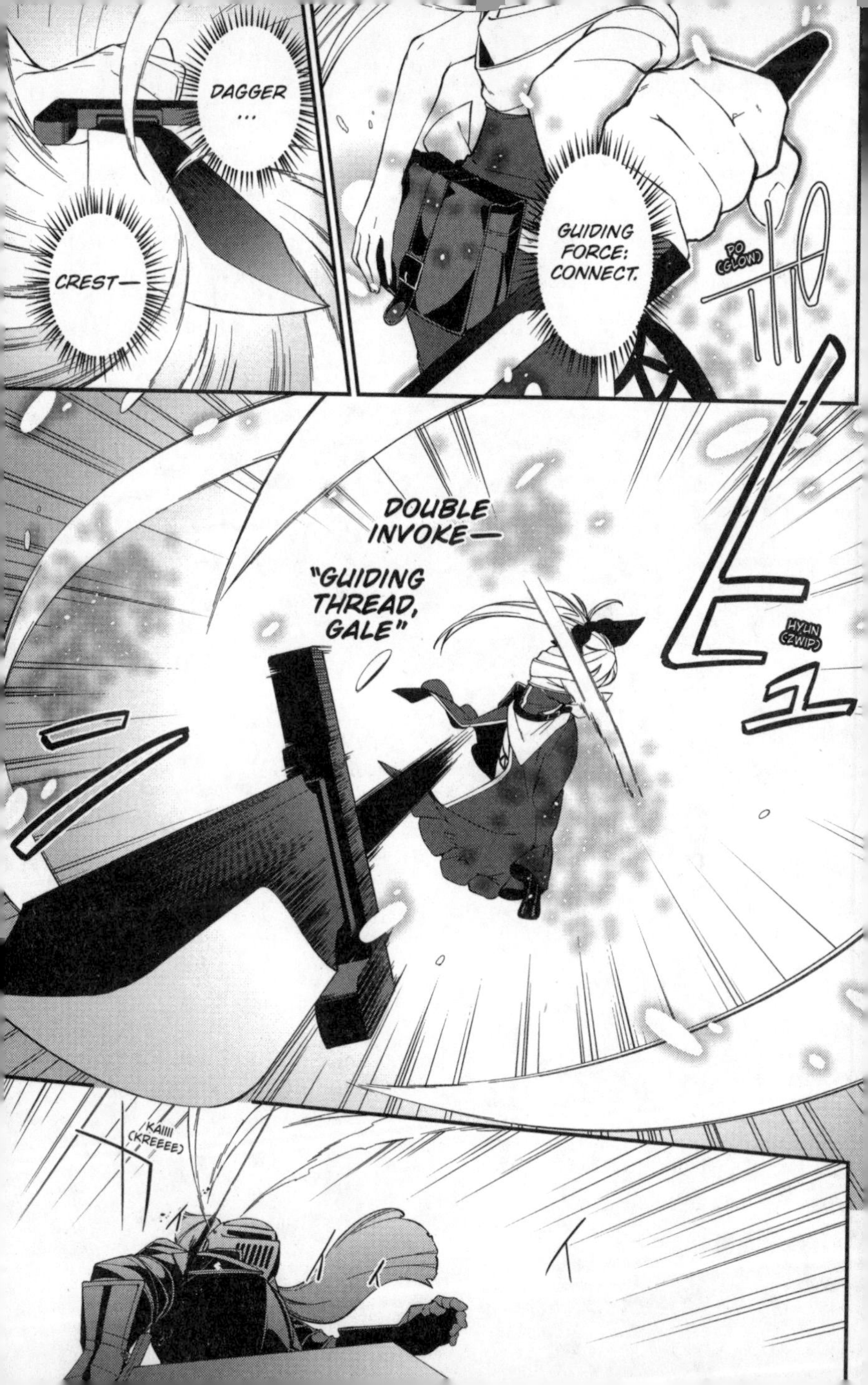
PO (GLOW)
GUIDING FORCE: CONNECT.
DAGGER ...
CREST—
HYUN (ZWIP)
DOUBLE INVOKE—
"GUIDING THREAD, GALE"
KAIIII (KREEEE)

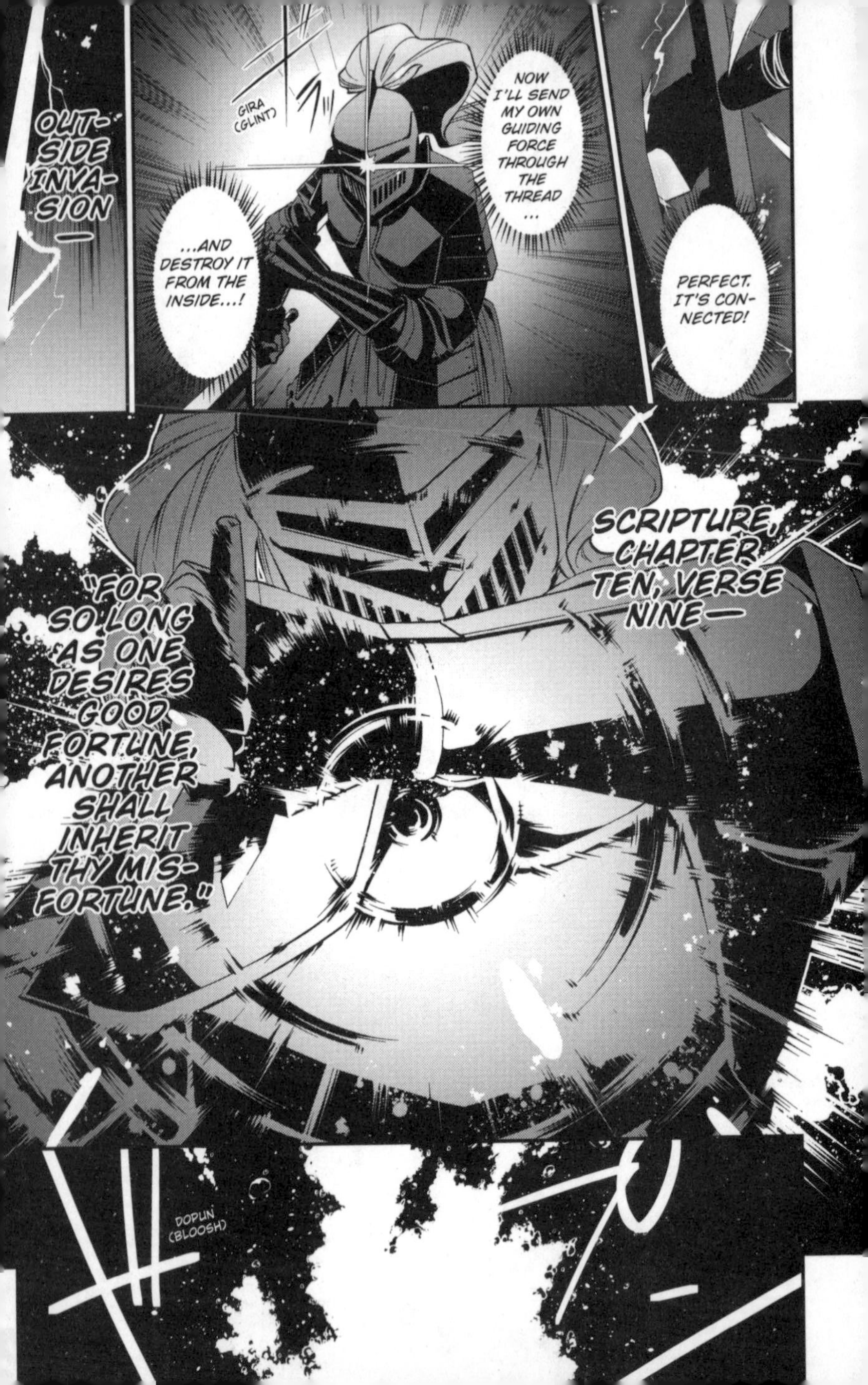
PERFECT. IT'S CON-NECTED!
NOW I'LL SEND MY OWN GUIDING FORCE THROUGH THE THREAD...
GIRA (GLINT)
...AND DESTROY IT FROM THE INSIDE...!
OUT-SIDE INVA-SION—
SCRIPTURE, CHAPTER TEN, VERSE NINE—
"FOR SO LONG AS ONE DESIRES GOOD FORTUNE, ANOTHER SHALL INHERIT THY MIS-FORTUNE."
DOPUN (BLOOSH)

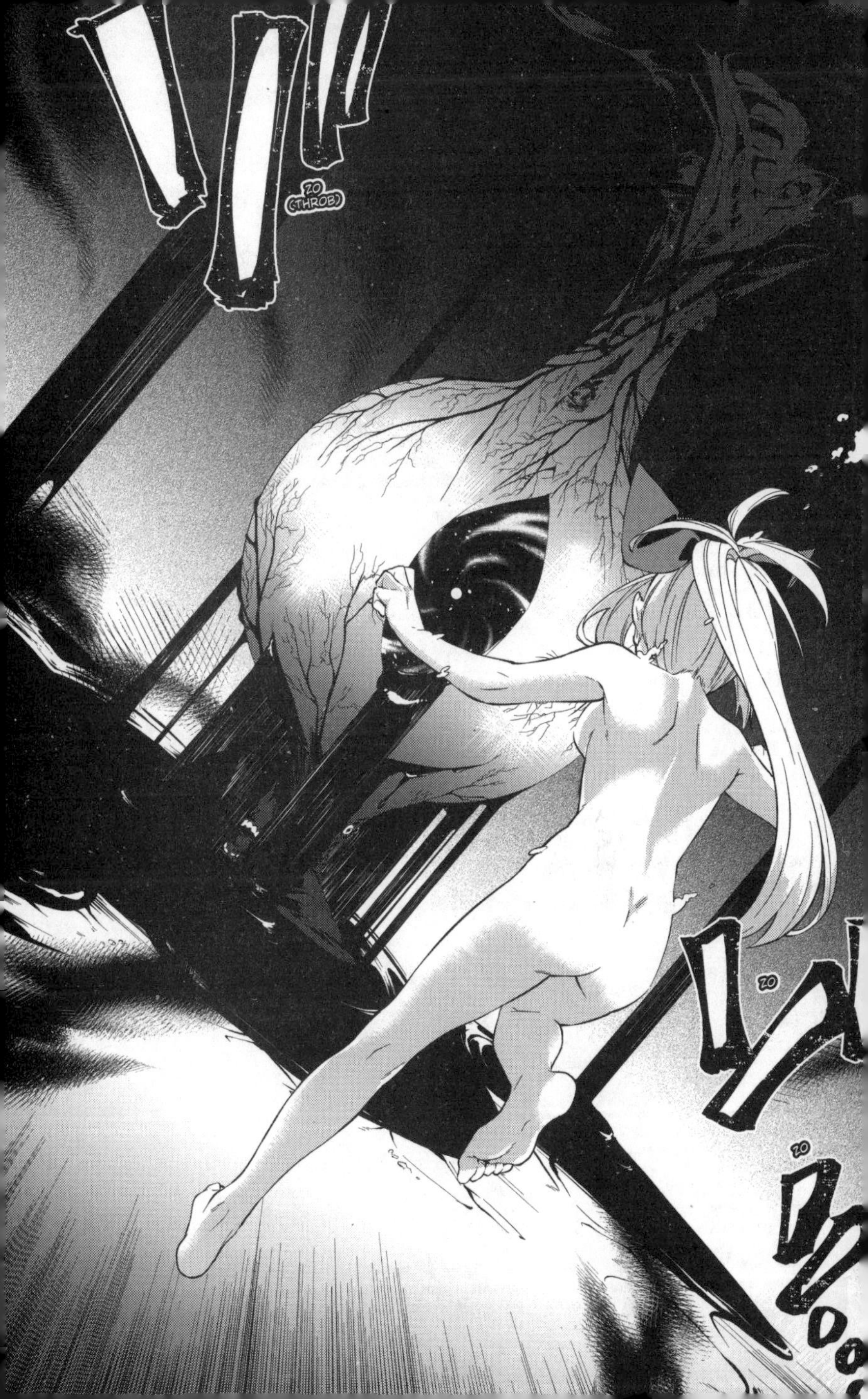
ZO
(THROB)
ZO
ZO

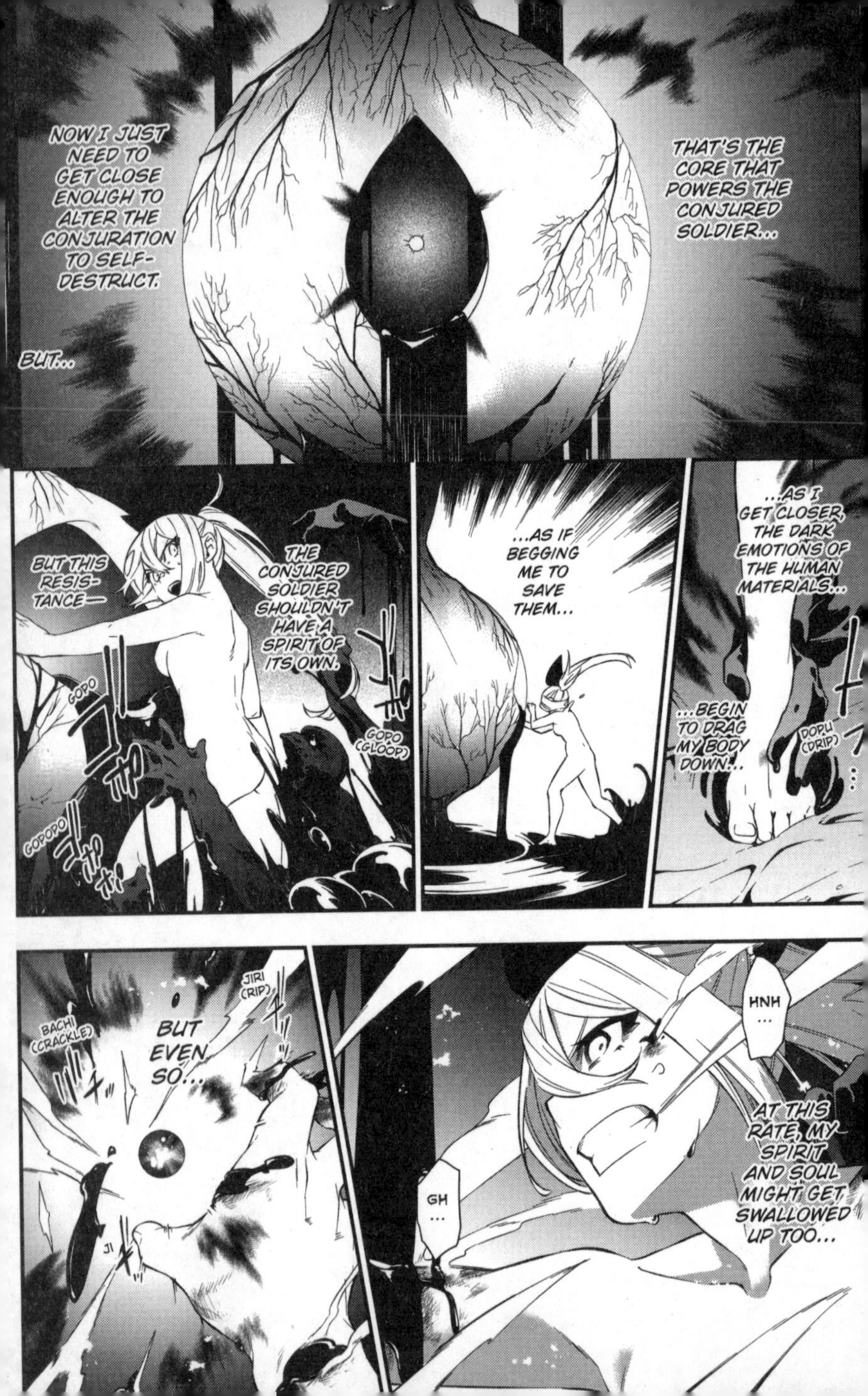
THAT'S THE CORE THAT POWERS THE CONJURED SOLDIER...
NOW I JUST NEED TO GET CLOSE ENOUGH TO ALTER THE CONJURATION TO SELF-DESTRUCT.
BUT...
...AS I GET CLOSER, THE DARK EMOTIONS OF THE HUMAN MATERIALS...
...BEGIN TO DRAG MY BODY DOWN...
DOPU (DRIP)
...AS IF BEGGING ME TO SAVE THEM...
THE CONJURED SOLDIER SHOULDN'T HAVE A SPIRIT OF ITS OWN.
BUT THIS RESIS-TANCE—
GOPO (GLOOP)
GOPO
GOPOPO
HNH...
AT THIS RATE, MY SPIRIT AND SOUL MIGHT GET SWALLOWED UP TOO...
GH...
JIRI (RIP)
BUT EVEN SO...
BACHI (CRACKLE)
JI

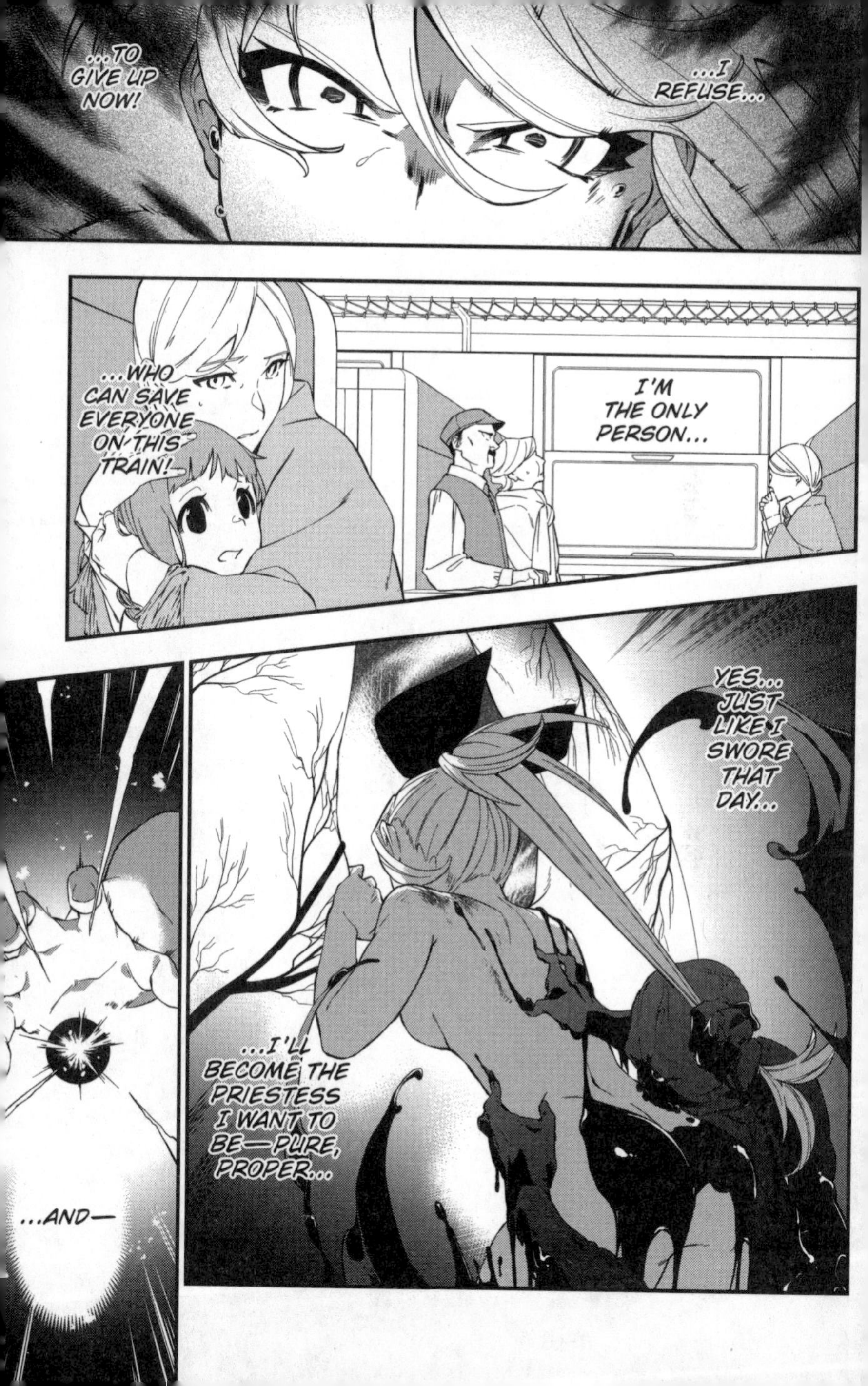
...I REFUSE...
...TO GIVE UP NOW!
I'M THE ONLY PERSON...
...WHO CAN SAVE EVERYONE ON THIS TRAIN!
YES... JUST LIKE I SWORE THAT DAY...
...I'LL BECOME THE PRIESTESS I WANT TO BE—PURE, PROPER...
...AND—

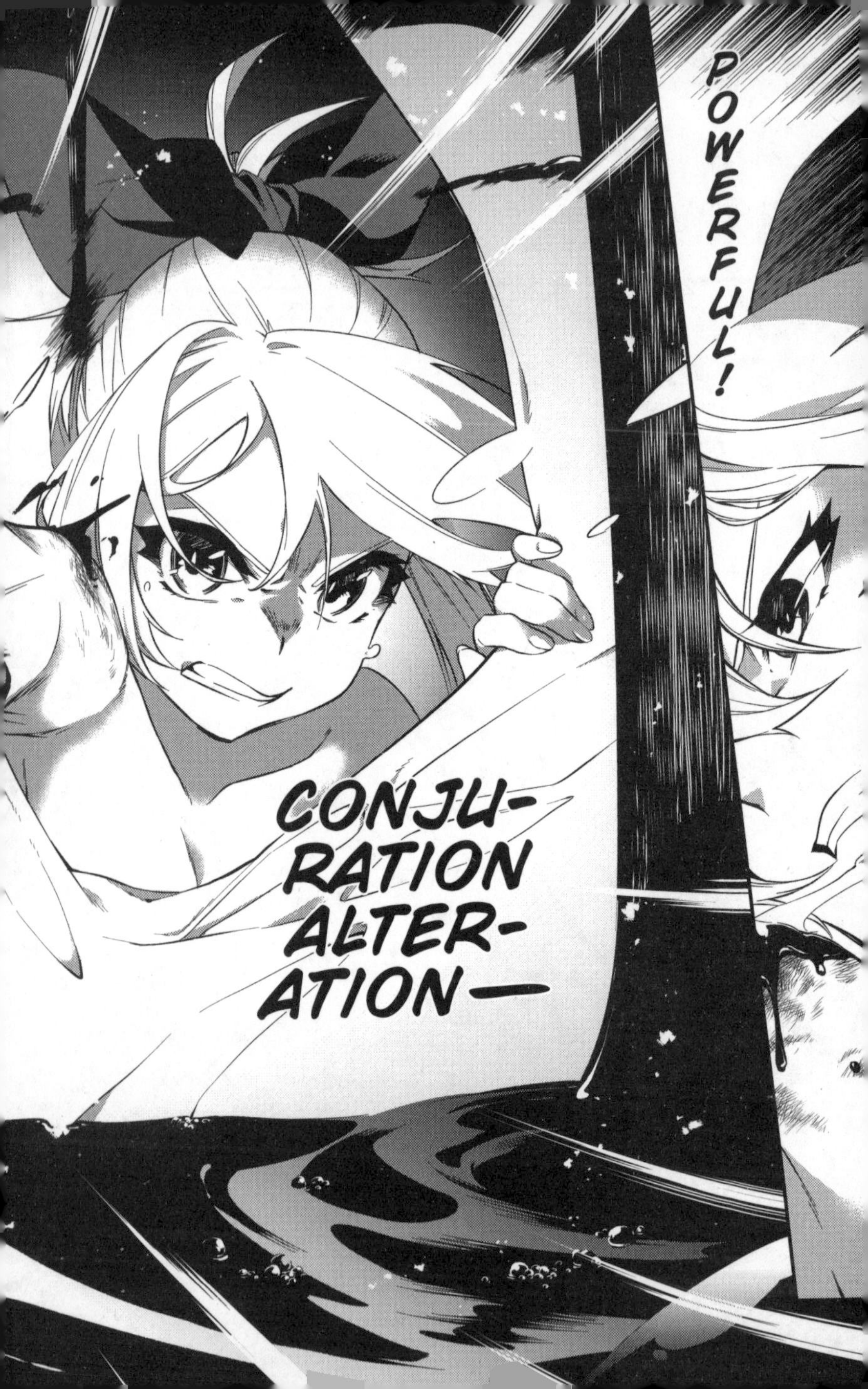
POWERFUL!
CONJU-RATION ALTER-ATION—

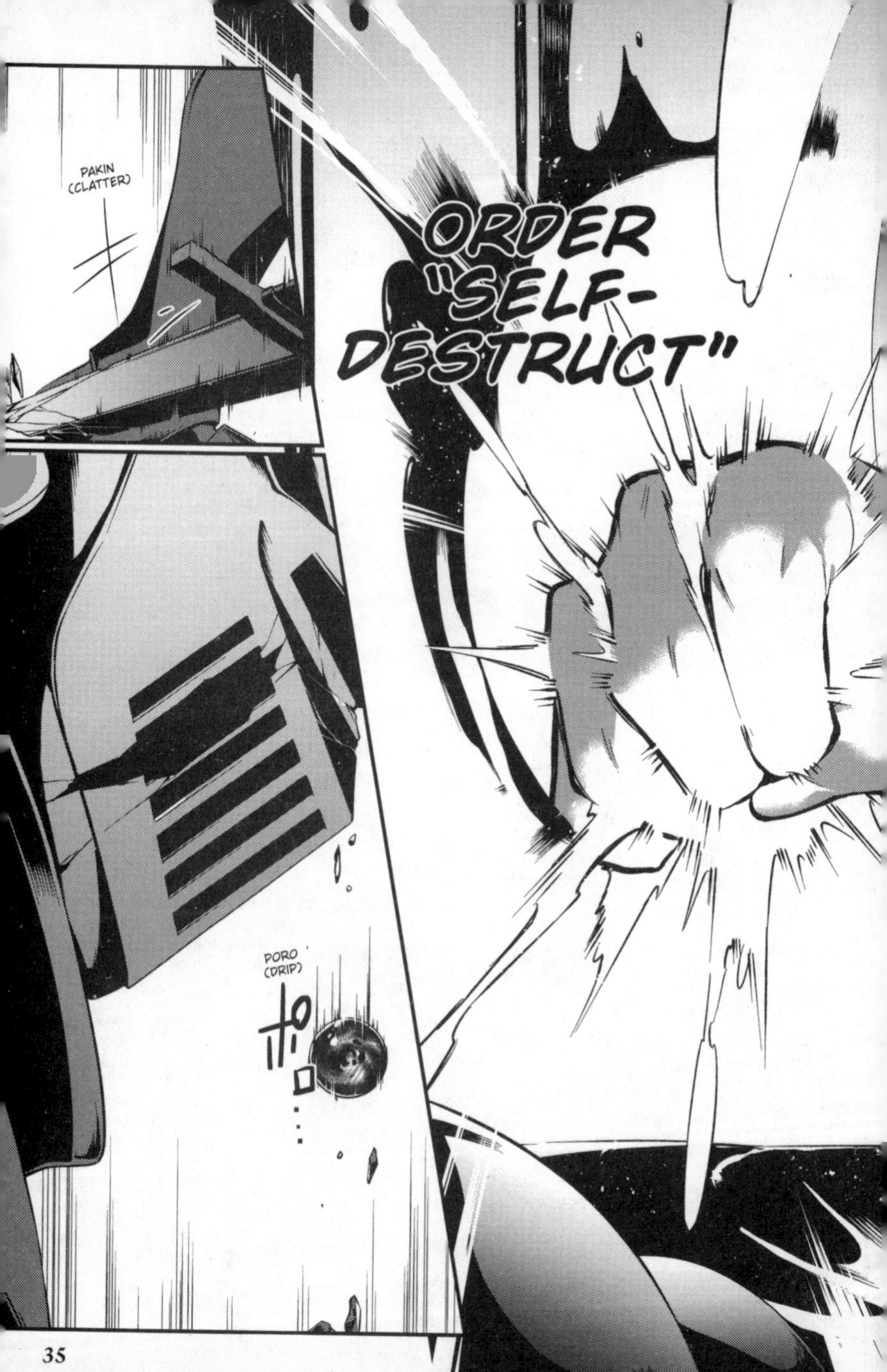
ORDER "SELF-DESTRUCT"
PAKIN (CLATTER)
PORO (DRIP)

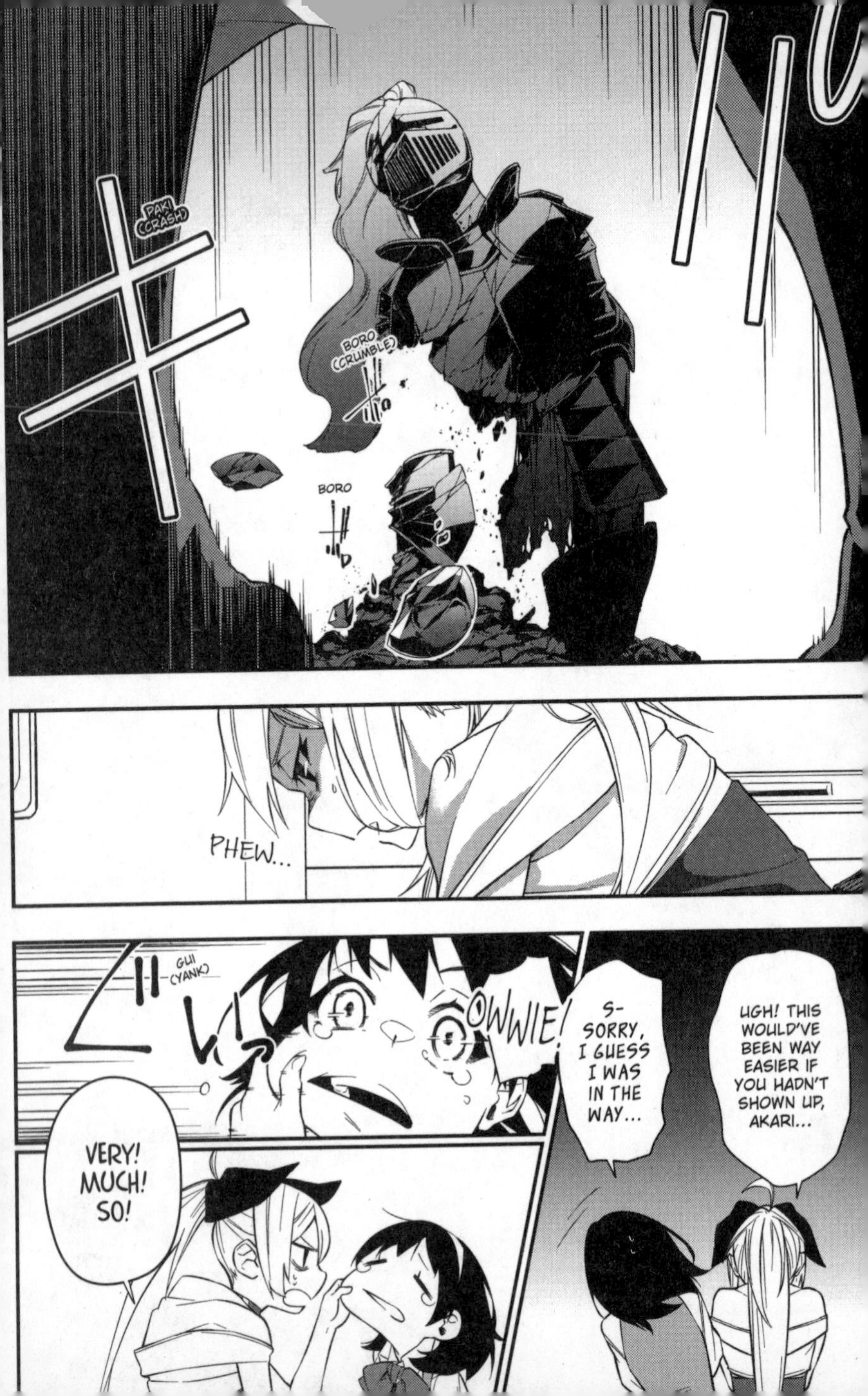
PAKI (CRASH)
BORO (CRUMBLE)
BORO
PHEW...
UGH! THIS WOULD'VE BEEN WAY EASIER IF YOU HADN'T SHOWN UP, AKARI...
S-SORRY, I GUESS I WAS IN THE WAY...
GUI (YANK)
OWWIE!
VERY! MUCH! SO!

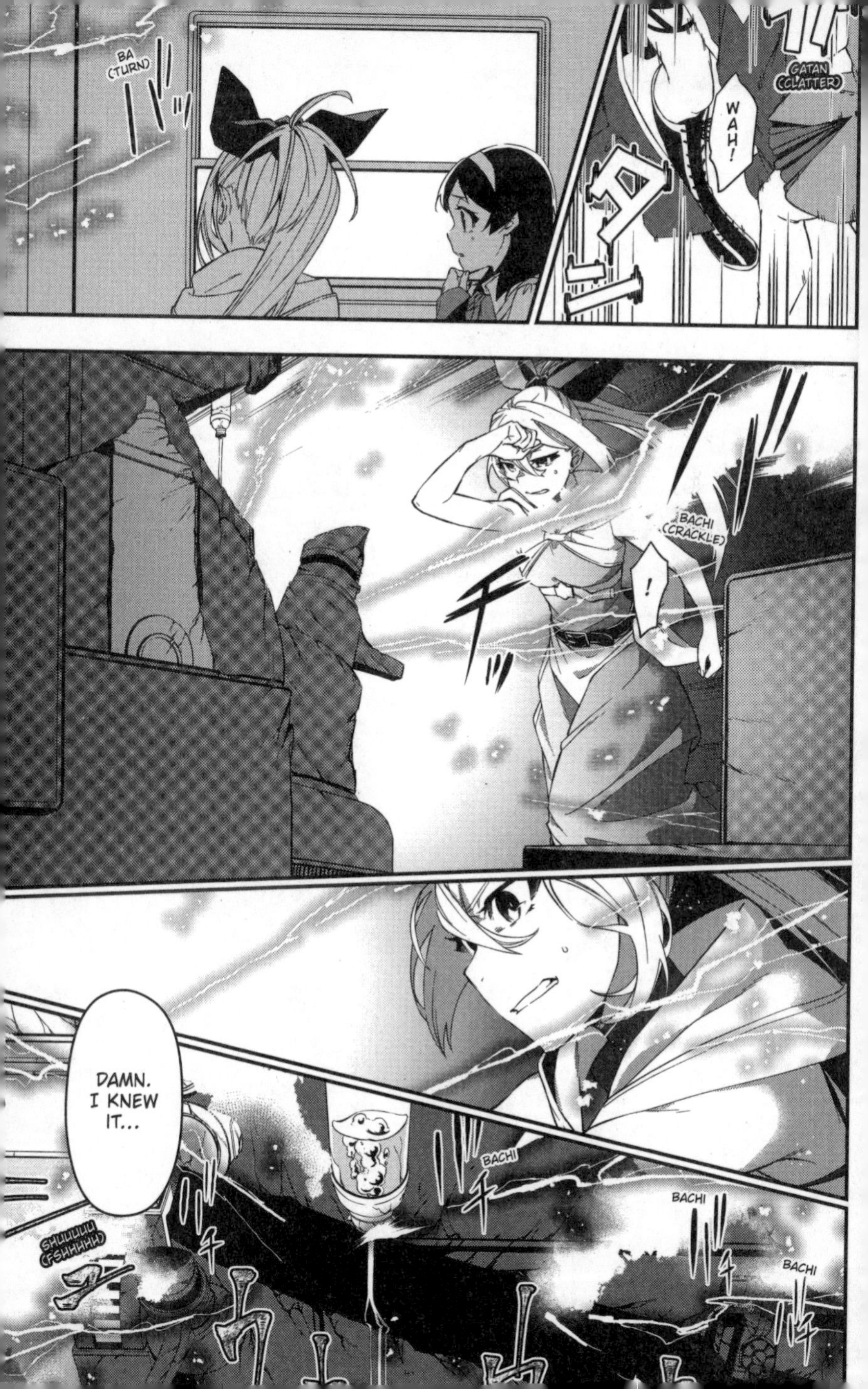
GATAN (CLATTER)
WAH!
BA (TURN)
BACHI (CRACKLE)
!
DAMN. I KNEW IT...
BACHI
BACHI
BACHI
SHUUUUU (FSHHHHH)

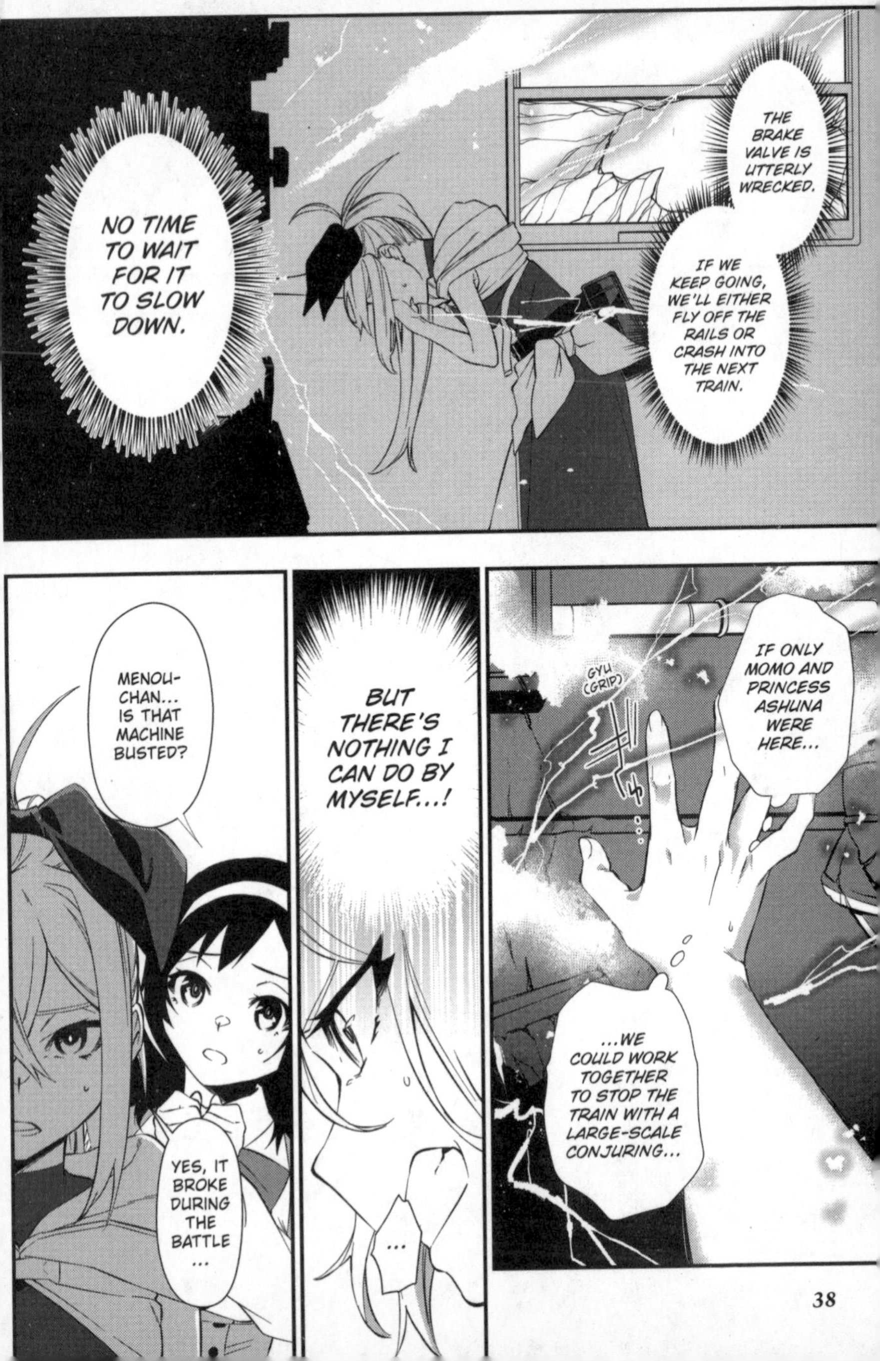
THE BRAKE VALVE IS UTTERLY WRECKED.
IF WE KEEP GOING, WE'LL EITHER FLY OFF THE RAILS OR CRASH INTO THE NEXT TRAIN.
NO TIME TO WAIT FOR IT TO SLOW DOWN.
IF ONLY MOMO AND PRINCESS ASHUNA WERE HERE...
GYU (GRIP)
...WE COULD WORK TOGETHER TO STOP THE TRAIN WITH A LARGE-SCALE CONJURING...
BUT THERE'S NOTHING I CAN DO BY MYSELF...!
...
MENOU-CHAN... IS THAT MACHINE BUSTED?
YES, IT BROKE DURING THE BATTLE ...

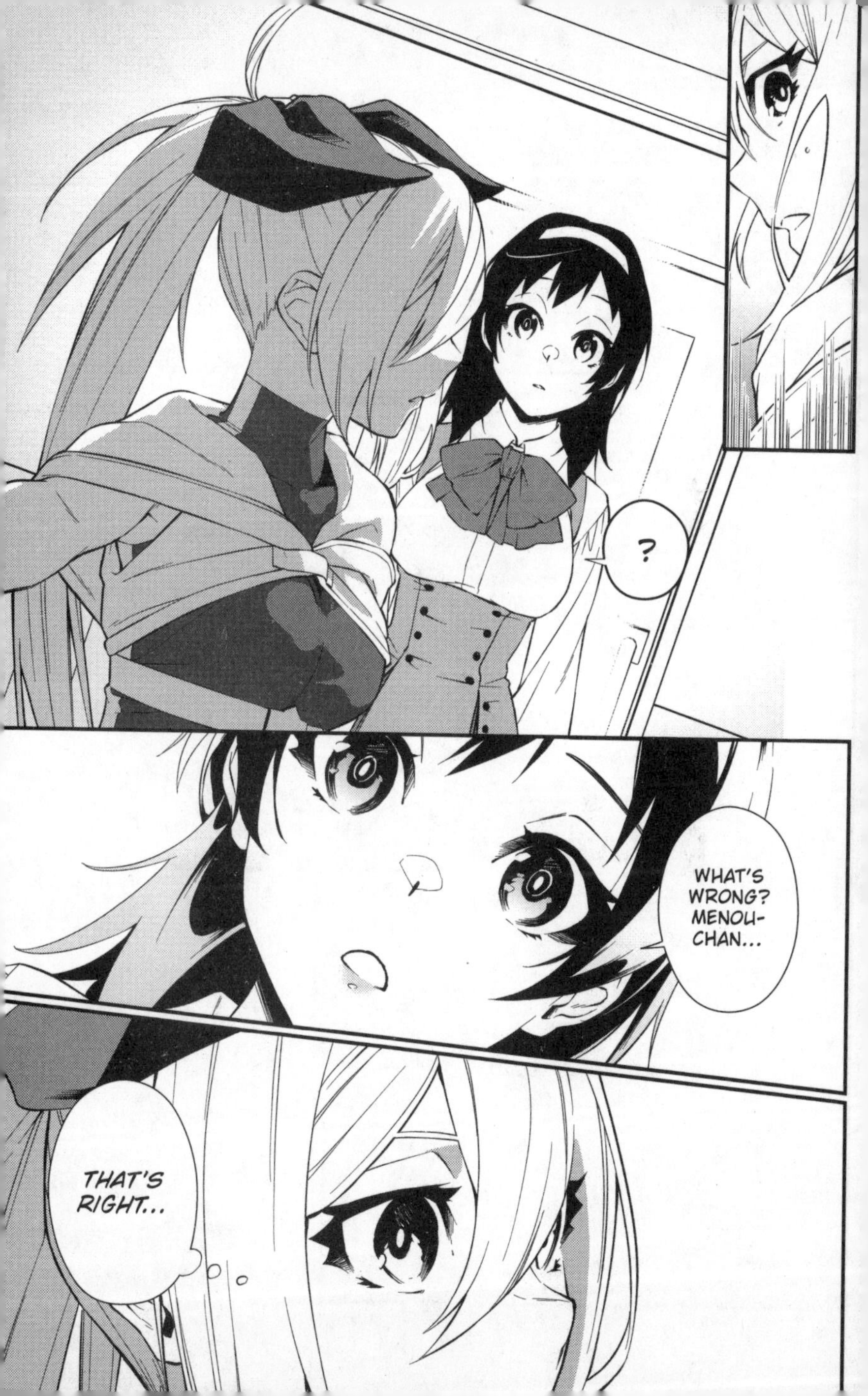
?
WHAT'S WRONG? MENOU-CHAN...
THAT'S RIGHT...

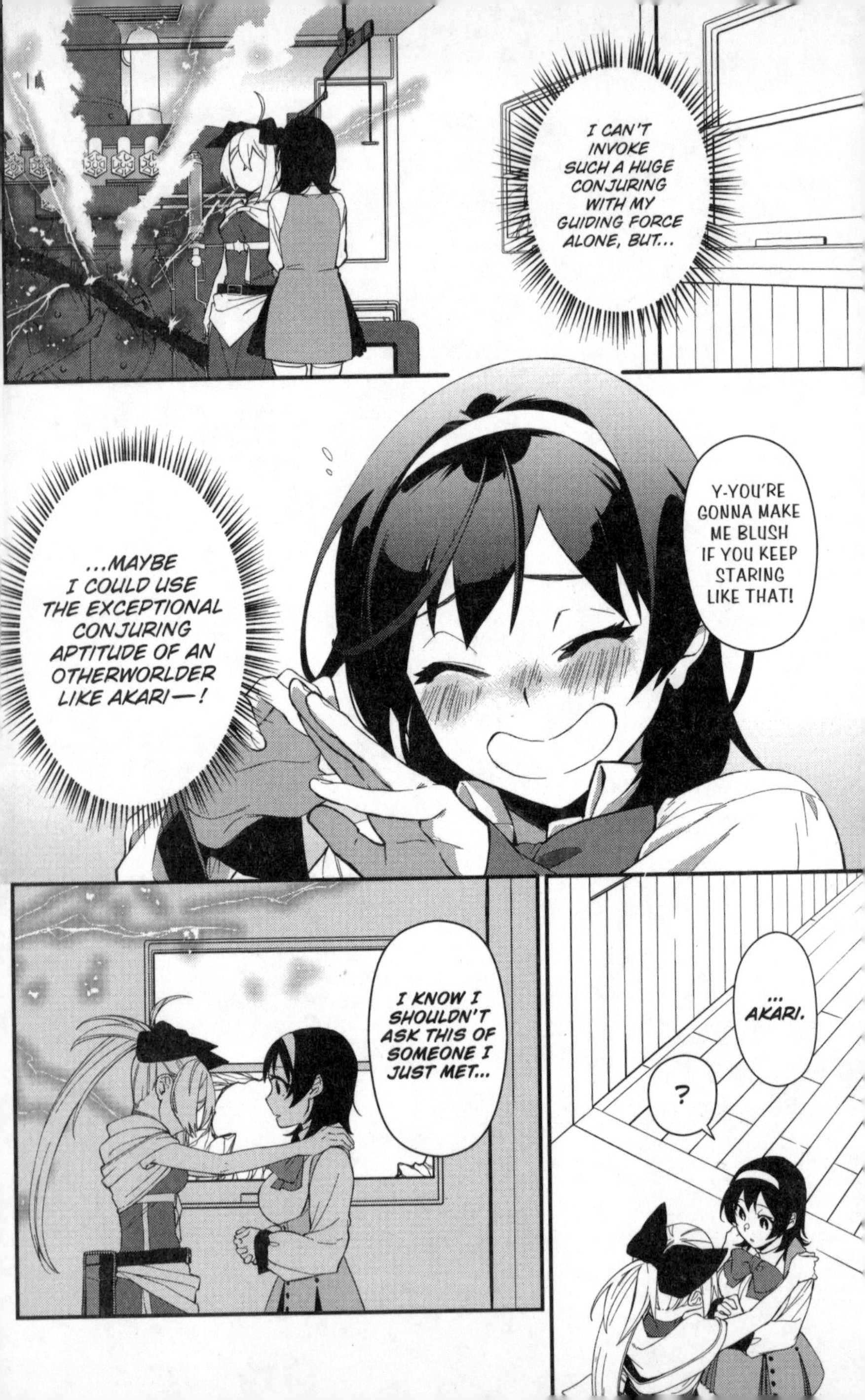
I CAN'T INVOKE SUCH A HUGE CONJURING WITH MY GUIDING FORCE ALONE, BUT...
Y-YOU'RE GONNA MAKE ME BLUSH IF YOU KEEP STARING LIKE THAT!
...MAYBE I COULD USE THE EXCEPTIONAL CONJURING APTITUDE OF AN OTHERWORLDER LIKE AKARI—!
... AKARI.
?
I KNOW I SHOULDN'T ASK THIS OF SOMEONE I JUST MET...

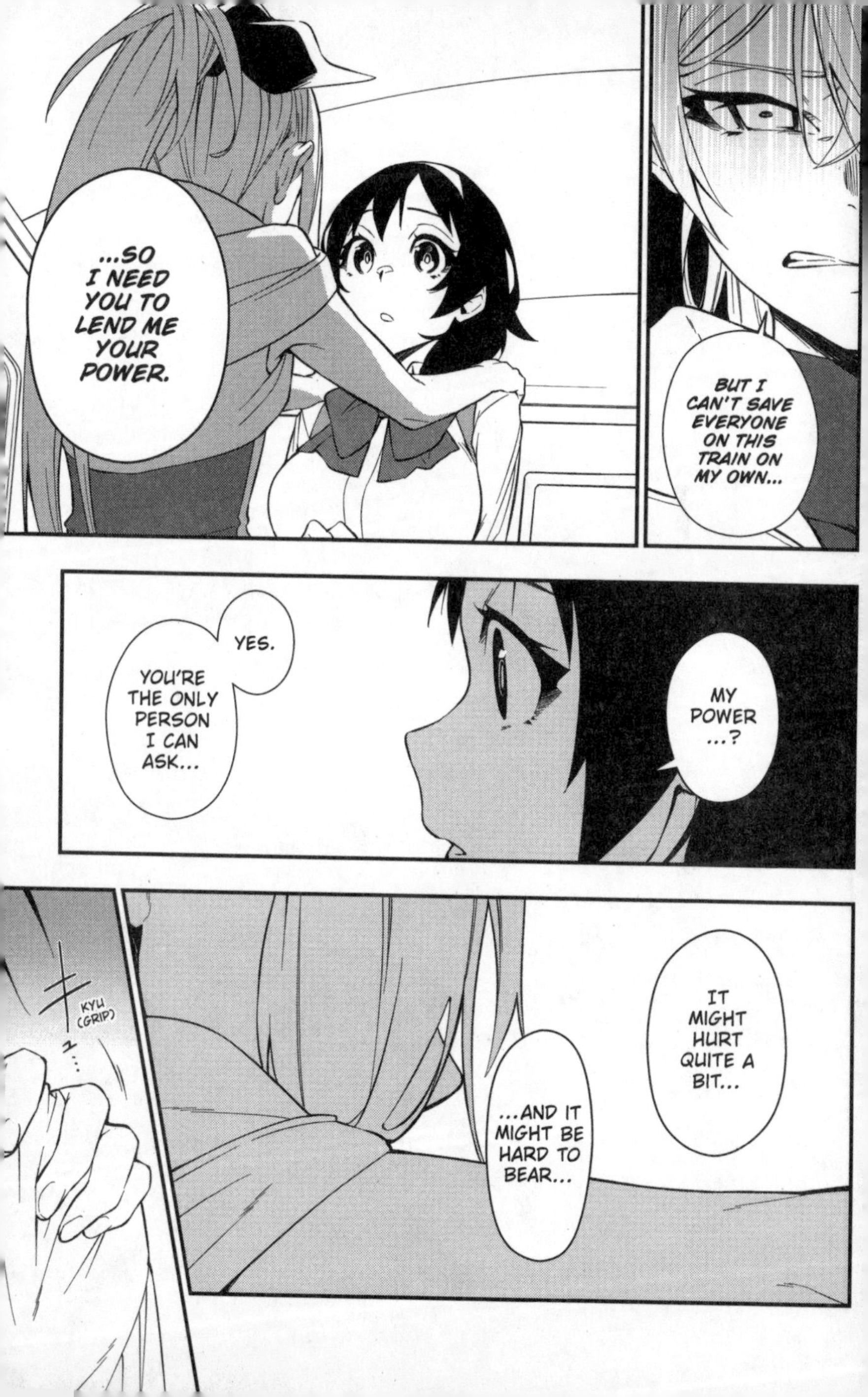
BUT I CAN'T SAVE EVERYONE ON THIS TRAIN ON MY OWN...
...SO I NEED YOU TO LEND ME YOUR POWER.
MY POWER ...?
YES.
YOU'RE THE ONLY PERSON I CAN ASK...
IT MIGHT HURT QUITE A BIT...
...AND IT MIGHT BE HARD TO BEAR...
KYU (GRIP)

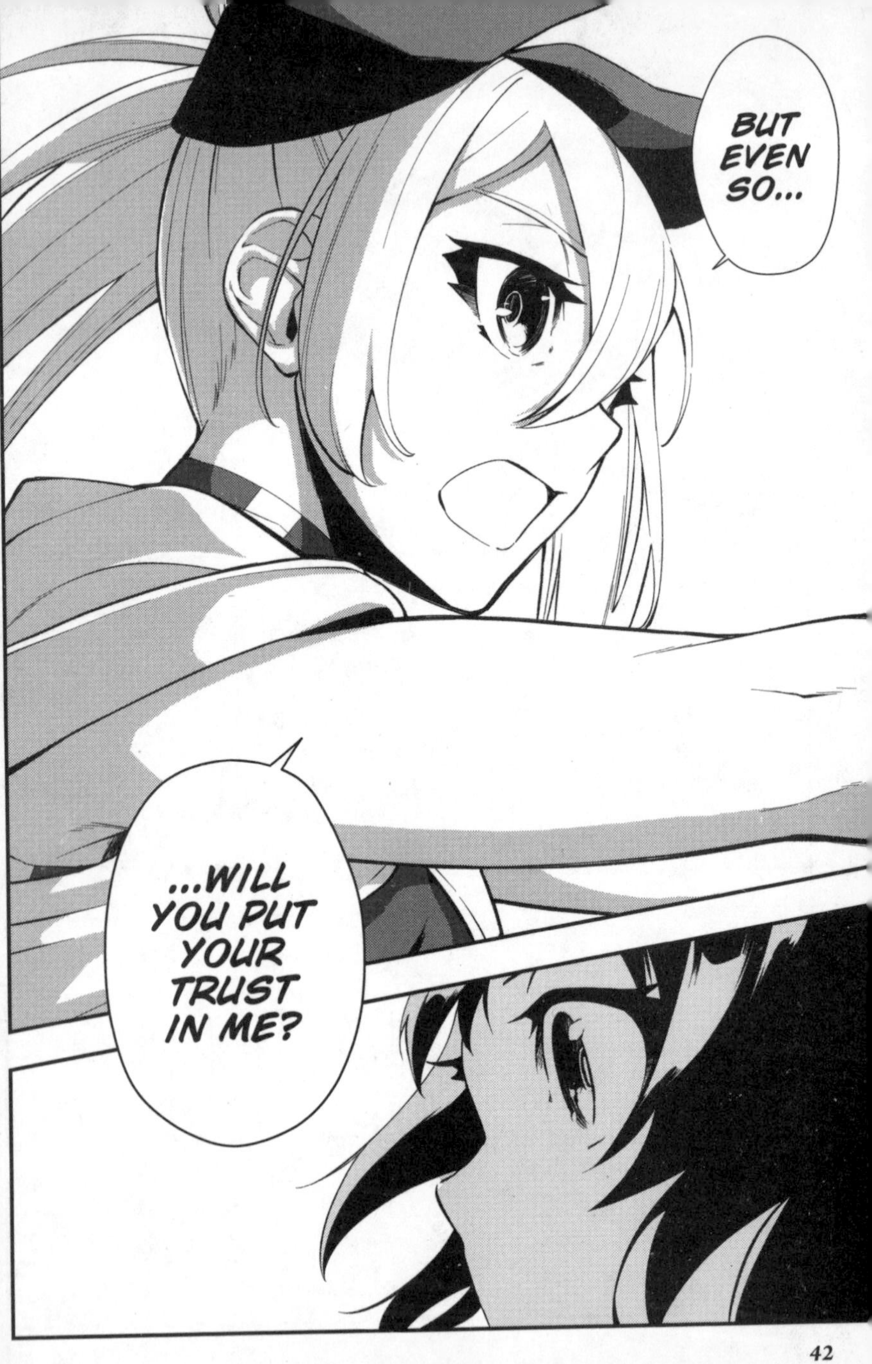
BUT EVEN SO...
...WILL YOU PUT YOUR TRUST IN ME?

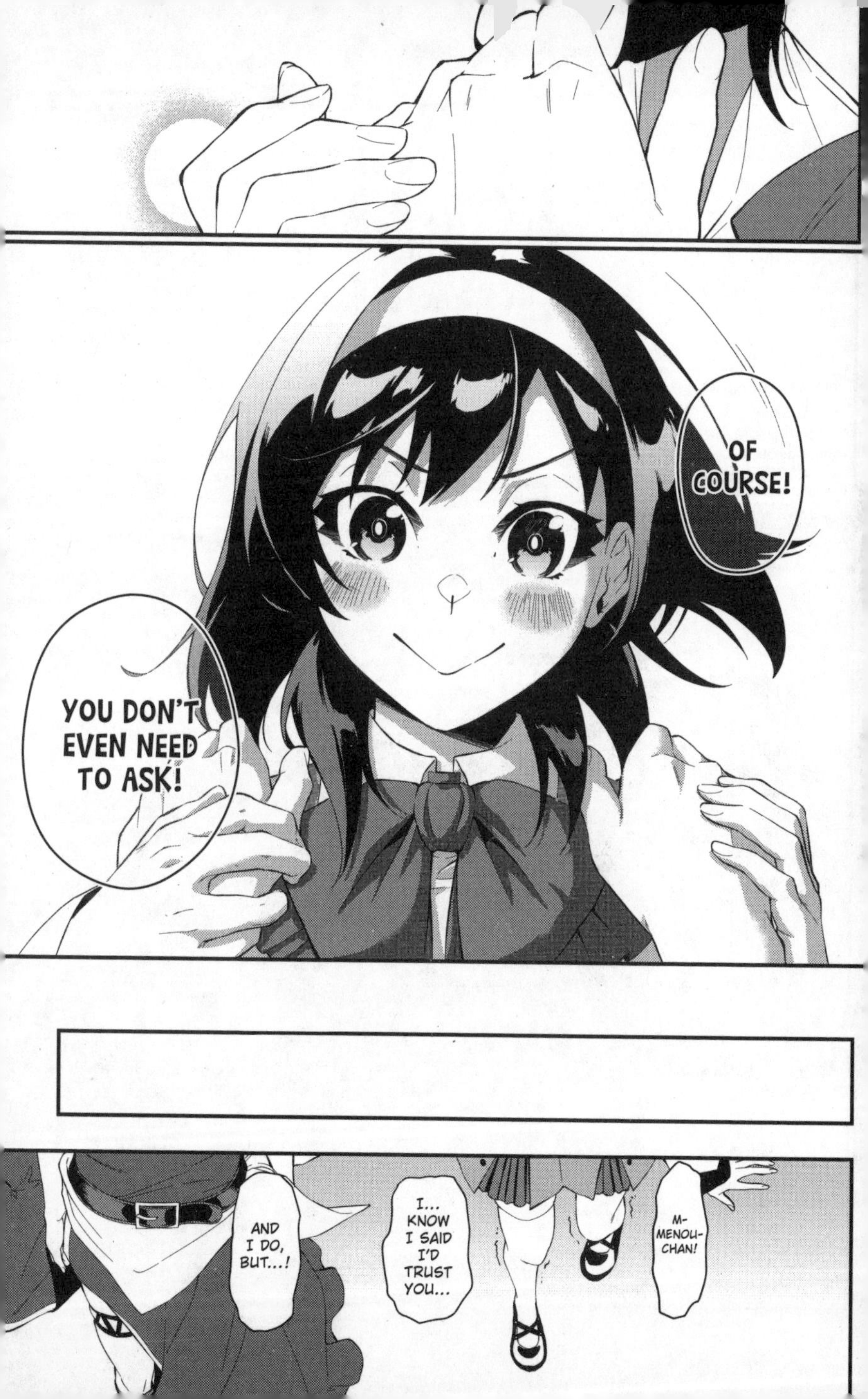
OF COURSE!
YOU DON'T EVEN NEED TO ASK!
M-MENOU-CHAN!
I... KNOW I SAID I'D TRUST YOU...
AND I DO, BUT...!

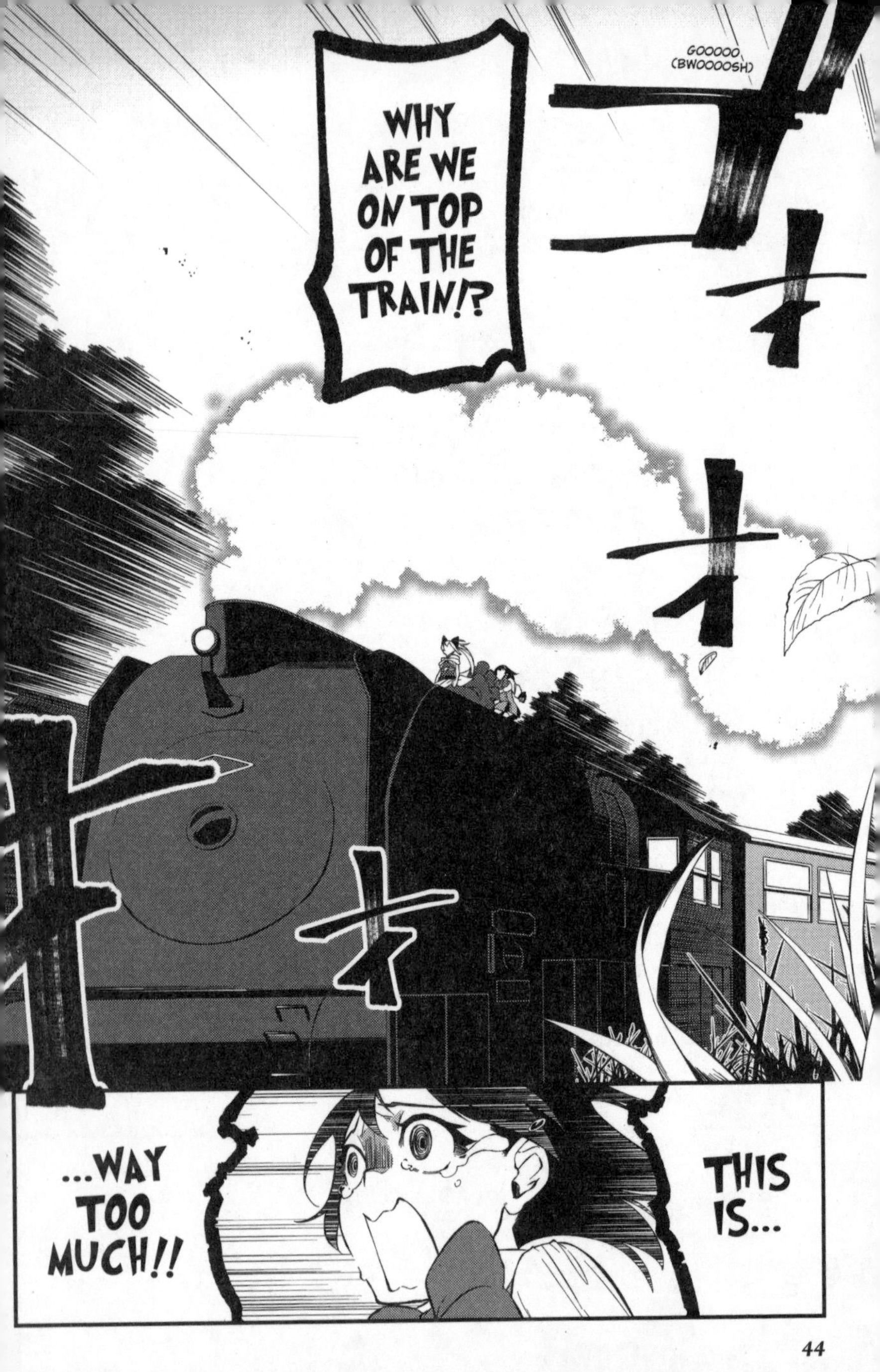
GOOOOO (BWOOOOSH)
WHY ARE WE ON TOP OF THE TRAIN!?
THIS IS...
...WAY TOO MUCH!!

The Executioner and Her Way of Life

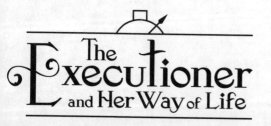

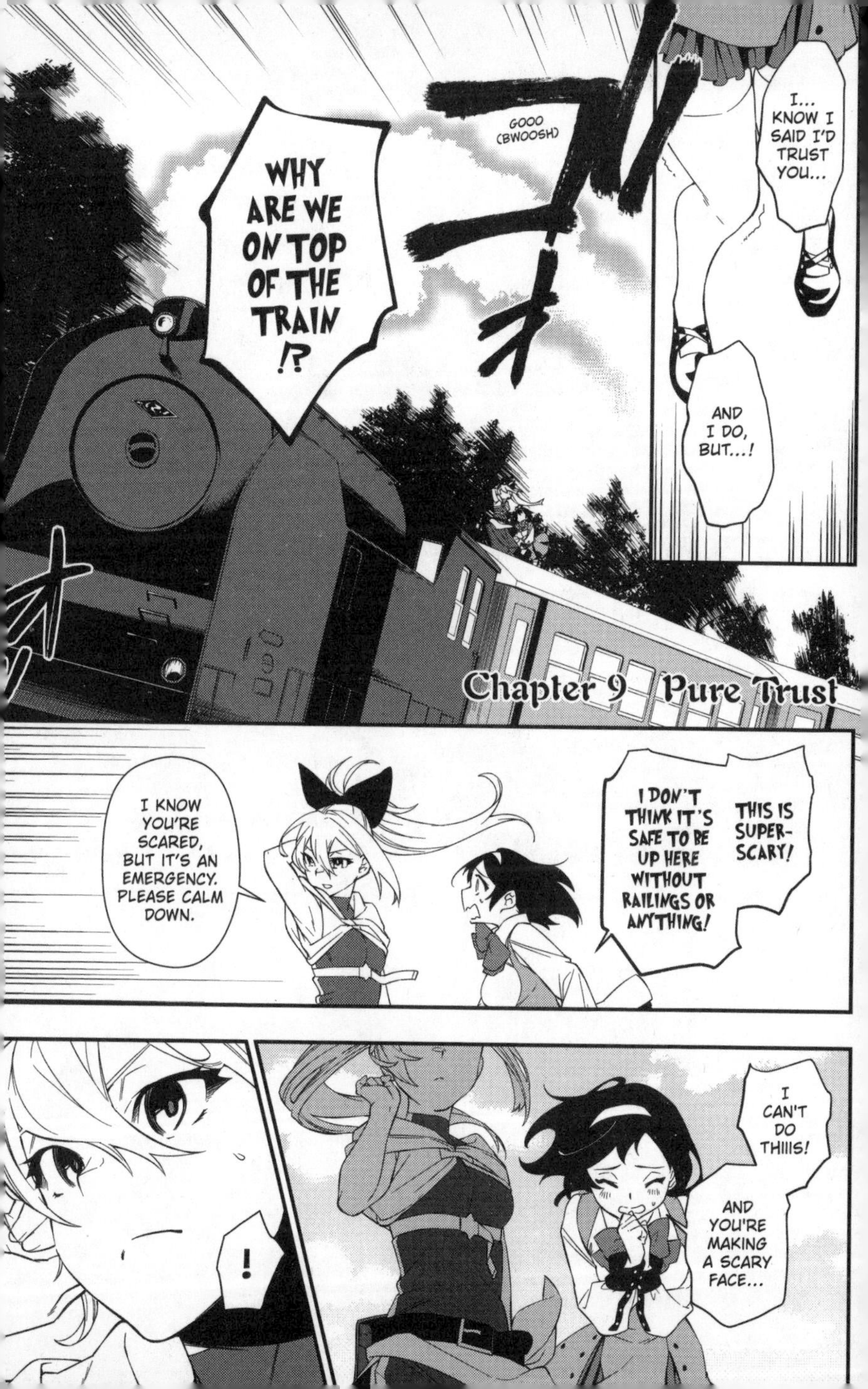
I... KNOW I SAID I'D TRUST YOU...
AND I DO, BUT...!
GOOO (BWOOSH)
WHY ARE WE ON TOP OF THE TRAIN ⁉
Chapter 9 Pure Trust
THIS IS SUPER-SCARY!
I DON'T THINK IT'S SAFE TO BE UP HERE WITHOUT RAILINGS OR ANYTHING!
I KNOW YOU'RE SCARED, BUT IT'S AN EMERGENCY. PLEASE CALM DOWN.
I CAN'T DO THIIIS!
AND YOU'RE MAKING A SCARY FACE...
!

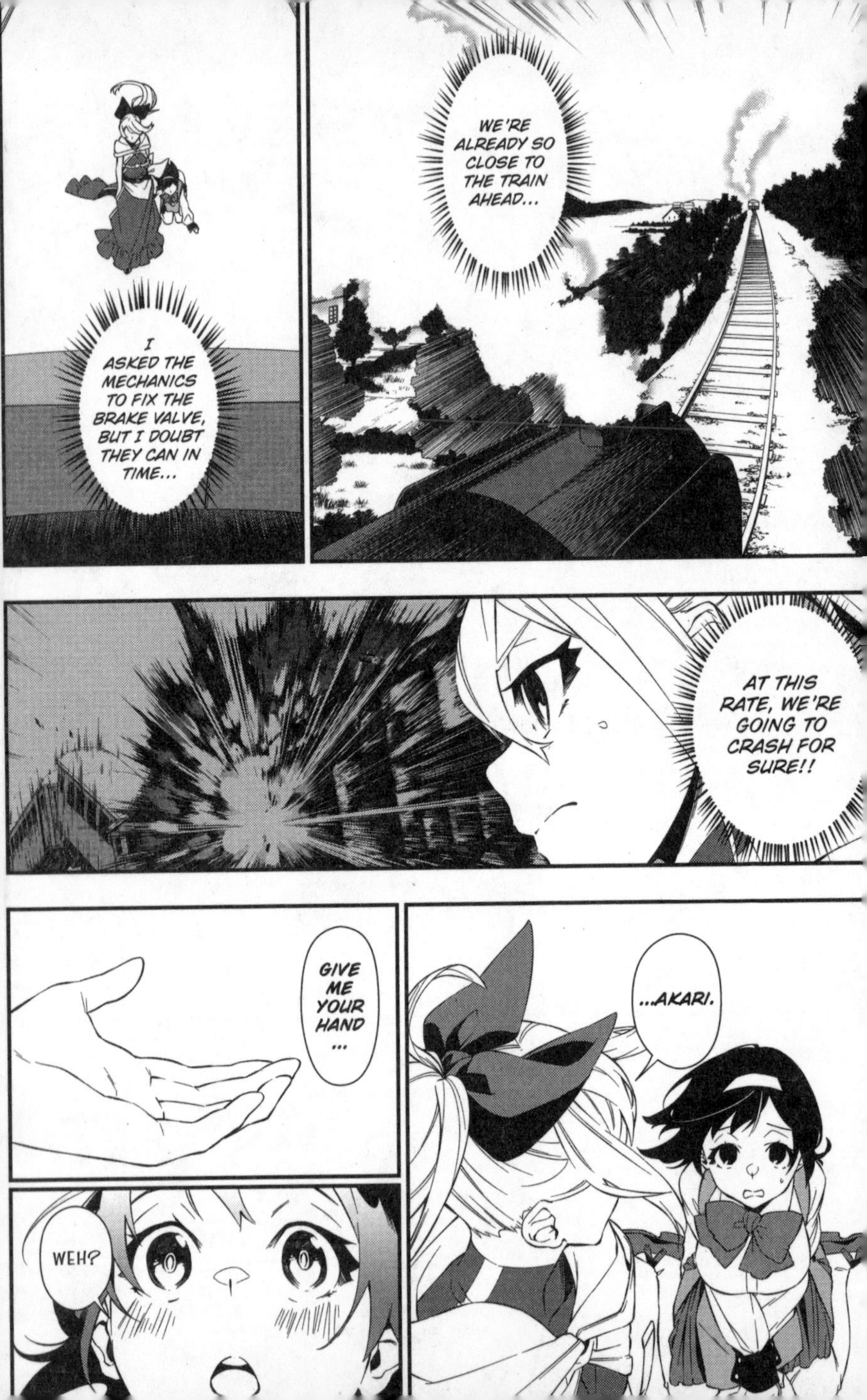
WE'RE ALREADY SO CLOSE TO THE TRAIN AHEAD...
I ASKED THE MECHANICS TO FIX THE BRAKE VALVE, BUT I DOUBT THEY CAN IN TIME...
AT THIS RATE, WE'RE GOING TO CRASH FOR SURE!!
...AKARI.
GIVE ME YOUR HAND ...
WEH?

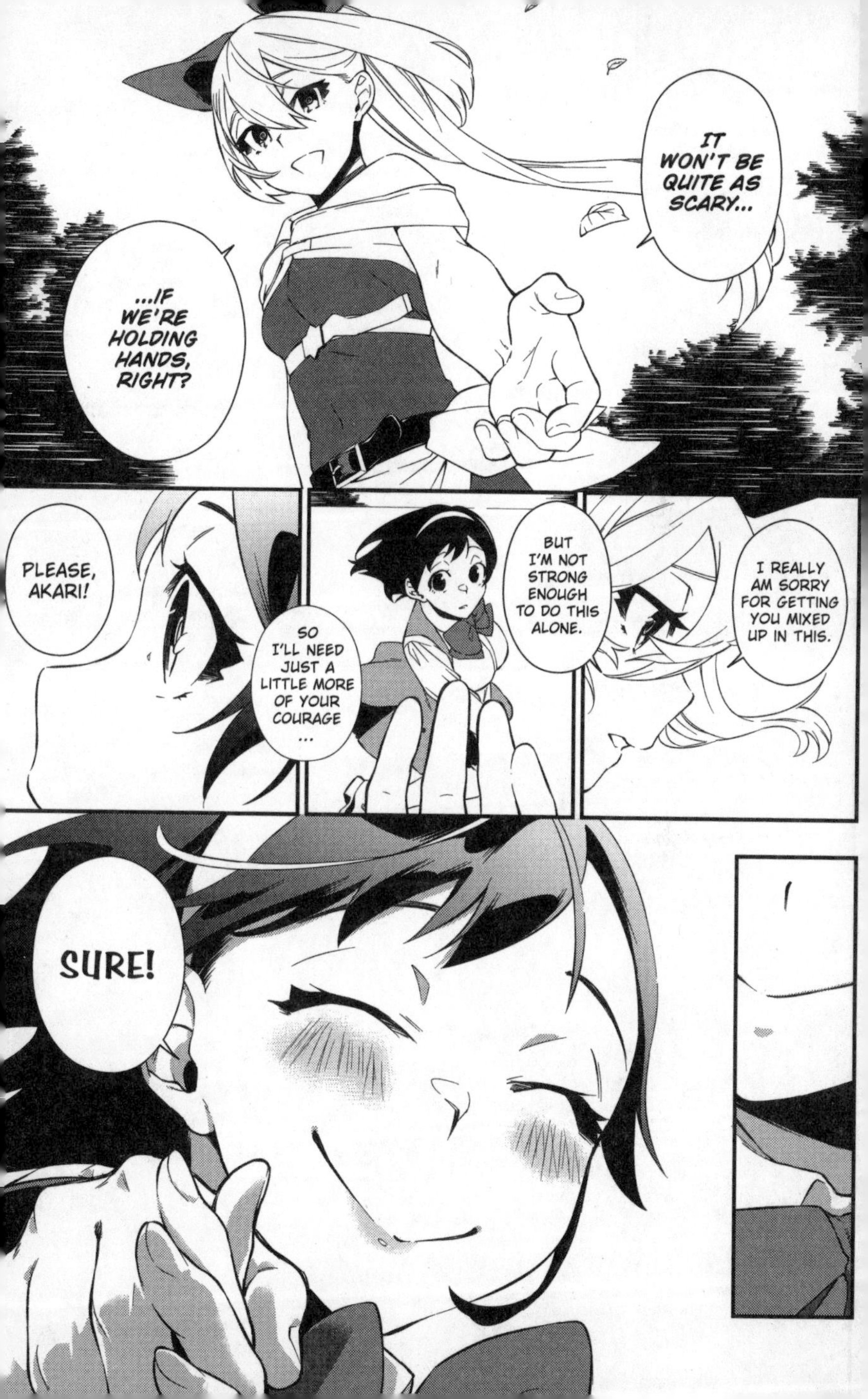
IT WON'T BE QUITE AS SCARY...
...IF WE'RE HOLDING HANDS, RIGHT?
I REALLY AM SORRY FOR GETTING YOU MIXED UP IN THIS.
BUT I'M NOT STRONG ENOUGH TO DO THIS ALONE.
SO I'LL NEED JUST A LITTLE MORE OF YOUR COURAGE ...
PLEASE, AKARI!
SURE!

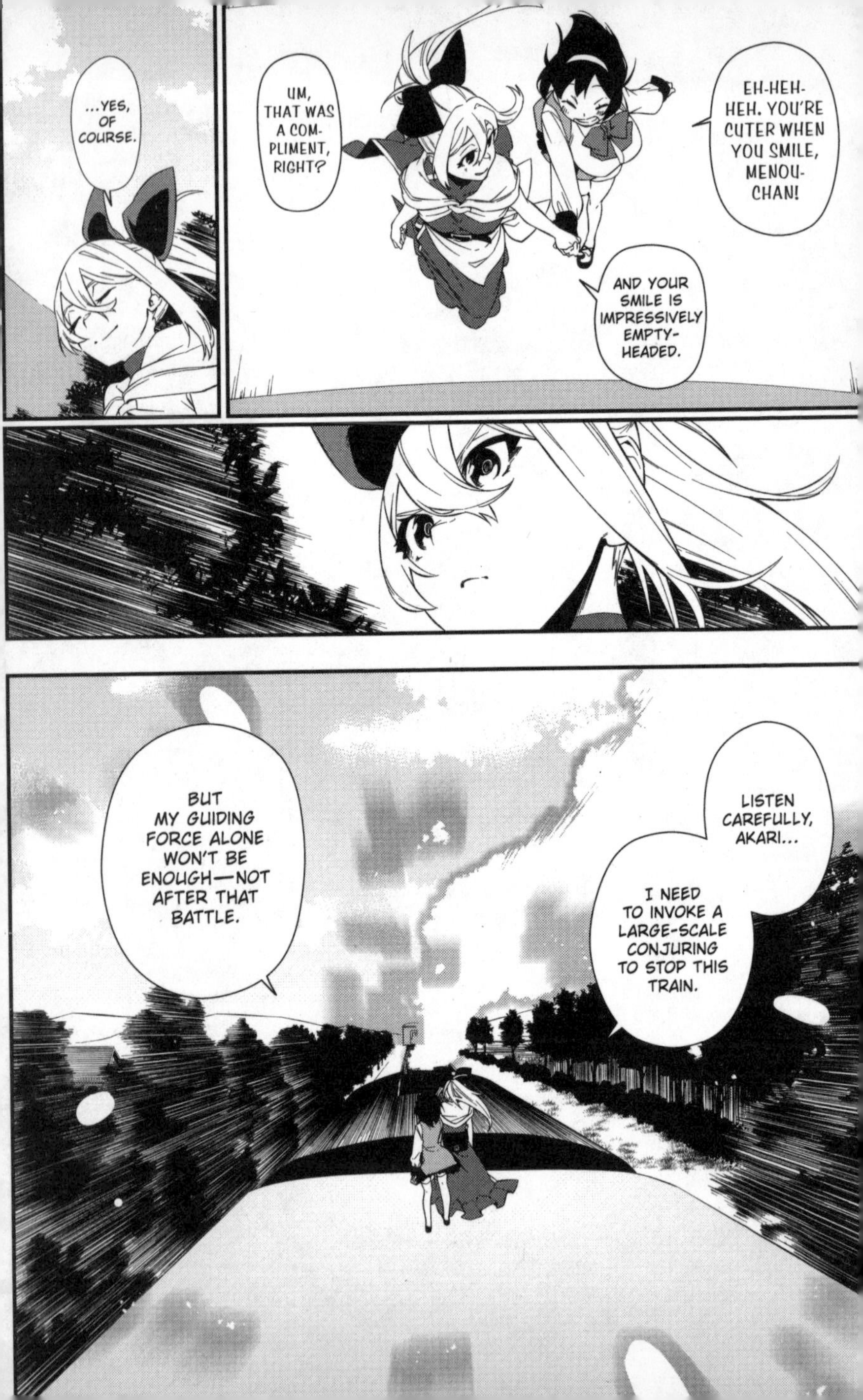
EH-HEH-HEH. YOU'RE CUTER WHEN YOU SMILE, MENOU-CHAN!
AND YOUR SMILE IS IMPRESSIVELY EMPTY-HEADED.
UM, THAT WAS A COMPLIMENT, RIGHT?
...YES, OF COURSE.
LISTEN CAREFULLY, AKARI...
I NEED TO INVOKE A LARGE-SCALE CONJURING TO STOP THIS TRAIN.
BUT MY GUIDING FORCE ALONE WON'T BE ENOUGH—NOT AFTER THAT BATTLE.

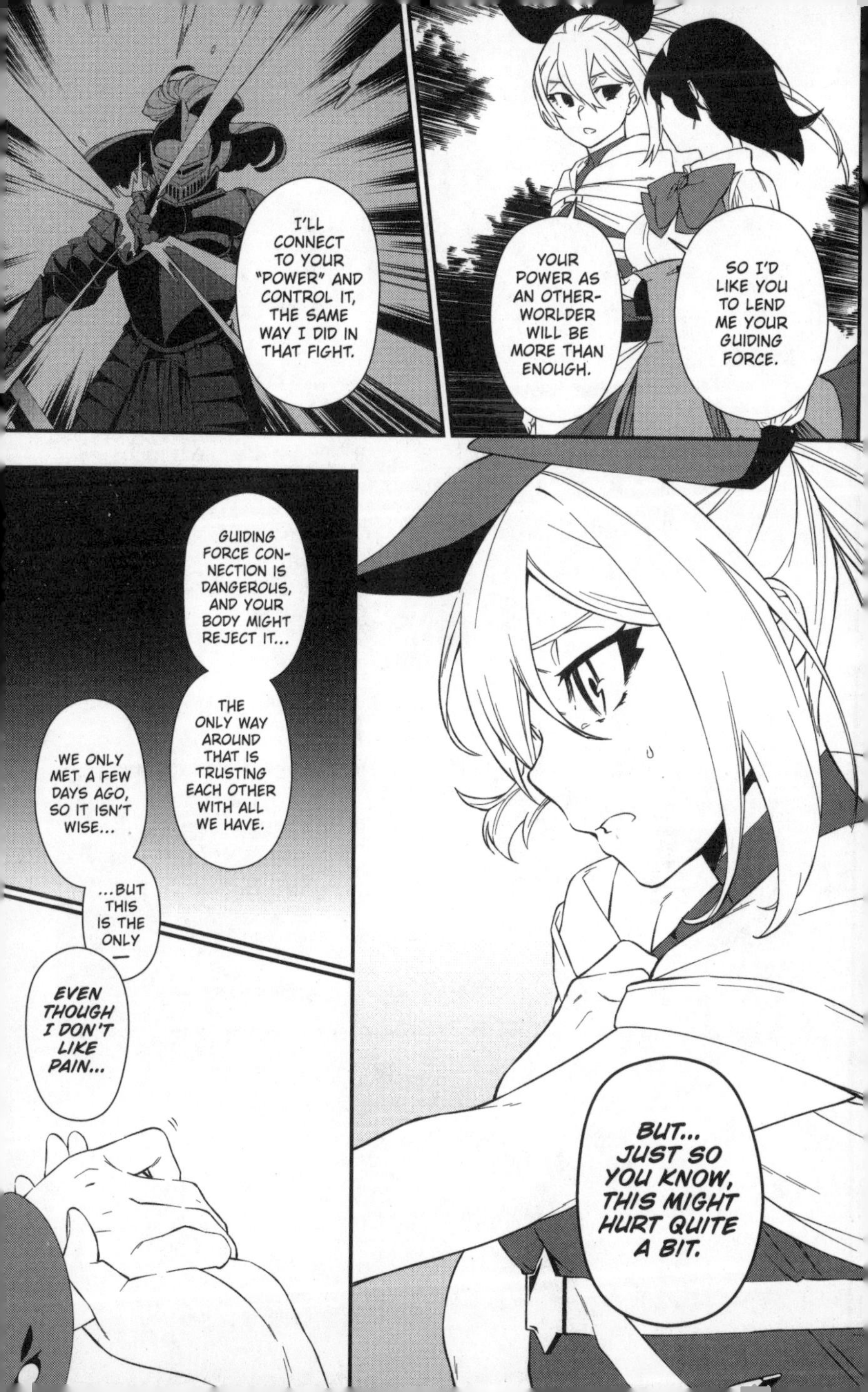
SO I'D LIKE YOU TO LEND ME YOUR GUIDING FORCE.
YOUR POWER AS AN OTHER-WORLDER WILL BE MORE THAN ENOUGH.
I'LL CONNECT TO YOUR "POWER" AND CONTROL IT, THE SAME WAY I DID IN THAT FIGHT.
BUT... JUST SO YOU KNOW, THIS MIGHT HURT QUITE A BIT.
GUIDING FORCE CON-NECTION IS DANGEROUS, AND YOUR BODY MIGHT REJECT IT...
THE ONLY WAY AROUND THAT IS TRUSTING EACH OTHER WITH ALL WE HAVE.
WE ONLY MET A FEW DAYS AGO, SO IT ISN'T WISE...
...BUT THIS IS THE ONLY—
EVEN THOUGH I DON'T LIKE PAIN...

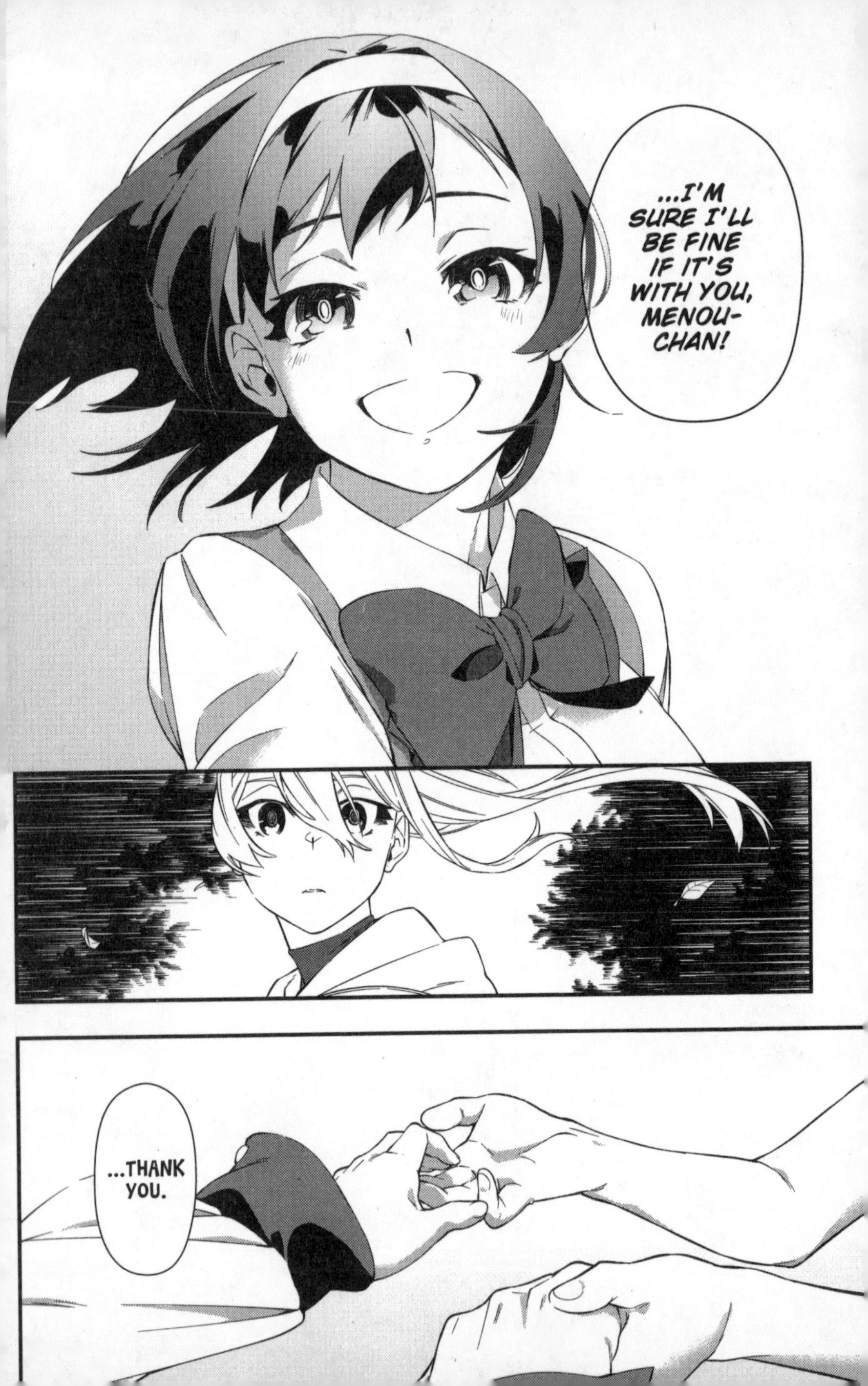
...I'M SURE I'LL BE FINE IF IT'S WITH YOU, MENOU-CHAN!
...THANK YOU.

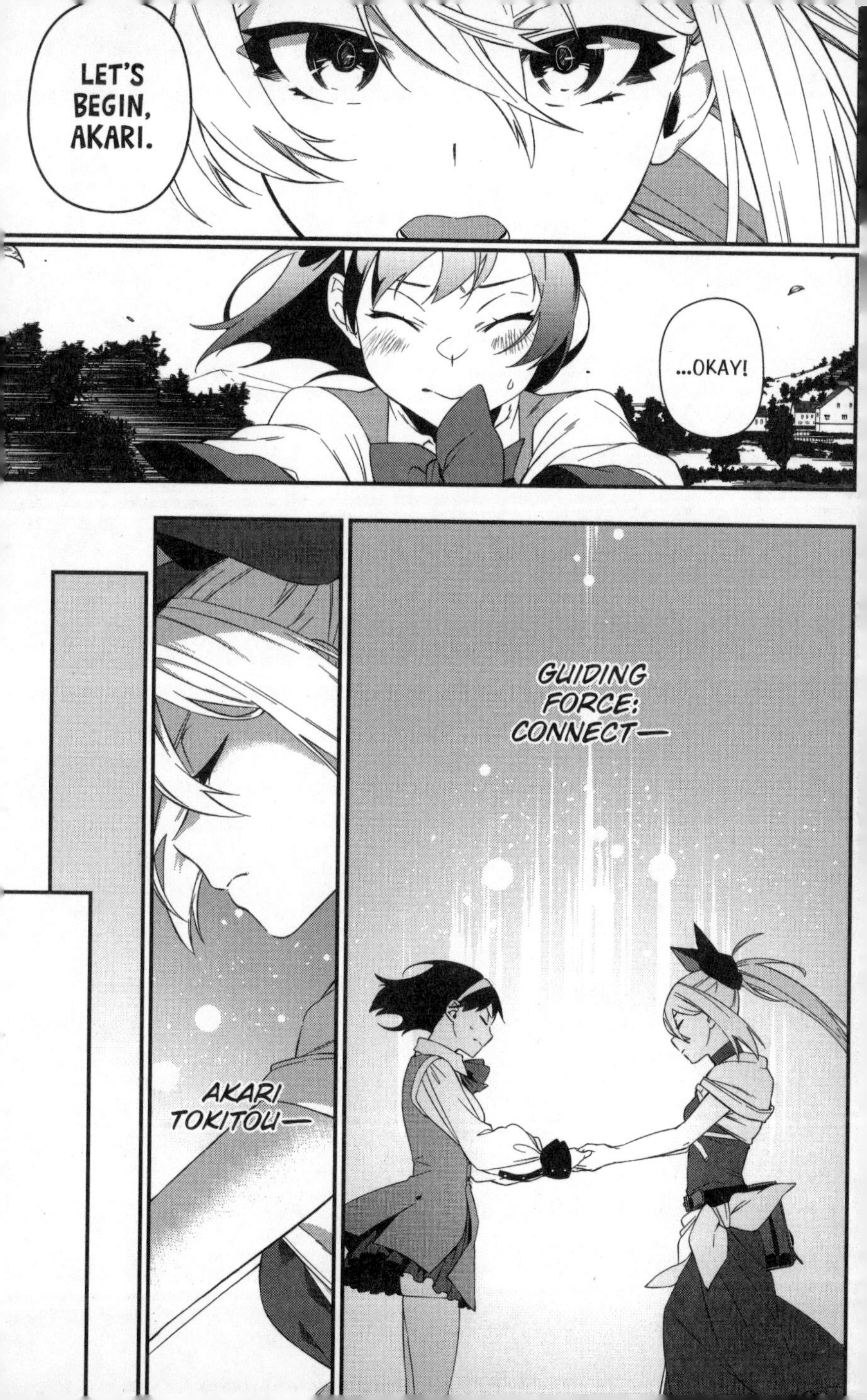
LET'S BEGIN, AKARI.
...OKAY!
GUIDING FORCE: CONNECT—
AKARI TOKITOU—

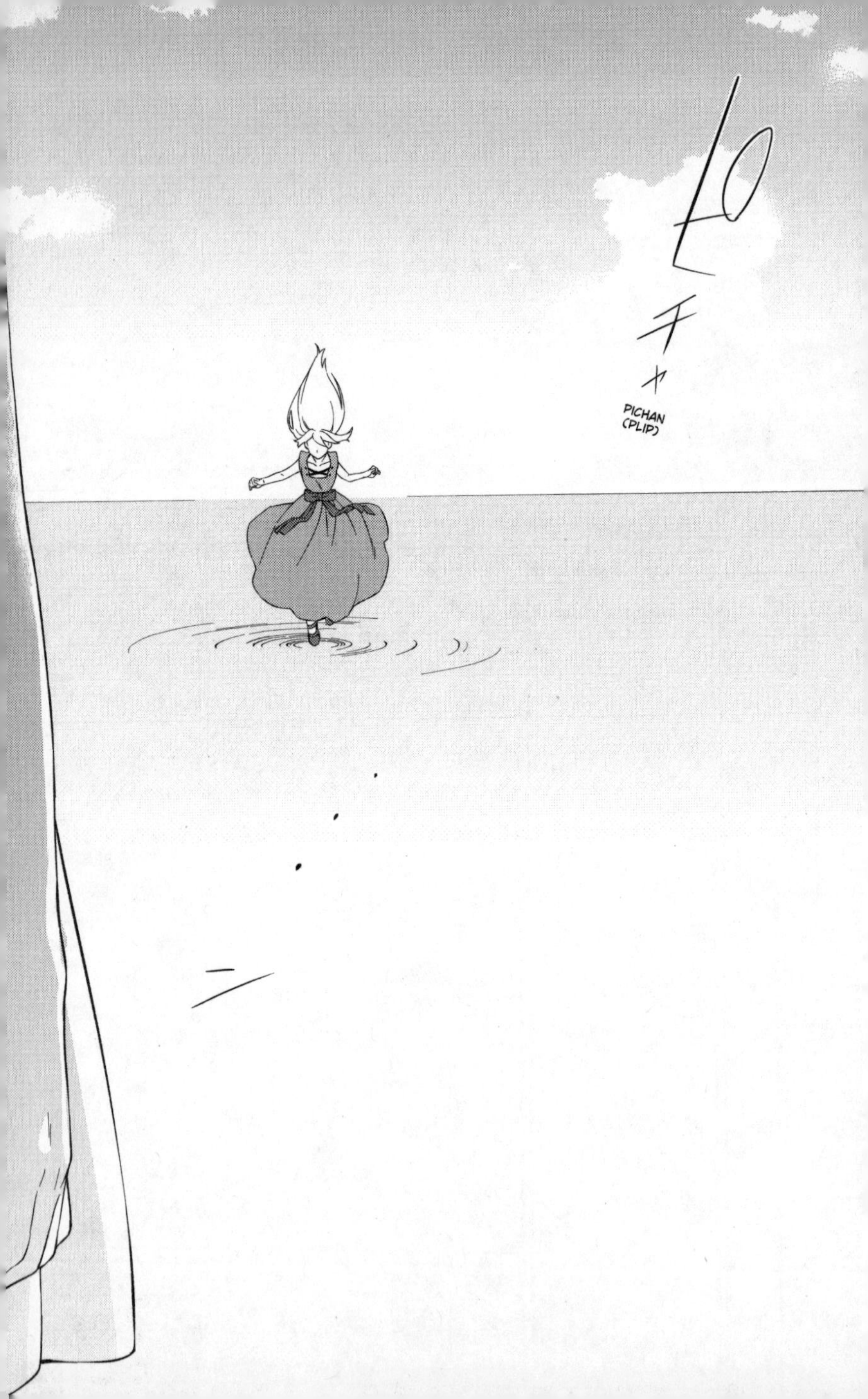
ピチャ
PICHAN
(PLIP)

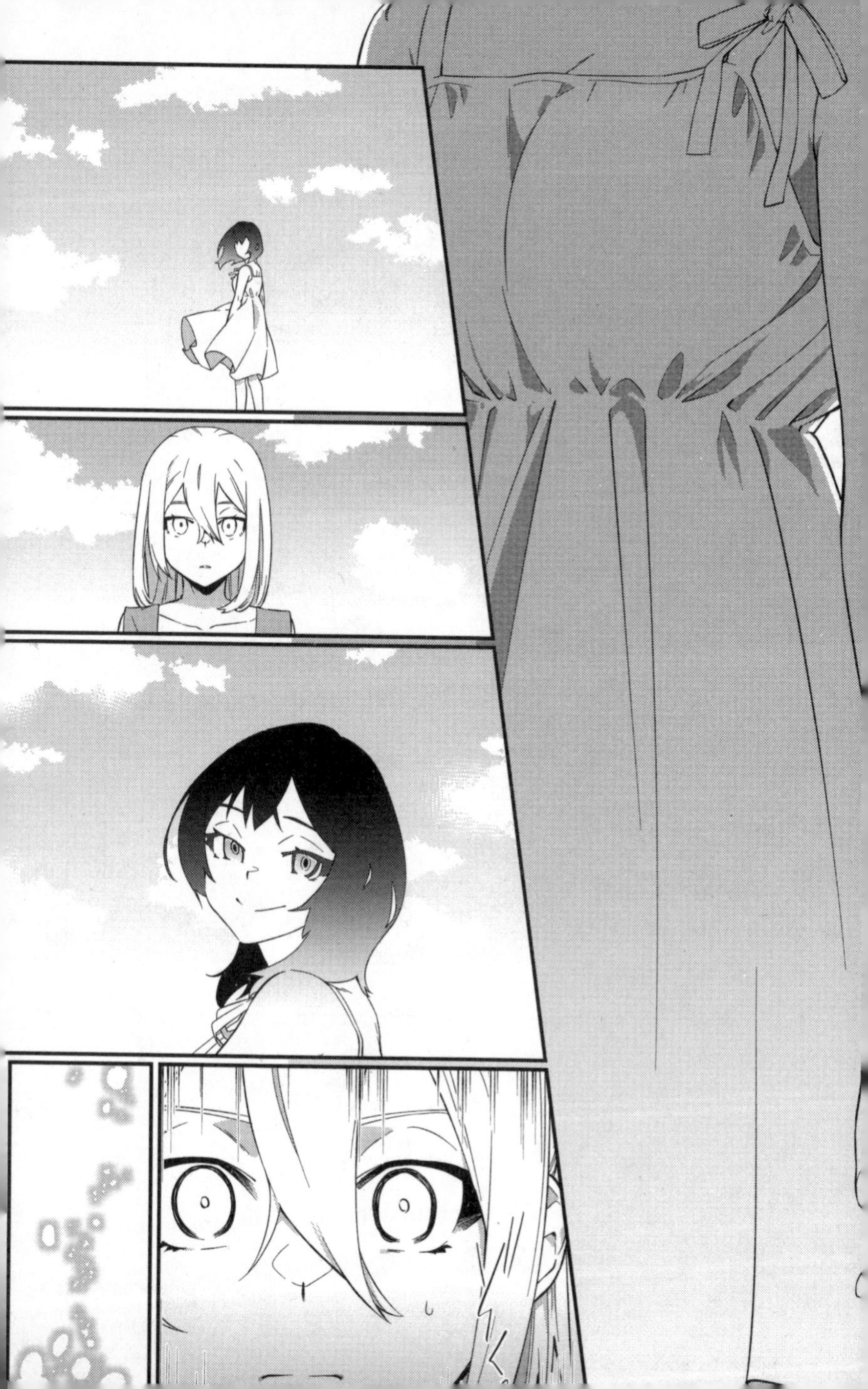

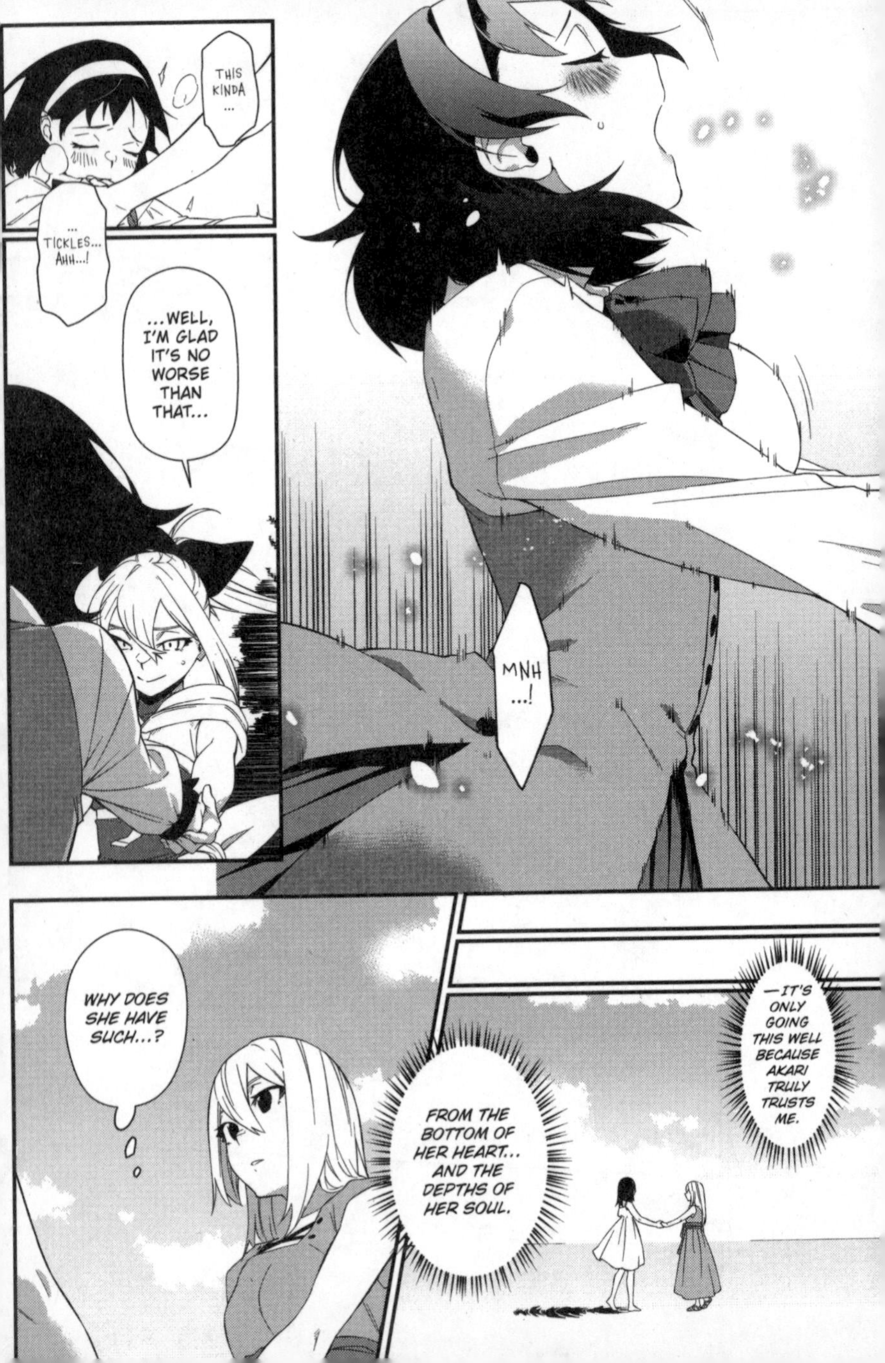
MNH...!
THIS KINDA...
...TICKLES... AHH...!
...WELL, I'M GLAD IT'S NO WORSE THAN THAT...
—IT'S ONLY GOING THIS WELL BECAUSE AKARI TRULY TRUSTS ME.
FROM THE BOTTOM OF HER HEART... AND THE DEPTHS OF HER SOUL.
WHY DOES SHE HAVE SUCH...?

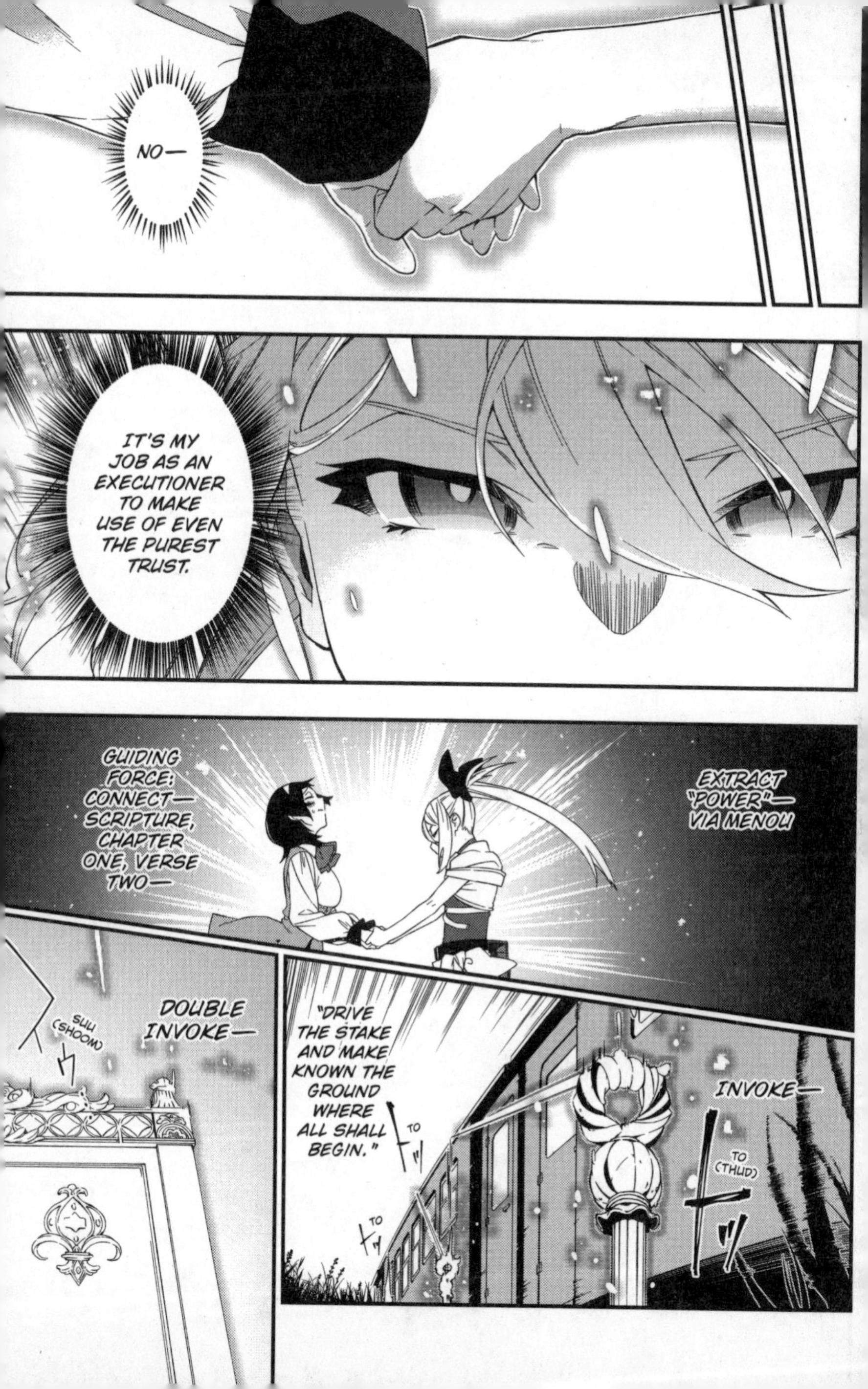
NO—
IT'S MY JOB AS AN EXECUTIONER TO MAKE USE OF EVEN THE PUREST TRUST.
EXTRACT "POWER"— VIA MENOU
GUIDING FORCE: CONNECT— SCRIPTURE, CHAPTER ONE, VERSE TWO—
INVOKE—
"DRIVE THE STAKE AND MAKE KNOWN THE GROUND WHERE ALL SHALL BEGIN."
TO
TO (THUD)
TO
DOUBLE INVOKE—
SUU (SHOOM)

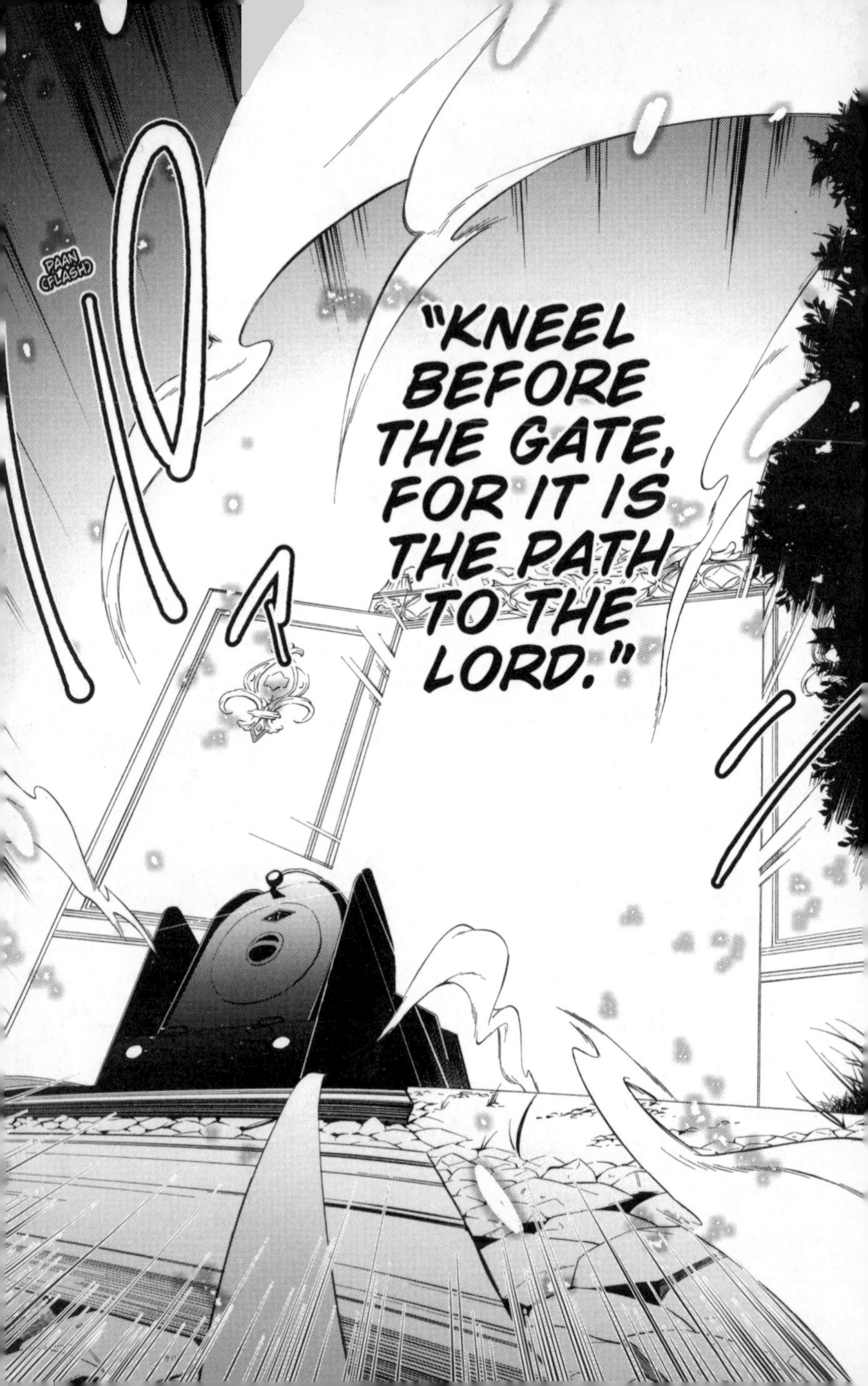

"KNEEL BEFORE THE GATE, FOR IT IS THE PATH TO THE LORD."
PAAN (FLASH)

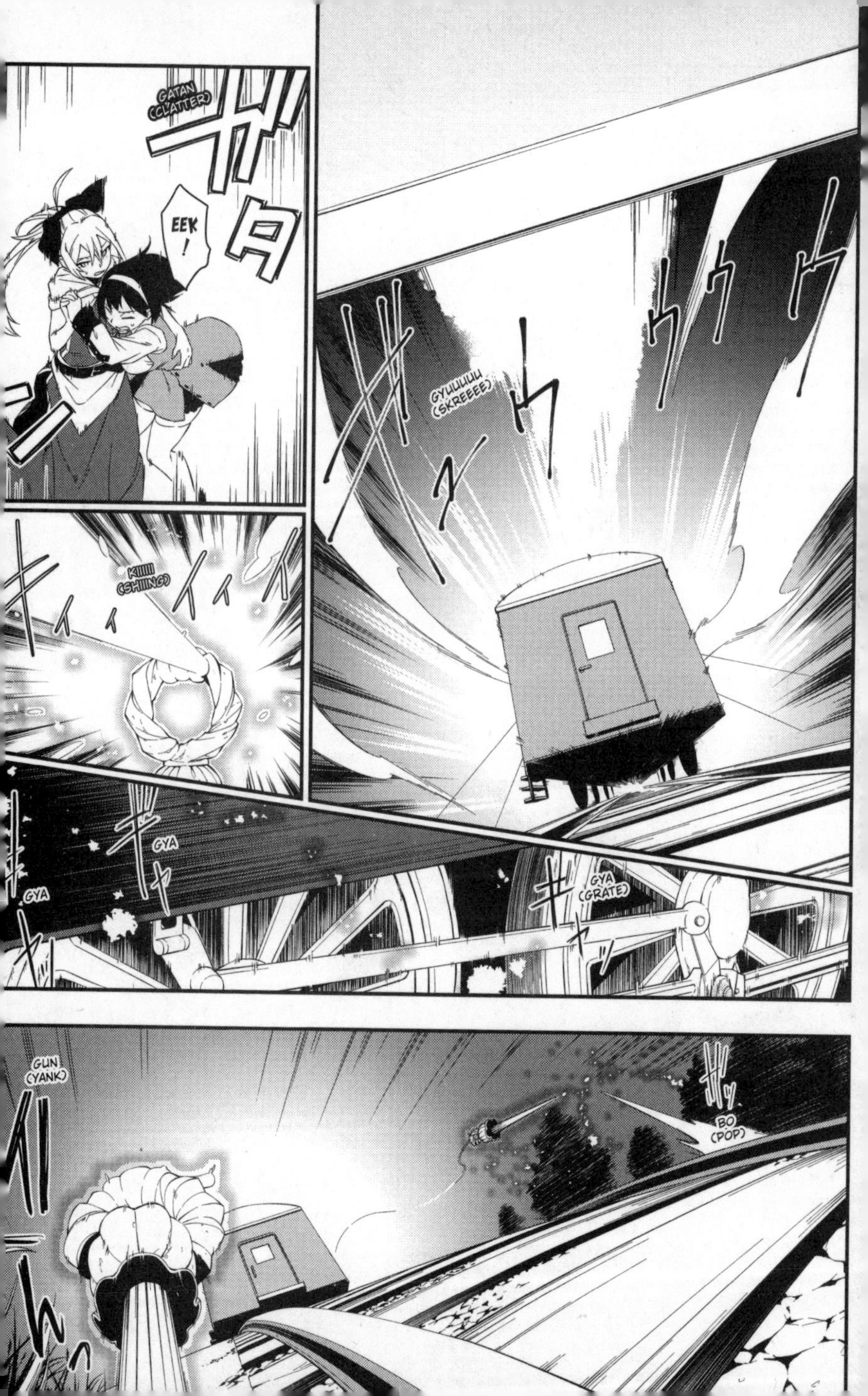
GYUUUUU (SKREEEE)
GATAN (CLATTER)
EEK!
KIIIIII (SHIIING)
GYA (GRATE)
GYA
GYA
BO (POP)
GUN (YANK)

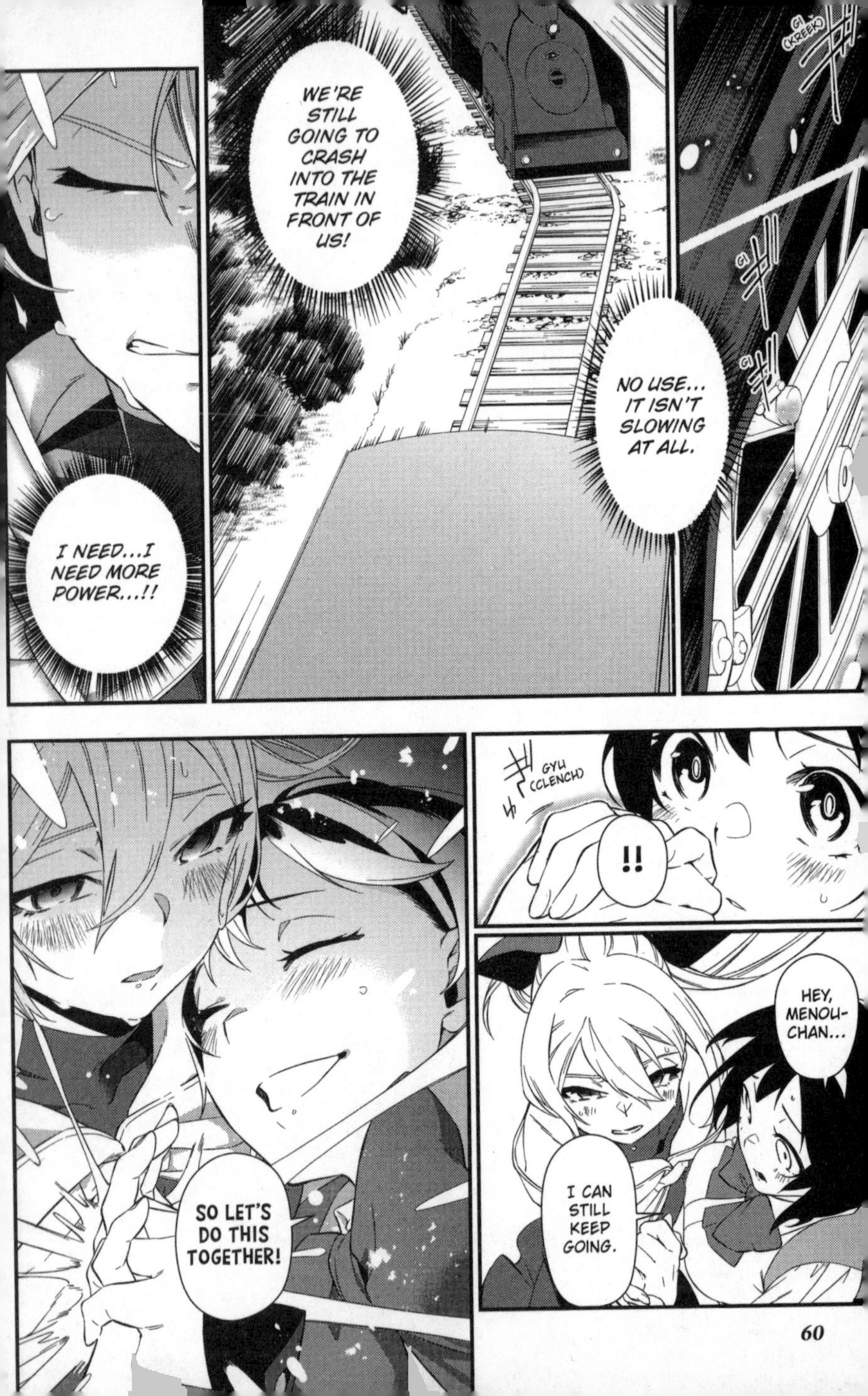
GI (KREEK)
GI
GI
NO USE... IT ISN'T SLOWING AT ALL.
WE'RE STILL GOING TO CRASH INTO THE TRAIN IN FRONT OF US!
I NEED...I NEED MORE POWER...!!
GYU (CLENCH)
!!
HEY, MENOU-CHAN...
I CAN STILL KEEP GOING.
SO LET'S DO THIS TOGETHER!

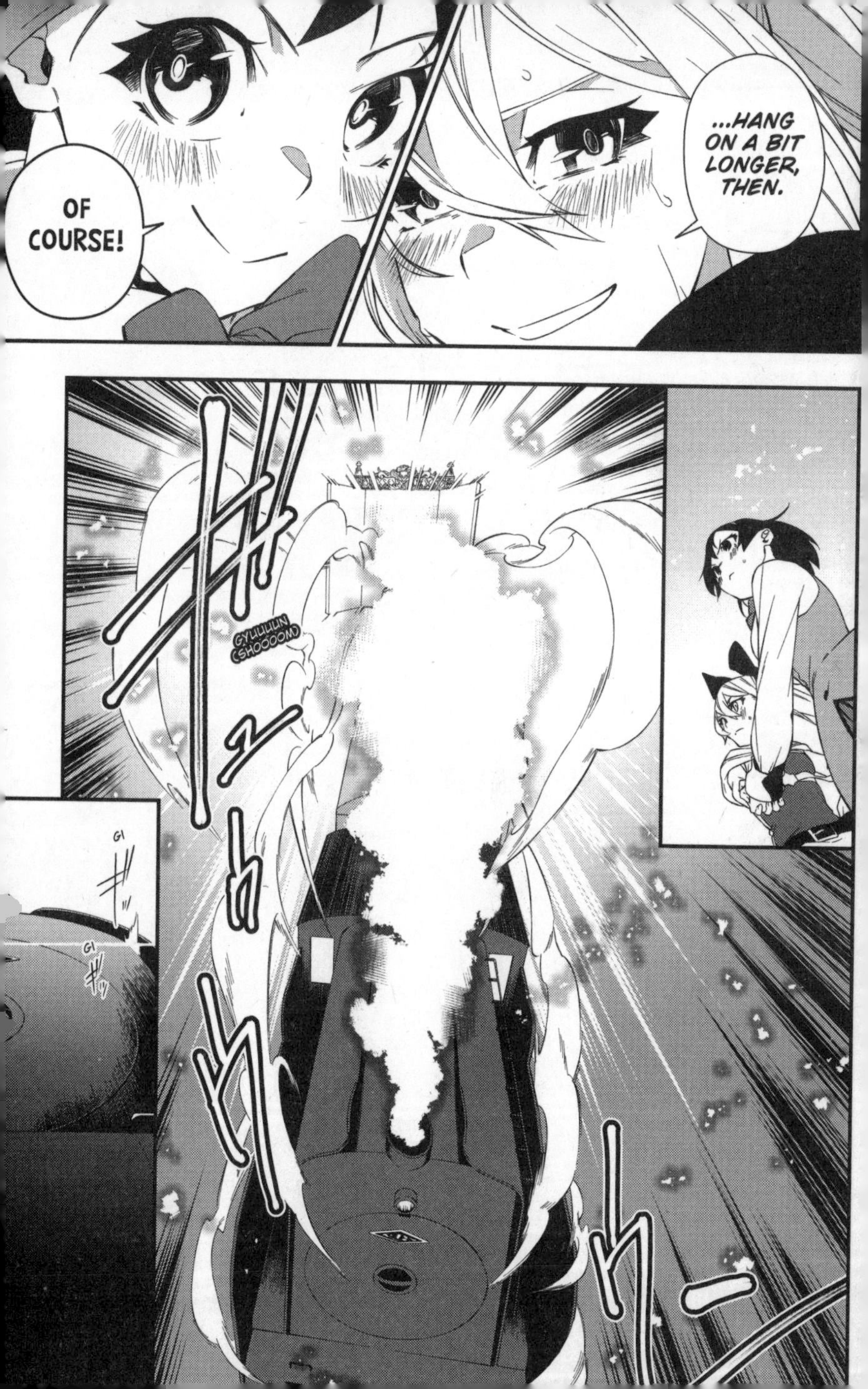
...HANG ON A BIT LONGER, THEN.
OF COURSE!
GYUUUUN (SHOOOOM)
GI
GI

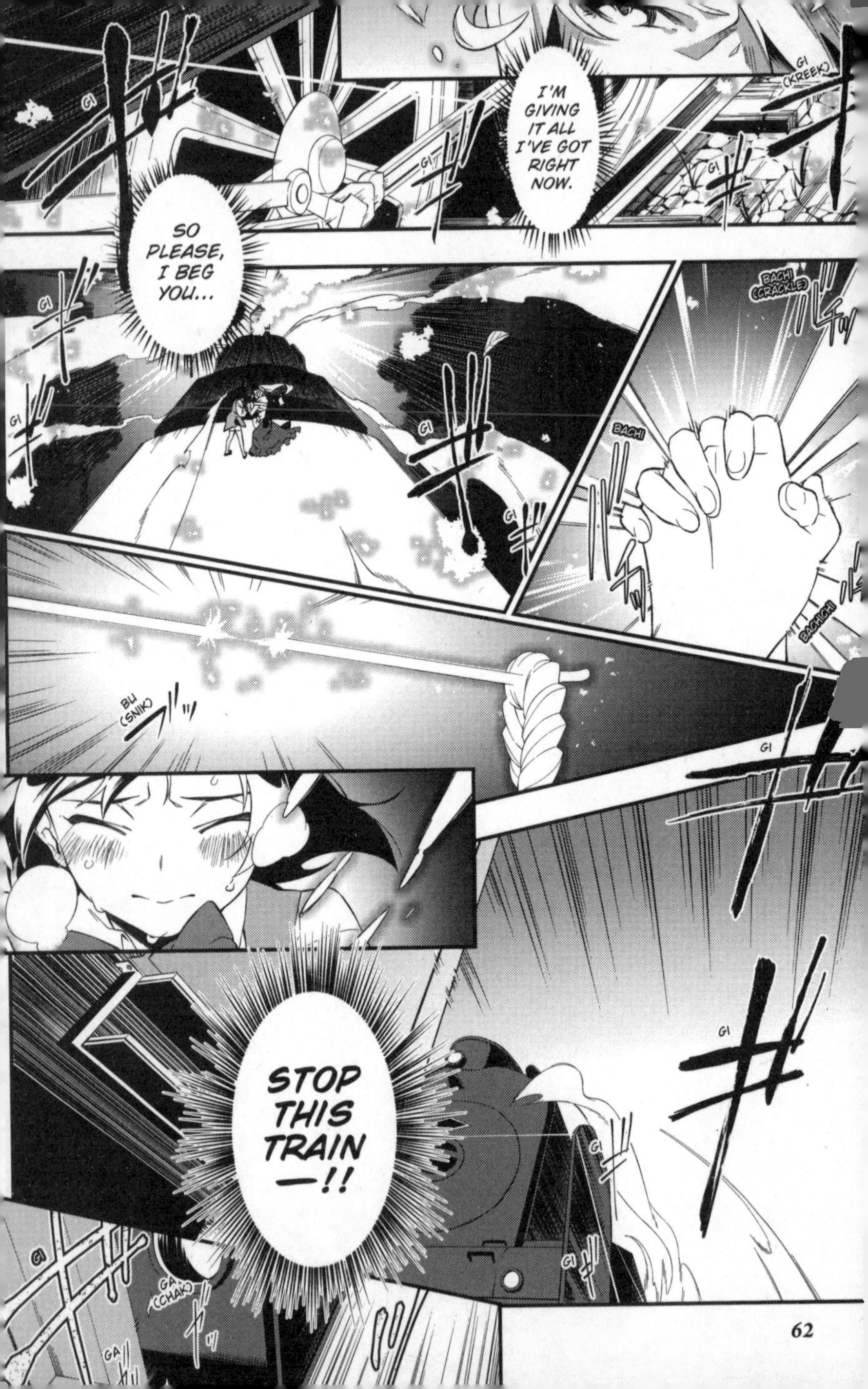
GI (KREEK)
I'M GIVING IT ALL I'VE GOT RIGHT NOW.
GI
GI
GI
SO PLEASE, I BEG YOU...
BACHI (CRACKLE)
BACHI
BACHICHI
GI
GI
GI
GI
GI
BU (SNIK)
GI
STOP THIS TRAIN—!!
GI
GI
GI
GA (CHAK)
GA

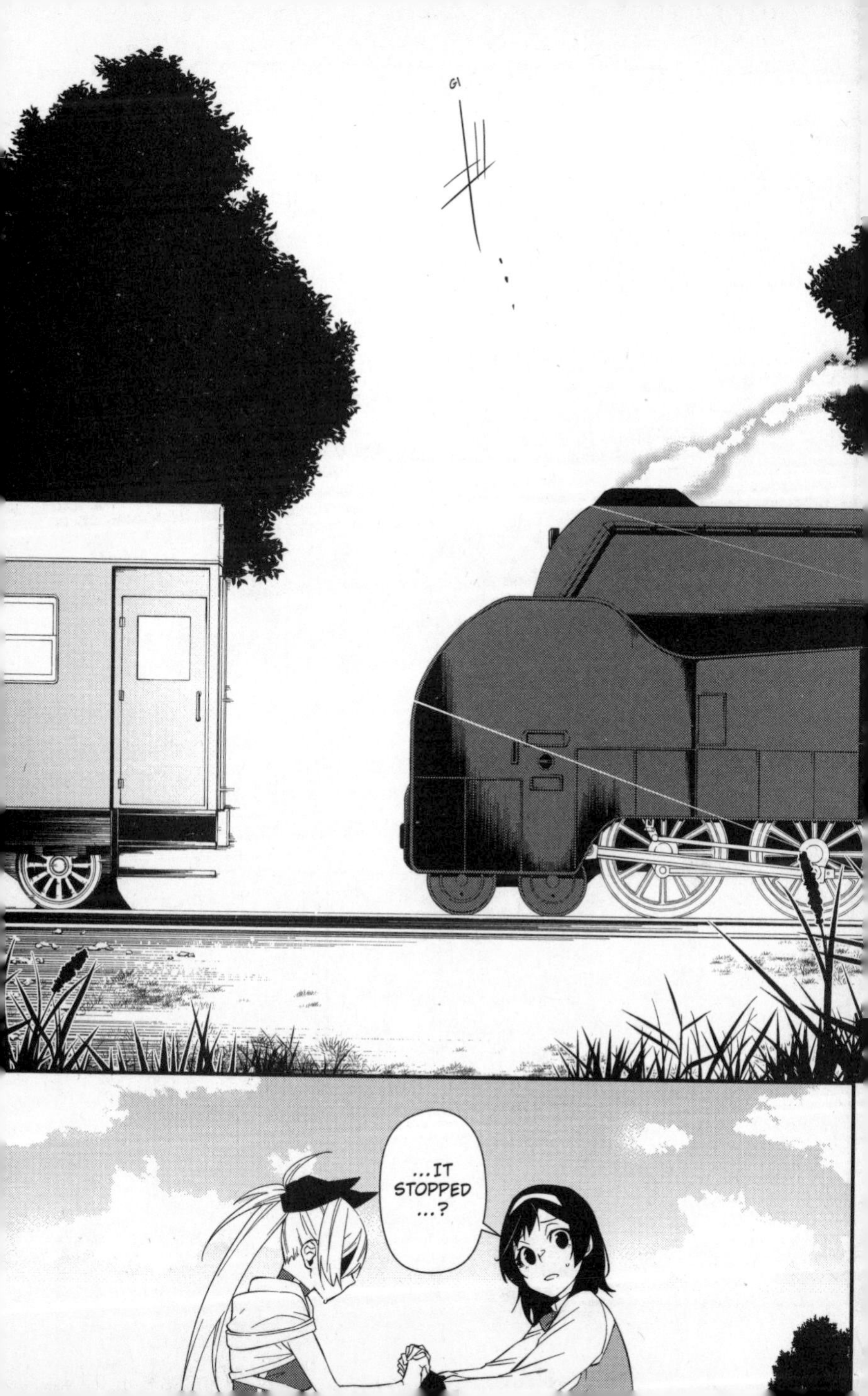
GI
...IT STOPPED ...?

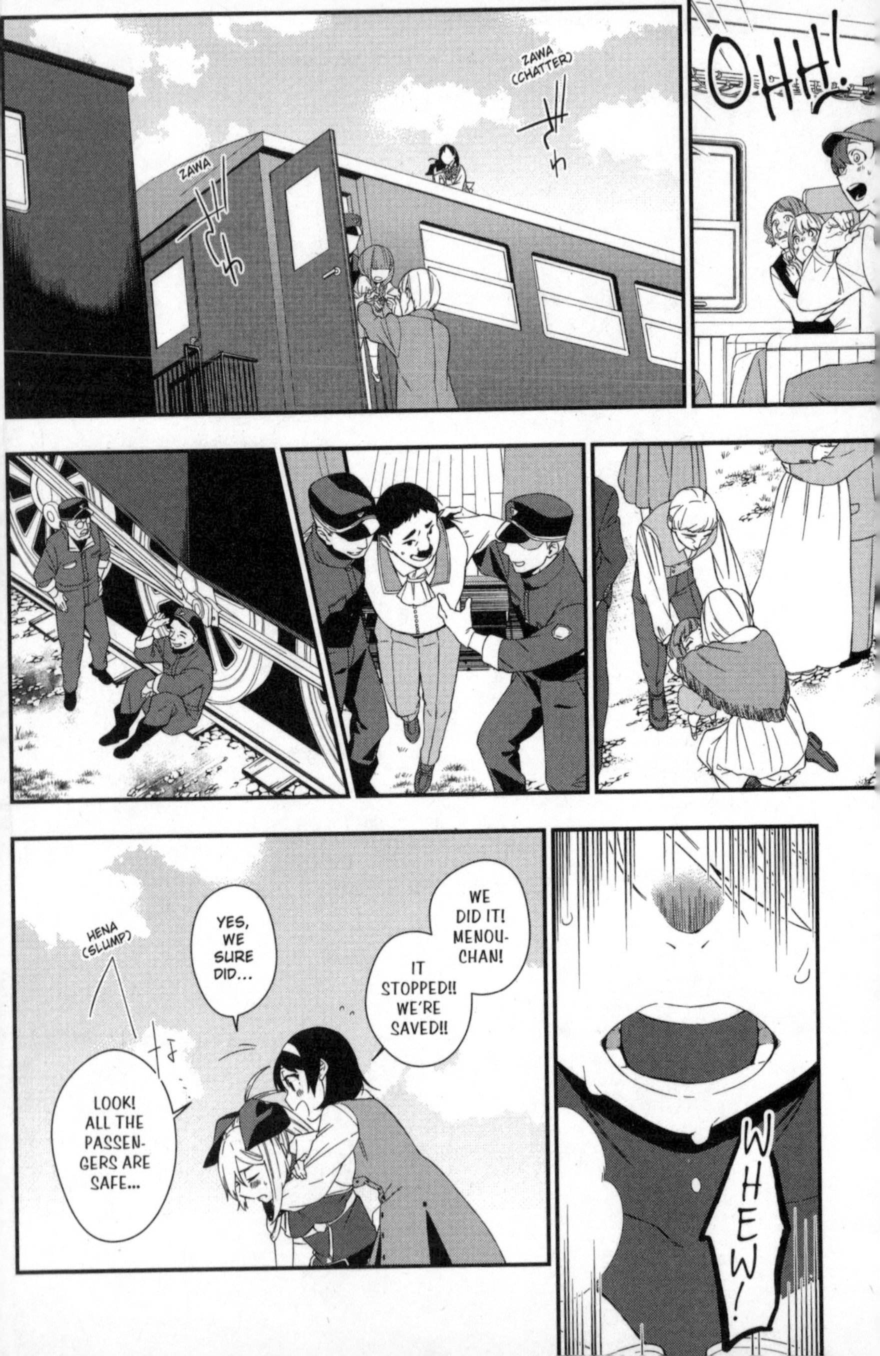
OHH!
ZAWA (CHATTER)
ZAWA
WHEW!
WE DID IT! MENOU-CHAN!
IT STOPPED!! WE'RE SAVED!!
YES, WE SURE DID...
HENA (SLUMP)
LOOK! ALL THE PASSEN-GERS ARE SAFE...

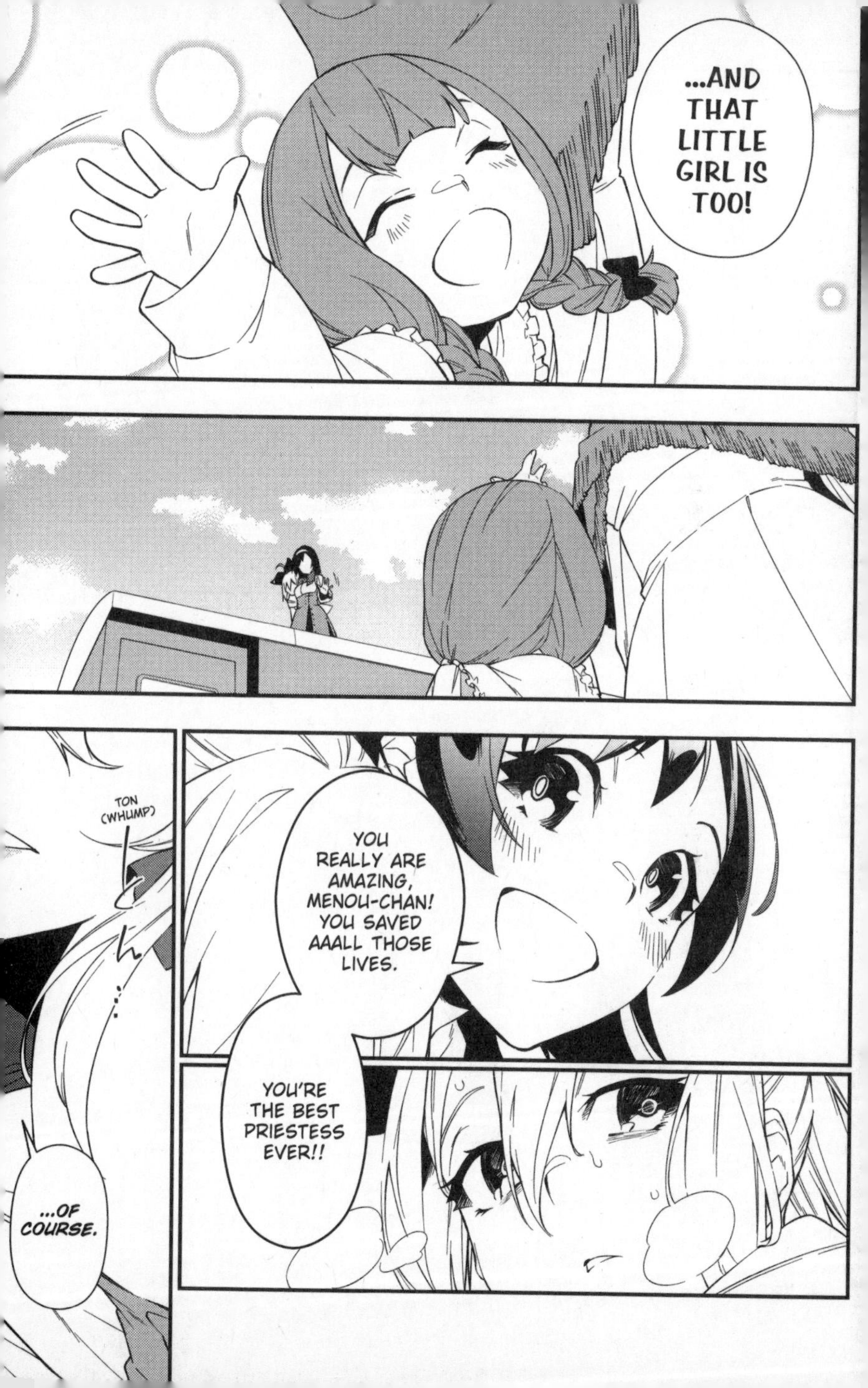
...AND THAT LITTLE GIRL IS TOO!
YOU REALLY ARE AMAZING, MENOU-CHAN! YOU SAVED AAALL THOSE LIVES.
YOU'RE THE BEST PRIESTESS EVER!!
TON (WHUMP)
...OF COURSE.

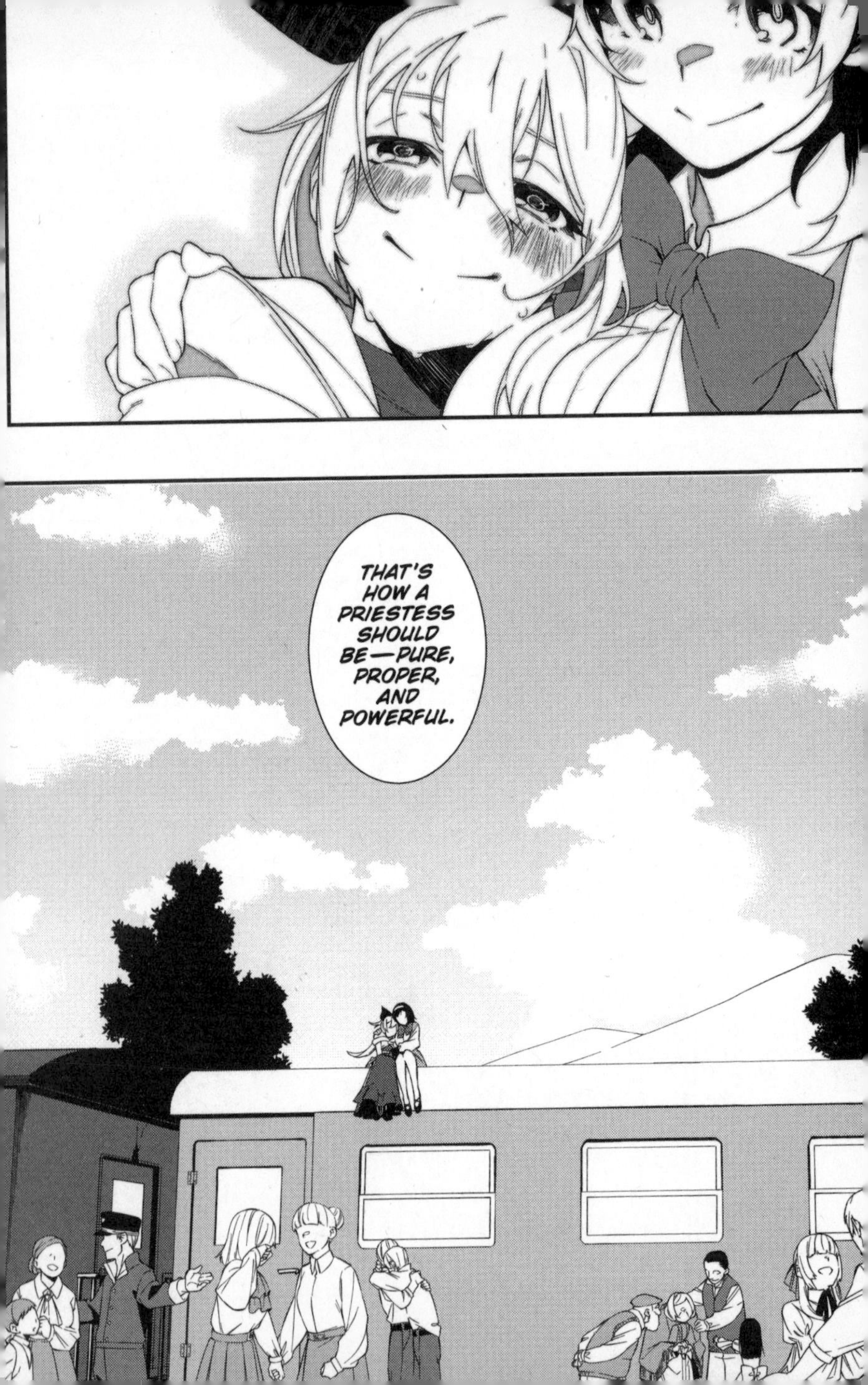
THAT'S HOW A PRIESTESS SHOULD BE—PURE, PROPER, AND POWERFUL.

The Executioner
and Her Way of Life

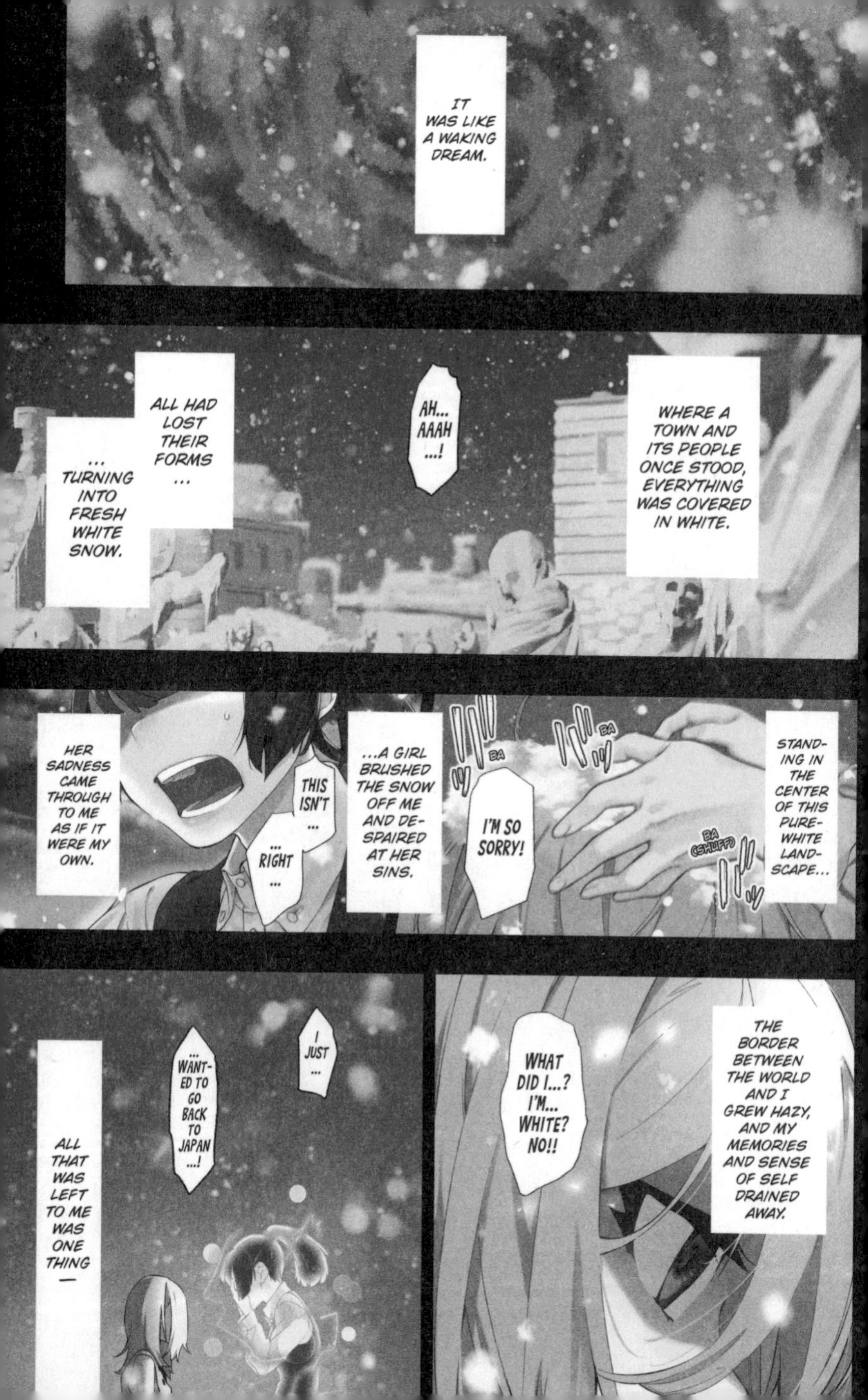
IT WAS LIKE A WAKING DREAM.
WHERE A TOWN AND ITS PEOPLE ONCE STOOD, EVERYTHING WAS COVERED IN WHITE.
AH... AAAH ...!
ALL HAD LOST THEIR FORMS ...
... TURNING INTO FRESH WHITE SNOW.
STANDING IN THE CENTER OF THIS PURE-WHITE LANDSCAPE...
BA
BA
BA (SHUFF)
I'M SO SORRY!
...A GIRL BRUSHED THE SNOW OFF ME AND DESPAIRED AT HER SINS.
THIS ISN'T ...
... RIGHT ...
HER SADNESS CAME THROUGH TO ME AS IF IT WERE MY OWN.
THE BORDER BETWEEN THE WORLD AND I GREW HAZY, AND MY MEMORIES AND SENSE OF SELF DRAINED AWAY.
WHAT DID I...? I'M... WHITE? NO!!
I JUST ...
... WANTED TO GO BACK TO JAPAN ...!
ALL THAT WAS LEFT TO ME WAS ONE THING —

Chapter 10 The Will to Walk On

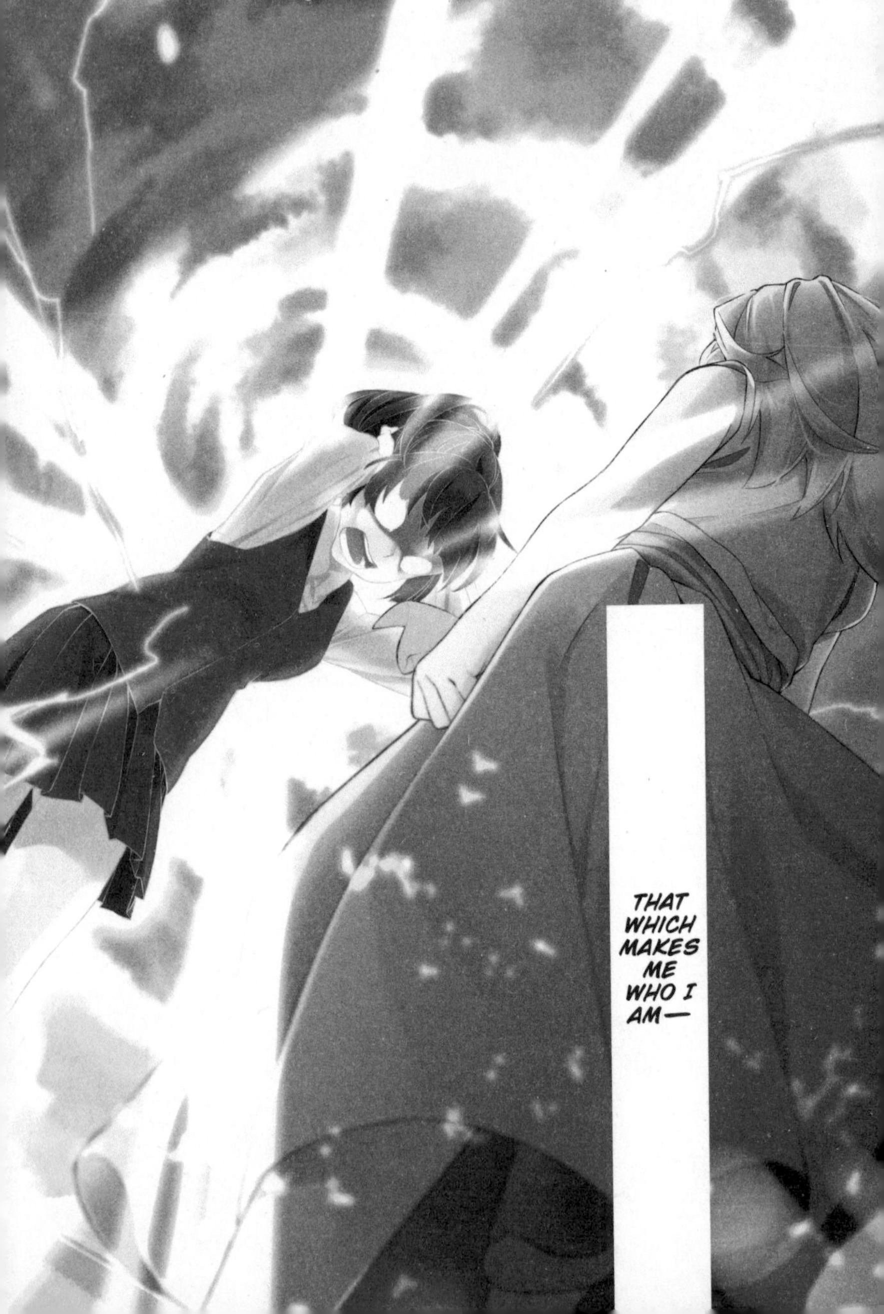
THAT WHICH MAKES ME WHO I AM—

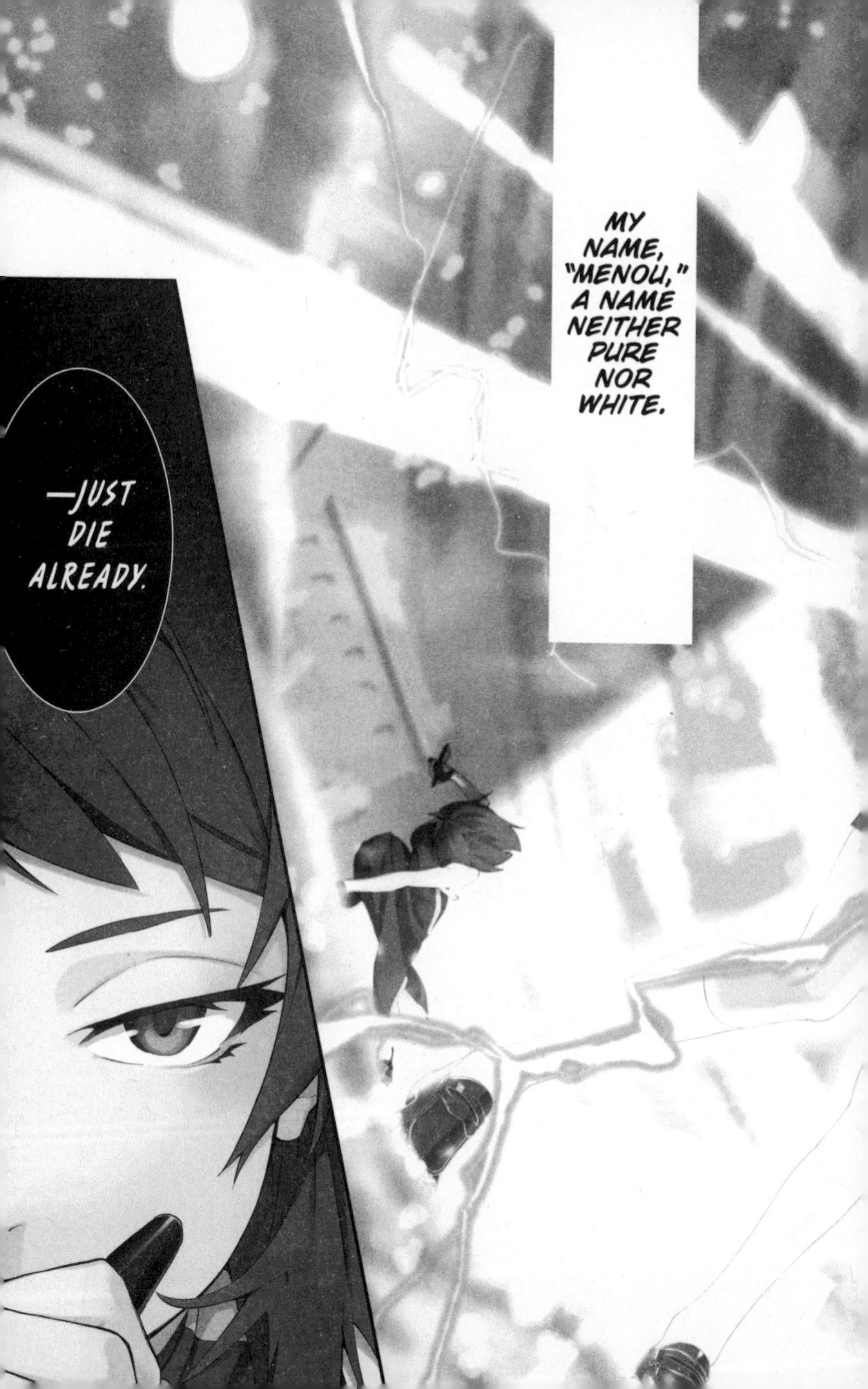
MY NAME, "MENOU," A NAME NEITHER PURE NOR WHITE.
—JUST DIE ALREADY.

The Executioner
and Her Way of Life

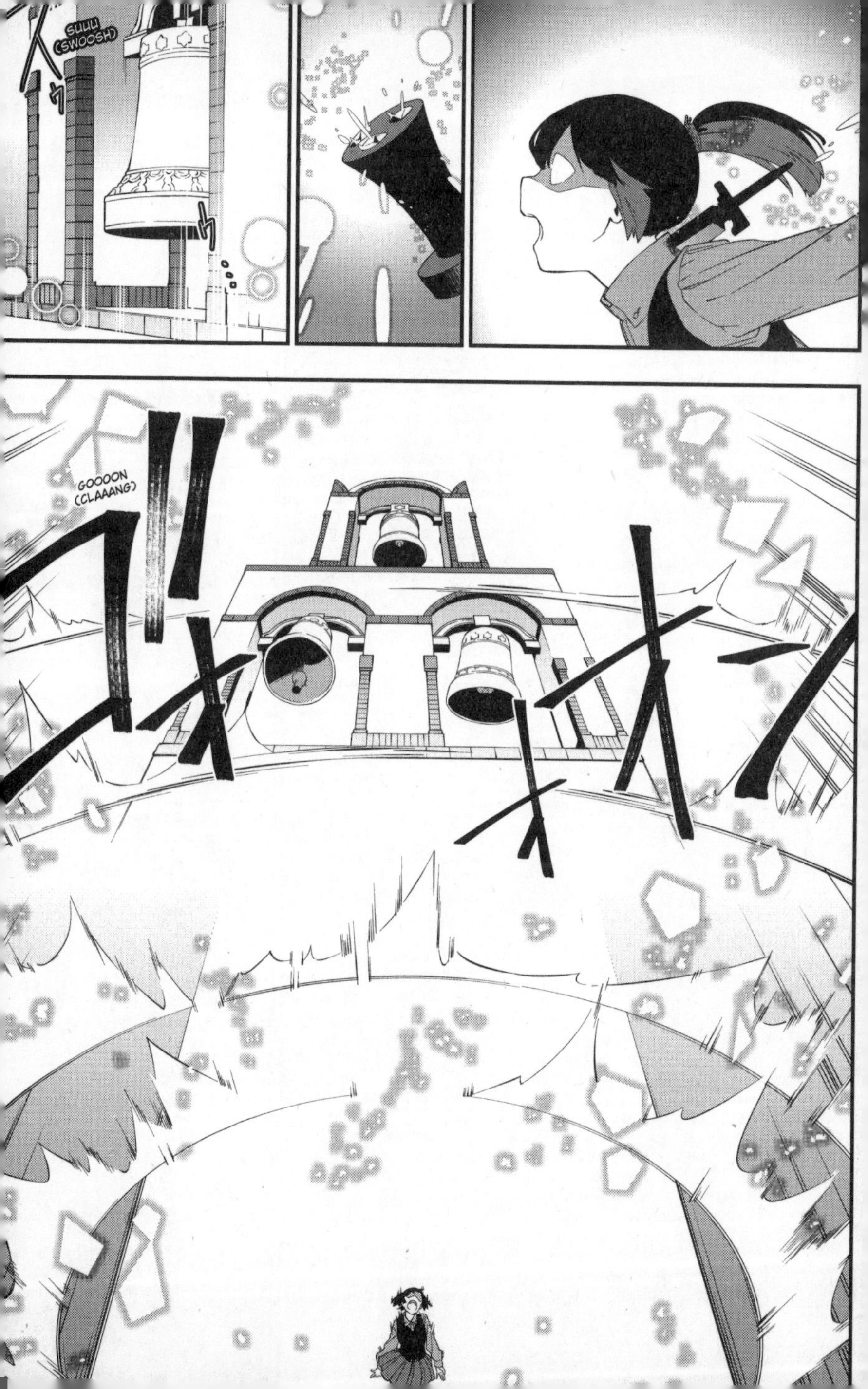
SUUU (SWOOSH)
GOOOON (CLAAANG)

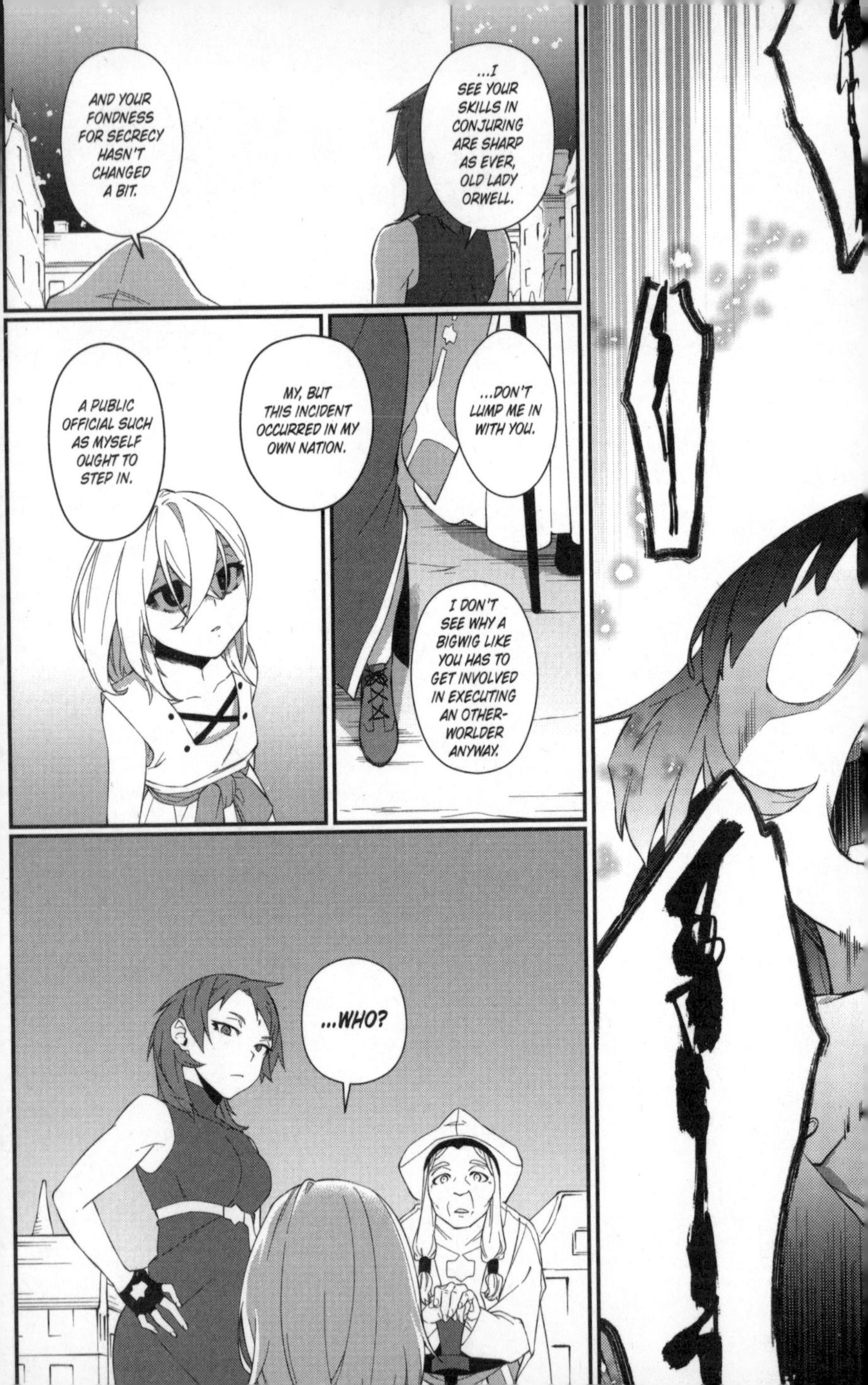
...I SEE YOUR SKILLS IN CONJURING ARE SHARP AS EVER, OLD LADY ORWELL.
AND YOUR FONDNESS FOR SECRECY HASN'T CHANGED A BIT.
...DON'T LUMP ME IN WITH YOU.
I DON'T SEE WHY A BIGWIG LIKE YOU HAS TO GET INVOLVED IN EXECUTING AN OTHER-WORLDER ANYWAY.
MY, BUT THIS INCIDENT OCCURRED IN MY OWN NATION.
A PUBLIC OFFICIAL SUCH AS MYSELF OUGHT TO STEP IN.
...WHO?

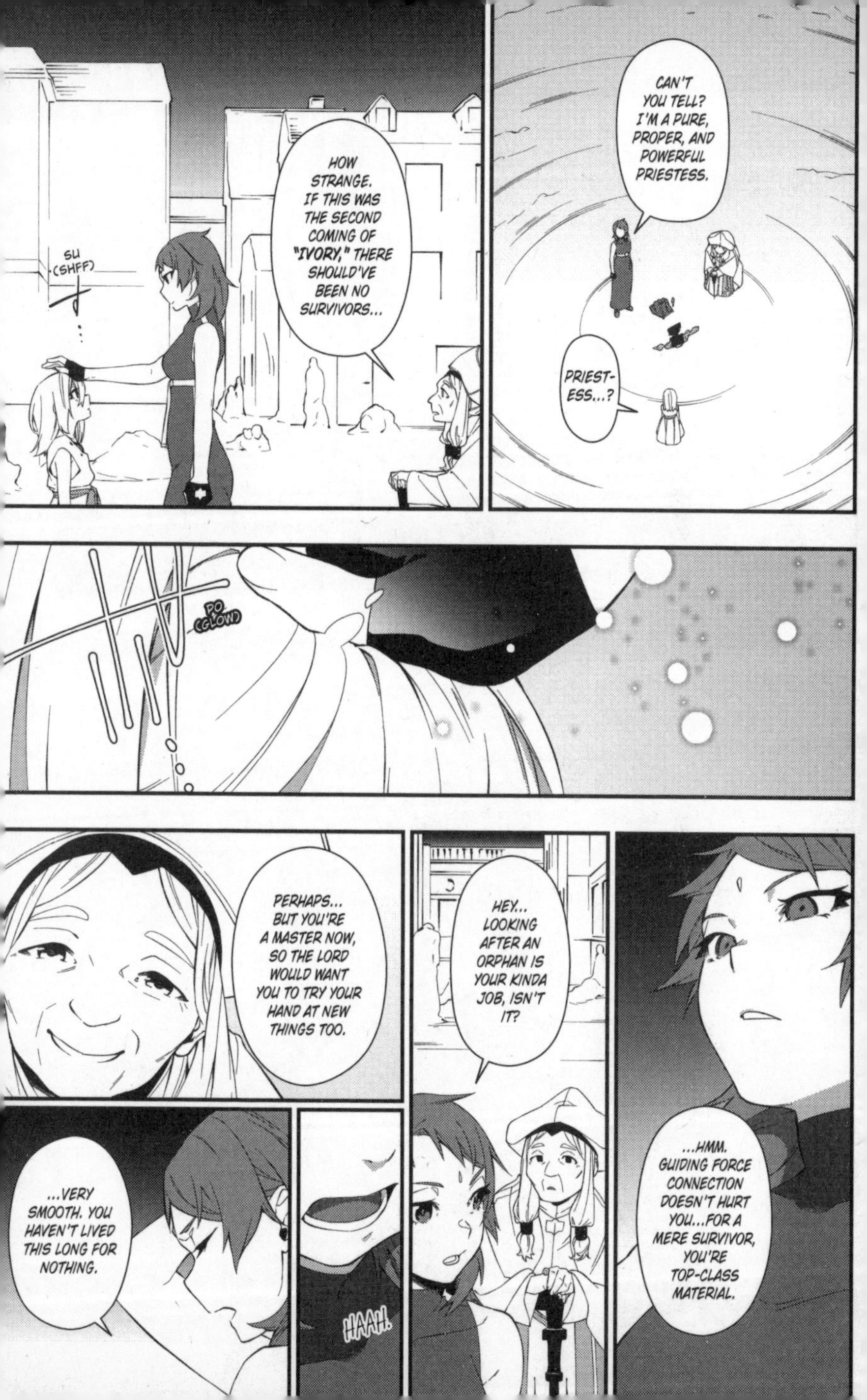
CAN'T YOU TELL? I'M A PURE, PROPER, AND POWERFUL PRIESTESS.
PRIEST-ESS...?
HOW STRANGE. IF THIS WAS THE SECOND COMING OF "IVORY," THERE SHOULD'VE BEEN NO SURVIVORS...
SU (SHFF)
PO (GLOW)
...HMM. GUIDING FORCE CONNECTION DOESN'T HURT YOU...FOR A MERE SURVIVOR, YOU'RE TOP-CLASS MATERIAL.
HEY... LOOKING AFTER AN ORPHAN IS YOUR KINDA JOB, ISN'T IT?
PERHAPS... BUT YOU'RE A MASTER NOW, SO THE LORD WOULD WANT YOU TO TRY YOUR HAND AT NEW THINGS TOO.
HAAH.
...VERY SMOOTH. YOU HAVEN'T LIVED THIS LONG FOR NOTHING.

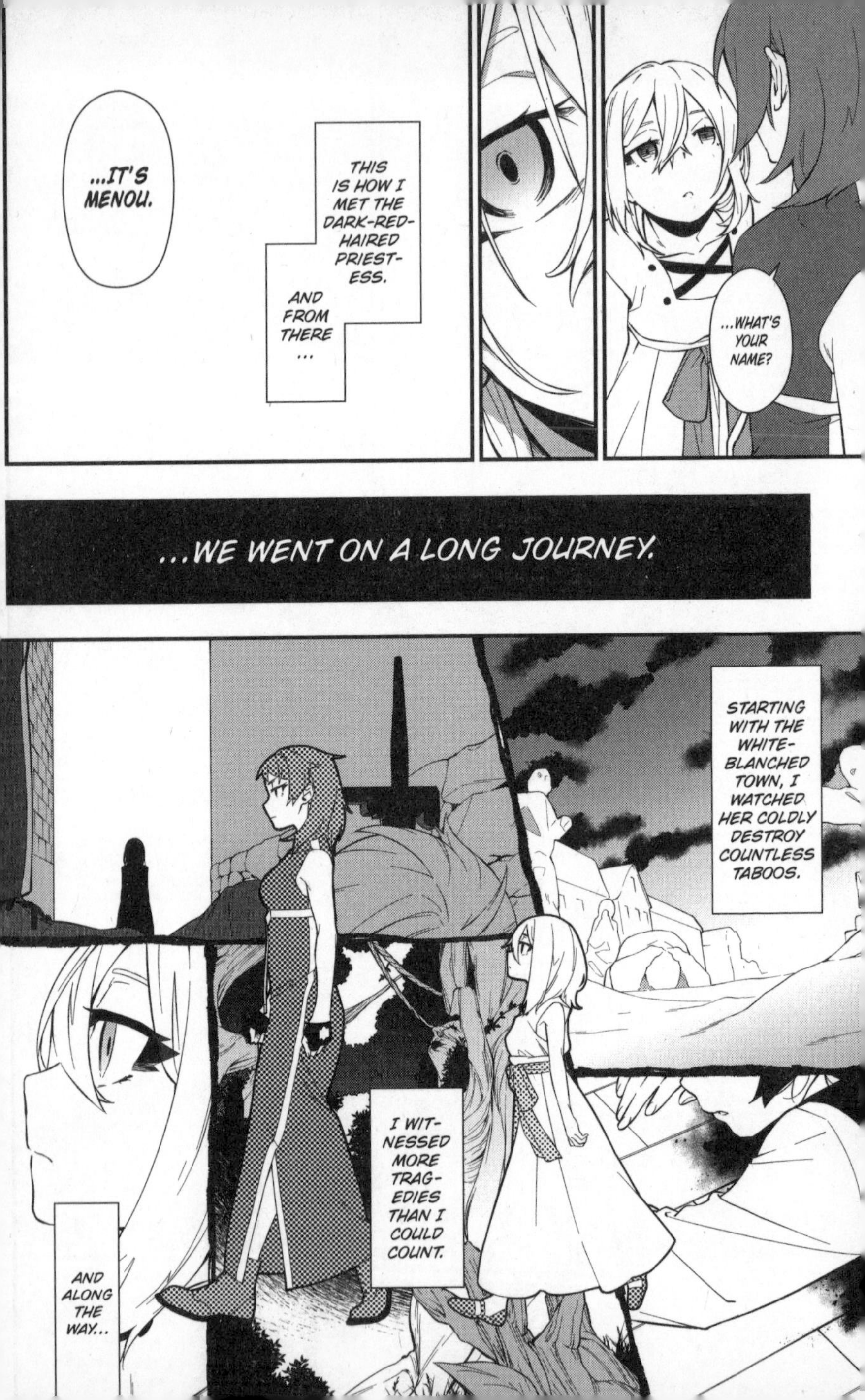
...WHAT'S YOUR NAME?
...IT'S MENOU.
THIS IS HOW I MET THE DARK-RED-HAIRED PRIEST-ESS.
AND FROM THERE ...
...WE WENT ON A LONG JOURNEY.
STARTING WITH THE WHITE-BLANCHED TOWN, I WATCHED HER COLDLY DESTROY COUNTLESS TABOOS.
I WIT-NESSED MORE TRAG-EDIES THAN I COULD COUNT.
AND ALONG THE WAY...

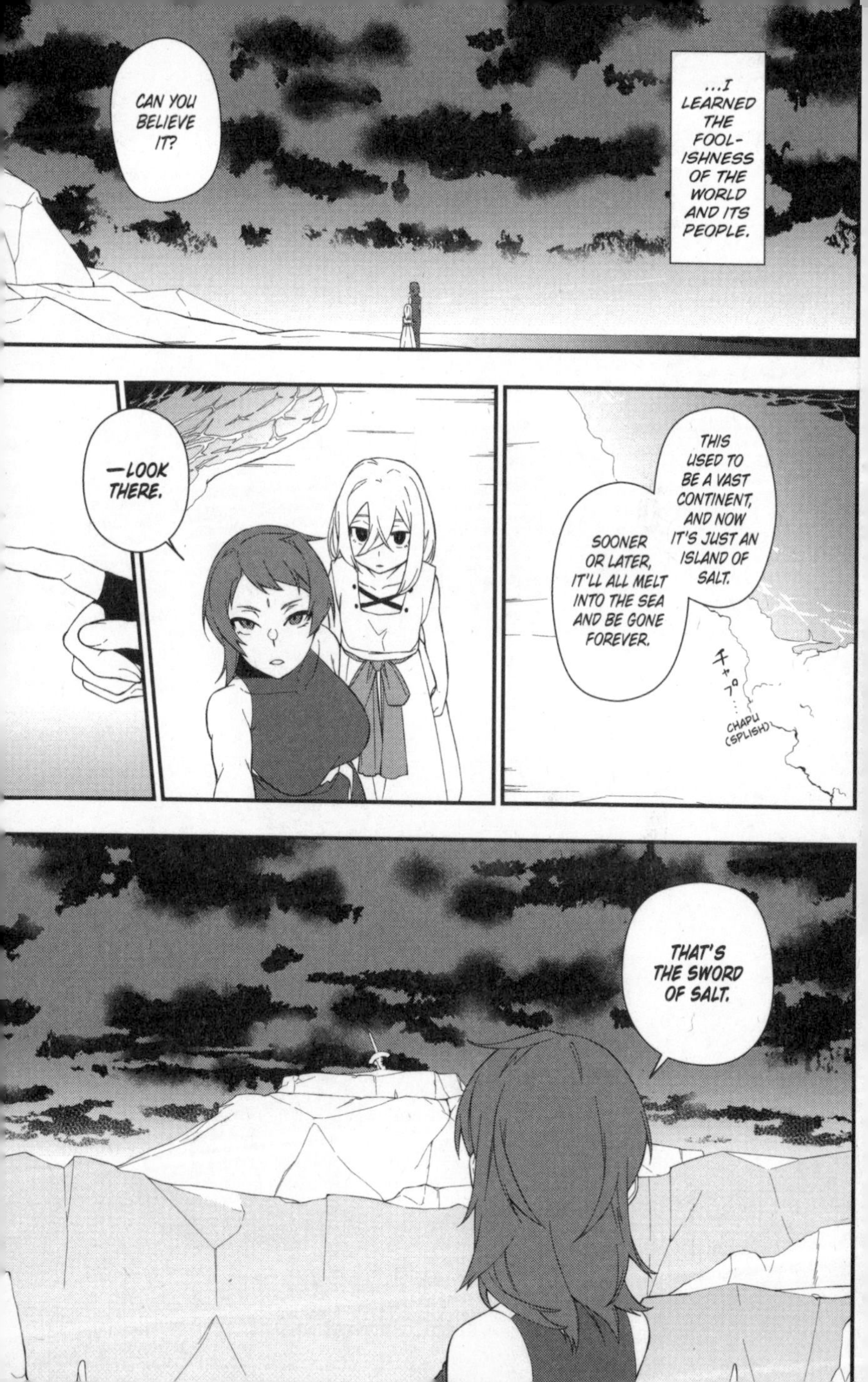
...I LEARNED THE FOOL-ISHNESS OF THE WORLD AND ITS PEOPLE.
CAN YOU BELIEVE IT?
THIS USED TO BE A VAST CONTINENT, AND NOW IT'S JUST AN ISLAND OF SALT.
SOONER OR LATER, IT'LL ALL MELT INTO THE SEA AND BE GONE FOREVER.
チャプ…
CHAPU (SPLISH)
—LOOK THERE.
THAT'S THE SWORD OF SALT.

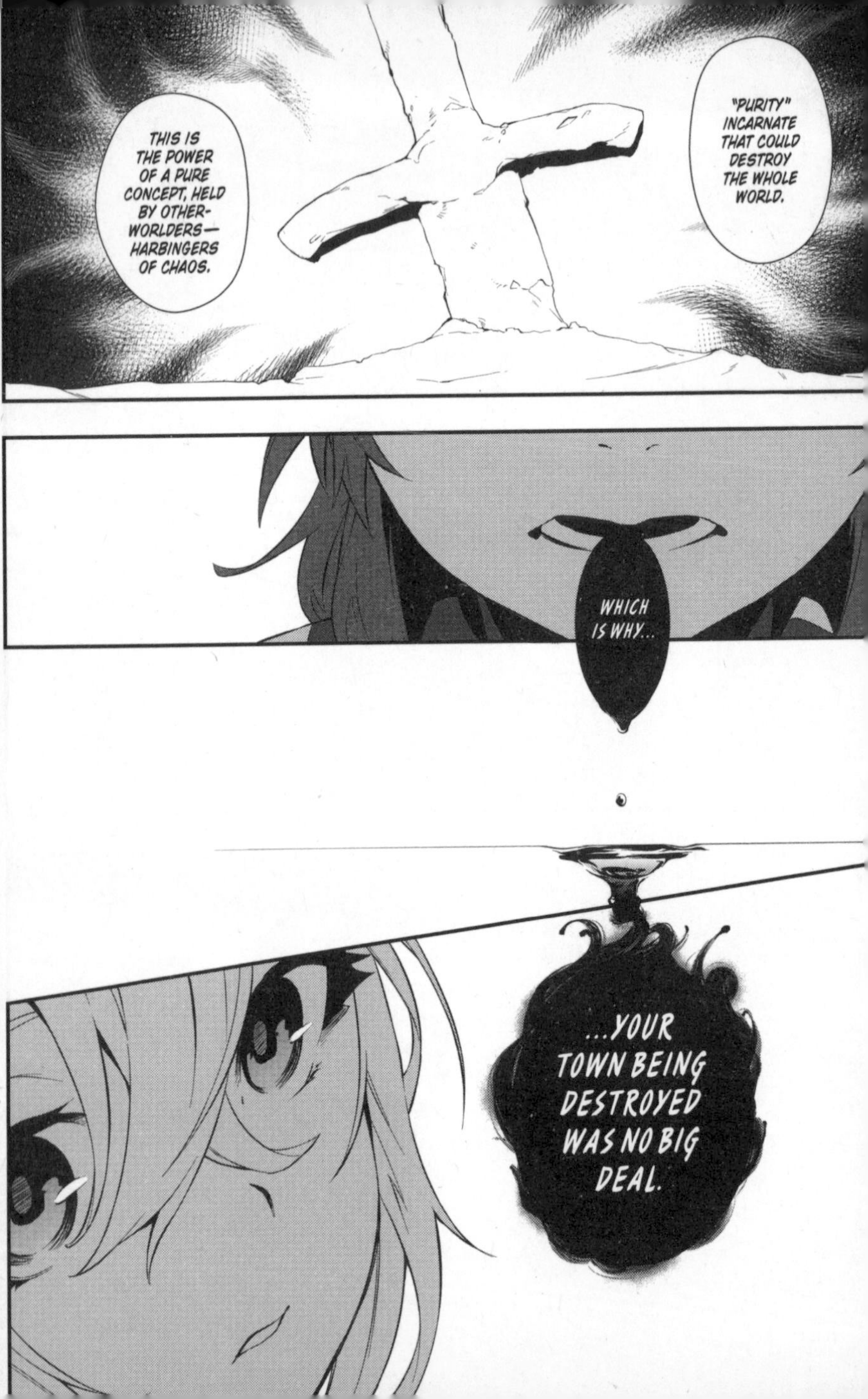
"PURITY" INCARNATE THAT COULD DESTROY THE WHOLE WORLD.
THIS IS THE POWER OF A PURE CONCEPT, HELD BY OTHER-WORLDERS—HARBINGERS OF CHAOS.
WHICH IS WHY...
...YOUR TOWN BEING DESTROYED WAS NO BIG DEAL.

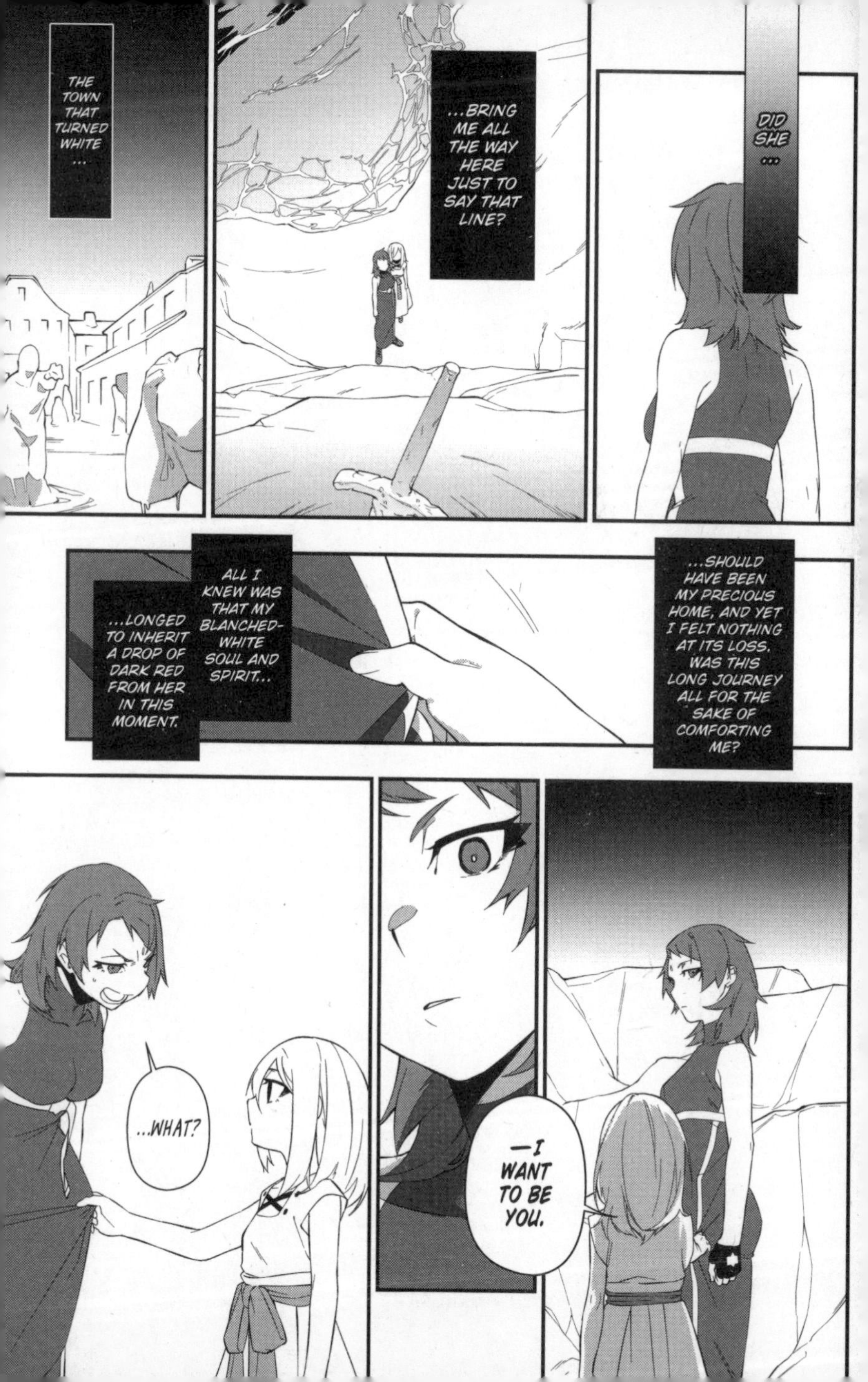
DID SHE ...
...BRING ME ALL THE WAY HERE JUST TO SAY THAT LINE?
THE TOWN THAT TURNED WHITE ...
...SHOULD HAVE BEEN MY PRECIOUS HOME, AND YET I FELT NOTHING AT ITS LOSS. WAS THIS LONG JOURNEY ALL FOR THE SAKE OF COMFORTING ME?
ALL I KNEW WAS THAT MY BLANCHED-WHITE SOUL AND SPIRIT...
...LONGED TO INHERIT A DROP OF DARK RED FROM HER IN THIS MOMENT.
—I WANT TO BE YOU.
...WHAT?

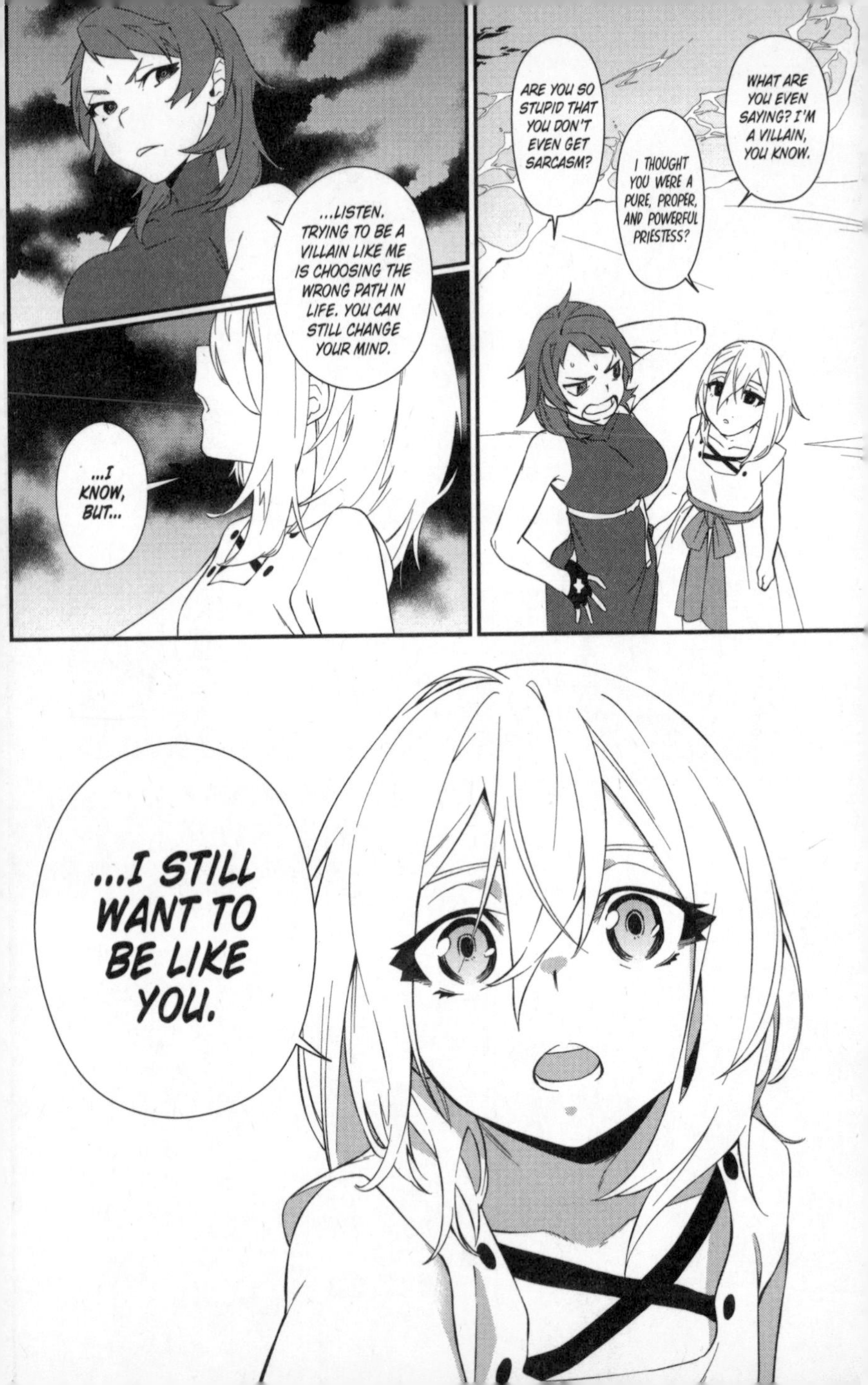
WHAT ARE YOU EVEN SAYING? I'M A VILLAIN, YOU KNOW.
I THOUGHT YOU WERE A PURE, PROPER, AND POWERFUL PRIESTESS?
ARE YOU SO STUPID THAT YOU DON'T EVEN GET SARCASM?
...LISTEN. TRYING TO BE A VILLAIN LIKE ME IS CHOOSING THE WRONG PATH IN LIFE. YOU CAN STILL CHANGE YOUR MIND.
...I KNOW, BUT...
...I STILL WANT TO BE LIKE YOU.

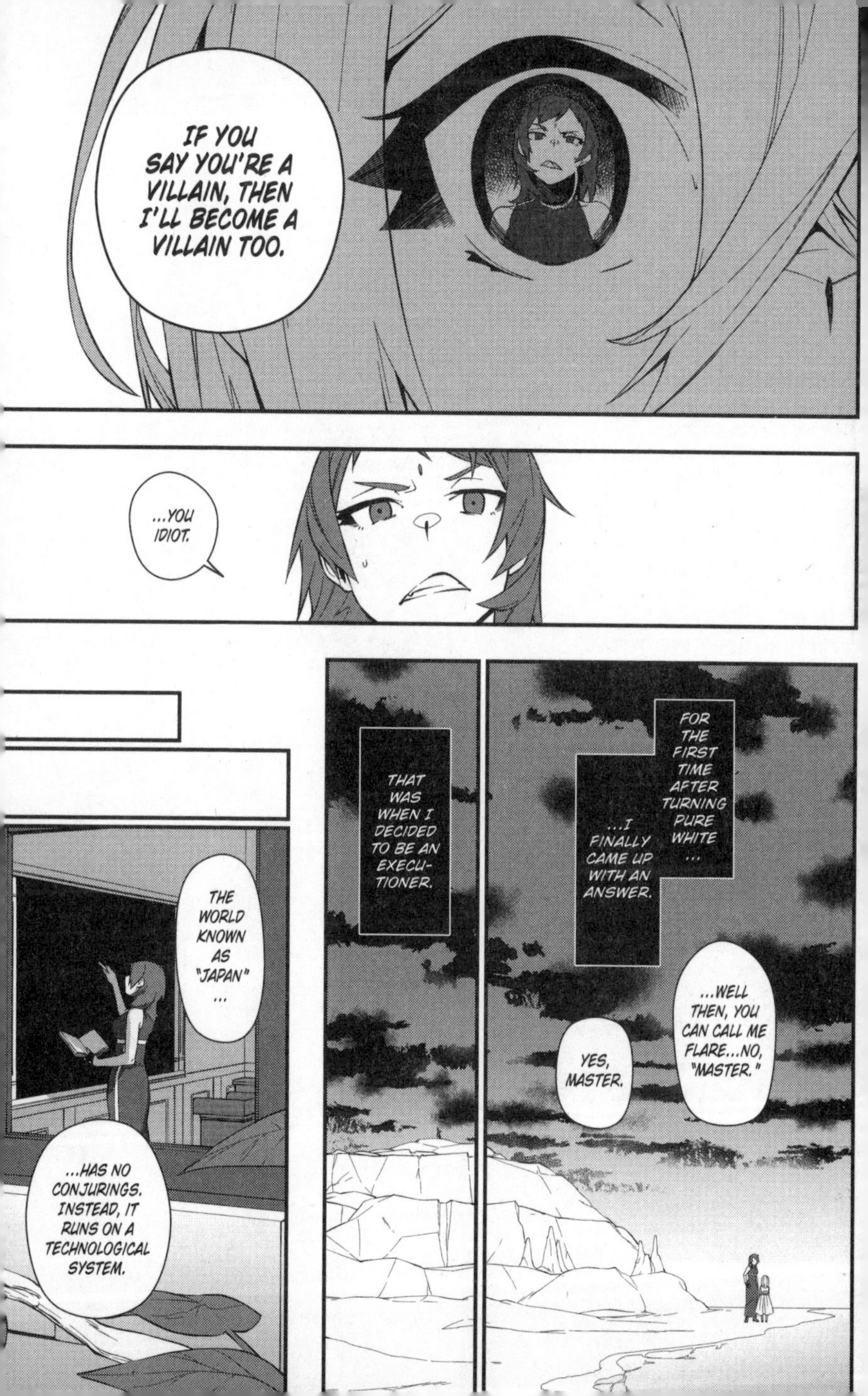
IF YOU SAY YOU'RE A VILLAIN, THEN I'LL BECOME A VILLAIN TOO.
...YOU IDIOT.
FOR THE FIRST TIME AFTER TURNING PURE WHITE...
...I FINALLY CAME UP WITH AN ANSWER.
...WELL THEN, YOU CAN CALL ME FLARE...NO, "MASTER."
YES, MASTER.
THAT WAS WHEN I DECIDED TO BE AN EXECU-TIONER.
THE WORLD KNOWN AS "JAPAN"...
...HAS NO CONJURINGS. INSTEAD, IT RUNS ON A TECHNOLOGICAL SYSTEM.

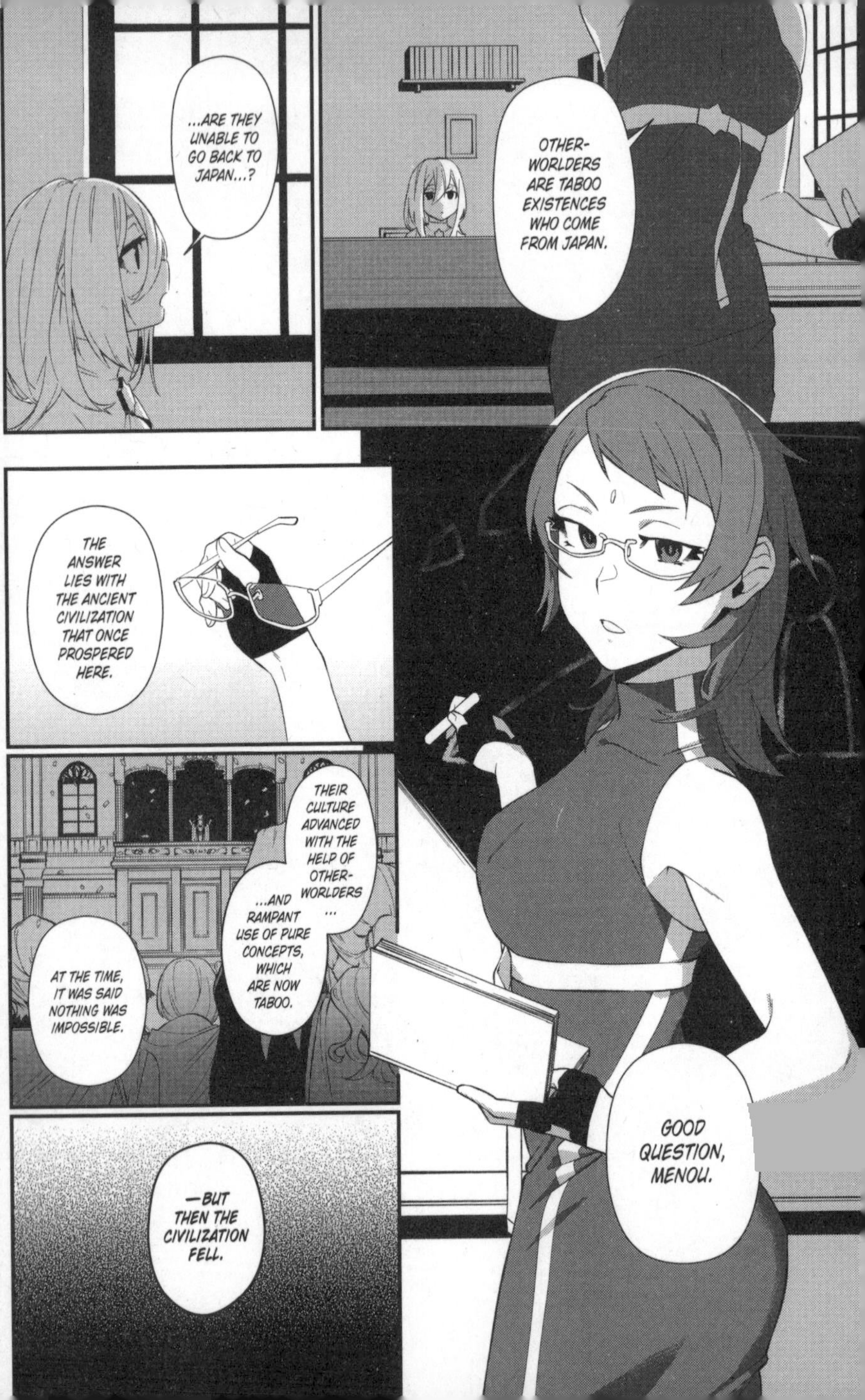
OTHER-WORLDERS ARE TABOO EXISTENCES WHO COME FROM JAPAN.
...ARE THEY UNABLE TO GO BACK TO JAPAN...?
GOOD QUESTION, MENOU.
THE ANSWER LIES WITH THE ANCIENT CIVILIZATION THAT ONCE PROSPERED HERE.
THEIR CULTURE ADVANCED WITH THE HELP OF OTHER-WORLDERS...
...AND RAMPANT USE OF PURE CONCEPTS, WHICH ARE NOW TABOO.
AT THE TIME, IT WAS SAID NOTHING WAS IMPOSSIBLE.
—BUT THEN THE CIVILIZATION FELL.

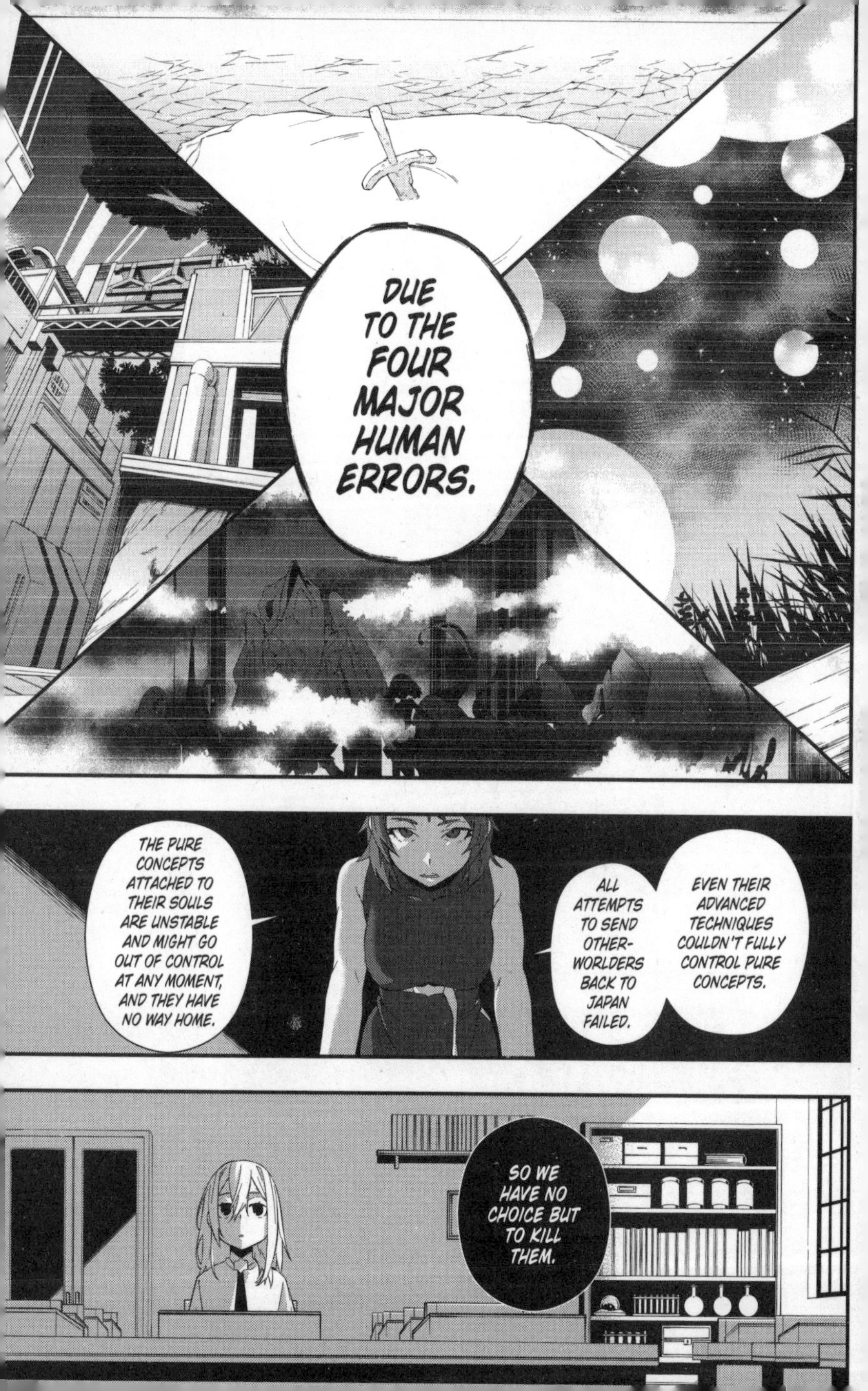
DUE TO THE FOUR MAJOR HUMAN ERRORS.
EVEN THEIR ADVANCED TECHNIQUES COULDN'T FULLY CONTROL PURE CONCEPTS.
ALL ATTEMPTS TO SEND OTHER-WORLDERS BACK TO JAPAN FAILED.
THE PURE CONCEPTS ATTACHED TO THEIR SOULS ARE UNSTABLE AND MIGHT GO OUT OF CONTROL AT ANY MOMENT, AND THEY HAVE NO WAY HOME.
SO WE HAVE NO CHOICE BUT TO KILL THEM.

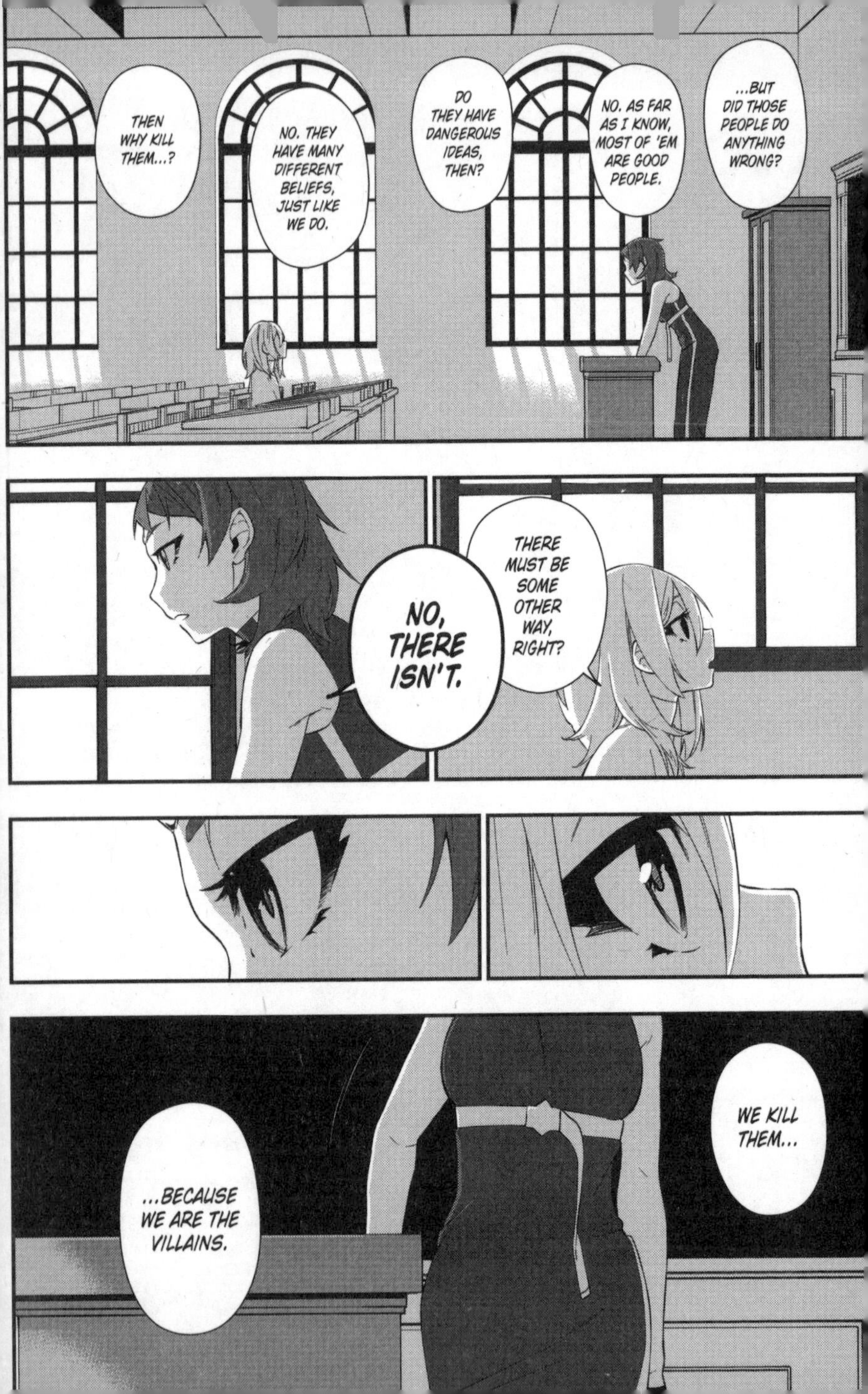
...BUT DID THOSE PEOPLE DO ANYTHING WRONG?
NO. AS FAR AS I KNOW, MOST OF 'EM ARE GOOD PEOPLE.
DO THEY HAVE DANGEROUS IDEAS, THEN?
NO. THEY HAVE MANY DIFFERENT BELIEFS, JUST LIKE WE DO.
THEN WHY KILL THEM...?
THERE MUST BE SOME OTHER WAY, RIGHT?
NO, THERE ISN'T.
WE KILL THEM...
...BECAUSE WE ARE THE VILLAINS.

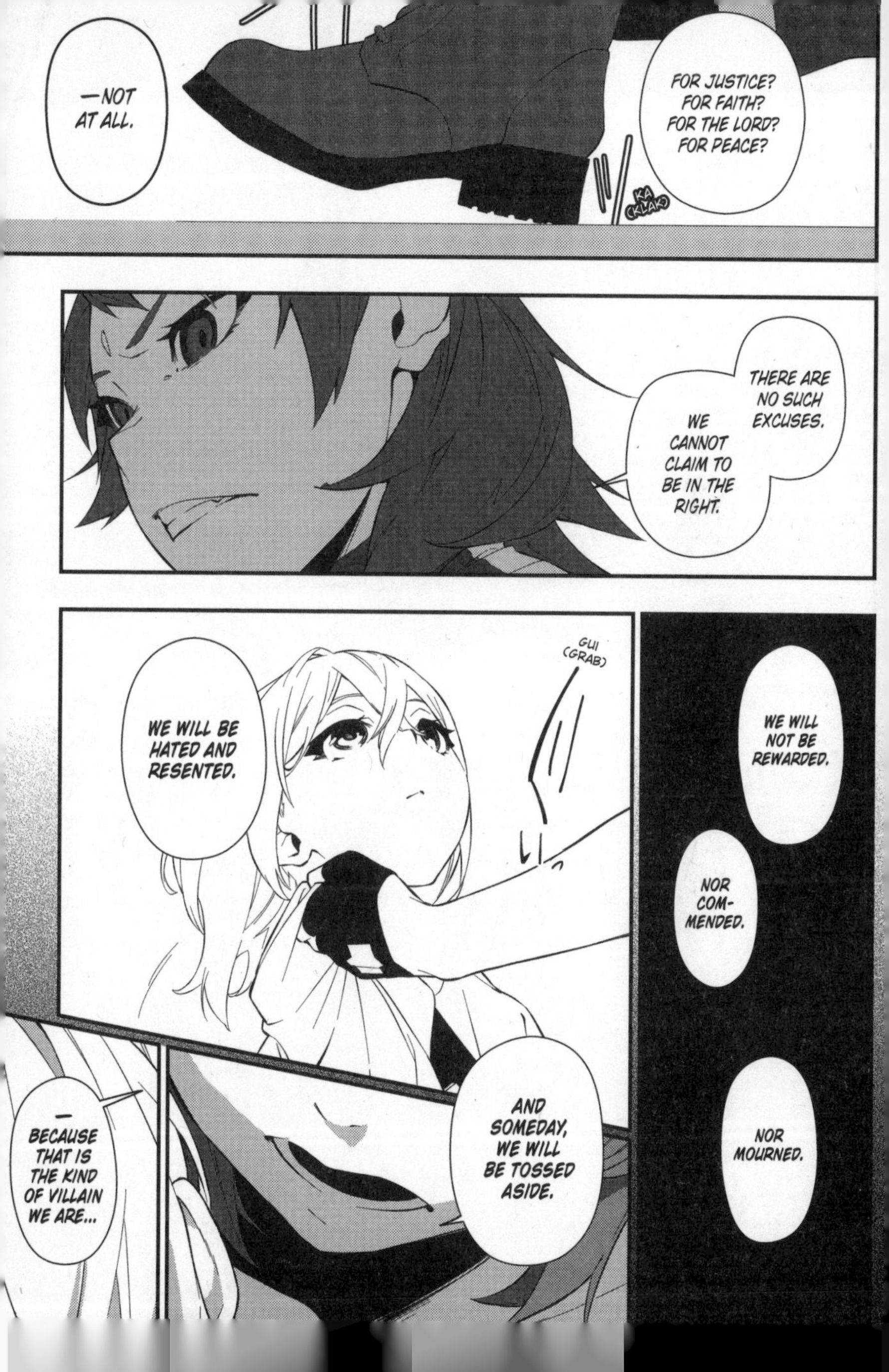
FOR JUSTICE? FOR FAITH? FOR THE LORD? FOR PEACE?
KA (KLAK)
—NOT AT ALL.
THERE ARE NO SUCH EXCUSES.
WE CANNOT CLAIM TO BE IN THE RIGHT.
WE WILL NOT BE REWARDED.
NOR COMMENDED.
NOR MOURNED.
GUI (GRAB)
WE WILL BE HATED AND RESENTED.
AND SOMEDAY, WE WILL BE TOSSED ASIDE.
—BECAUSE THAT IS THE KIND OF VILLAIN WE ARE...

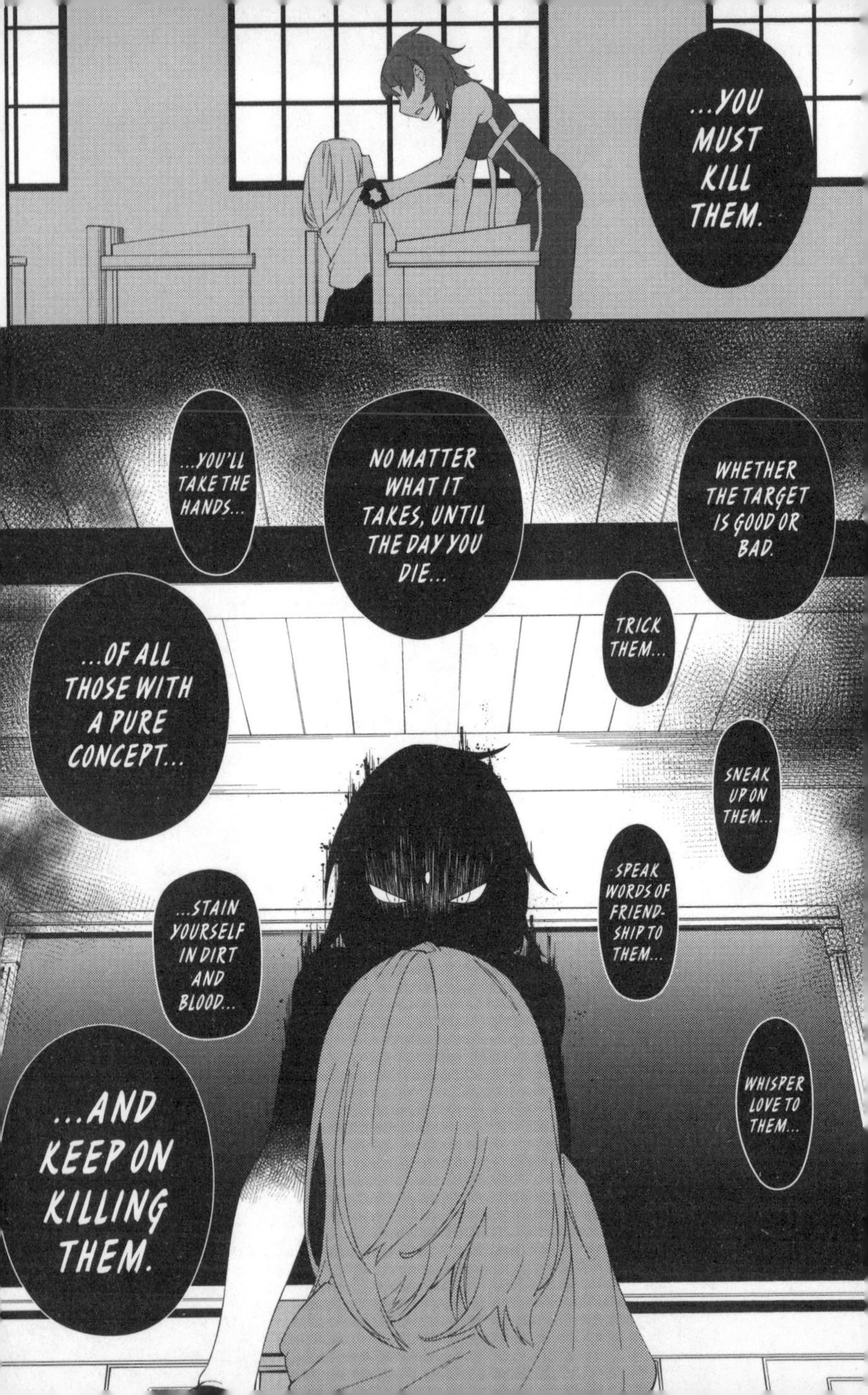
...YOU MUST KILL THEM.
WHETHER THE TARGET IS GOOD OR BAD.
NO MATTER WHAT IT TAKES, UNTIL THE DAY YOU DIE...
...YOU'LL TAKE THE HANDS...
...OF ALL THOSE WITH A PURE CONCEPT...
TRICK THEM...
SNEAK UP ON THEM...
SPEAK WORDS OF FRIEND-SHIP TO THEM...
WHISPER LOVE TO THEM...
...STAIN YOURSELF IN DIRT AND BLOOD...
...AND KEEP ON KILLING THEM.

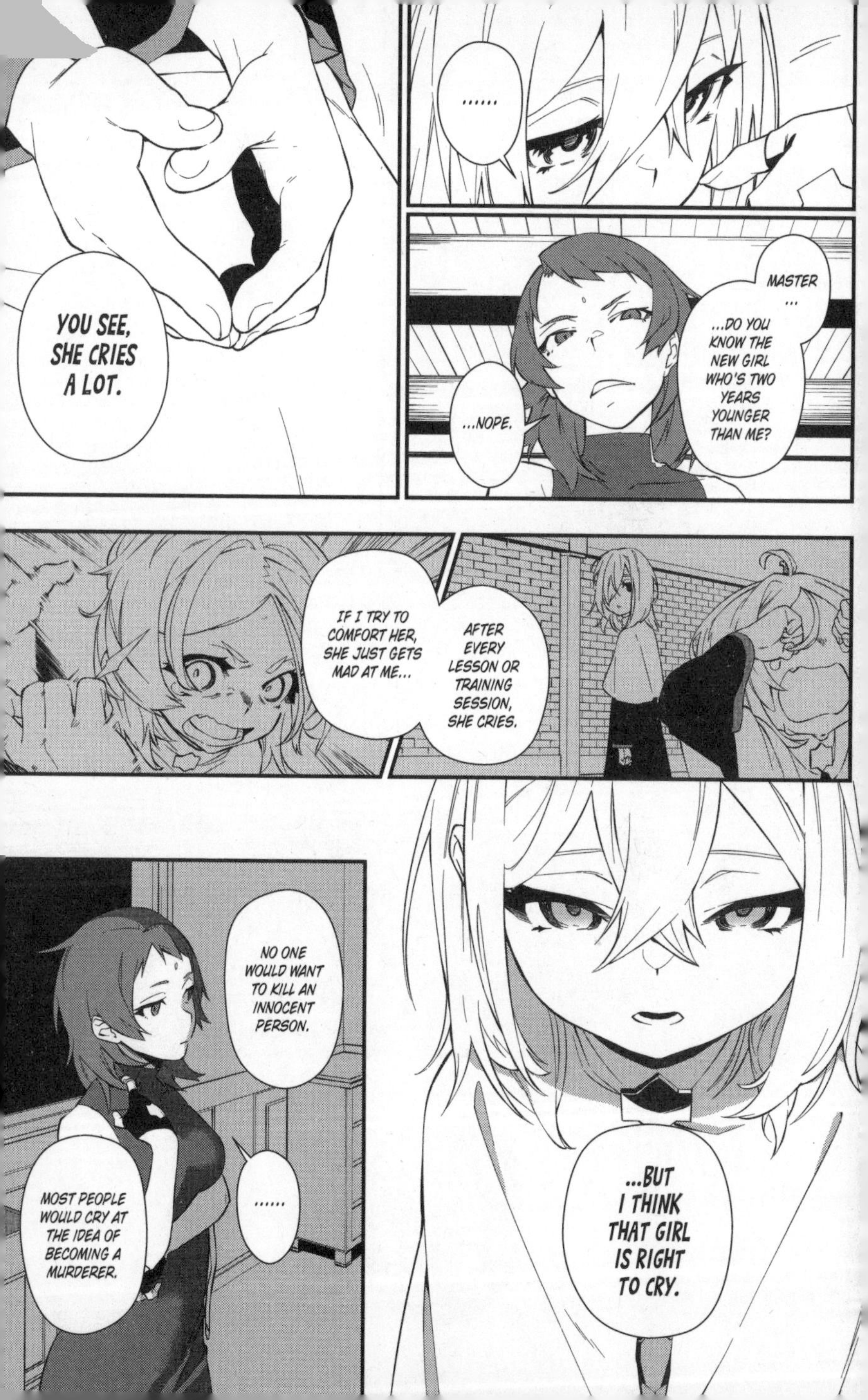
......
MASTER ...
...DO YOU KNOW THE NEW GIRL WHO'S TWO YEARS YOUNGER THAN ME?
...NOPE.
YOU SEE, SHE CRIES A LOT.
AFTER EVERY LESSON OR TRAINING SESSION, SHE CRIES.
IF I TRY TO COMFORT HER, SHE JUST GETS MAD AT ME...
...BUT I THINK THAT GIRL IS RIGHT TO CRY.
NO ONE WOULD WANT TO KILL AN INNOCENT PERSON.
......
MOST PEOPLE WOULD CRY AT THE IDEA OF BECOMING A MURDERER.

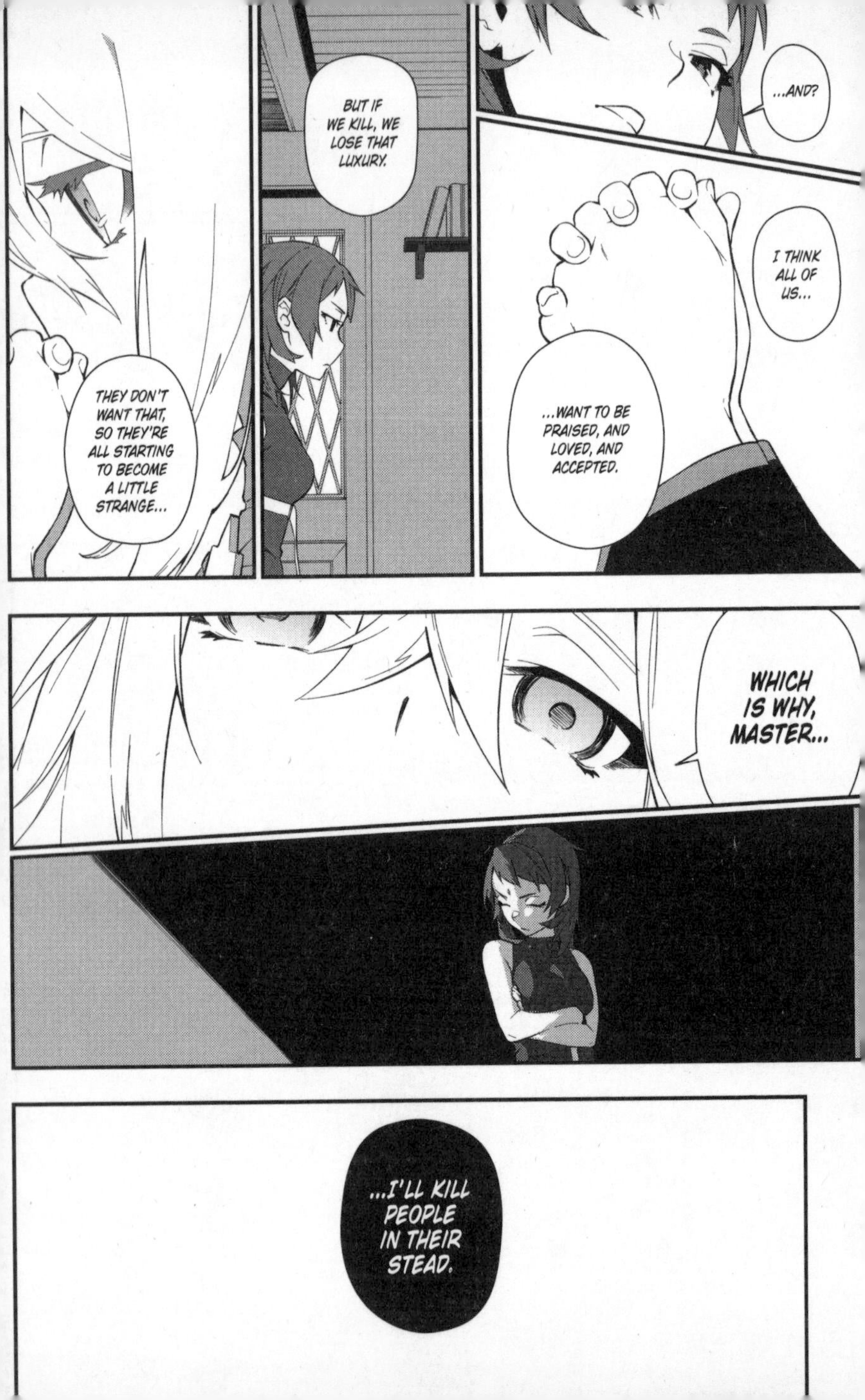
...AND?
I THINK ALL OF US...
...WANT TO BE PRAISED, AND LOVED, AND ACCEPTED.
BUT IF WE KILL, WE LOSE THAT LUXURY.
THEY DON'T WANT THAT, SO THEY'RE ALL STARTING TO BECOME A LITTLE STRANGE...
WHICH IS WHY, MASTER...
...I'LL KILL PEOPLE IN THEIR STEAD.

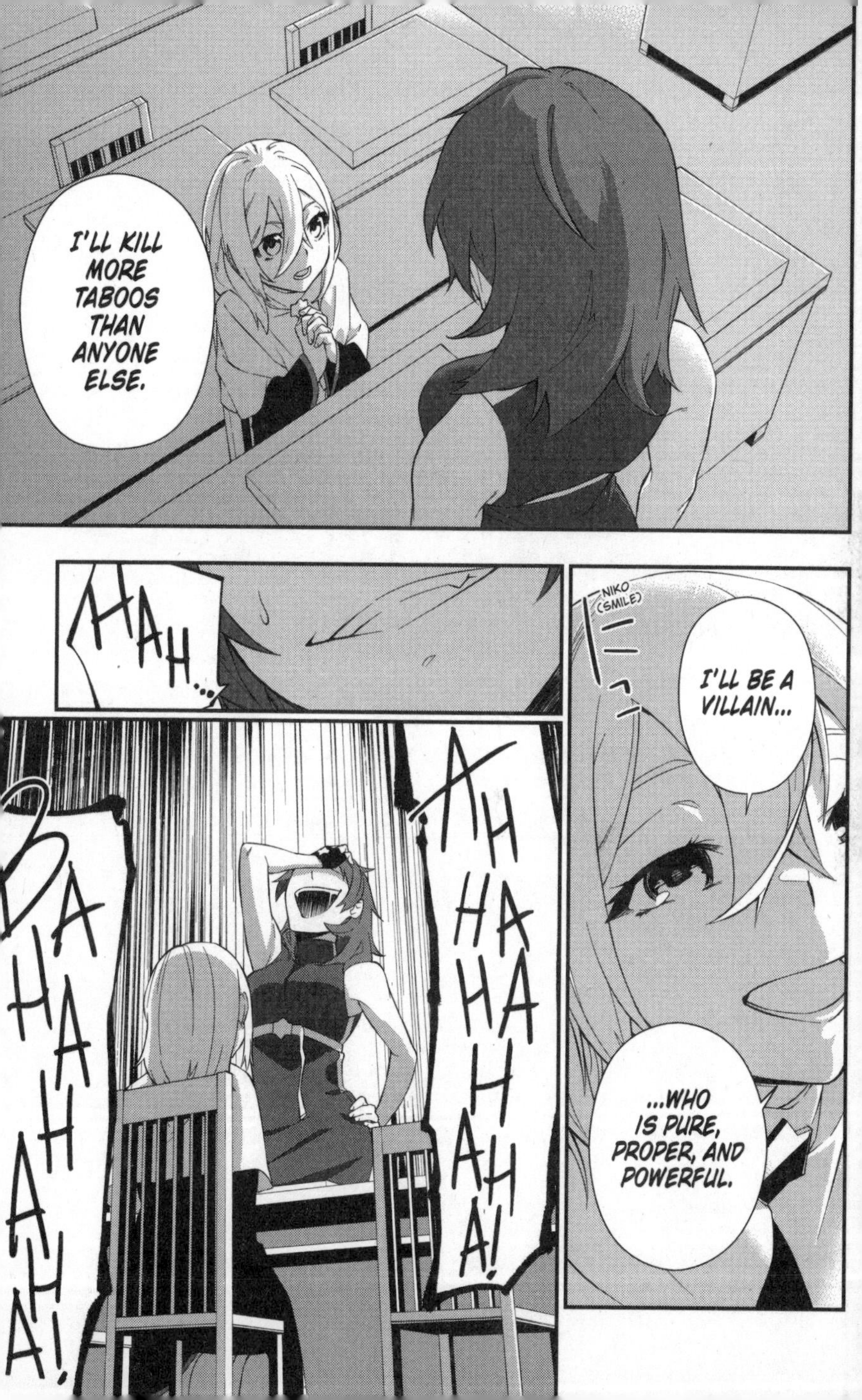
I'LL KILL MORE TABOOS THAN ANYONE ELSE.
NIKO (SMILE)
I'LL BE A VILLAIN...
...WHO IS PURE, PROPER, AND POWERFUL.
HAH...
AHAHAHAHAHAHA!
AHAHAHAHAHAHA!

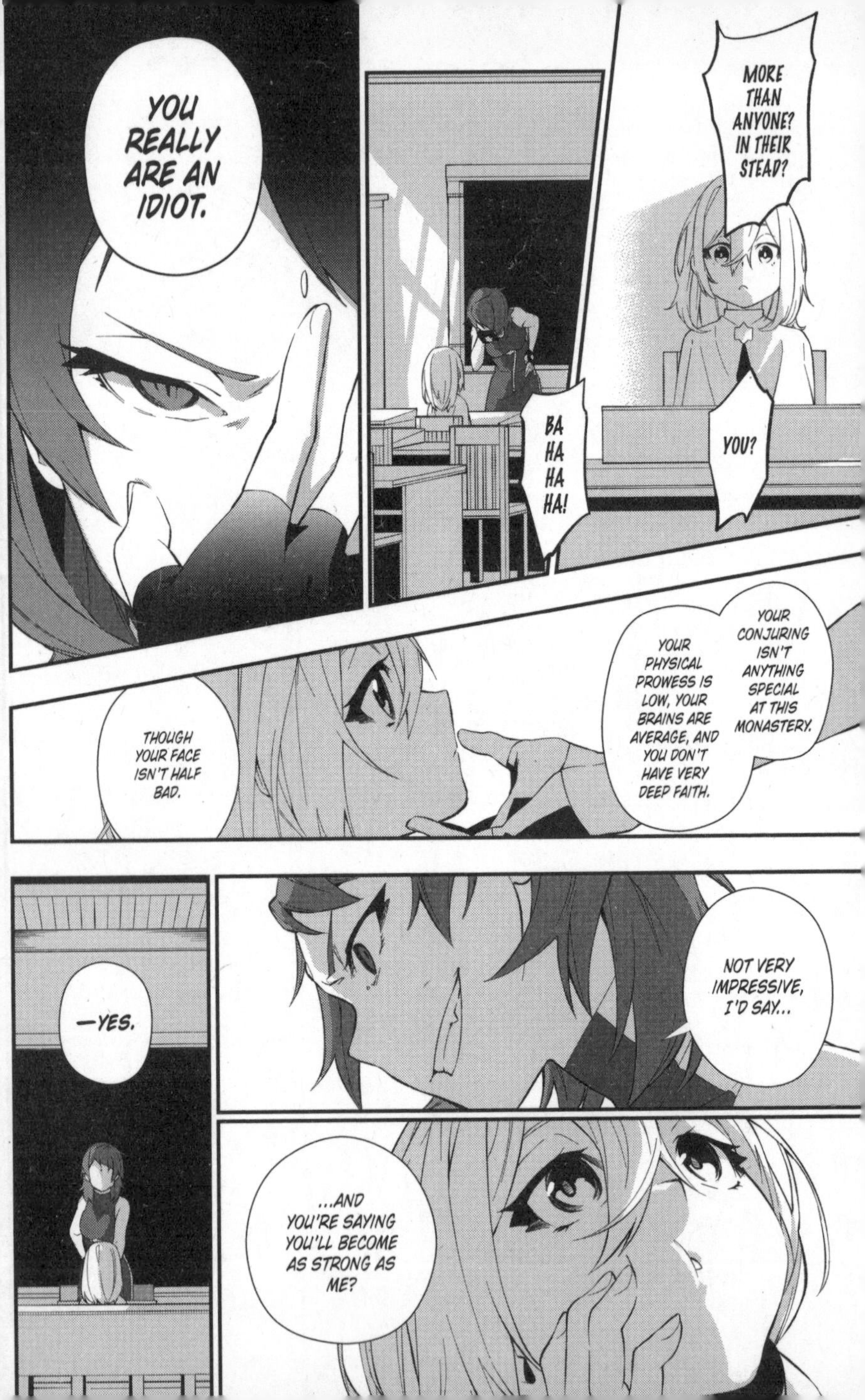
MORE THAN ANYONE? IN THEIR STEAD?
YOU?
BA HA HA HA!
YOU REALLY ARE AN IDIOT.
YOUR CONJURING ISN'T ANYTHING SPECIAL AT THIS MONASTERY.
YOUR PHYSICAL PROWESS IS LOW, YOUR BRAINS ARE AVERAGE, AND YOU DON'T HAVE VERY DEEP FAITH.
THOUGH YOUR FACE ISN'T HALF BAD.
NOT VERY IMPRESSIVE, I'D SAY...
...AND YOU'RE SAYING YOU'LL BECOME AS STRONG AS ME?
—YES.

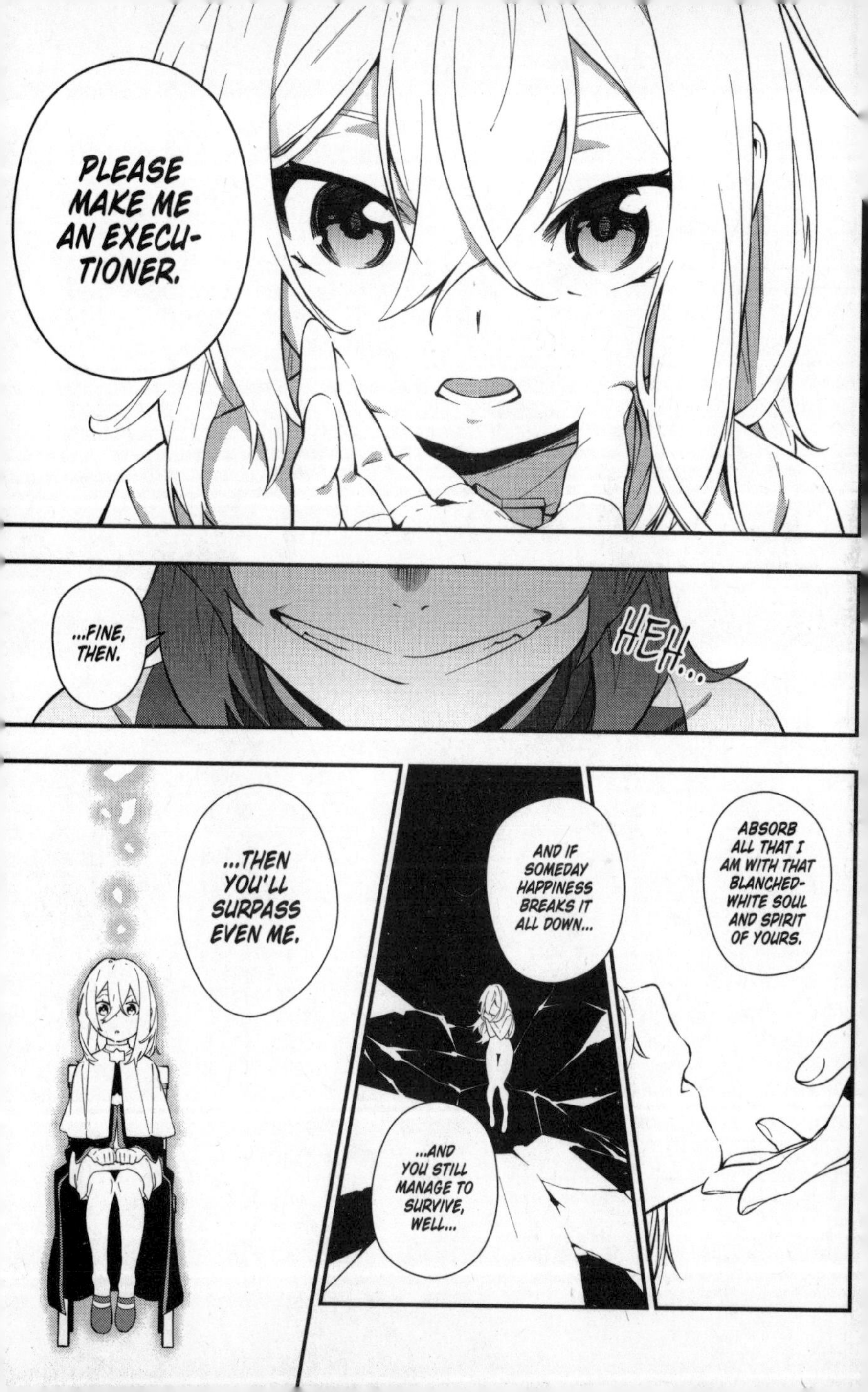
PLEASE MAKE ME AN EXECUTIONER.
HEH...
...FINE, THEN.
ABSORB ALL THAT I AM WITH THAT BLANCHED-WHITE SOUL AND SPIRIT OF YOURS.
AND IF SOMEDAY HAPPINESS BREAKS IT ALL DOWN...
...AND YOU STILL MANAGE TO SURVIVE, WELL...
...THEN YOU'LL SURPASS EVEN ME.

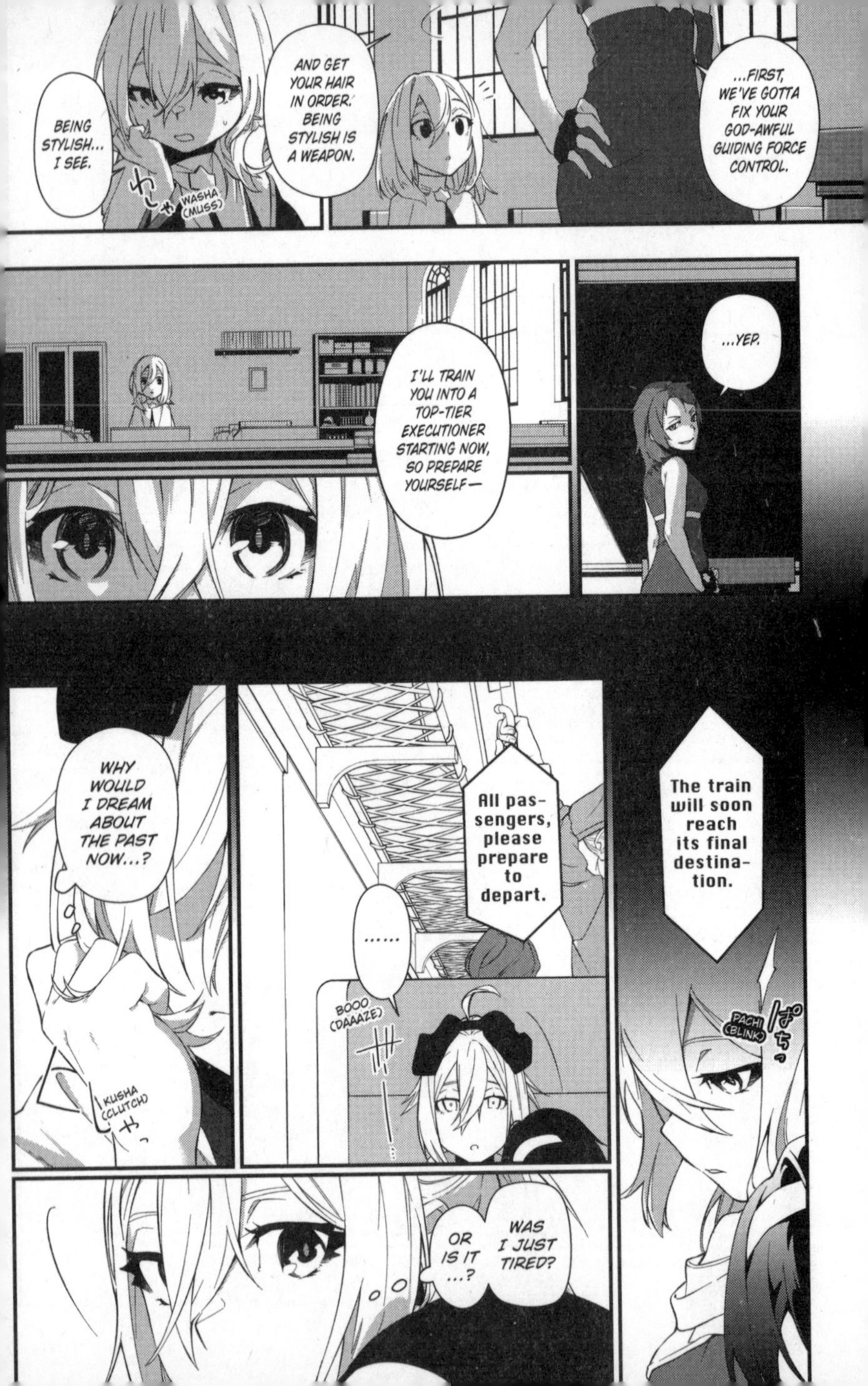
...FIRST, WE'VE GOTTA FIX YOUR GOD-AWFUL GUIDING FORCE CONTROL.
AND GET YOUR HAIR IN ORDER. BEING STYLISH IS A WEAPON.
BEING STYLISH... I SEE.
WASHA (MUSS)
...YEP.
I'LL TRAIN YOU INTO A TOP-TIER EXECUTIONER STARTING NOW, SO PREPARE YOURSELF—
The train will soon reach its final destination.
PACHI (BLINK)
All passengers, please prepare to depart.
......
BOOO (DAAAZE)
WHY WOULD I DREAM ABOUT THE PAST NOW...?
KUSHA (CLUTCH)
WAS I JUST TIRED?
OR IS IT ...?

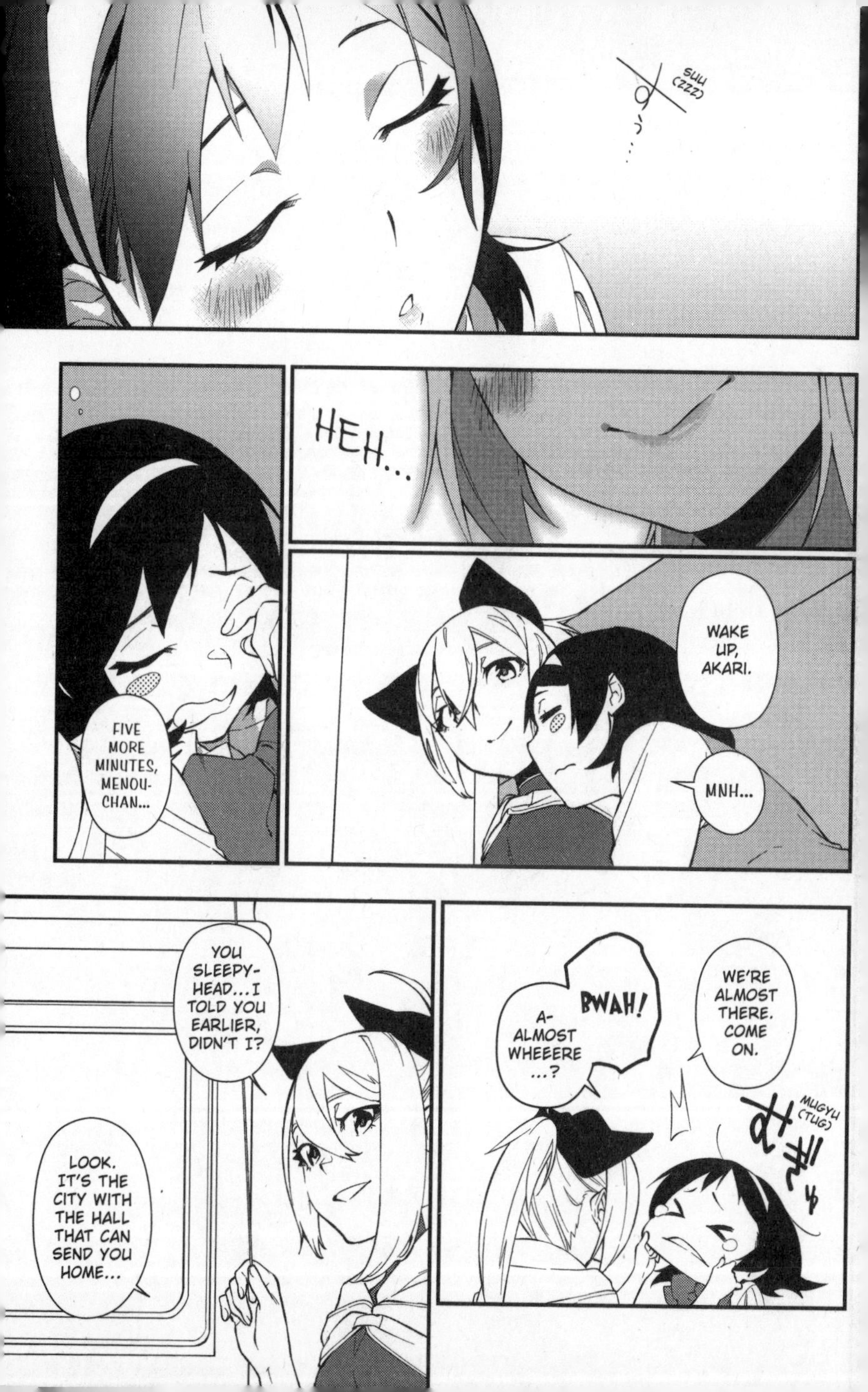
すぅ…
SUU (ZZZ)
HEH...
WAKE UP, AKARI.
MNH...
FIVE MORE MINUTES, MENOU-CHAN...
WE'RE ALMOST THERE. COME ON.
むぎゅ
MUGYU (TUG)
BWAH!
A-ALMOST WHEEERE ...?
YOU SLEEPY-HEAD...I TOLD YOU EARLIER, DIDN'T I?
LOOK. IT'S THE CITY WITH THE HALL THAT CAN SEND YOU HOME...

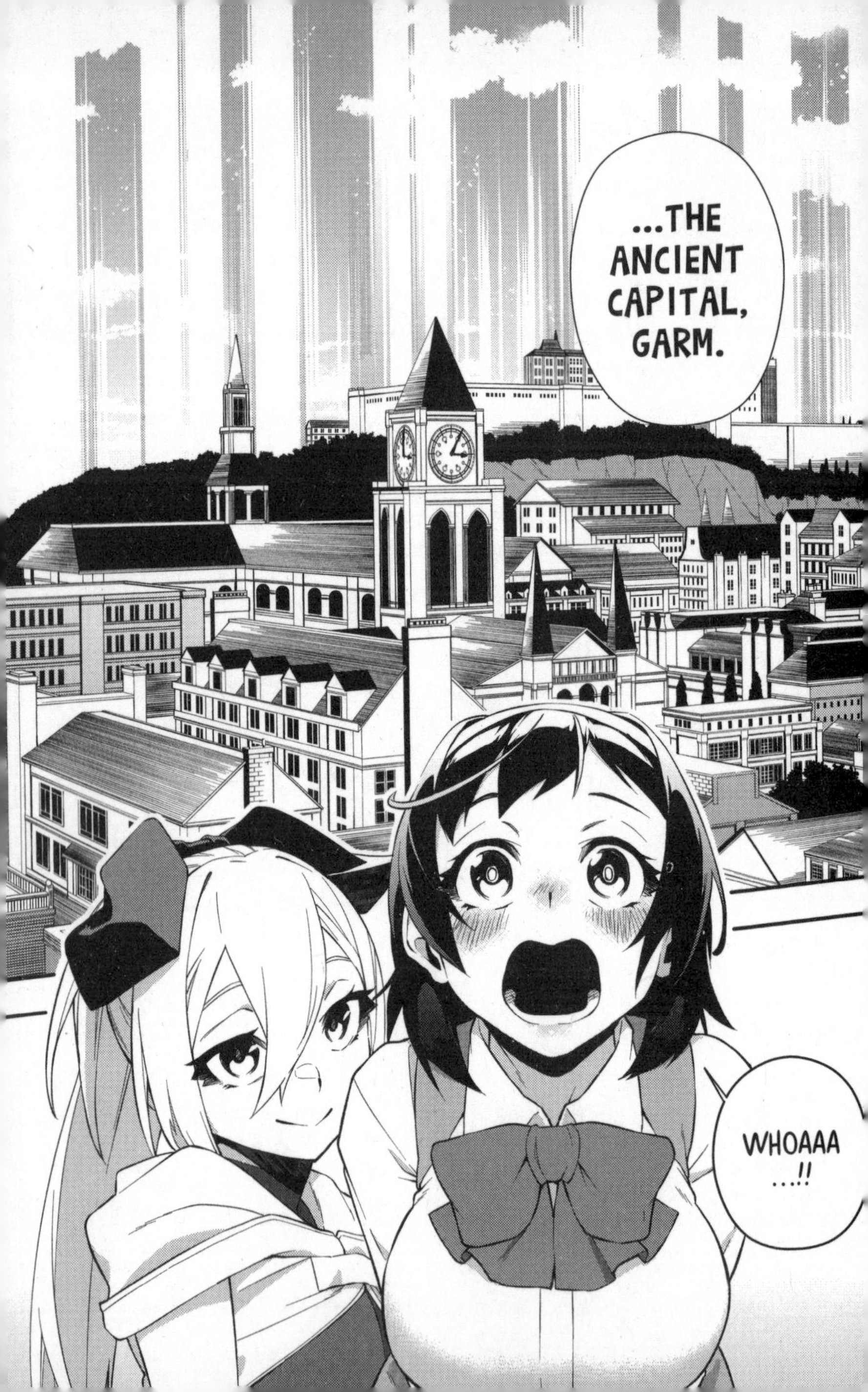
...THE ANCIENT CAPITAL, GARM.
WHOAAA ...!!

The Executioner and Her Way of Life

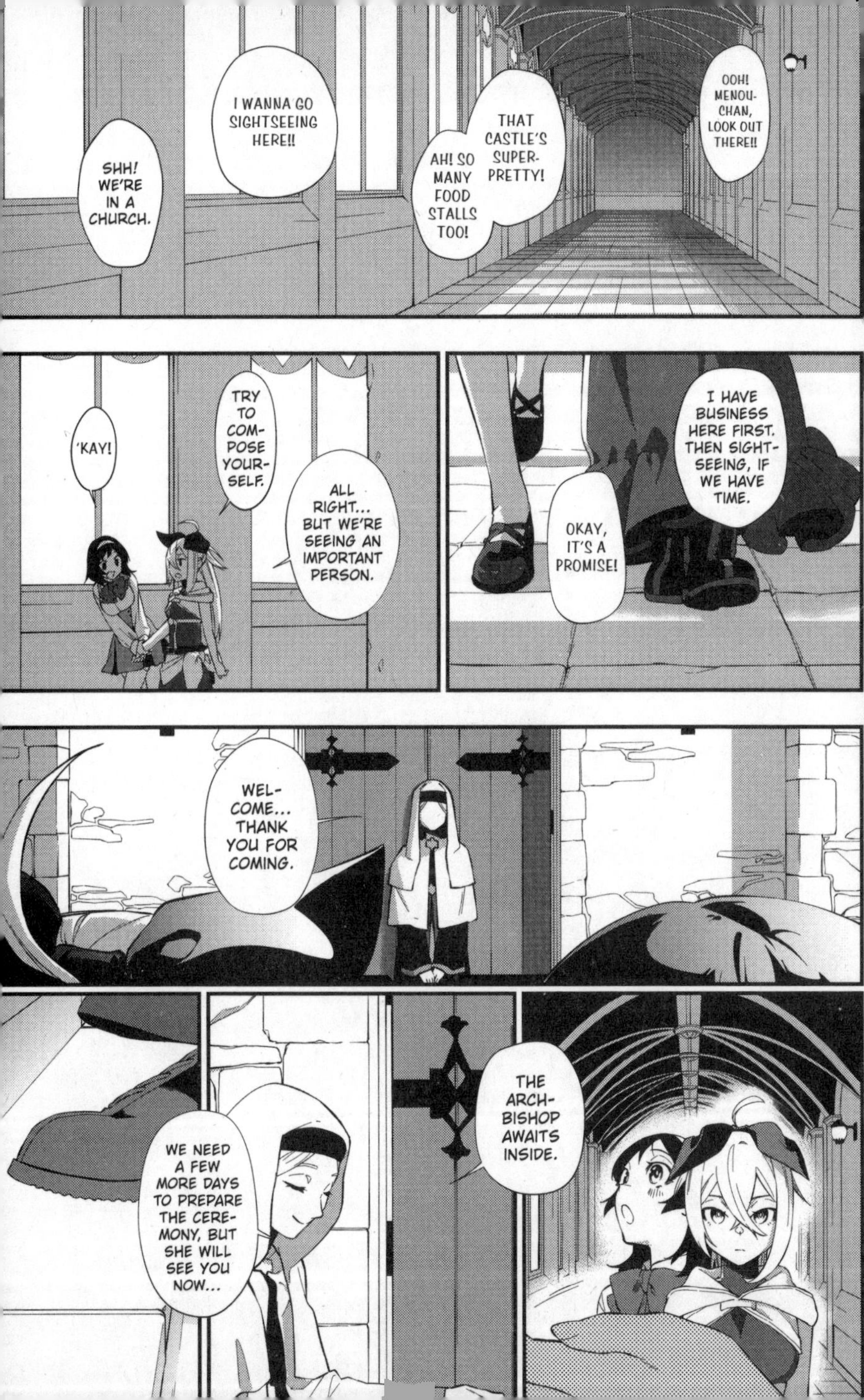
OOH! MENOU-CHAN, LOOK OUT THERE!!
THAT CASTLE'S SUPER-PRETTY!
AH! SO MANY FOOD STALLS TOO!
I WANNA GO SIGHTSEEING HERE!!
SHH! WE'RE IN A CHURCH.
I HAVE BUSINESS HERE FIRST. THEN SIGHT-SEEING, IF WE HAVE TIME.
OKAY, IT'S A PROMISE!
TRY TO COM-POSE YOUR-SELF.
'KAY!
ALL RIGHT... BUT WE'RE SEEING AN IMPORTANT PERSON.
WEL-COME... THANK YOU FOR COMING.
THE ARCH-BISHOP AWAITS INSIDE.
WE NEED A FEW MORE DAYS TO PREPARE THE CERE-MONY, BUT SHE WILL SEE YOU NOW...

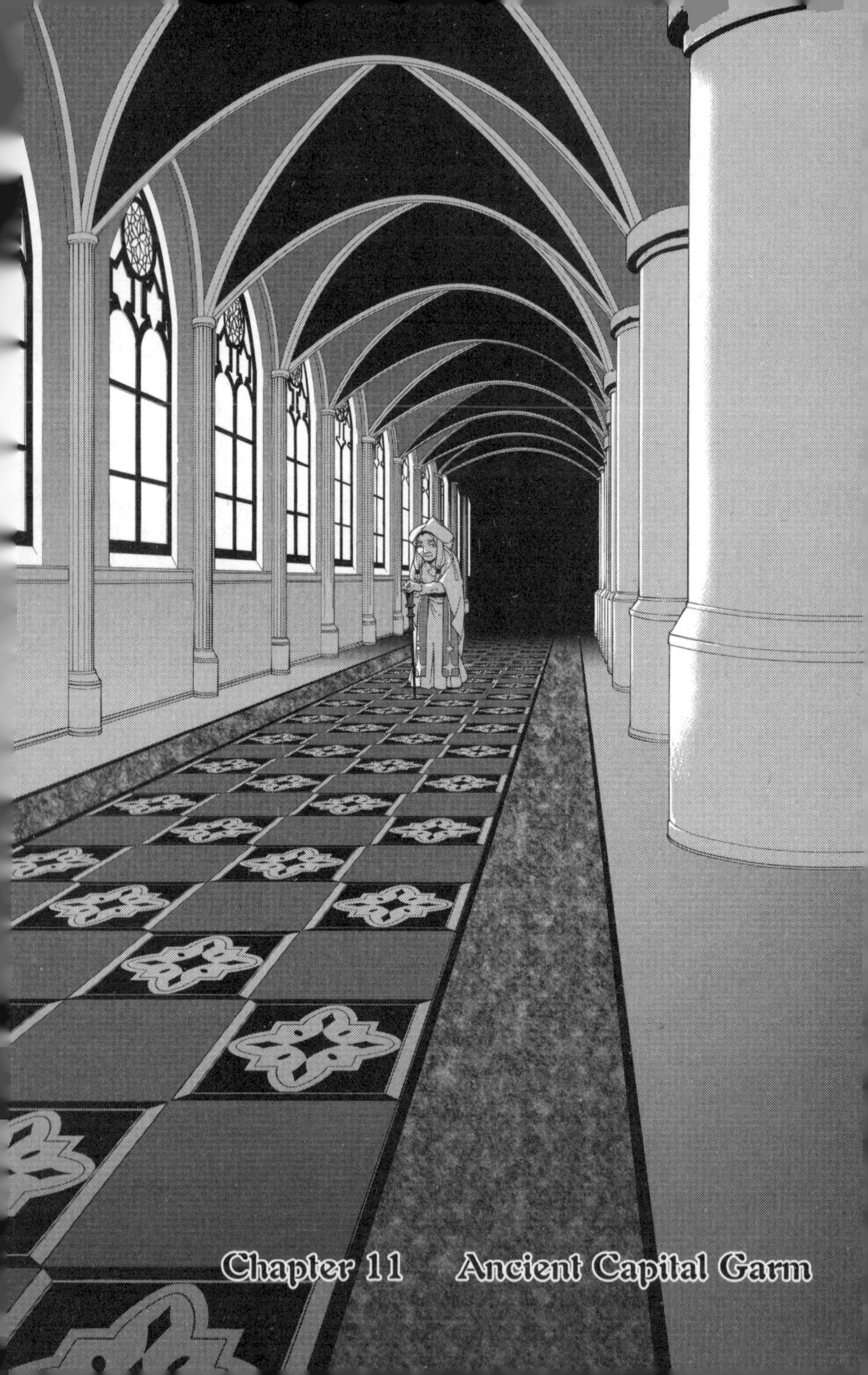
Chapter 11 Ancient Capital Garm

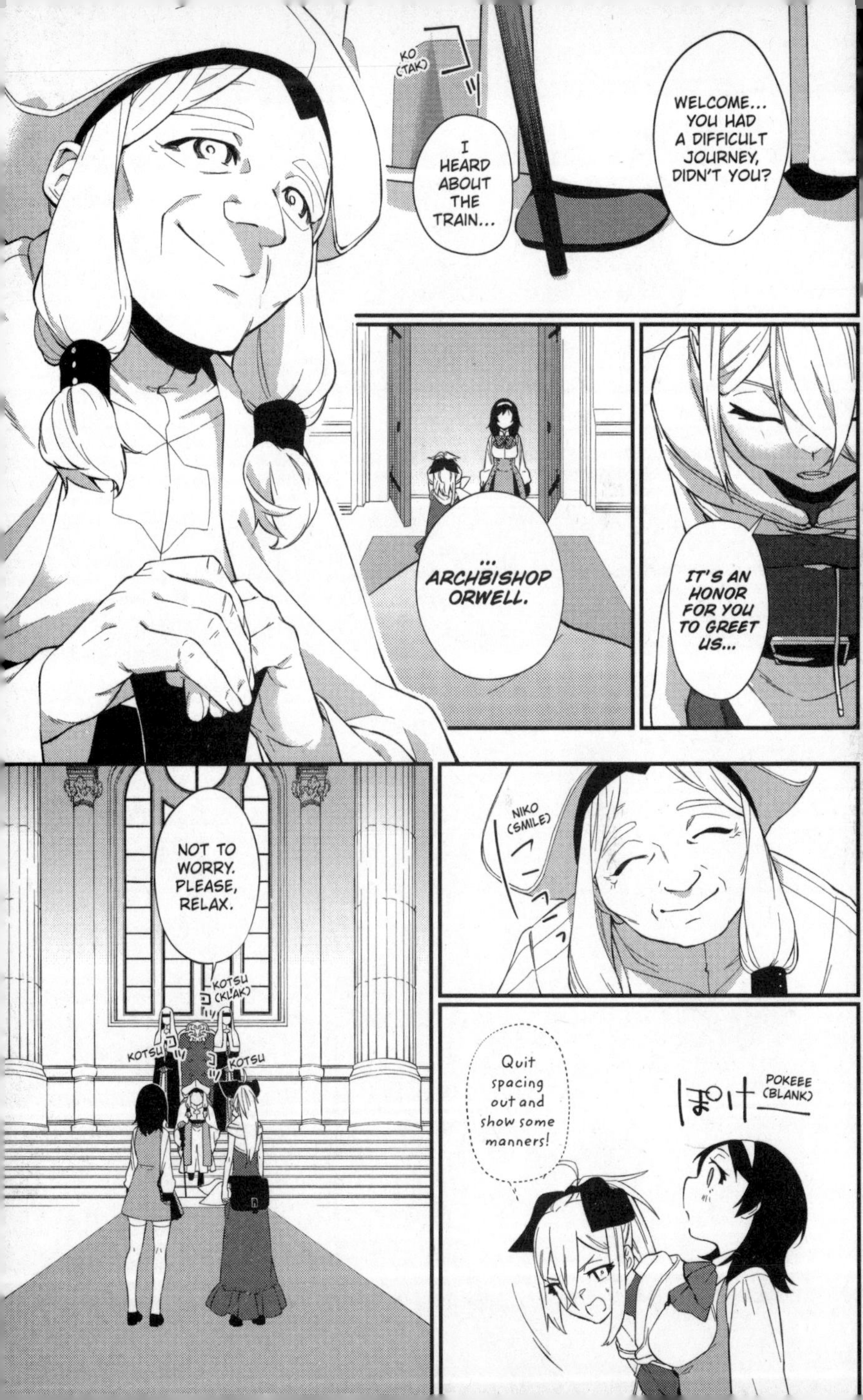
KO (TAK)
WELCOME... YOU HAD A DIFFICULT JOURNEY, DIDN'T YOU?
I HEARD ABOUT THE TRAIN...
IT'S AN HONOR FOR YOU TO GREET US...
... ARCHBISHOP ORWELL.
NIKO (SMILE)
POKEEE (BLANK)
Quit spacing out and show some manners!
NOT TO WORRY. PLEASE, RELAX.
KOTSU (KLAK)
KOTSU
KOTSU

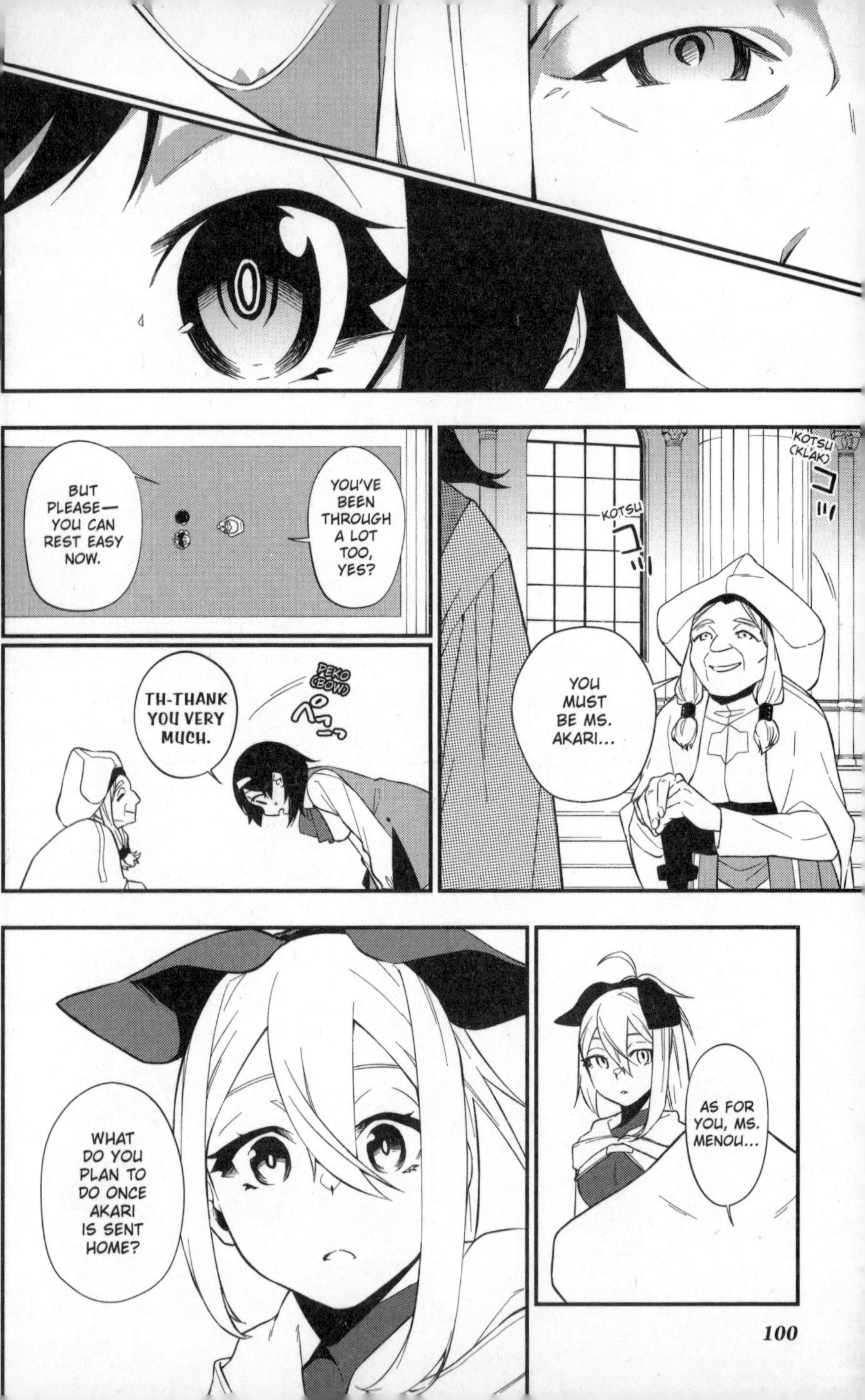
KOTSU (KLAK)
KOTSU
YOU MUST BE MS. AKARI...
YOU'VE BEEN THROUGH A LOT TOO, YES?
BUT PLEASE—YOU CAN REST EASY NOW.
PEKO (BOW)
TH-THANK YOU VERY MUCH.
AS FOR YOU, MS. MENOU...
WHAT DO YOU PLAN TO DO ONCE AKARI IS SENT HOME?

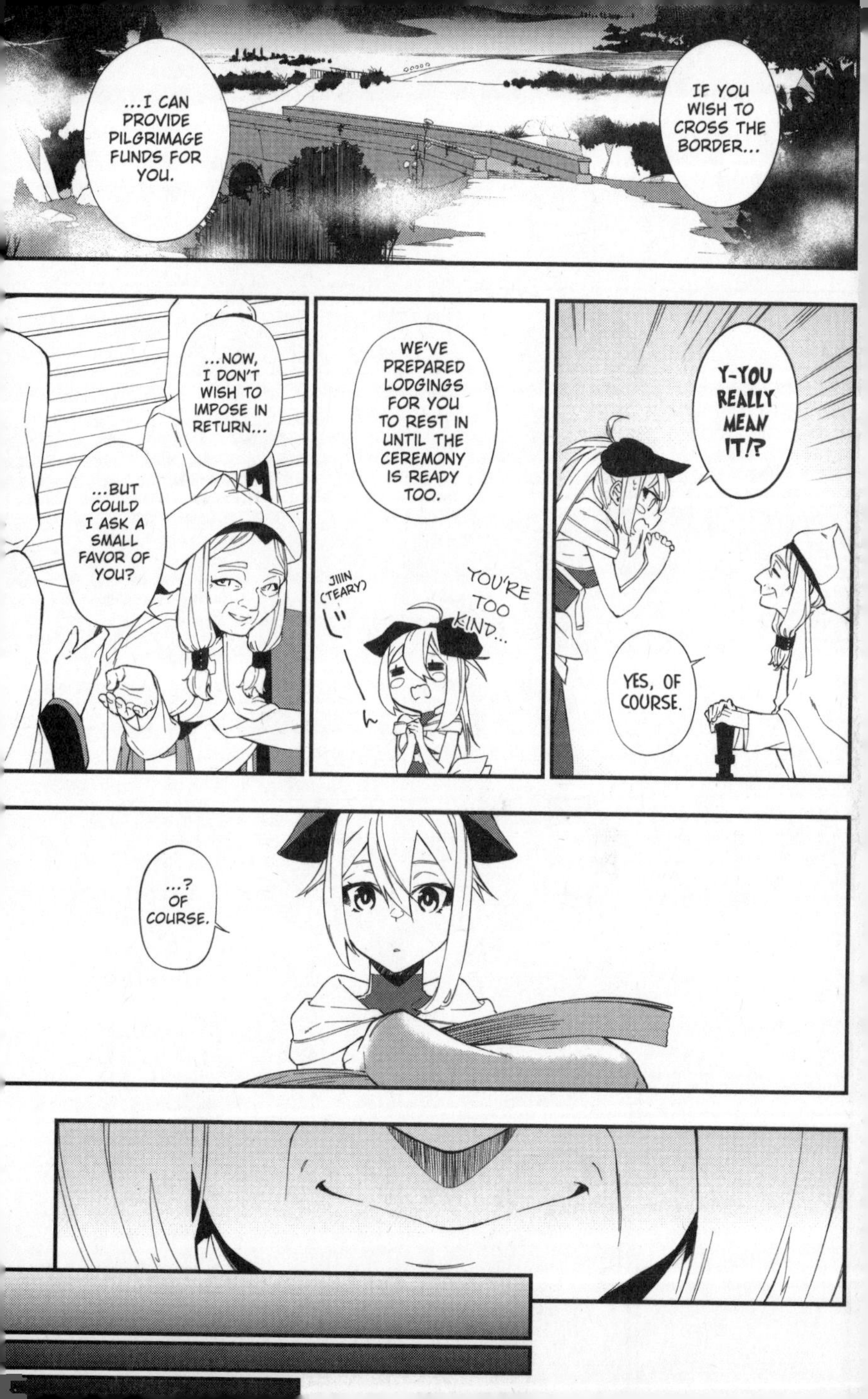
IF YOU WISH TO CROSS THE BORDER...
...I CAN PROVIDE PILGRIMAGE FUNDS FOR YOU.
Y-YOU REALLY MEAN IT!?
YES, OF COURSE.
WE'VE PREPARED LODGINGS FOR YOU TO REST IN UNTIL THE CEREMONY IS READY TOO.
YOU'RE TOO KIND...
JIIIN (TEARY)
...NOW, I DON'T WISH TO IMPOSE IN RETURN...
...BUT COULD I ASK A SMALL FAVOR OF YOU?
...? OF COURSE.

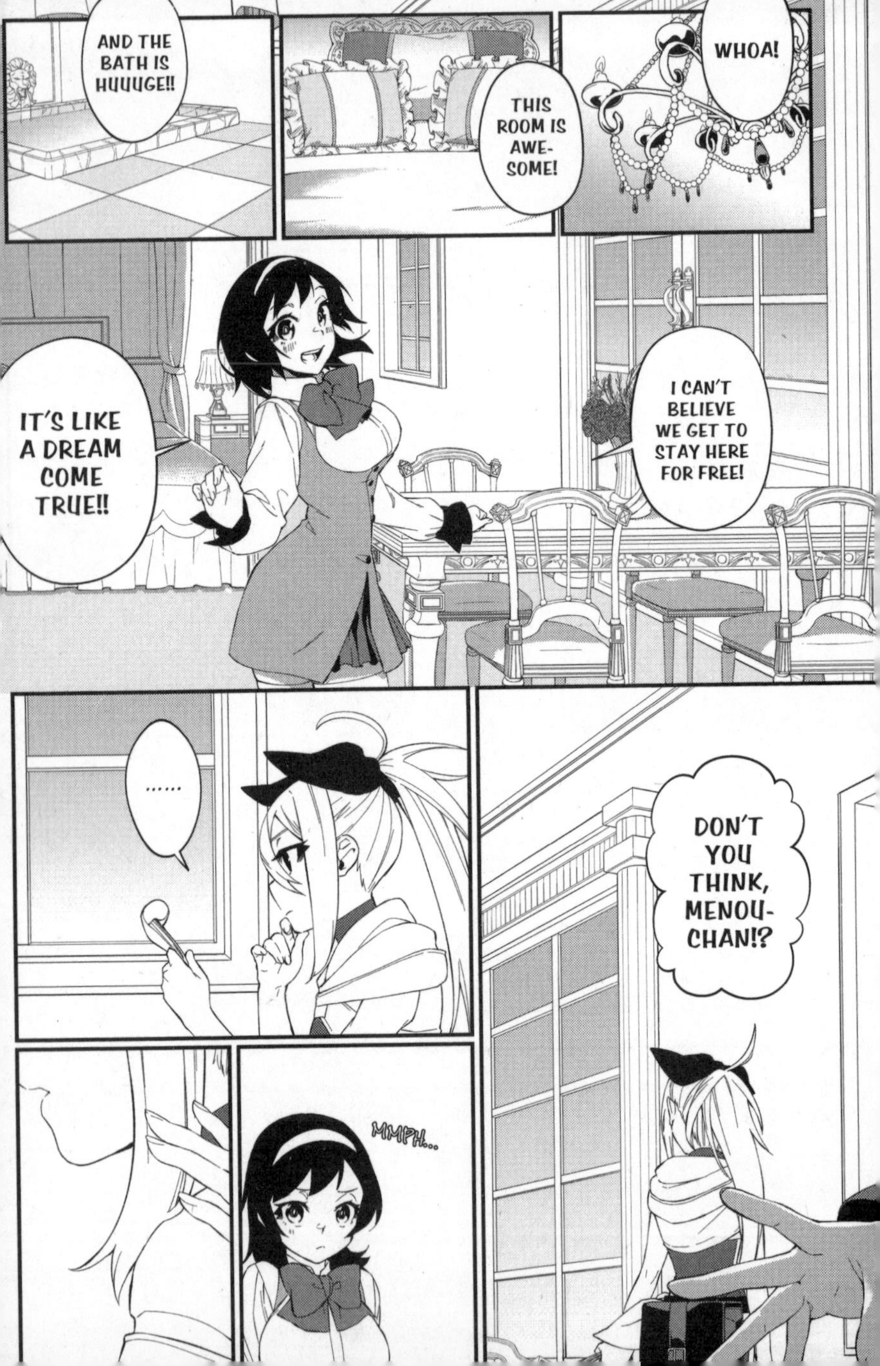
WHOA!
THIS ROOM IS AWE-SOME!
AND THE BATH IS HUUUGE!!
I CAN'T BELIEVE WE GET TO STAY HERE FOR FREE!
IT'S LIKE A DREAM COME TRUE!!
DON'T YOU THINK, MENOU-CHAN!?
......
MMPH...

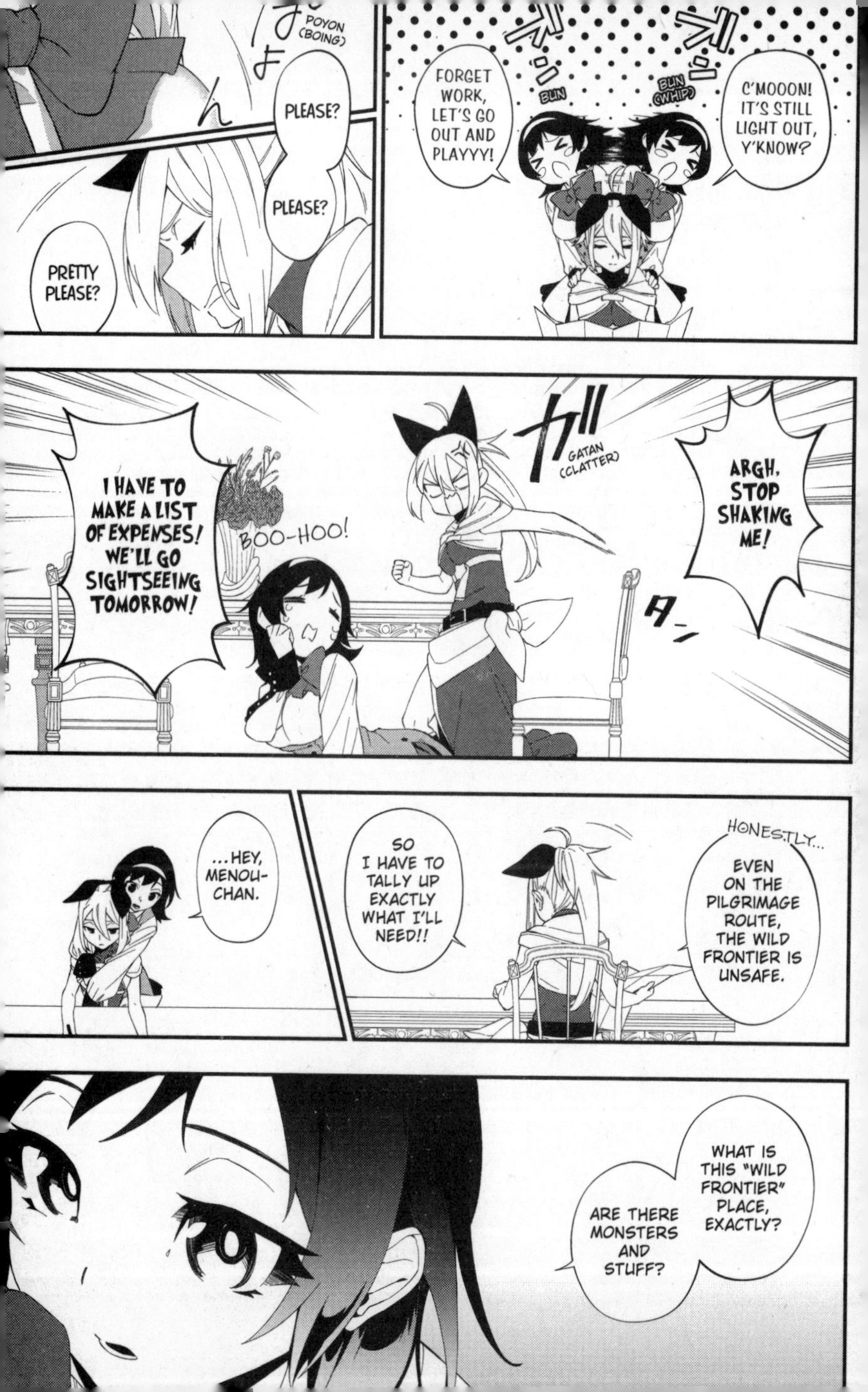
BUN (WHIP)
BUN
C'MOOON! IT'S STILL LIGHT OUT, Y'KNOW?
FORGET WORK, LET'S GO OUT AND PLAYYY!
POYON (BOING)
PLEASE?
PLEASE?
PRETTY PLEASE?
ARGH. STOP SHAKING ME!
GATAN (CLATTER)
BOO-HOO!
I HAVE TO MAKE A LIST OF EXPENSES! WE'LL GO SIGHTSEEING TOMORROW!
HONESTLY...
EVEN ON THE PILGRIMAGE ROUTE, THE WILD FRONTIER IS UNSAFE.
SO I HAVE TO TALLY UP EXACTLY WHAT I'LL NEED!!
...HEY, MENOU-CHAN.
WHAT IS THIS "WILD FRONTIER" PLACE, EXACTLY?
ARE THERE MONSTERS AND STUFF?

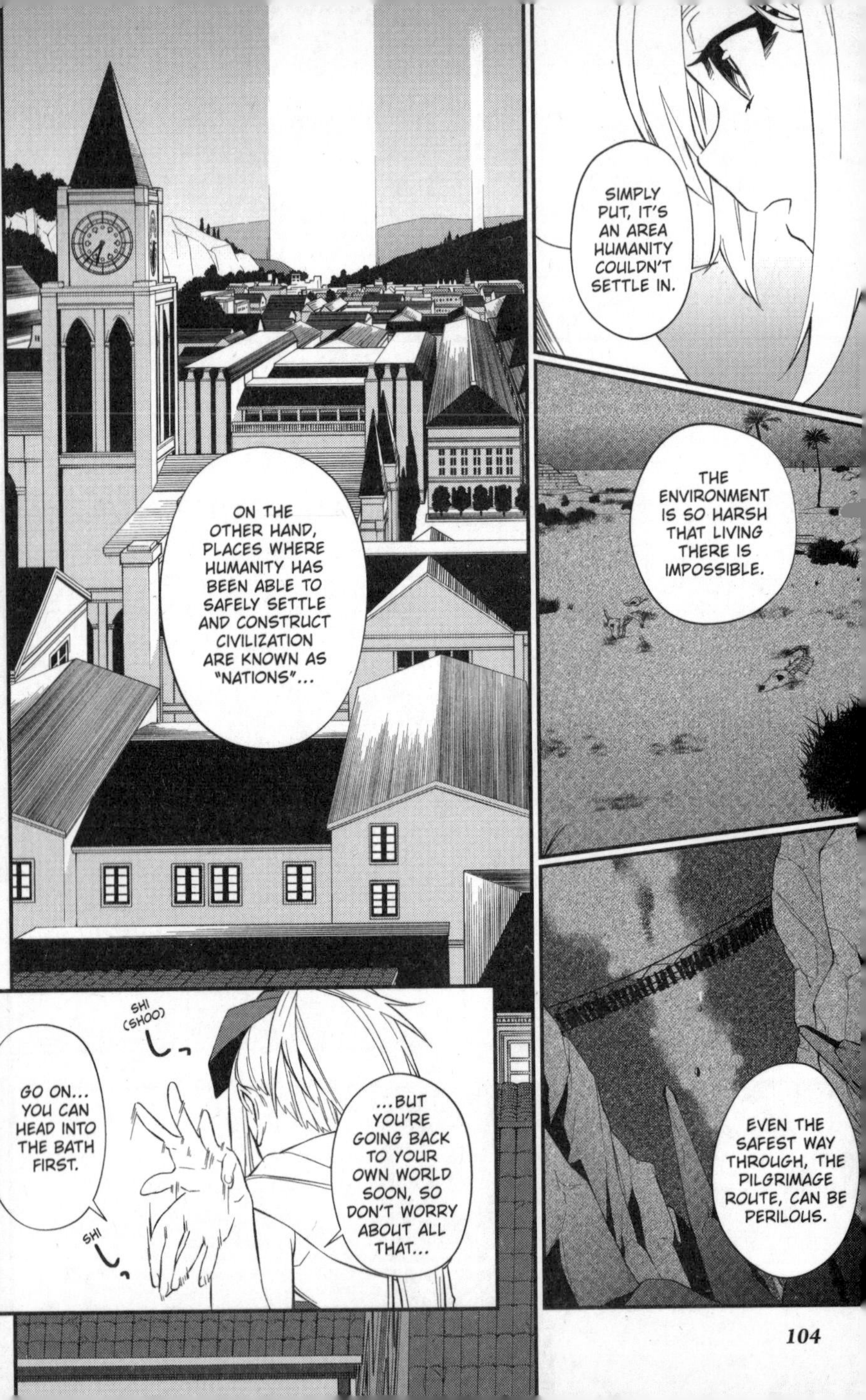
SIMPLY PUT, IT'S AN AREA HUMANITY COULDN'T SETTLE IN.
THE ENVIRONMENT IS SO HARSH THAT LIVING THERE IS IMPOSSIBLE.
EVEN THE SAFEST WAY THROUGH, THE PILGRIMAGE ROUTE, CAN BE PERILOUS.
ON THE OTHER HAND, PLACES WHERE HUMANITY HAS BEEN ABLE TO SAFELY SETTLE AND CONSTRUCT CIVILIZATION ARE KNOWN AS "NATIONS"...
...BUT YOU'RE GOING BACK TO YOUR OWN WORLD SOON, SO DON'T WORRY ABOUT ALL THAT...
SHI (SHOO)
GO ON... YOU CAN HEAD INTO THE BATH FIRST.
SHI

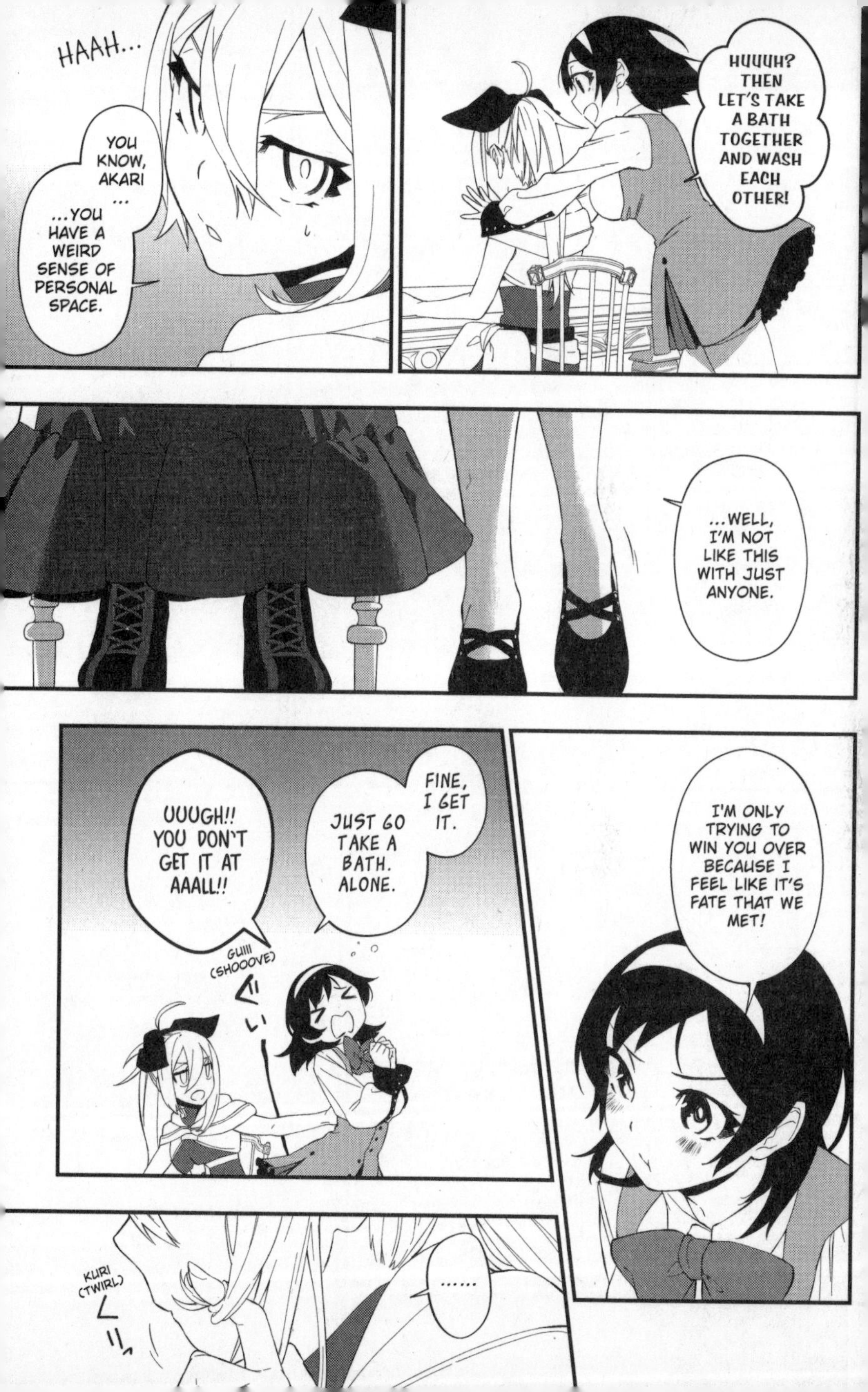
HUUUH? THEN LET'S TAKE A BATH TOGETHER AND WASH EACH OTHER!
HAAAH...
YOU KNOW, AKARI ...
...YOU HAVE A WEIRD SENSE OF PERSONAL SPACE.
...WELL, I'M NOT LIKE THIS WITH JUST ANYONE.
I'M ONLY TRYING TO WIN YOU OVER BECAUSE I FEEL LIKE IT'S FATE THAT WE MET!
FINE, I GET IT.
JUST GO TAKE A BATH. ALONE.
UUUGH!! YOU DON'T GET IT AT AAALL!!
GUIII (SHOOOVE)
......
KURI (TWIRL)

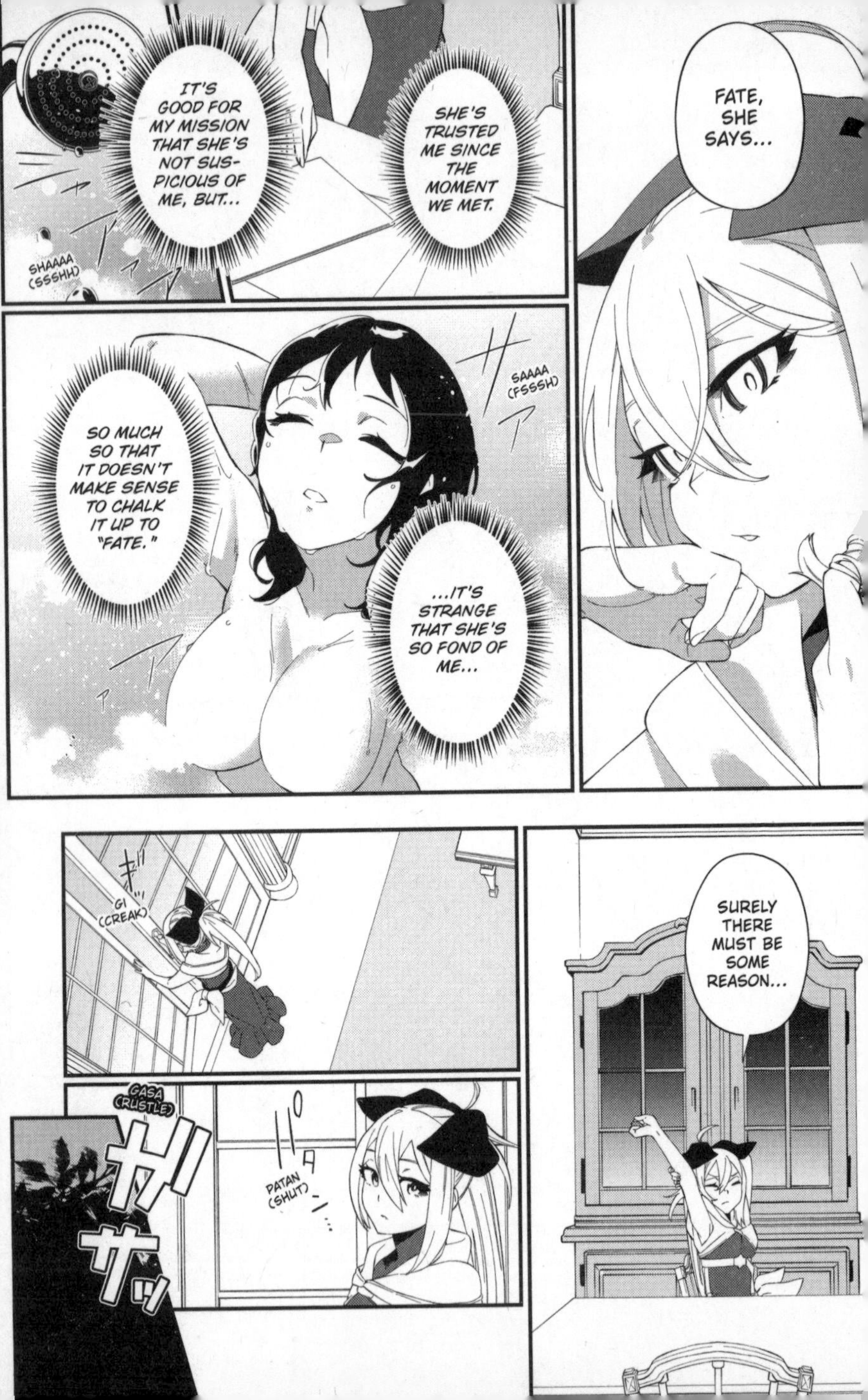
FATE, SHE SAYS...
SHE'S TRUSTED ME SINCE THE MOMENT WE MET.
IT'S GOOD FOR MY MISSION THAT SHE'S NOT SUS-PICIOUS OF ME, BUT...
SHAAAA (SSSHH)
SAAAA (FSSSH)
...IT'S STRANGE THAT SHE'S SO FOND OF ME...
SO MUCH SO THAT IT DOESN'T MAKE SENSE TO CHALK IT UP TO "FATE."
SURELY THERE MUST BE SOME REASON...
GI (CREAK)
PATAN (SHUT)
GASA (RUSTLE)

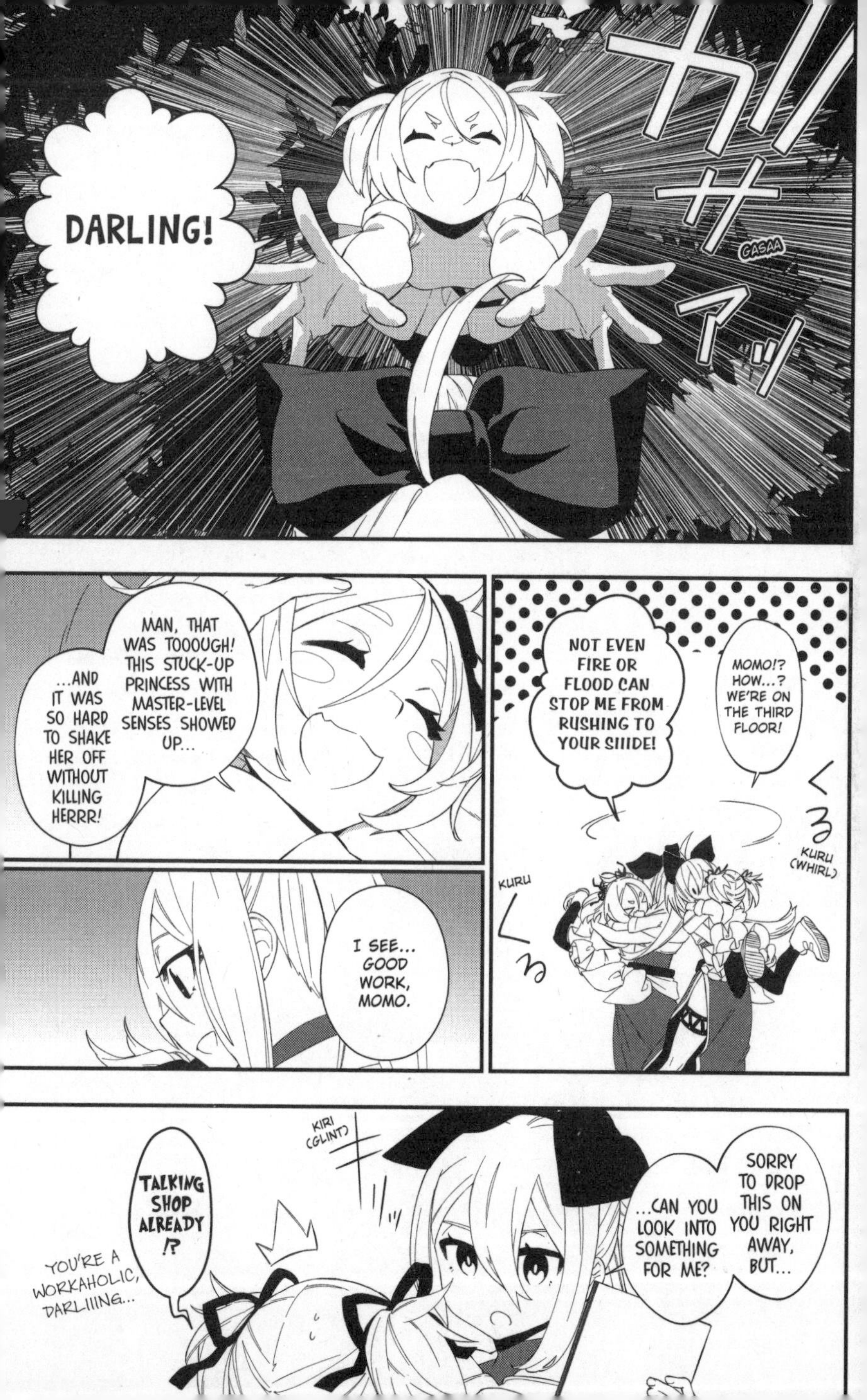
カサァッ
GASAA
DARLING!
MOMO!? HOW...? WE'RE ON THE THIRD FLOOR!
NOT EVEN FIRE OR FLOOD CAN STOP ME FROM RUSHING TO YOUR SIIIDE!
くる
KURU (WHIRL)
KURU
くる
MAN, THAT WAS TOOOUGH! THIS STUCK-UP PRINCESS WITH MASTER-LEVEL SENSES SHOWED UP...
...AND IT WAS SO HARD TO SHAKE HER OFF WITHOUT KILLING HERRR!
I SEE... GOOD WORK, MOMO.
SORRY TO DROP THIS ON YOU RIGHT AWAY, BUT...
...CAN YOU LOOK INTO SOMETHING FOR ME?
KIRI (GLINT)
TALKING SHOP ALREADY!?
YOU'RE A WORKAHOLIC, DARLIIING...

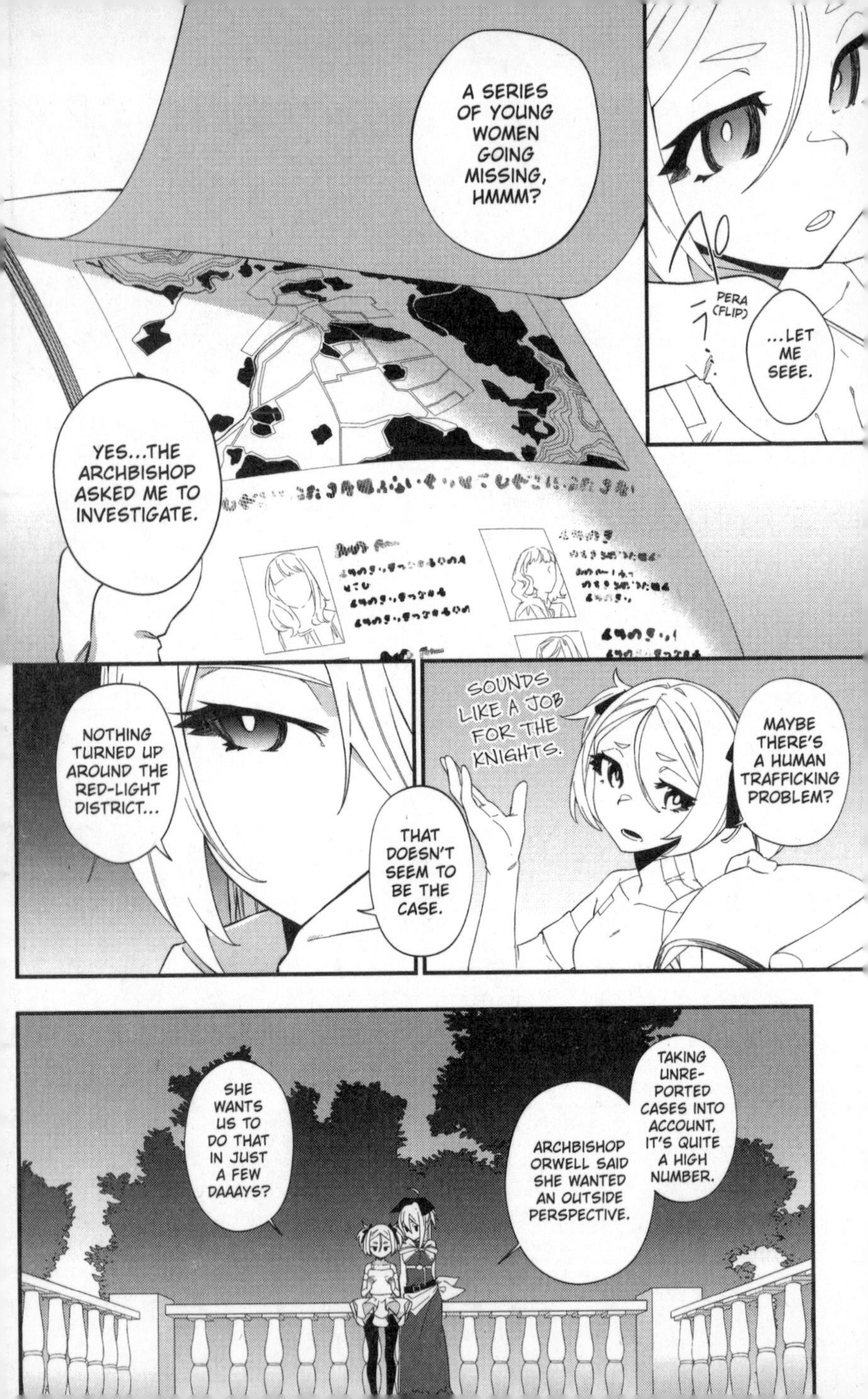
PERA (FLIP)
...LET ME SEEE.
A SERIES OF YOUNG WOMEN GOING MISSING, HMMM?
YES...THE ARCHBISHOP ASKED ME TO INVESTIGATE.
MAYBE THERE'S A HUMAN TRAFFICKING PROBLEM?
SOUNDS LIKE A JOB FOR THE KNIGHTS.
THAT DOESN'T SEEM TO BE THE CASE.
NOTHING TURNED UP AROUND THE RED-LIGHT DISTRICT...
TAKING UNRE-PORTED CASES INTO ACCOUNT, IT'S QUITE A HIGH NUMBER.
ARCHBISHOP ORWELL SAID SHE WANTED AN OUTSIDE PERSPECTIVE.
SHE WANTS US TO DO THAT IN JUST A FEW DAAAYS?

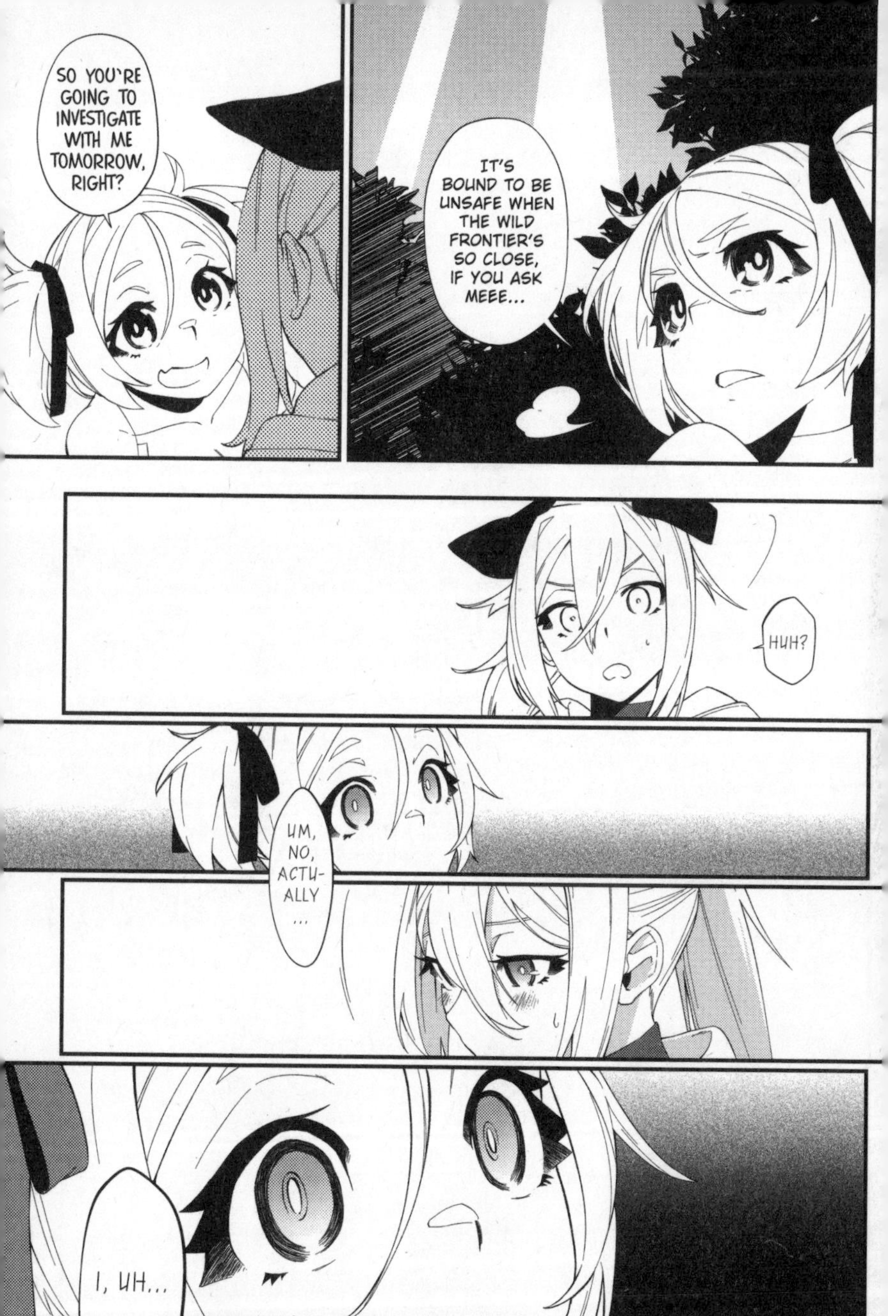
IT'S BOUND TO BE UNSAFE WHEN THE WILD FRONTIER'S SO CLOSE, IF YOU ASK MEEE...
SO YOU'RE GOING TO INVESTIGATE WITH ME TOMORROW, RIGHT?
HUH?
UM, NO, ACTU-ALLY...
I, UH...

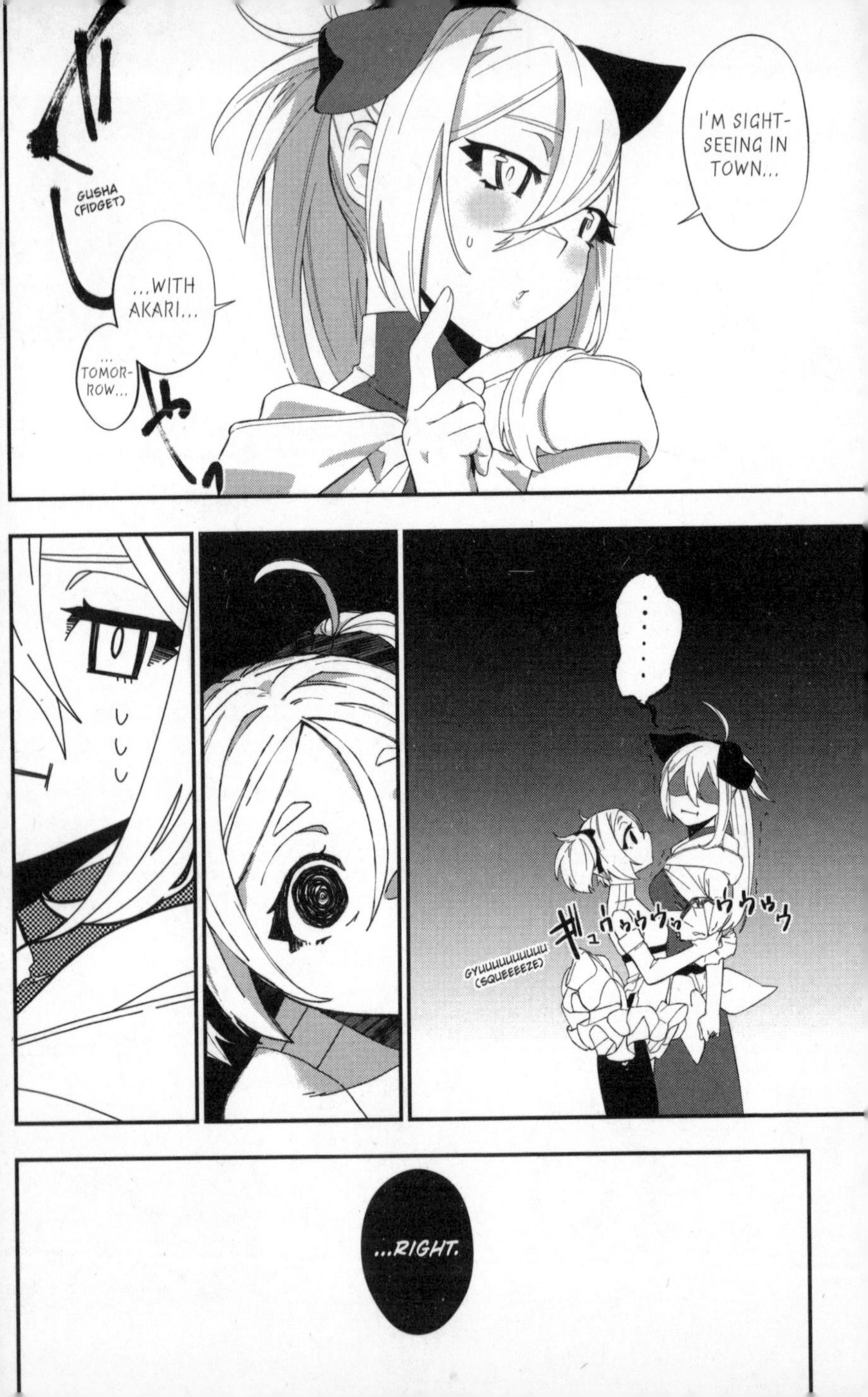
I'M SIGHT-SEEING IN TOWN...
GUSHA (FIDGET)
...WITH AKARI...
...TOMORROW...
......
GYUUUUUUUUUU (SQUEEEEZE)
...RIGHT.

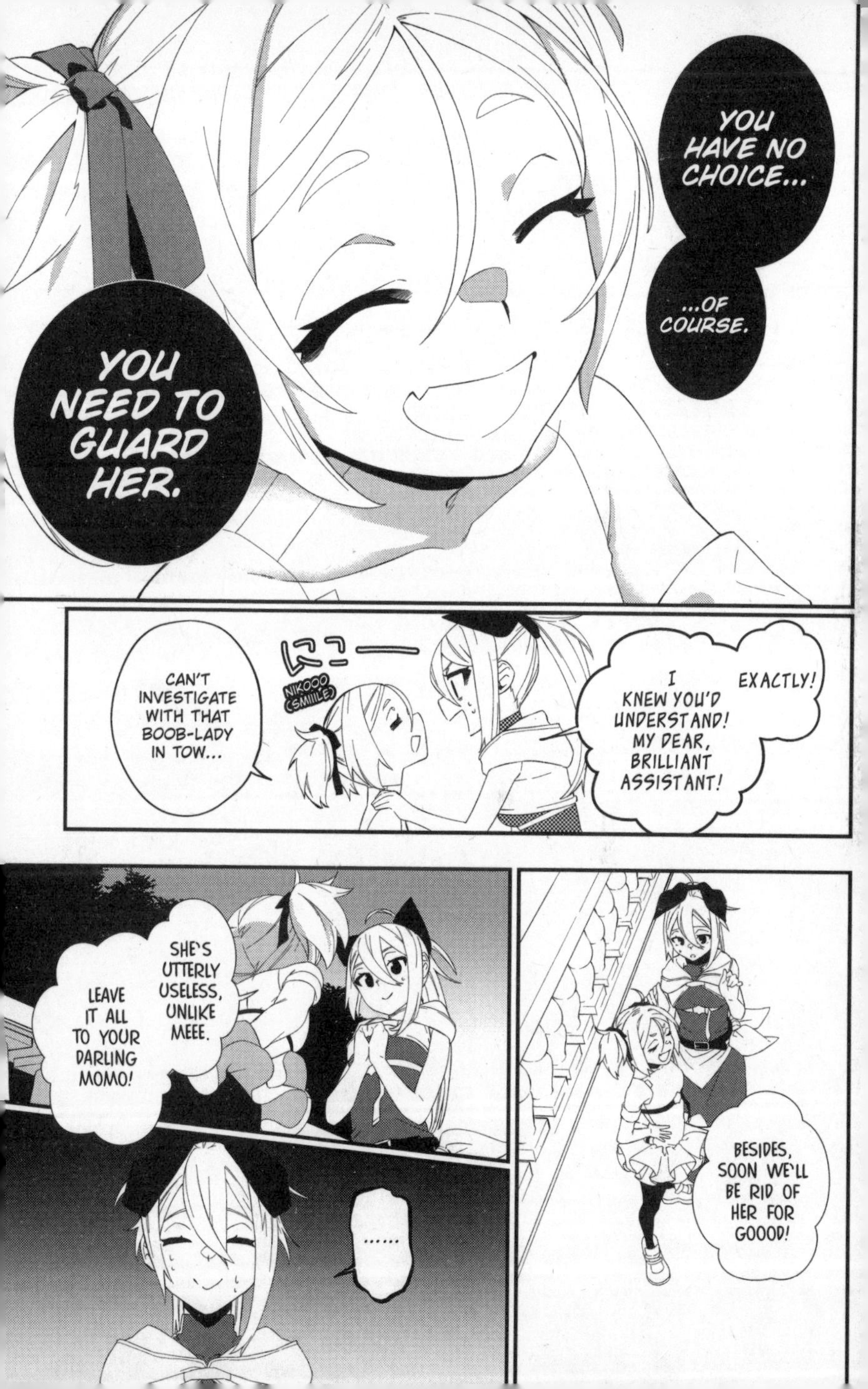
YOU HAVE NO CHOICE...
...OF COURSE.
YOU NEED TO GUARD HER.
EXACTLY!
I KNEW YOU'D UNDERSTAND! MY DEAR, BRILLIANT ASSISTANT!
にこーー
NIKOOO (SMIIILE)
CAN'T INVESTIGATE WITH THAT BOOB-LADY IN TOW...
BESIDES, SOON WE'LL BE RID OF HER FOR GOOOD!
SHE'S UTTERLY USELESS, UNLIKE MEEE.
LEAVE IT ALL TO YOUR DARLING MOMO!
......

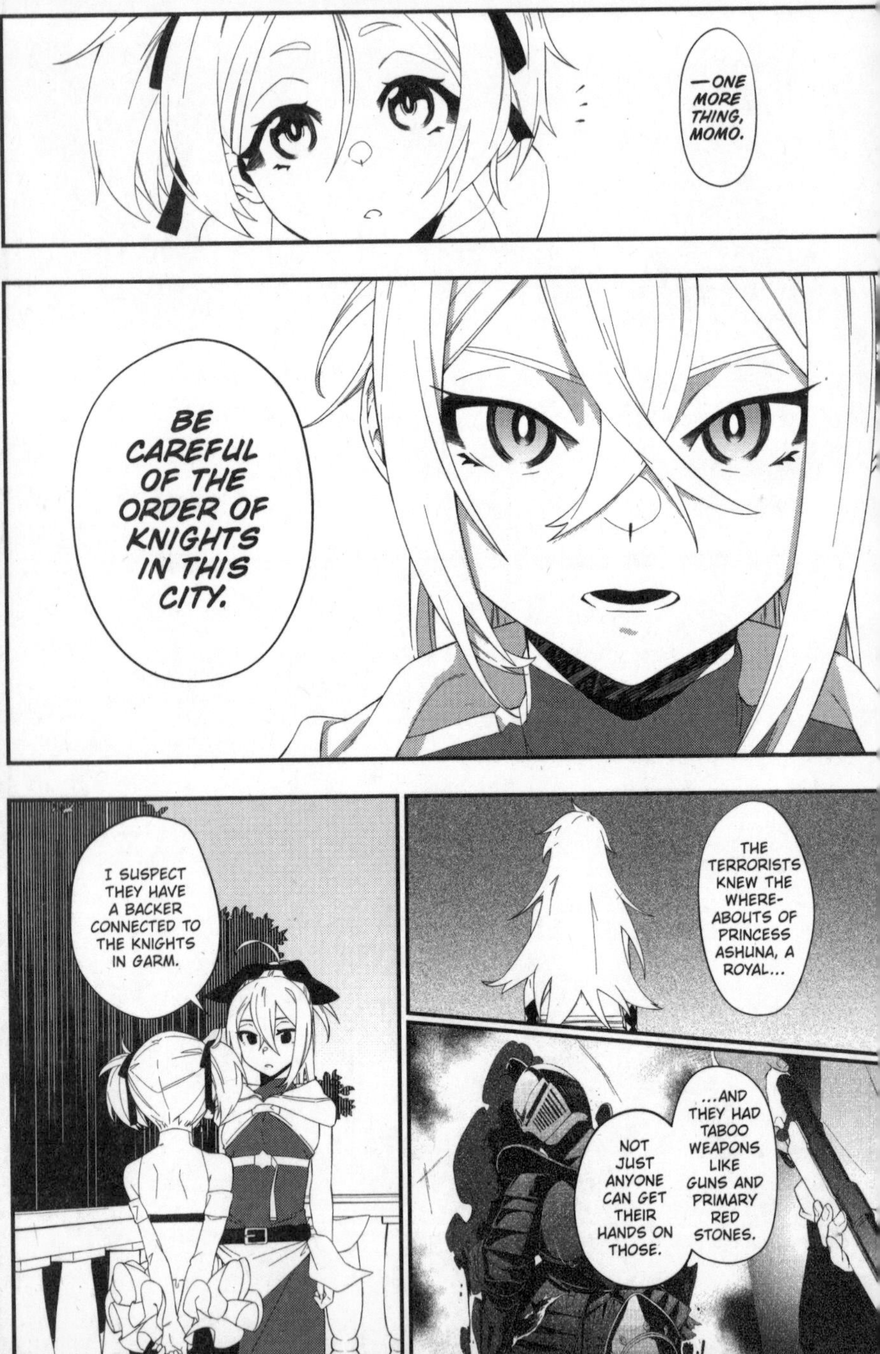
—ONE MORE THING, MOMO.
BE CAREFUL OF THE ORDER OF KNIGHTS IN THIS CITY.
THE TERRORISTS KNEW THE WHERE-ABOUTS OF PRINCESS ASHUNA, A ROYAL...
...AND THEY HAD TABOO WEAPONS LIKE GUNS AND PRIMARY RED STONES.
NOT JUST ANYONE CAN GET THEIR HANDS ON THOSE.
I SUSPECT THEY HAVE A BACKER CONNECTED TO THE KNIGHTS IN GARM.

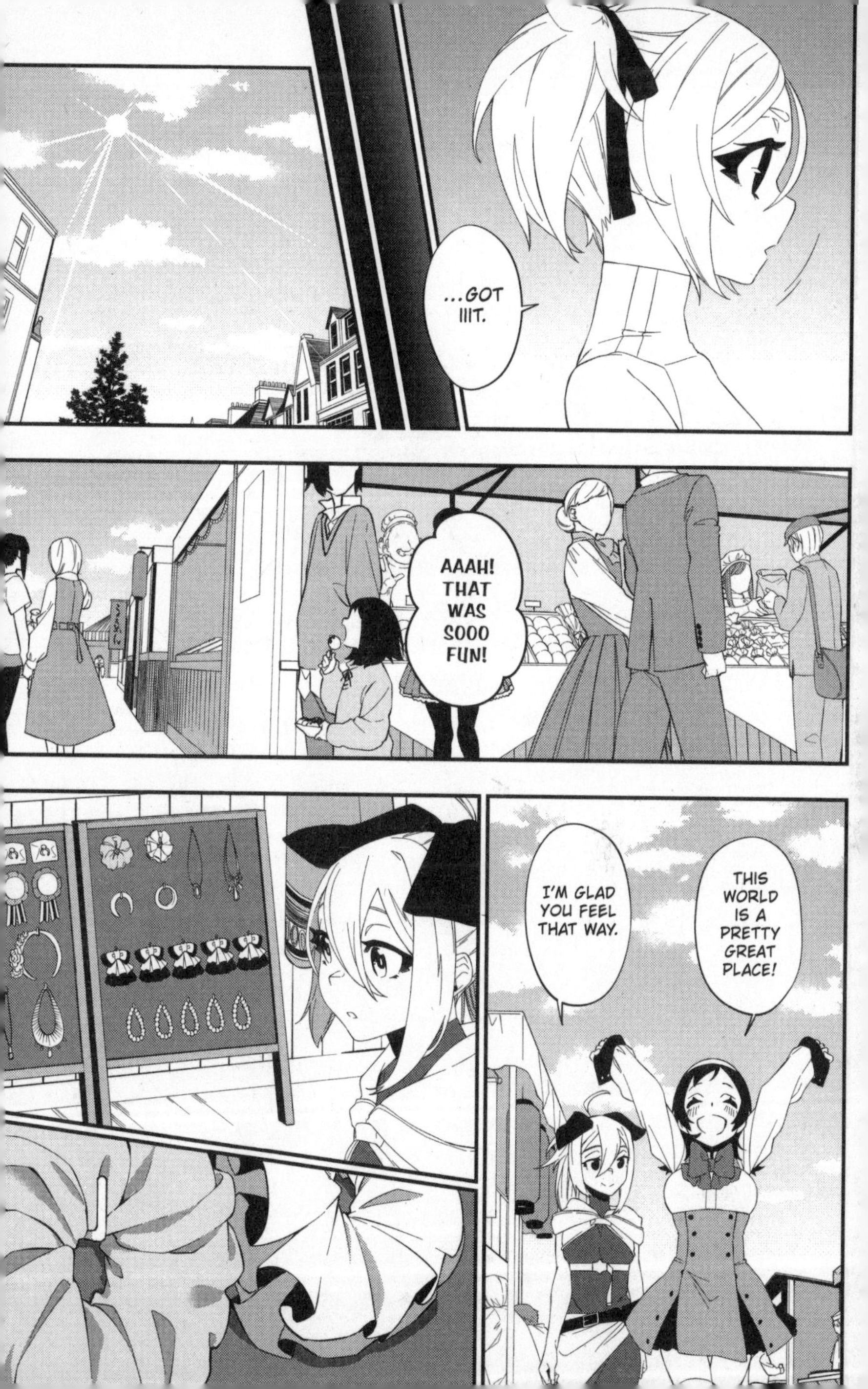
...GOT IIIT.
AAAH! THAT WAS SOOO FUN!
THIS WORLD IS A PRETTY GREAT PLACE!
I'M GLAD YOU FEEL THAT WAY.

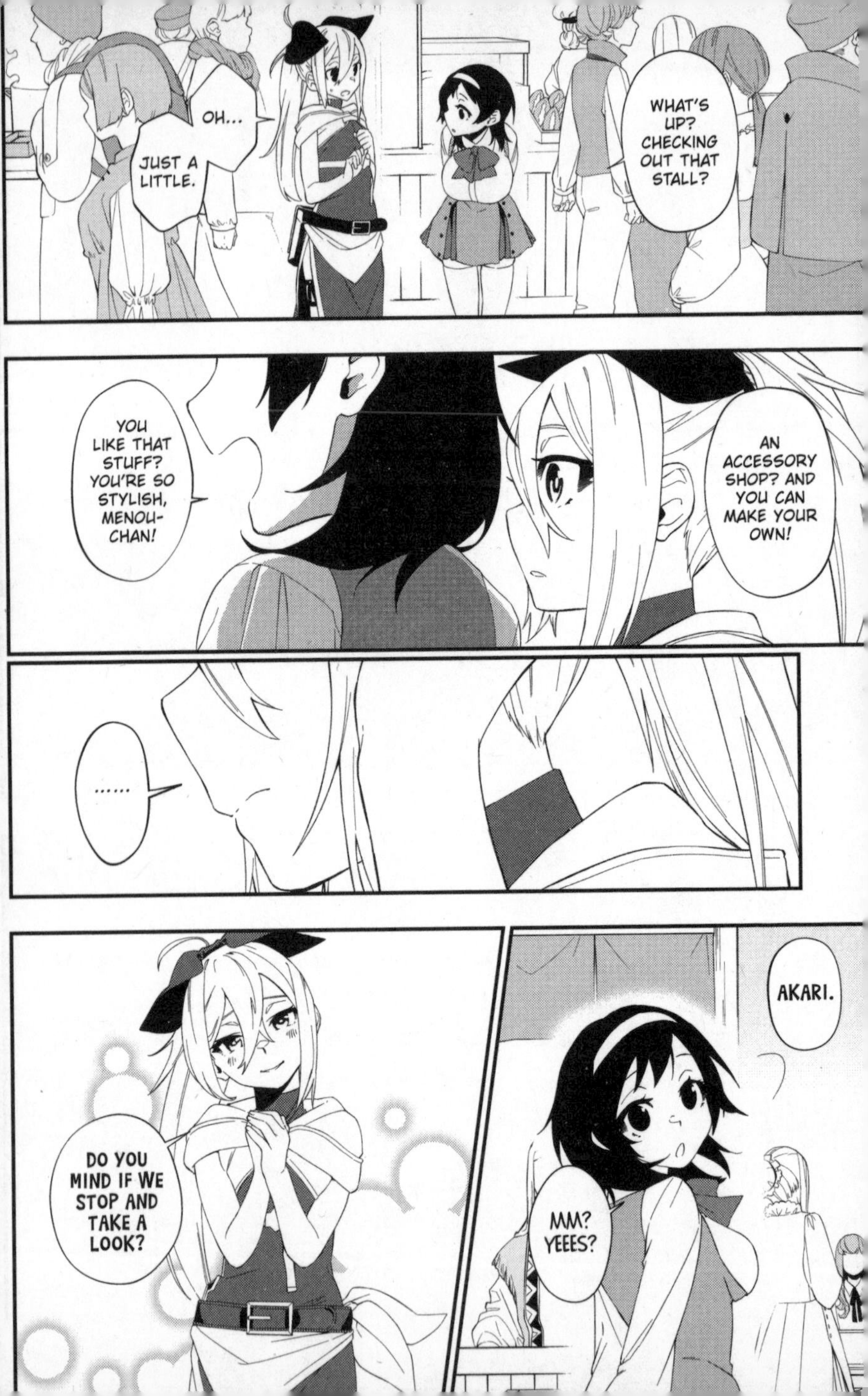
WHAT'S UP? CHECKING OUT THAT STALL?
OH... JUST A LITTLE.
AN ACCESSORY SHOP? AND YOU CAN MAKE YOUR OWN!
YOU LIKE THAT STUFF? YOU'RE SO STYLISH, MENOU-CHAN!
......
AKARI.
MM? YEEES?
DO YOU MIND IF WE STOP AND TAKE A LOOK?

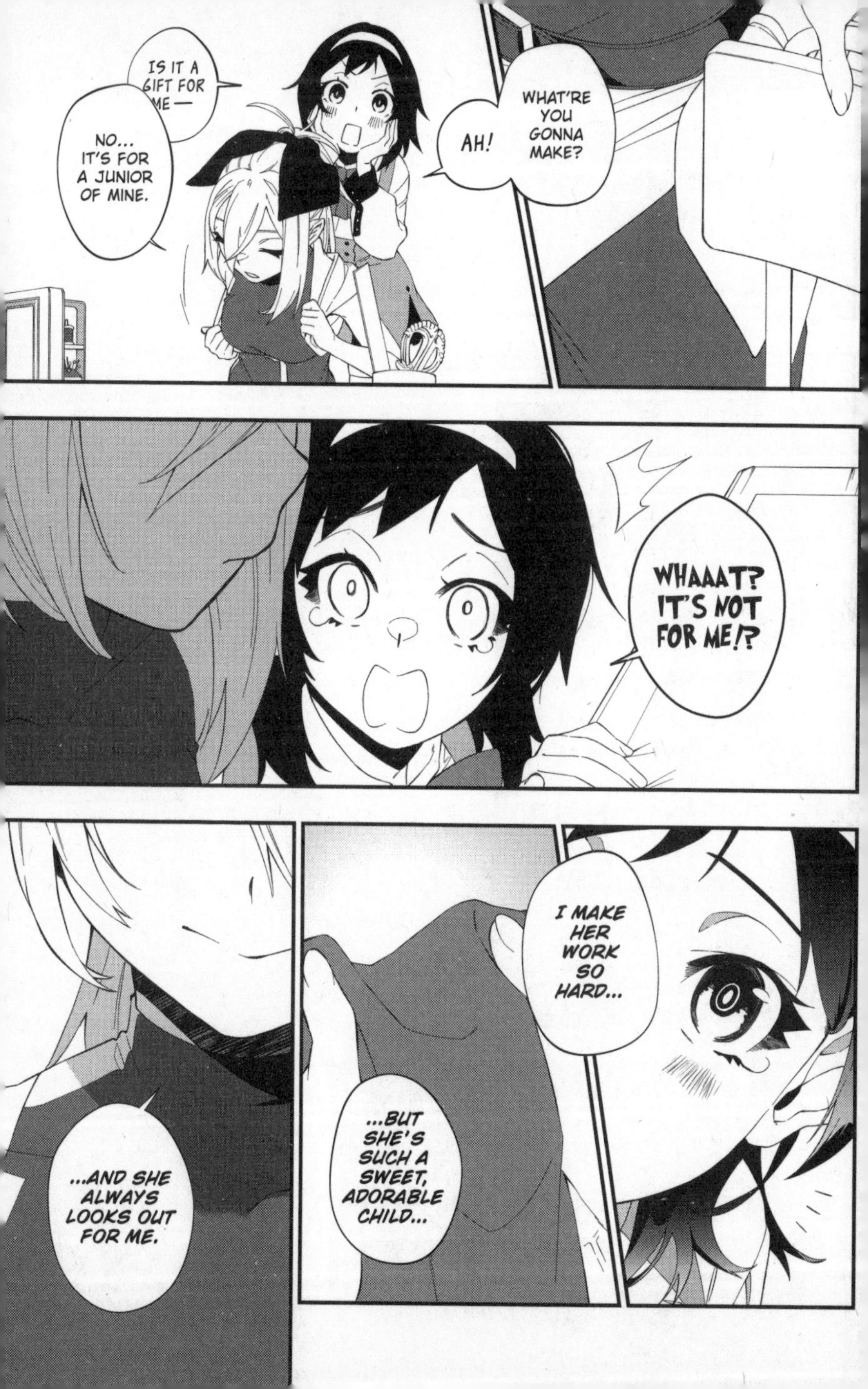
WHAT'RE YOU GONNA MAKE?
AH!
IS IT A GIFT FOR ME—
NO... IT'S FOR A JUNIOR OF MINE.
WHAAAT? IT'S NOT FOR ME!?
I MAKE HER WORK SO HARD...
...BUT SHE'S SUCH A SWEET, ADORABLE CHILD...
...AND SHE ALWAYS LOOKS OUT FOR ME.

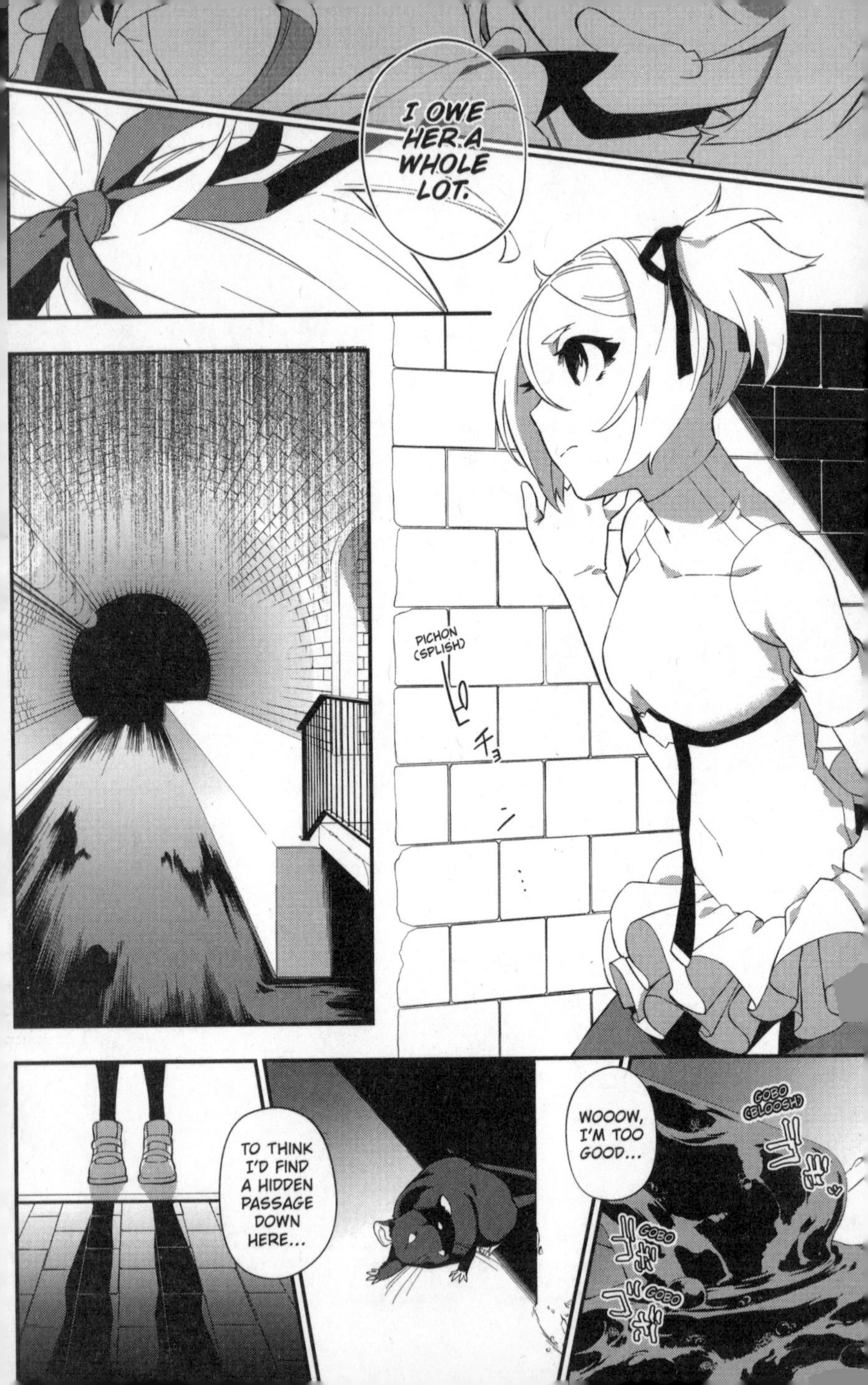
I OWE HER A WHOLE LOT.
PICHON (SPLISH)
GOBO (BLOOSH)
WOOOW, I'M TOO GOOD...
GOBO
GOBO
TO THINK I'D FIND A HIDDEN PASSAGE DOWN HERE...

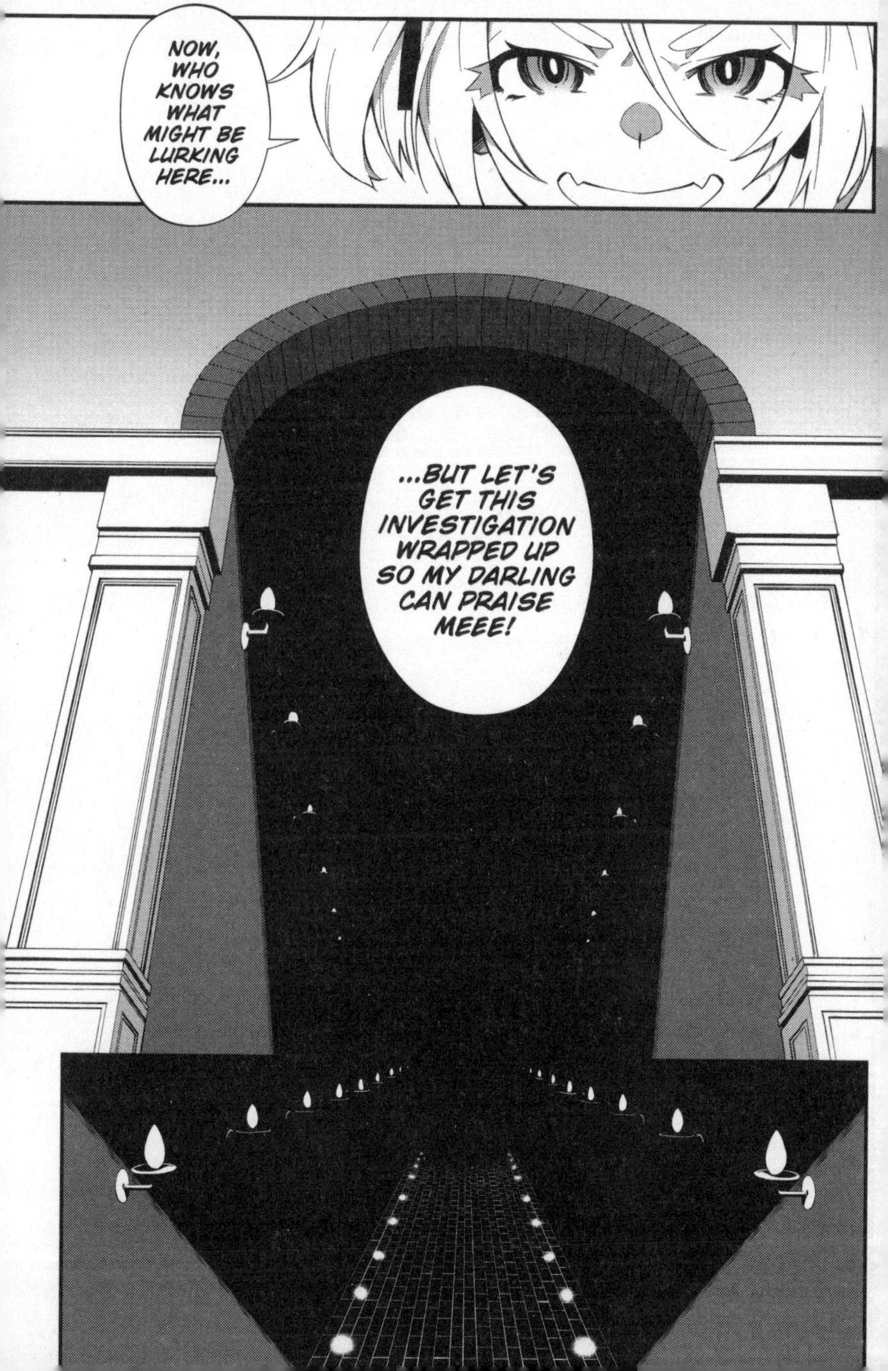
NOW, WHO KNOWS WHAT MIGHT BE LURKING HERE...
...BUT LET'S GET THIS INVESTIGATION WRAPPED UP SO MY DARLING CAN PRAISE MEEE!

The Executioner and Her Way of Life

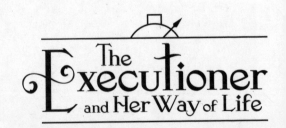

Chapter 12 Guiding Figure

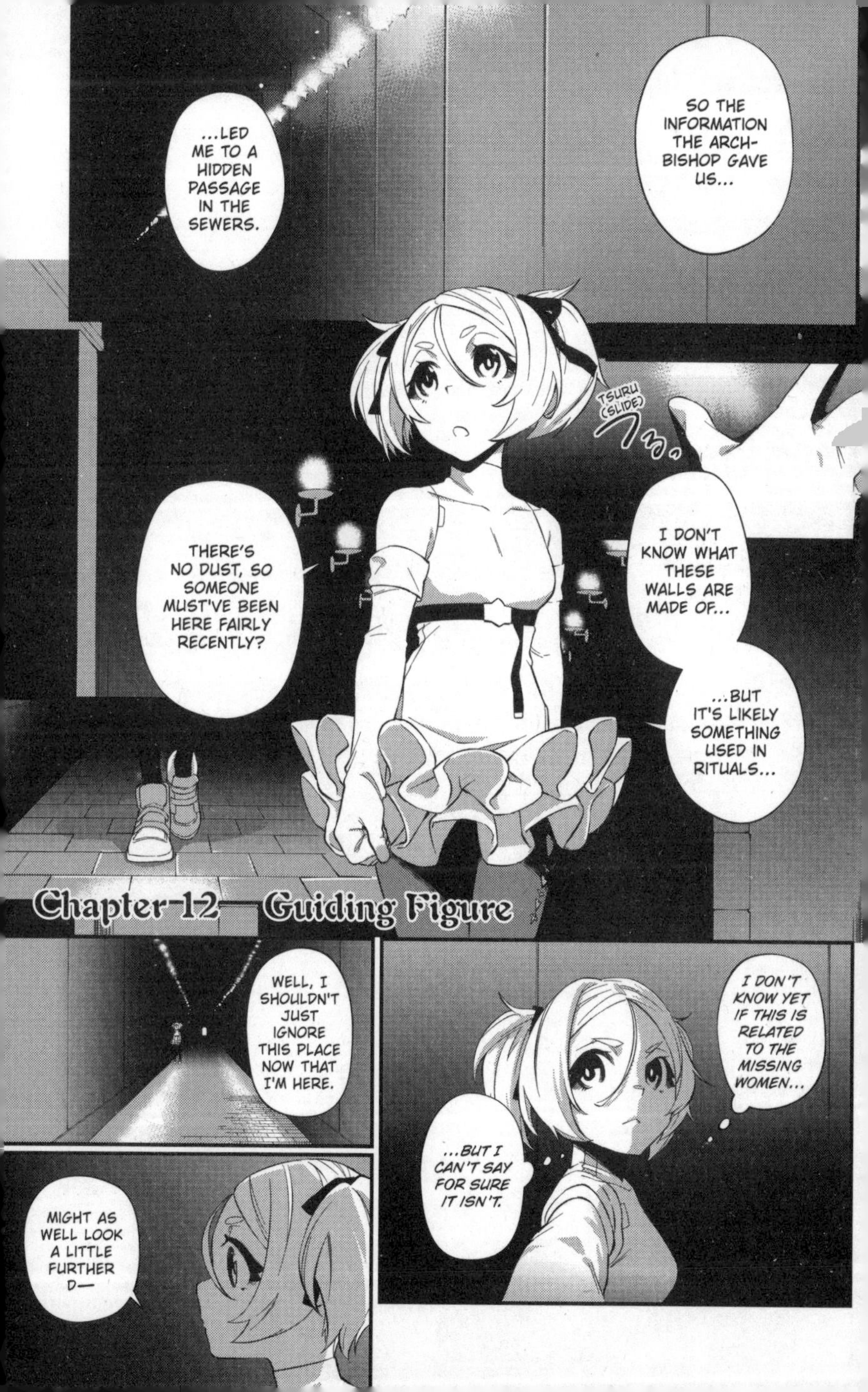
SO THE INFORMATION THE ARCH-BISHOP GAVE US...
...LED ME TO A HIDDEN PASSAGE IN THE SEWERS.
TSURU (SLIDE)
I DON'T KNOW WHAT THESE WALLS ARE MADE OF...
...BUT IT'S LIKELY SOMETHING USED IN RITUALS...
THERE'S NO DUST, SO SOMEONE MUST'VE BEEN HERE FAIRLY RECENTLY?
I DON'T KNOW YET IF THIS IS RELATED TO THE MISSING WOMEN...
...BUT I CAN'T SAY FOR SURE IT ISN'T.
WELL, I SHOULDN'T JUST IGNORE THIS PLACE NOW THAT I'M HERE.
MIGHT AS WELL LOOK A LITTLE FURTHER D—

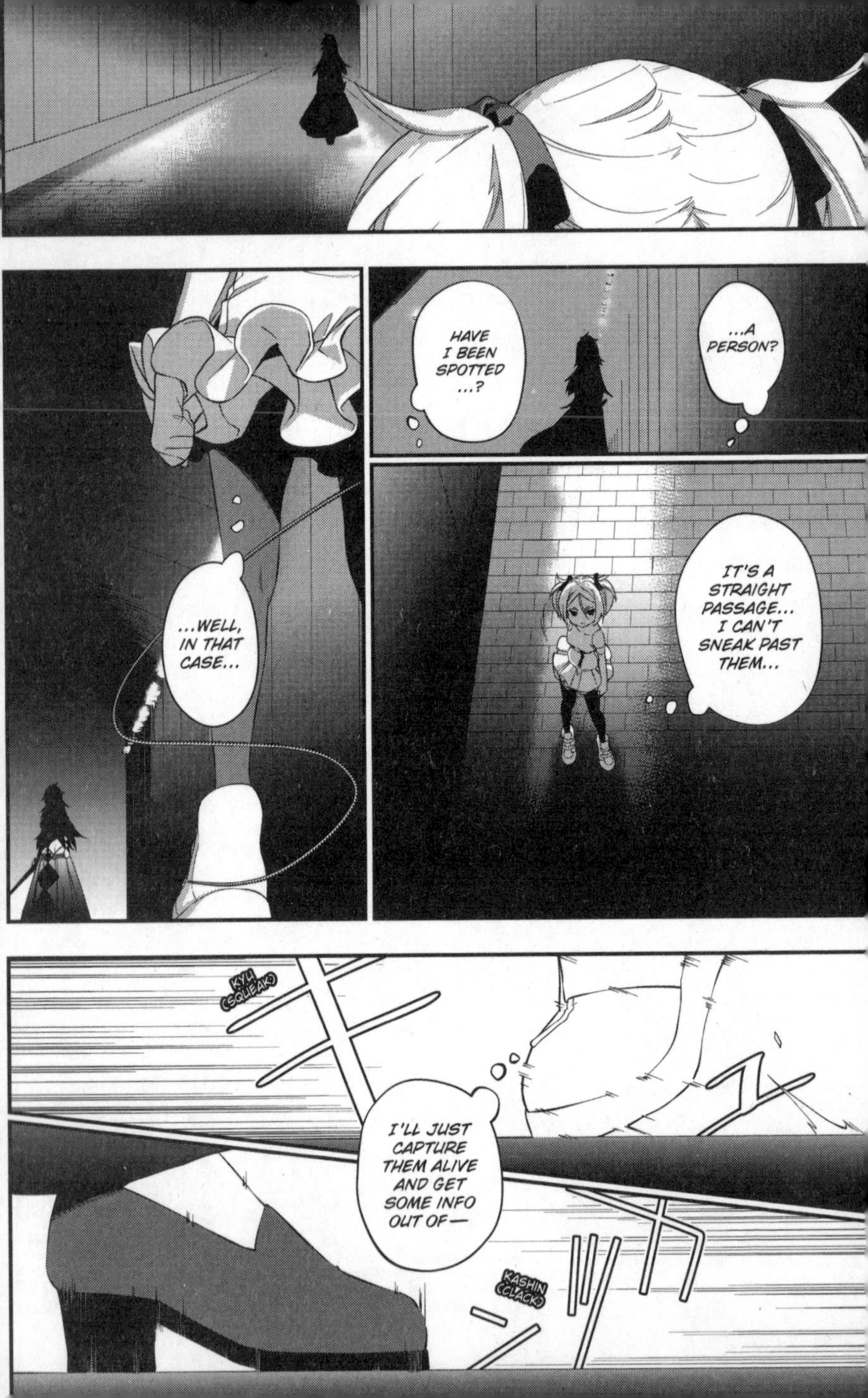
...A PERSON?
HAVE I BEEN SPOTTED ...?
IT'S A STRAIGHT PASSAGE... I CAN'T SNEAK PAST THEM...
...WELL, IN THAT CASE...
KYU (SQUEAK)
I'LL JUST CAPTURE THEM ALIVE AND GET SOME INFO OUT OF—
KASHIN (CLACK)

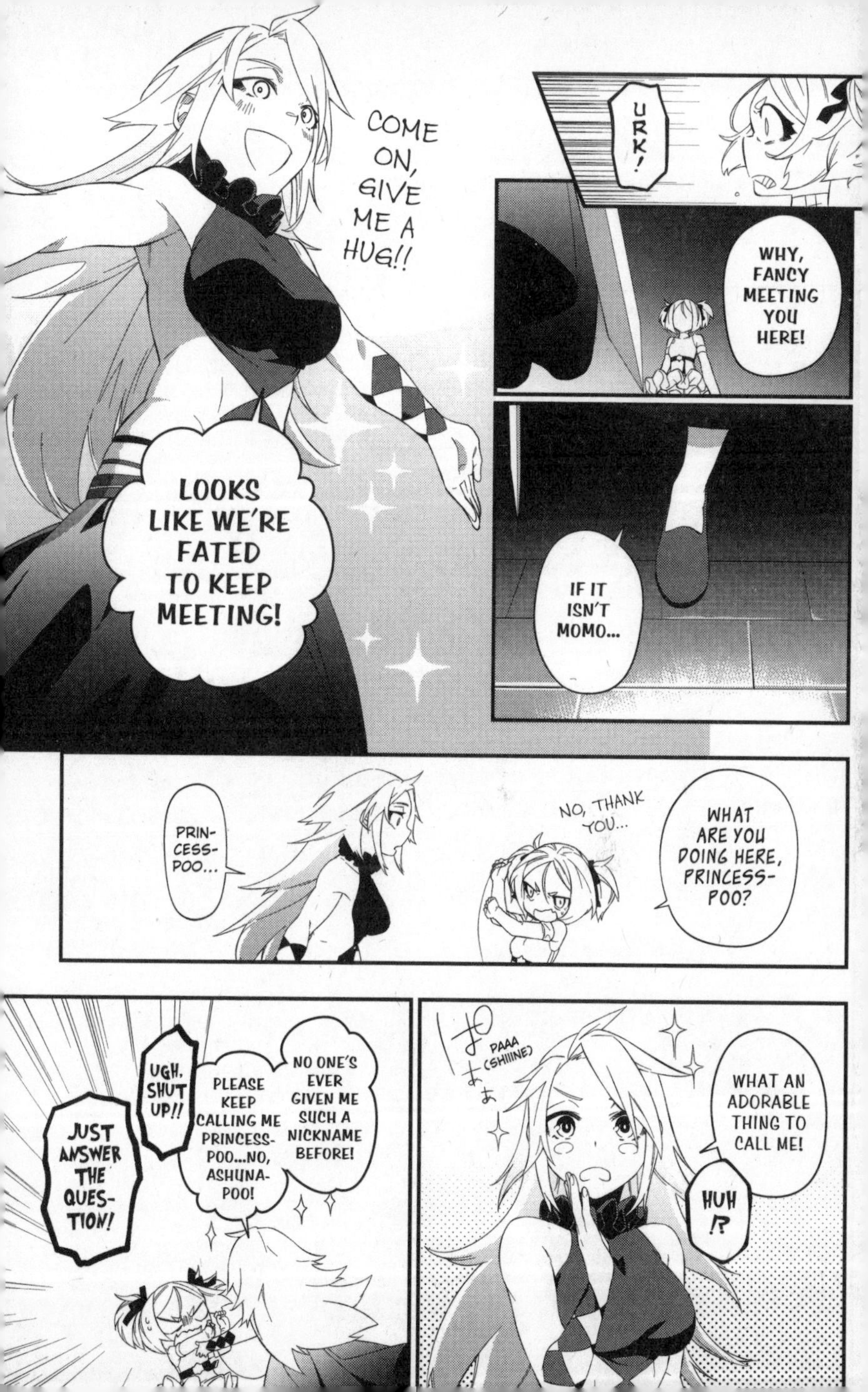
URK!
WHY, FANCY MEETING YOU HERE!
IF IT ISN'T MOMO...
COME ON, GIVE ME A HUG!!
LOOKS LIKE WE'RE FATED TO KEEP MEETING!
NO, THANK YOU...
WHAT ARE YOU DOING HERE, PRINCESS-POO?
PRIN-CESS-POO...
PAAA (SHIIINE)
WHAT AN ADORABLE THING TO CALL ME!
HUH!?
NO ONE'S EVER GIVEN ME SUCH A NICKNAME BEFORE!
PLEASE KEEP CALLING ME PRINCESS-POO...NO, ASHUNA-POO!
UGH, SHUT UP!!
JUST ANSWER THE QUES-TION!

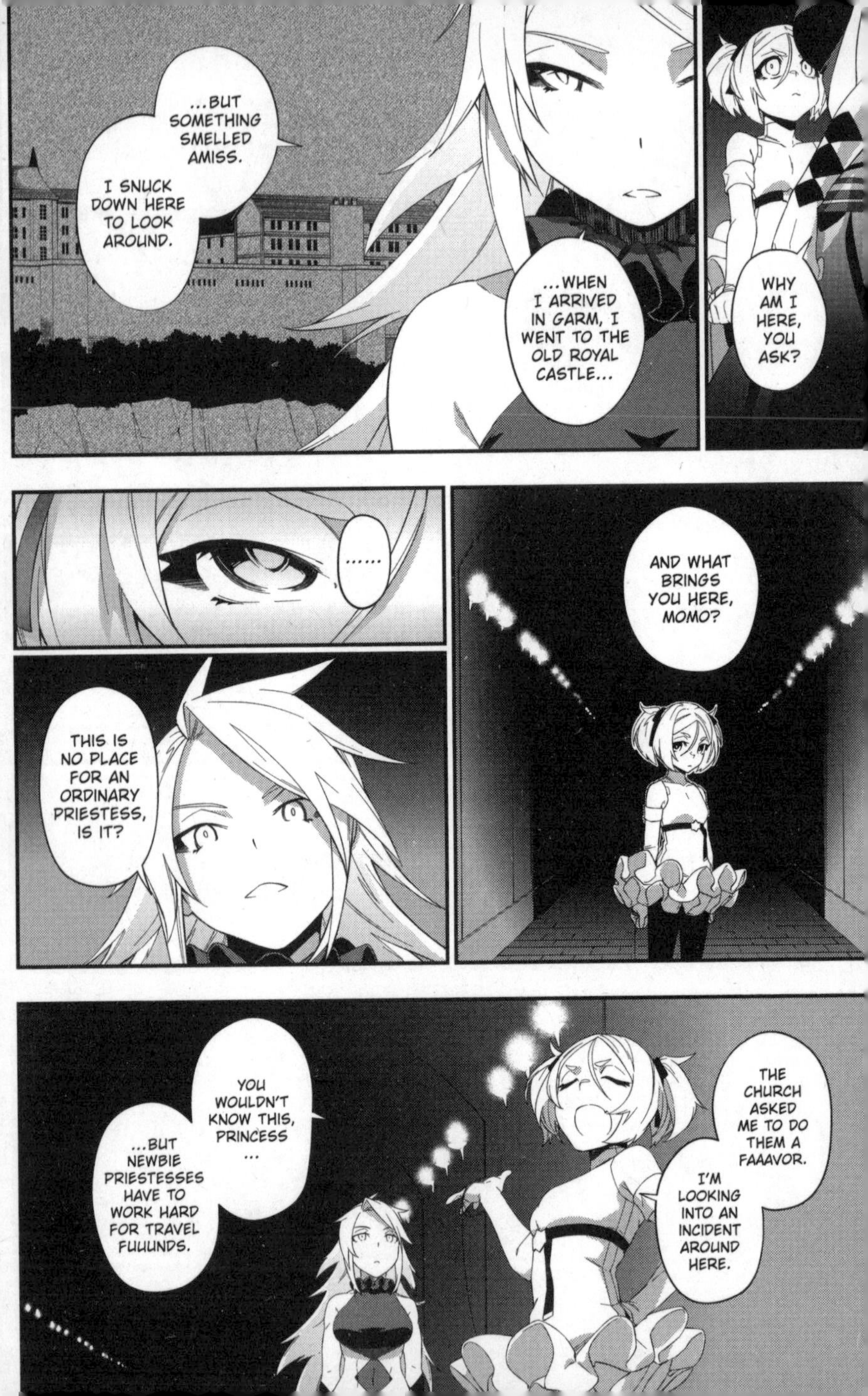
WHY AM I HERE, YOU ASK?
...WHEN I ARRIVED IN GARM, I WENT TO THE OLD ROYAL CASTLE...
...BUT SOMETHING SMELLED AMISS.
I SNUCK DOWN HERE TO LOOK AROUND.
AND WHAT BRINGS YOU HERE, MOMO?
......
THIS IS NO PLACE FOR AN ORDINARY PRIESTESS, IS IT?
THE CHURCH ASKED ME TO DO THEM A FAAAVOR.
I'M LOOKING INTO AN INCIDENT AROUND HERE.
YOU WOULDN'T KNOW THIS, PRINCESS ...
...BUT NEWBIE PRIESTESSES HAVE TO WORK HARD FOR TRAVEL FUUUNDS.

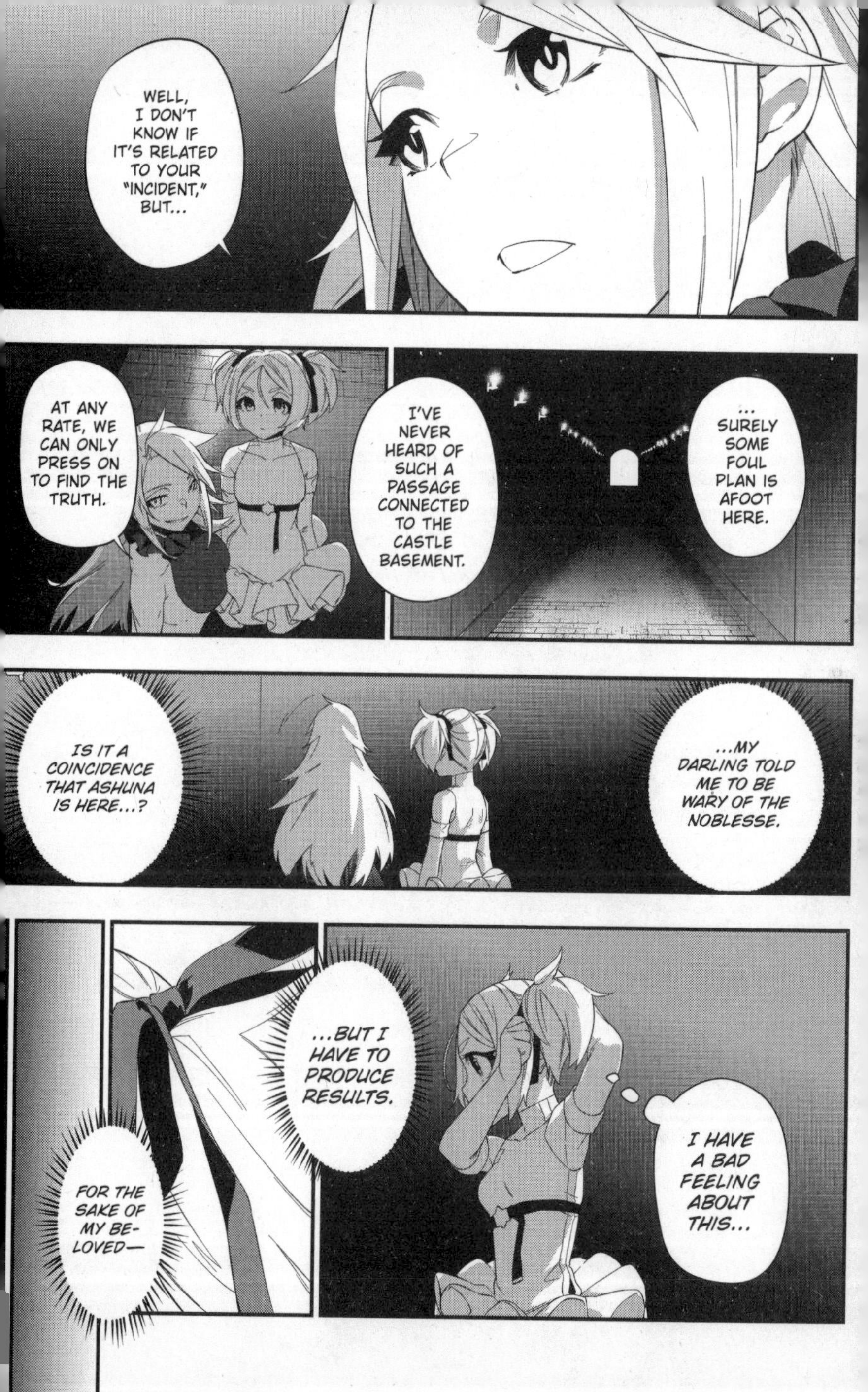
WELL, I DON'T KNOW IF IT'S RELATED TO YOUR "INCIDENT," BUT...
... SURELY SOME FOUL PLAN IS AFOOT HERE.
I'VE NEVER HEARD OF SUCH A PASSAGE CONNECTED TO THE CASTLE BASEMENT.
AT ANY RATE, WE CAN ONLY PRESS ON TO FIND THE TRUTH.
...MY DARLING TOLD ME TO BE WARY OF THE NOBLESSE.
IS IT A COINCIDENCE THAT ASHUNA IS HERE...?
I HAVE A BAD FEELING ABOUT THIS...
...BUT I HAVE TO PRODUCE RESULTS.
FOR THE SAKE OF MY BE-LOVED—

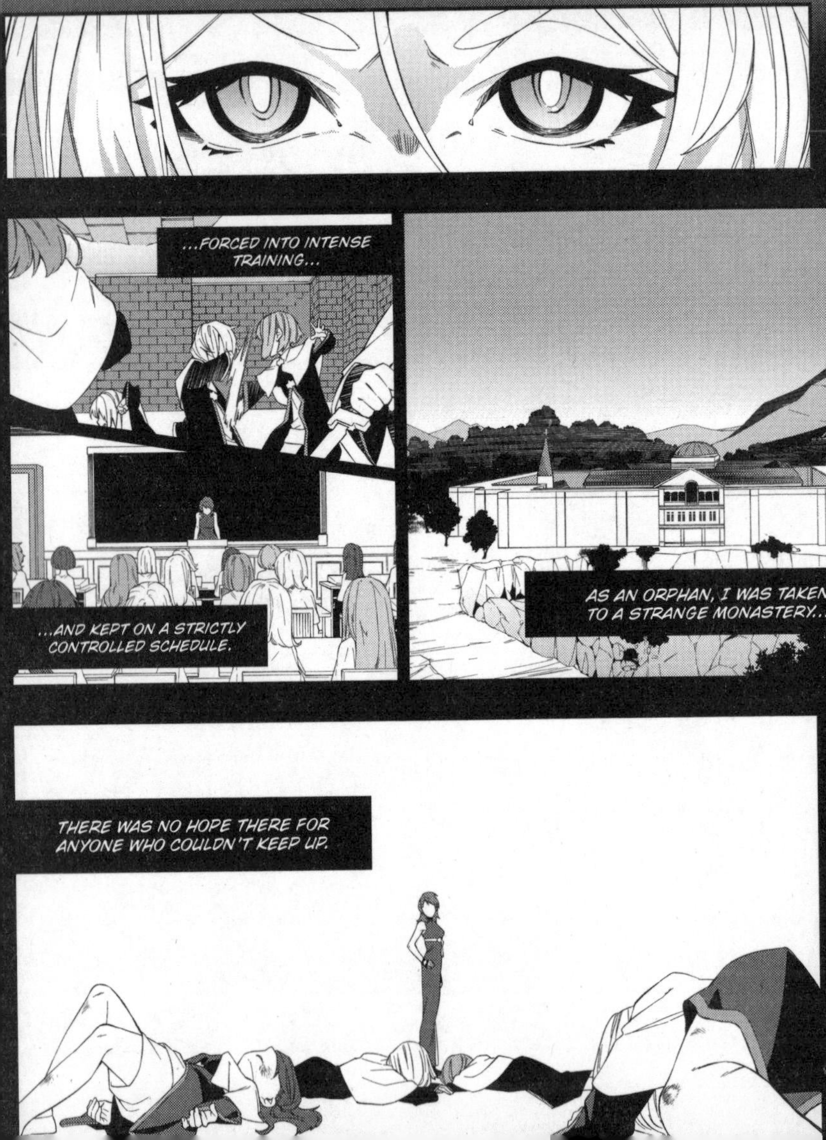
AS AN ORPHAN, I WAS TAKEN TO A STRANGE MONASTERY...
...FORCED INTO INTENSE TRAINING...
...AND KEPT ON A STRICTLY CONTROLLED SCHEDULE.
THERE WAS NO HOPE THERE FOR ANYONE WHO COULDN'T KEEP UP.

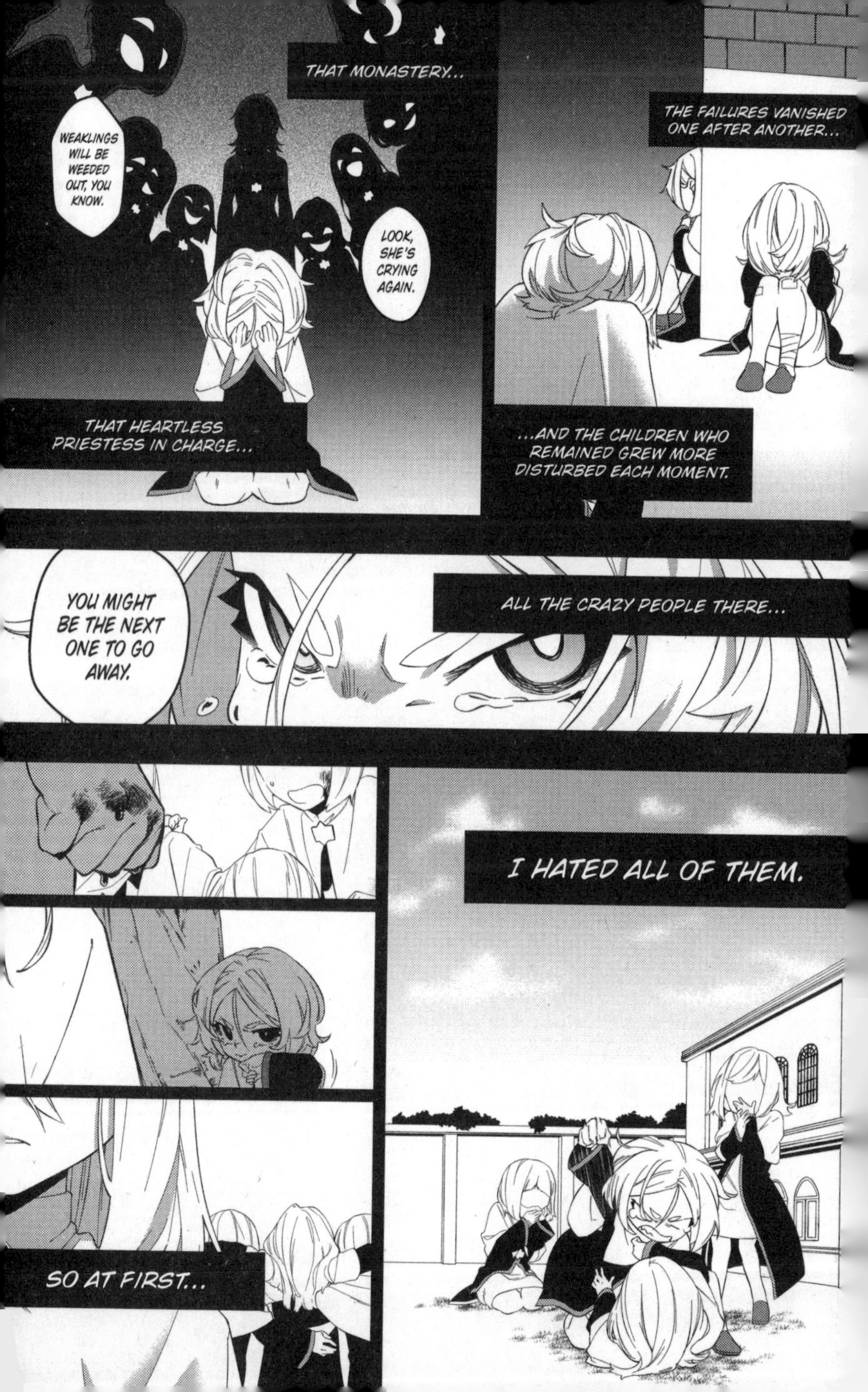
THE FAILURES VANISHED ONE AFTER ANOTHER...
...AND THE CHILDREN WHO REMAINED GREW MORE DISTURBED EACH MOMENT.
THAT MONASTERY...
LOOK, SHE'S CRYING AGAIN.
WEAKLINGS WILL BE WEEDED OUT, YOU KNOW.
THAT HEARTLESS PRIESTESS IN CHARGE...
ALL THE CRAZY PEOPLE THERE...
YOU MIGHT BE THE NEXT ONE TO GO AWAY.
I HATED ALL OF THEM.
SO AT FIRST...

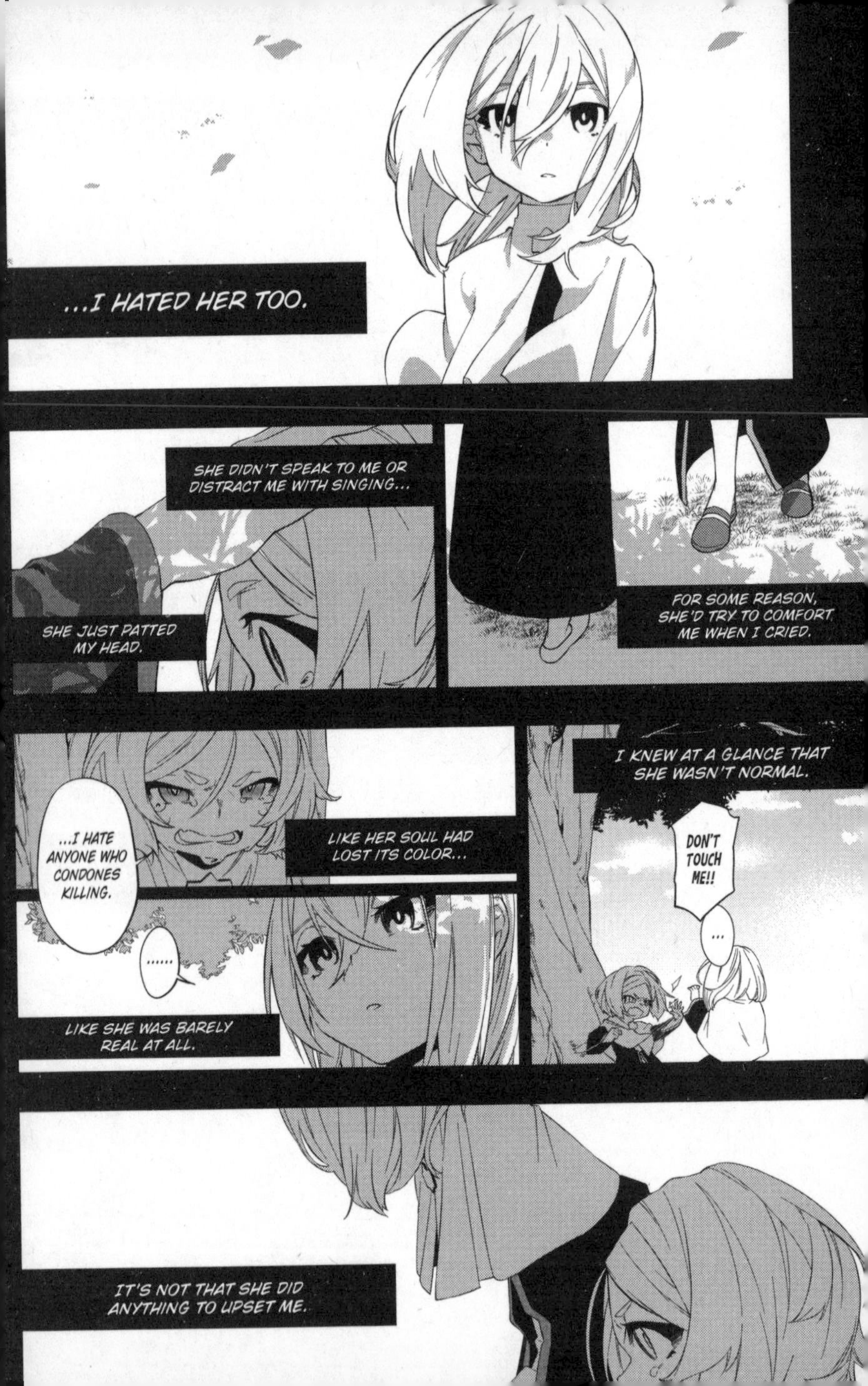
...I HATED HER TOO.
FOR SOME REASON, SHE'D TRY TO COMFORT ME WHEN I CRIED.
SHE DIDN'T SPEAK TO ME OR DISTRACT ME WITH SINGING...
SHE JUST PATTED MY HEAD.
I KNEW AT A GLANCE THAT SHE WASN'T NORMAL.
DON'T TOUCH ME!!
...
LIKE HER SOUL HAD LOST ITS COLOR...
...I HATE ANYONE WHO CONDONES KILLING.
......
LIKE SHE WAS BARELY REAL AT ALL.
IT'S NOT THAT SHE DID ANYTHING TO UPSET ME.

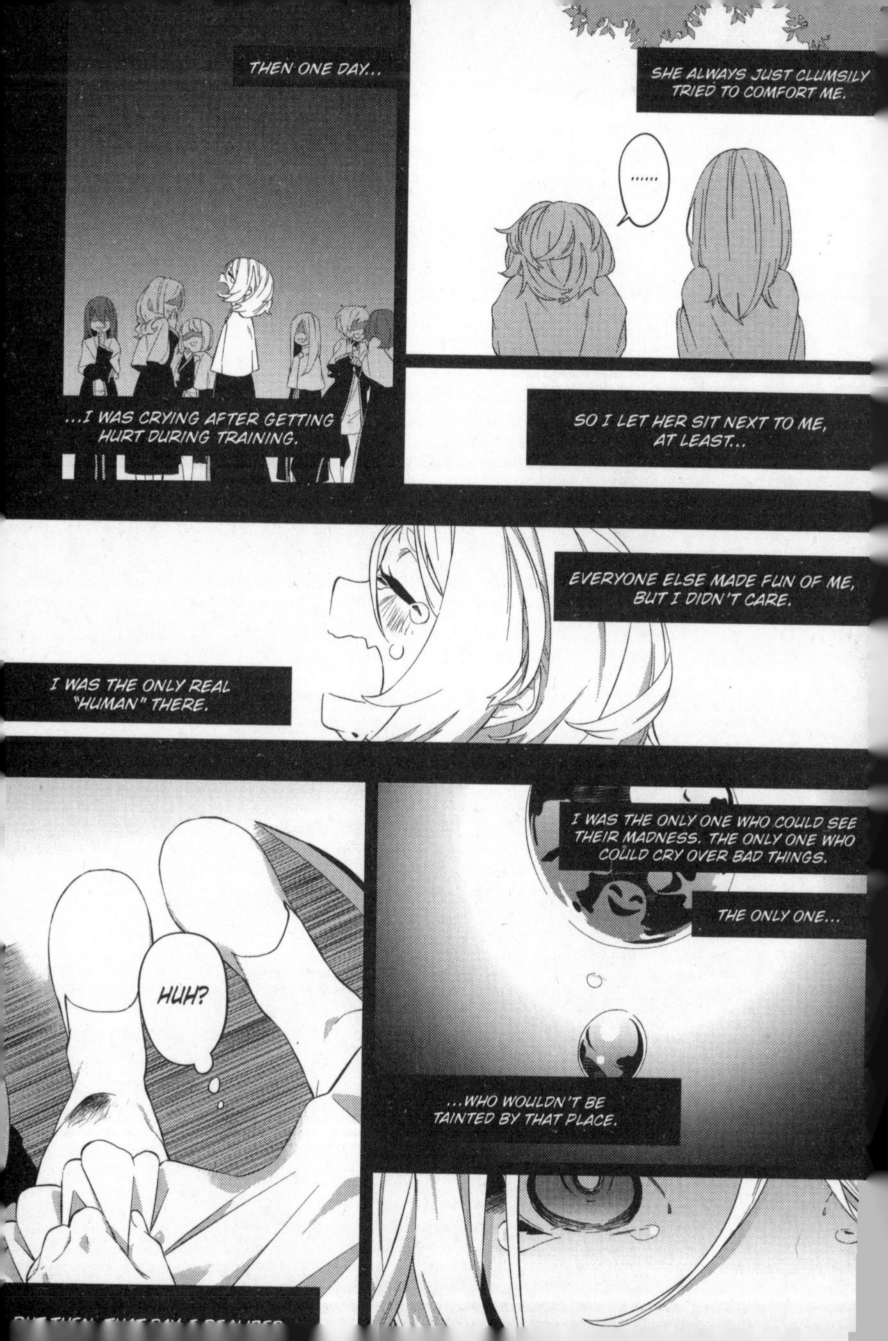
SHE ALWAYS JUST CLUMSILY TRIED TO COMFORT ME.
......
SO I LET HER SIT NEXT TO ME, AT LEAST...
THEN ONE DAY...
...I WAS CRYING AFTER GETTING HURT DURING TRAINING.
EVERYONE ELSE MADE FUN OF ME, BUT I DIDN'T CARE.
I WAS THE ONLY REAL "HUMAN" THERE.
I WAS THE ONLY ONE WHO COULD SEE THEIR MADNESS. THE ONLY ONE WHO COULD CRY OVER BAD THINGS.
THE ONLY ONE...
...WHO WOULDN'T BE TAINTED BY THAT PLACE.
HUH?

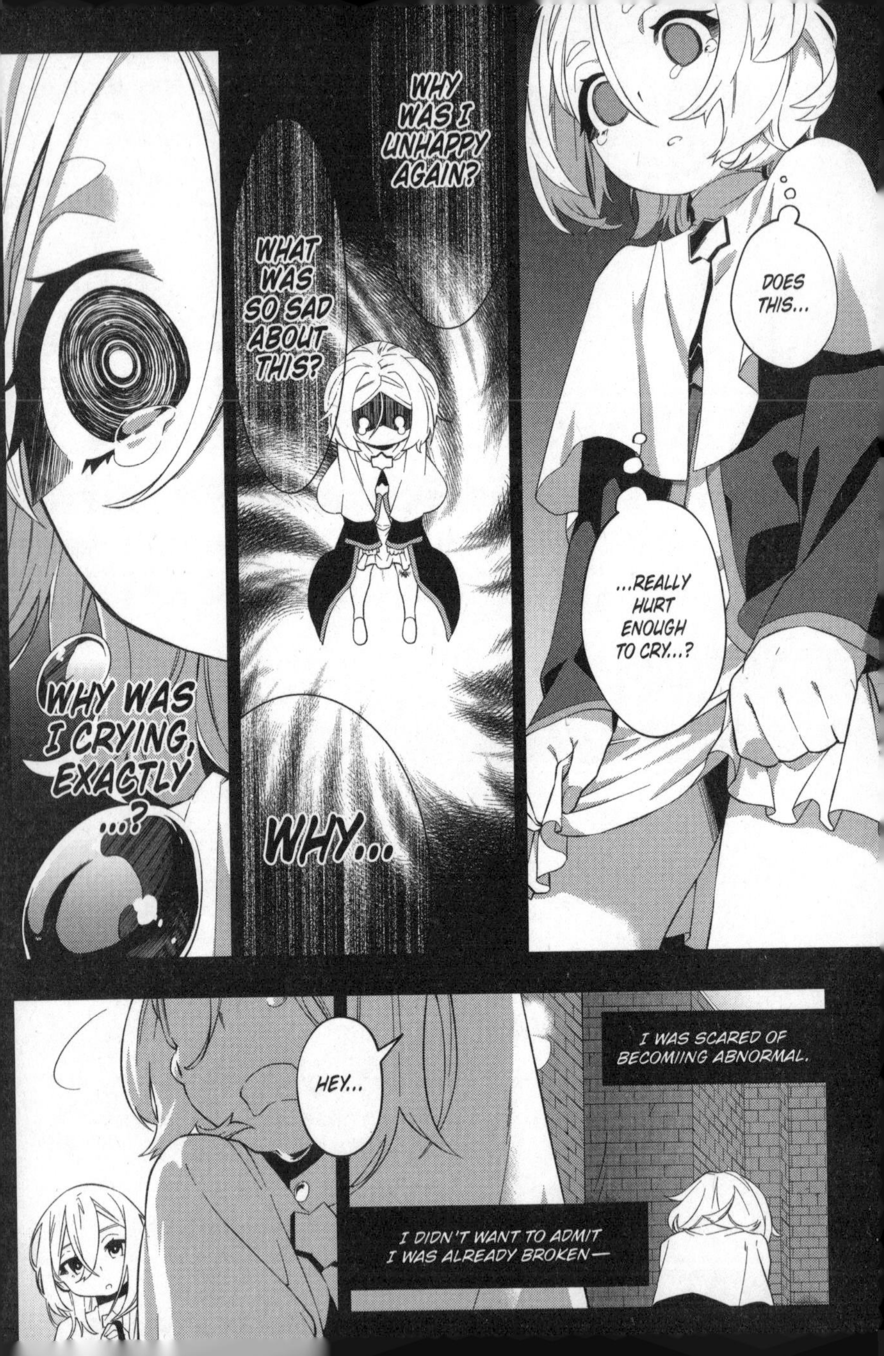
DOES THIS...
...REALLY HURT ENOUGH TO CRY...?
WHY WAS I UNHAPPY AGAIN?
WHAT WAS SO SAD ABOUT THIS?
WHY...
WHY WAS I CRYING, EXACTLY ...?
I WAS SCARED OF BECOMIING ABNORMAL.
I DIDN'T WANT TO ADMIT I WAS ALREADY BROKEN—
HEY...

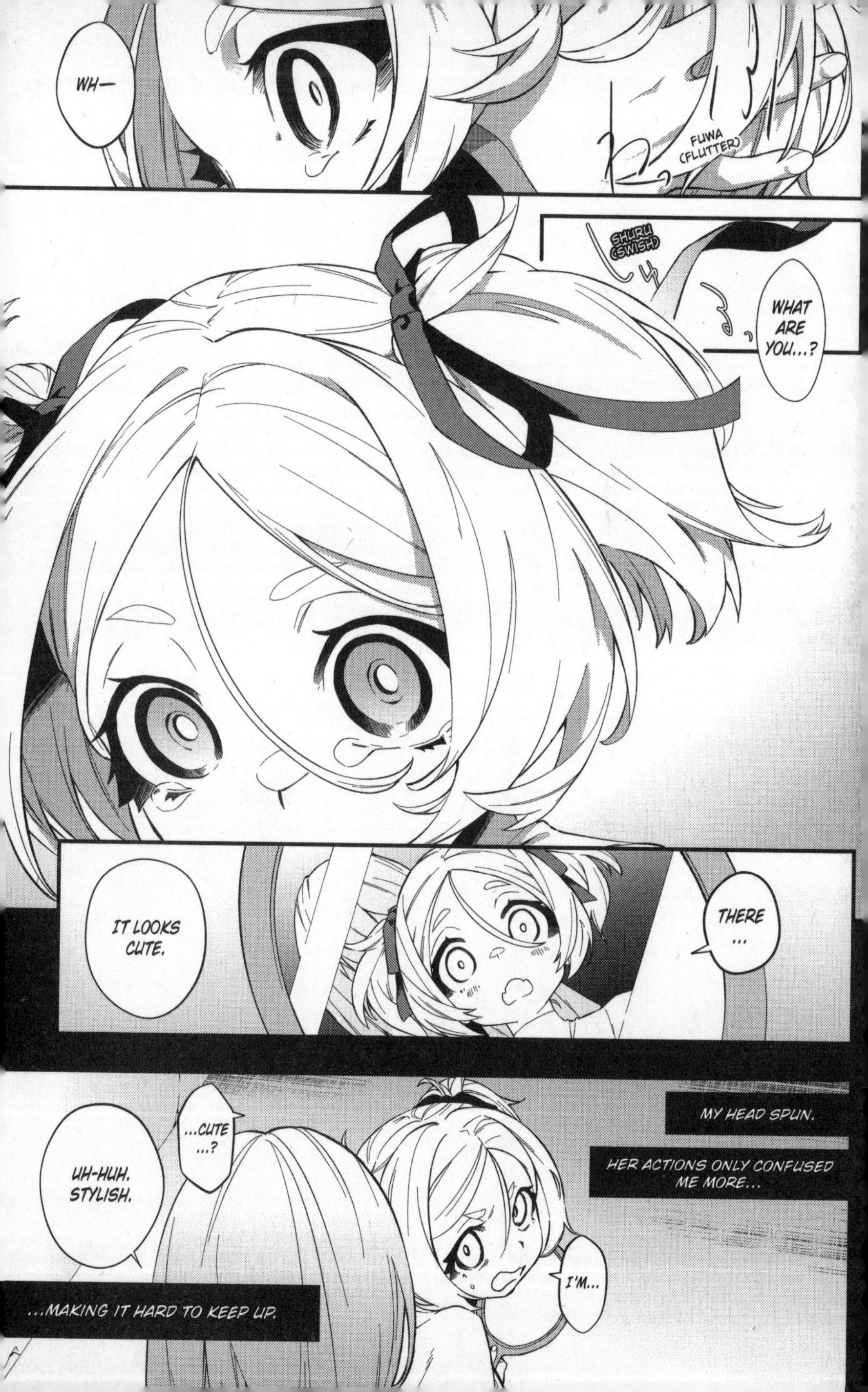
FUWA (FLUTTER)
WH—
SHURU (SWISH)
WHAT ARE YOU...?
THERE ...
IT LOOKS CUTE.
MY HEAD SPUN.
HER ACTIONS ONLY CONFUSED ME MORE...
...CUTE ...?
UH-HUH. STYLISH.
I'M...
...MAKING IT HARD TO KEEP UP.

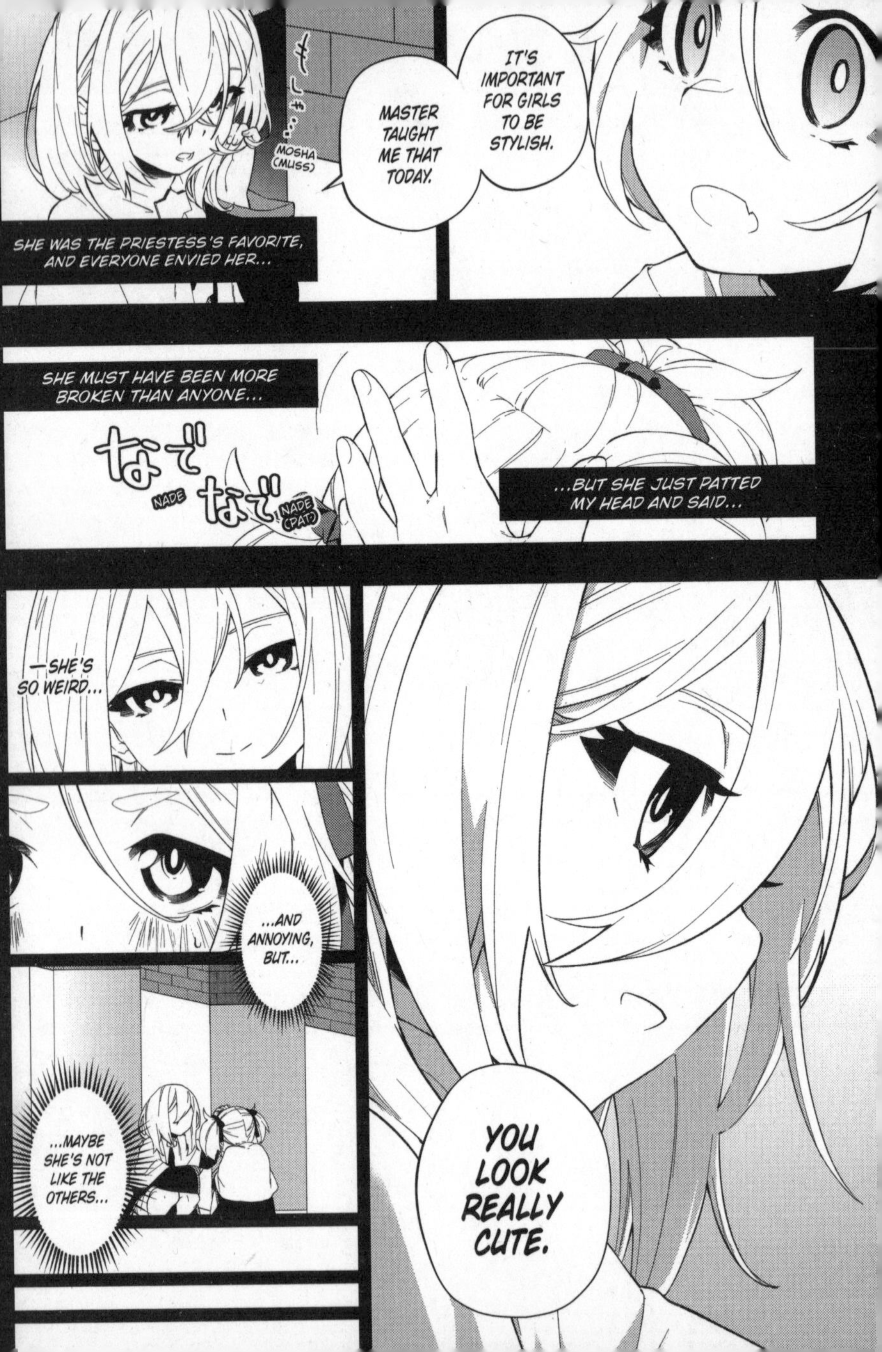
IT'S IMPORTANT FOR GIRLS TO BE STYLISH.
MASTER TAUGHT ME THAT TODAY.
もしゃ…
MOSHA (MUSS)
SHE WAS THE PRIESTESS'S FAVORITE, AND EVERYONE ENVIED HER...
SHE MUST HAVE BEEN MORE BROKEN THAN ANYONE...
なで NADE
なで NADE (PAT)
...BUT SHE JUST PATTED MY HEAD AND SAID...
YOU LOOK REALLY CUTE.
—SHE'S SO WEIRD...
...AND ANNOYING, BUT...
...MAYBE SHE'S NOT LIKE THE OTHERS...

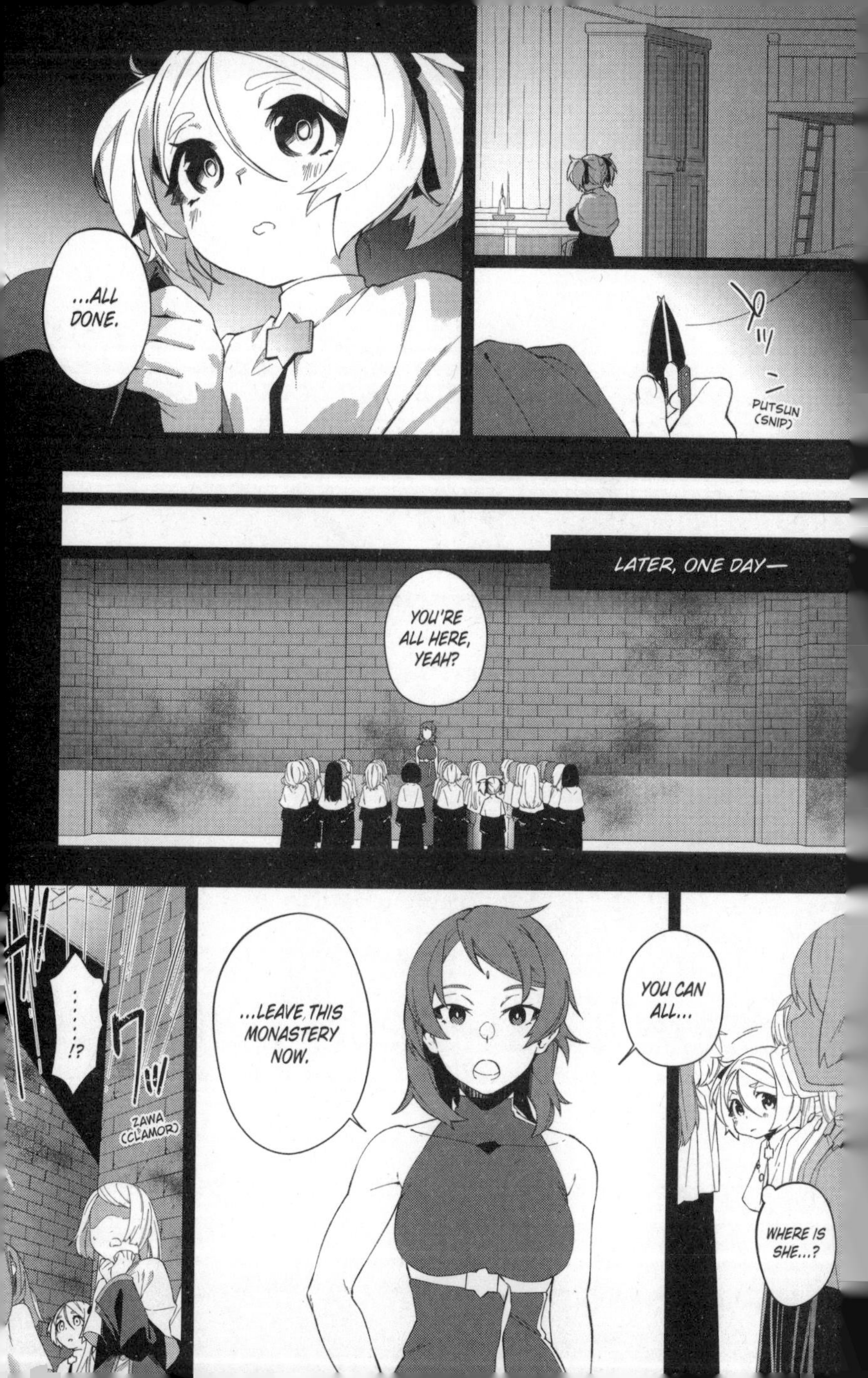
PUTSUN (SNIP)
...ALL DONE.
LATER, ONE DAY—
YOU'RE ALL HERE, YEAH?
YOU CAN ALL...
WHERE IS SHE...?
...LEAVE THIS MONASTERY NOW.
......!?
ZAWA (CLAMOR)

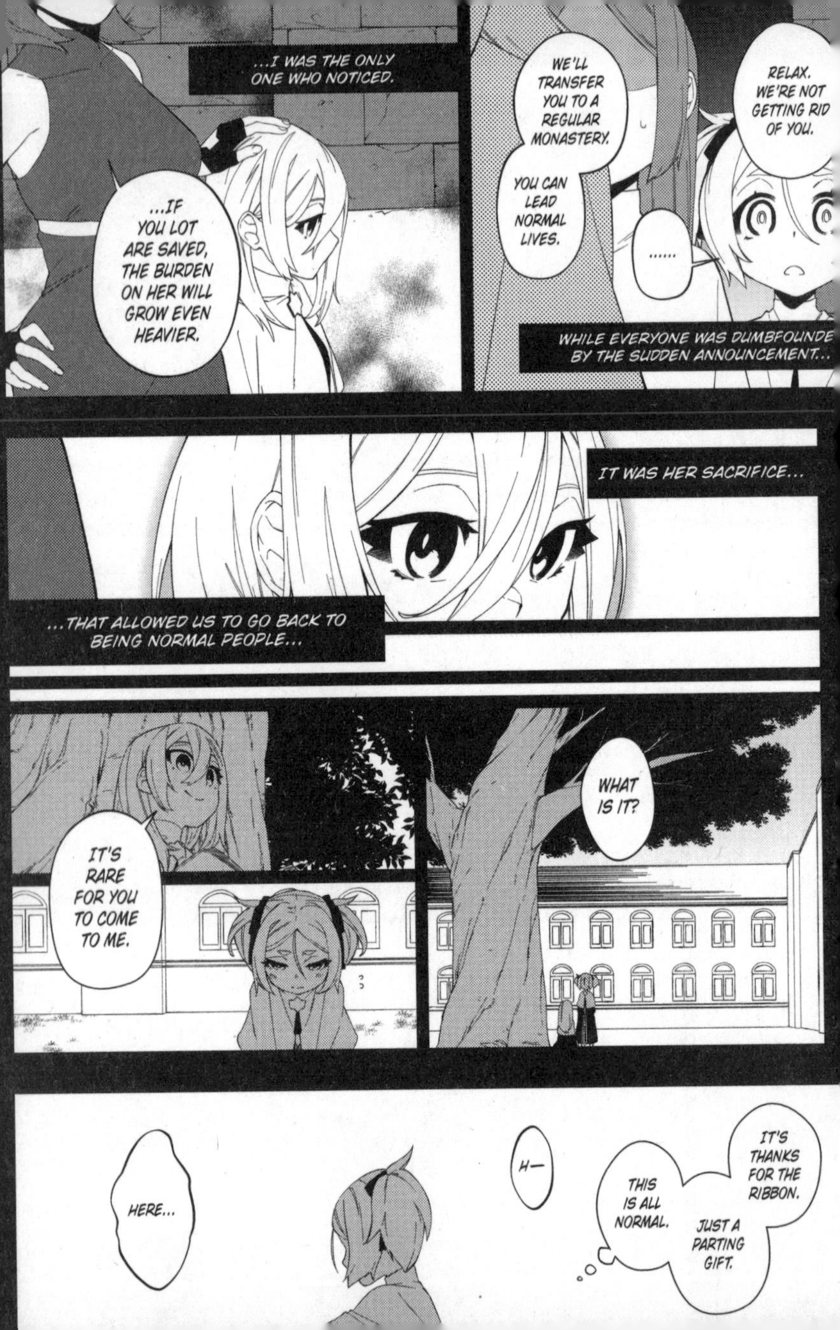
RELAX. WE'RE NOT GETTING RID OF YOU.
WE'LL TRANSFER YOU TO A REGULAR MONASTERY.
YOU CAN LEAD NORMAL LIVES.
......
WHILE EVERYONE WAS DUMBFOUNDE BY THE SUDDEN ANNOUNCEMENT...
...I WAS THE ONLY ONE WHO NOTICED.
...IF YOU LOT ARE SAVED, THE BURDEN ON HER WILL GROW EVEN HEAVIER.
IT WAS HER SACRIFICE...
...THAT ALLOWED US TO GO BACK TO BEING NORMAL PEOPLE...
WHAT IS IT?
IT'S RARE FOR YOU TO COME TO ME.
IT'S THANKS FOR THE RIBBON.
THIS IS ALL NORMAL.
JUST A PARTING GIFT.
H—
HERE...

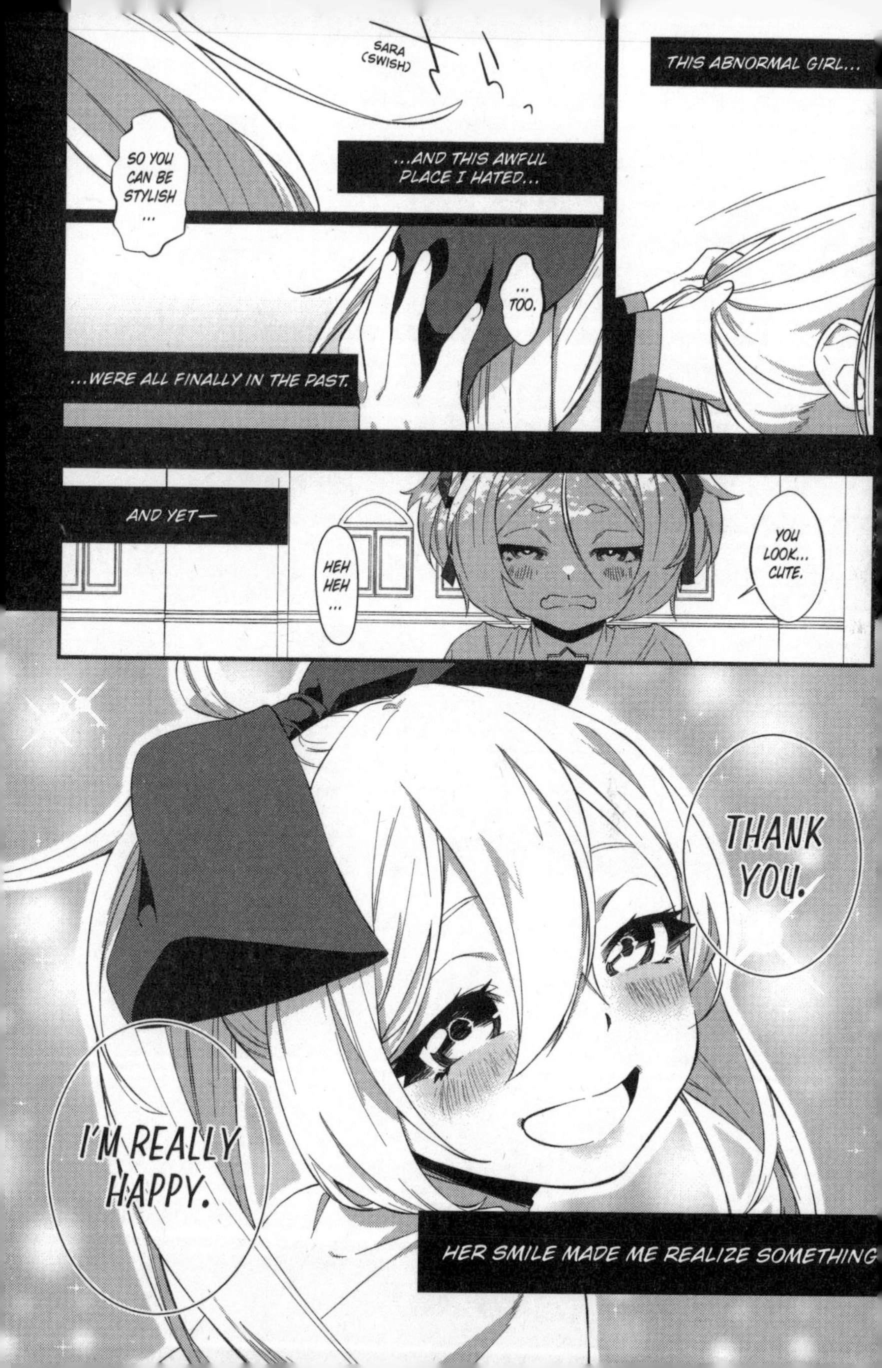
THIS ABNORMAL GIRL...
SARA (SWISH)
...AND THIS AWFUL PLACE I HATED...
SO YOU CAN BE STYLISH ...
... TOO.
...WERE ALL FINALLY IN THE PAST.
YOU LOOK... CUTE.
HEH HEH ...
AND YET—
THANK YOU.
I'M REALLY HAPPY.
HER SMILE MADE ME REALIZE SOMETHING

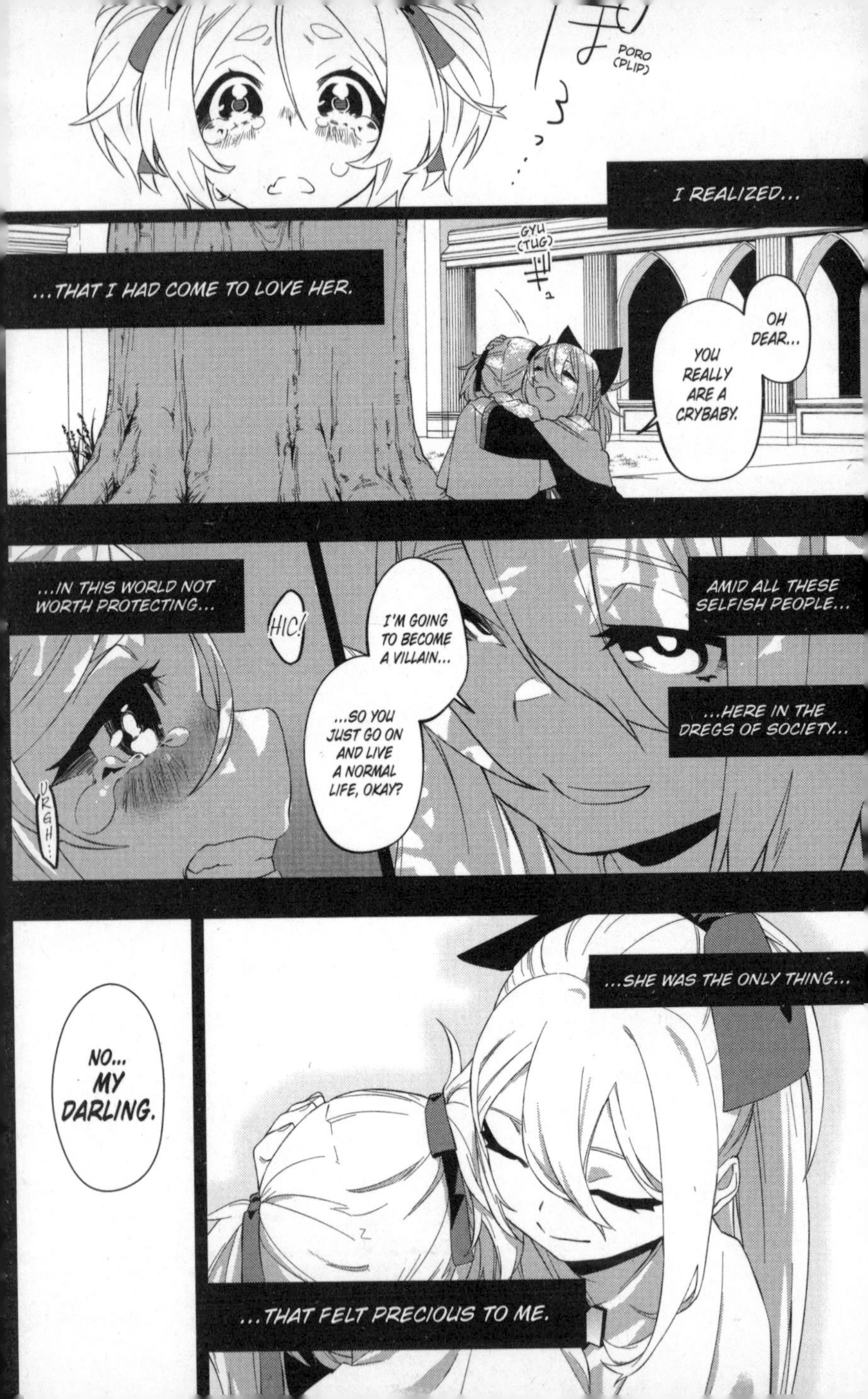
PORO (PLIP)
I REALIZED...
GYU (TUG)
OH DEAR... YOU REALLY ARE A CRYBABY.
...THAT I HAD COME TO LOVE HER.
AMID ALL THESE SELFISH PEOPLE...
...HERE IN THE DREGS OF SOCIETY...
I'M GOING TO BECOME A VILLAIN...
...SO YOU JUST GO ON AND LIVE A NORMAL LIFE, OKAY?
HIC!
...IN THIS WORLD NOT WORTH PROTECTING...
URGH...
...SHE WAS THE ONLY THING...
...THAT FELT PRECIOUS TO ME.
NO... MY DARLING.

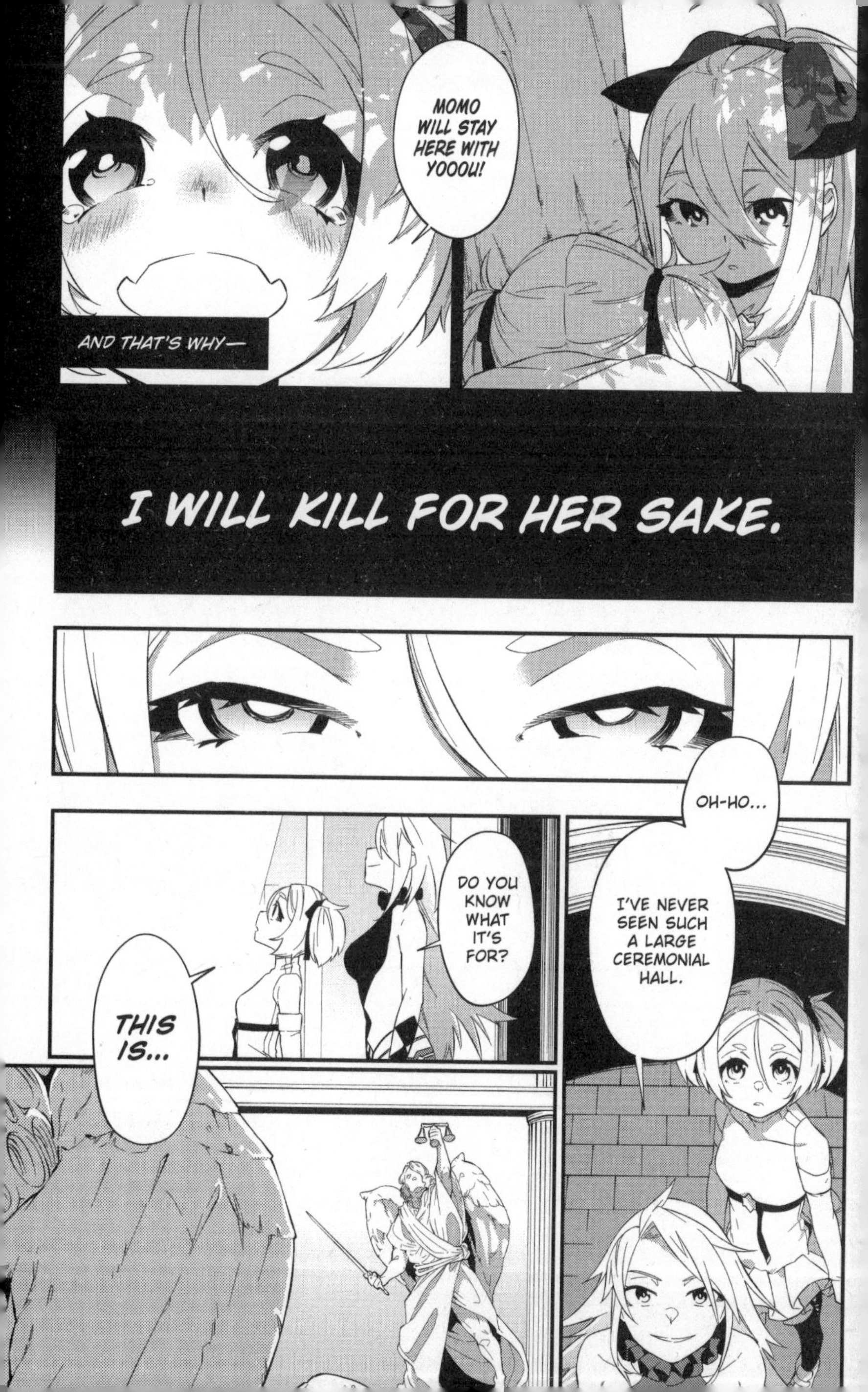
MOMO WILL STAY HERE WITH YOOOU!
AND THAT'S WHY—
I WILL KILL FOR HER SAKE.
OH-HO...
I'VE NEVER SEEN SUCH A LARGE CEREMONIAL HALL.
DO YOU KNOW WHAT IT'S FOR?
THIS IS...

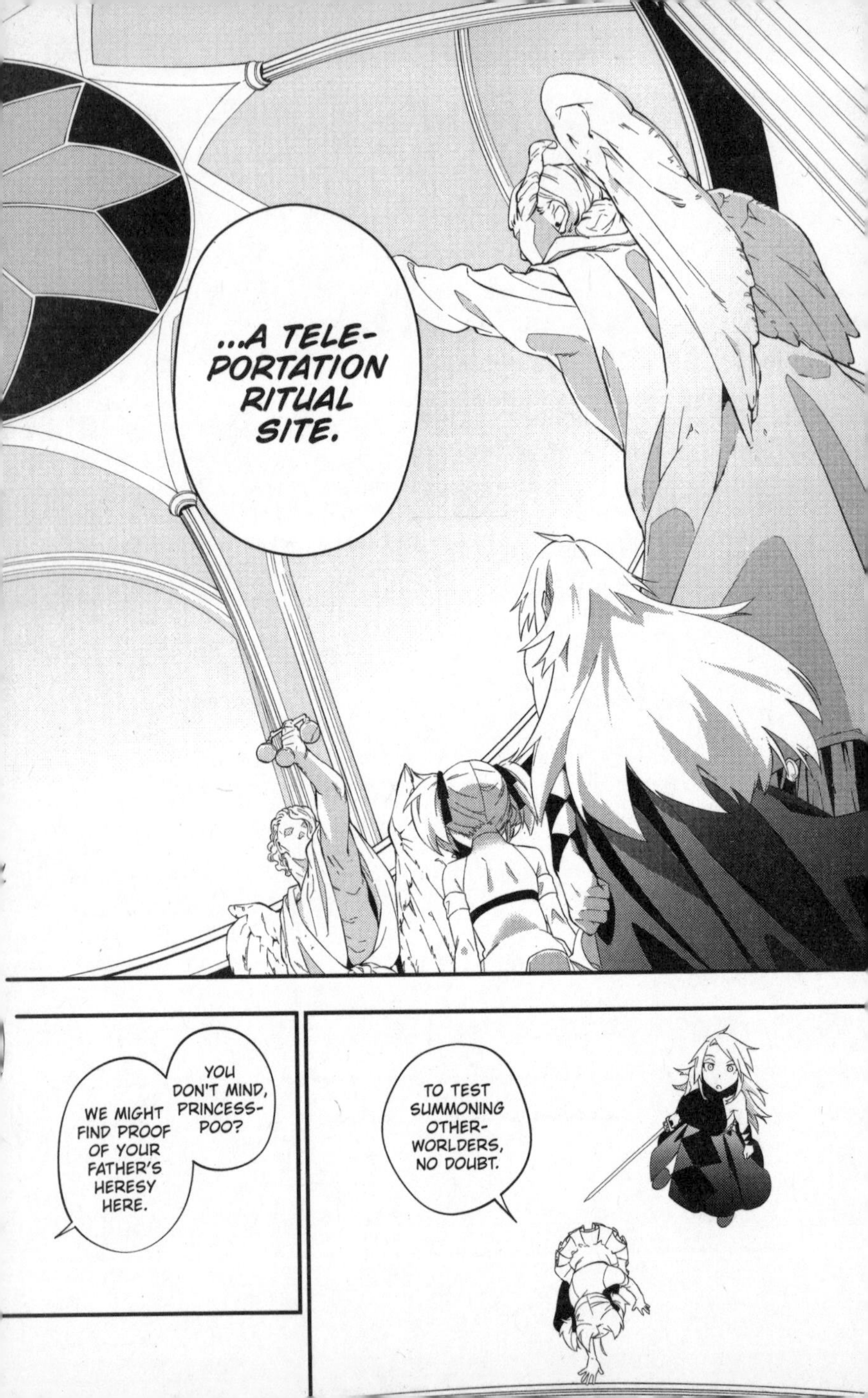
...A TELE-PORTATION RITUAL SITE.
TO TEST SUMMONING OTHER-WORLDERS, NO DOUBT.
YOU DON'T MIND, PRINCESS-POO?
WE MIGHT FIND PROOF OF YOUR FATHER'S HERESY HERE.

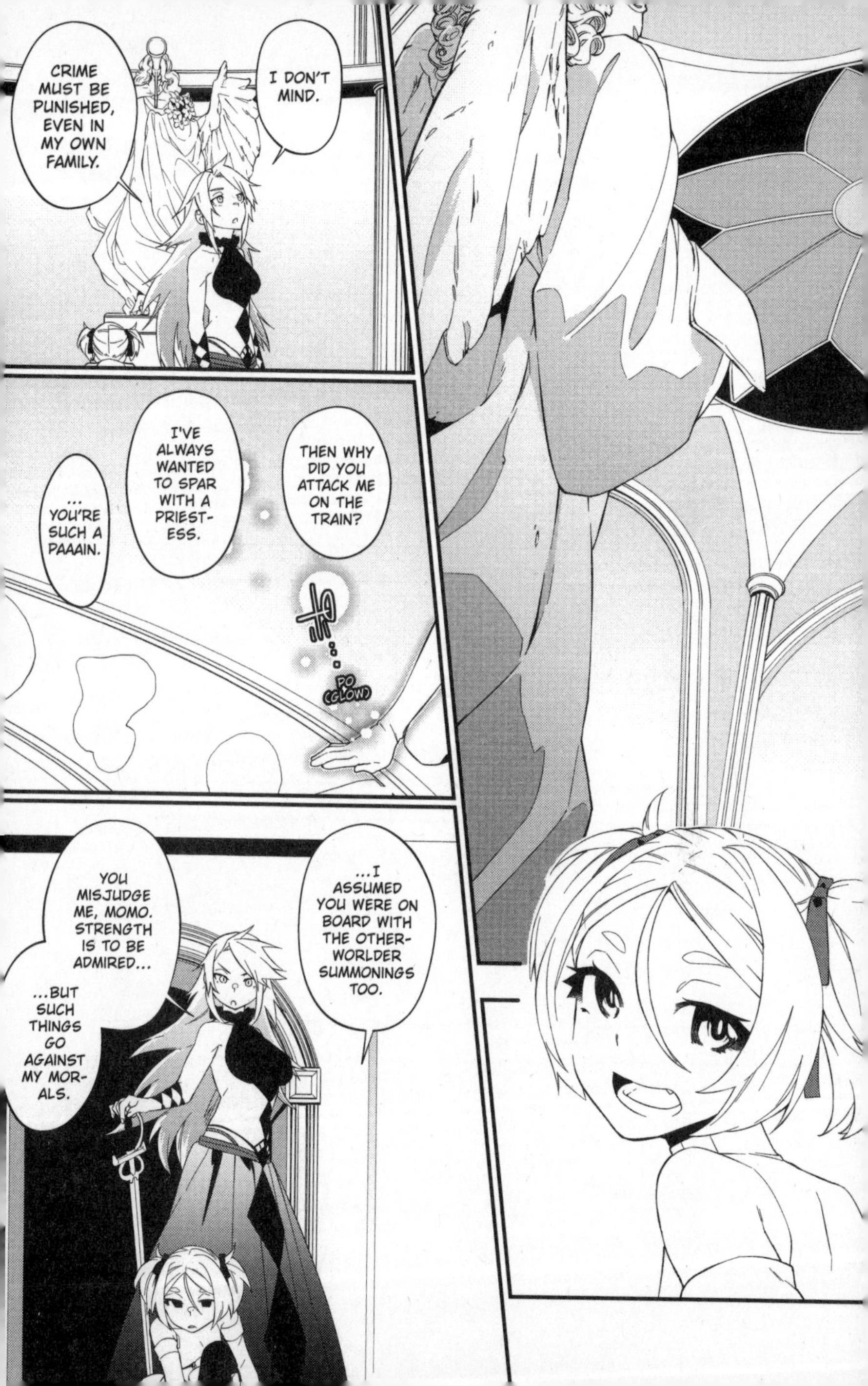
I DON'T MIND.
CRIME MUST BE PUNISHED, EVEN IN MY OWN FAMILY.
THEN WHY DID YOU ATTACK ME ON THE TRAIN?
I'VE ALWAYS WANTED TO SPAR WITH A PRIEST-ESS.
...YOU'RE SUCH A PAAAIN.
PO (GLOW)
...I ASSUMED YOU WERE ON BOARD WITH THE OTHER-WORLDER SUMMONINGS TOO.
YOU MISJUDGE ME, MOMO. STRENGTH IS TO BE ADMIRED...
...BUT SUCH THINGS GO AGAINST MY MOR-ALS.

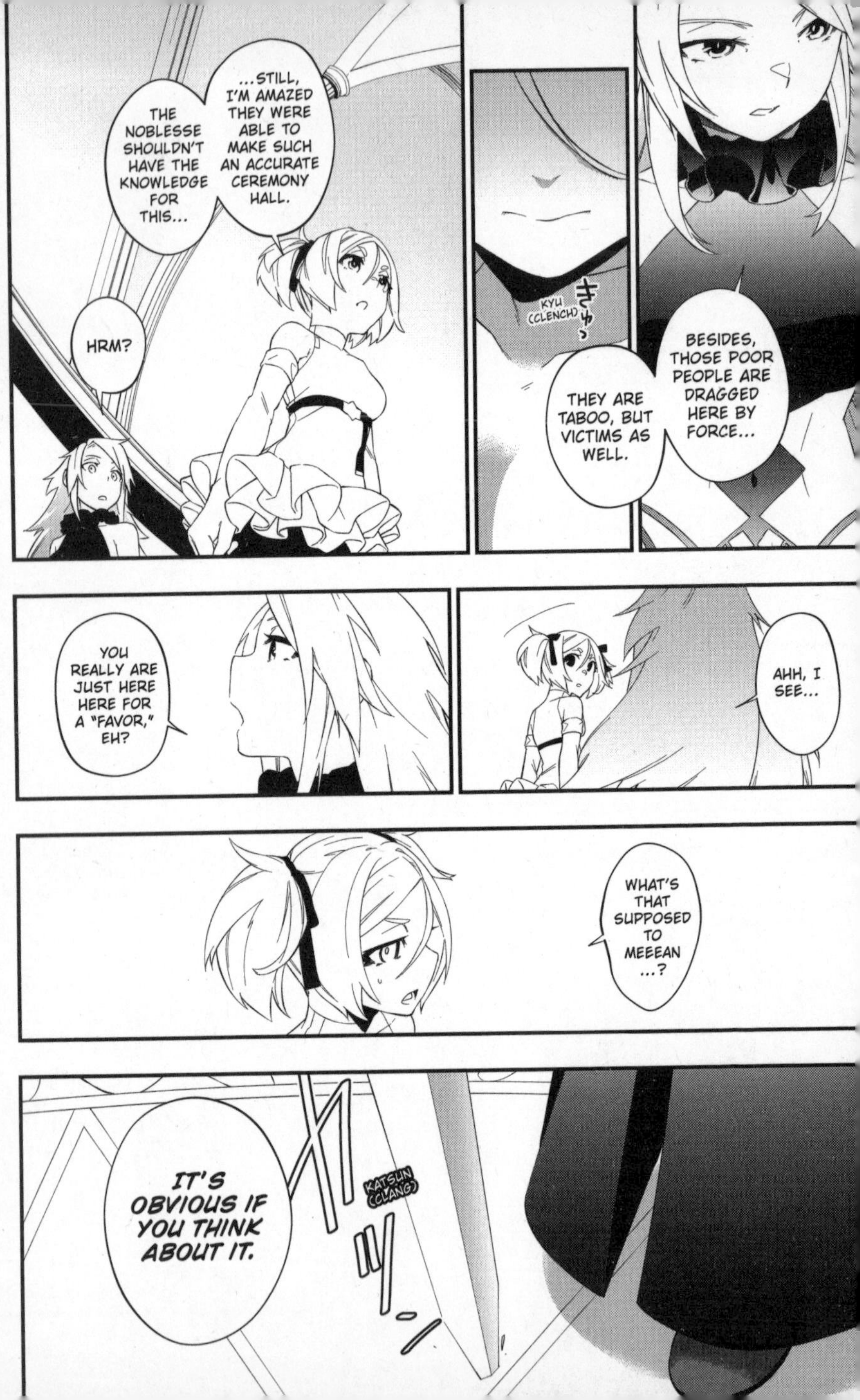
BESIDES, THOSE POOR PEOPLE ARE DRAGGED HERE BY FORCE...
KYU (CLENCH)
THEY ARE TABOO, BUT VICTIMS AS WELL.
...STILL, I'M AMAZED THEY WERE ABLE TO MAKE SUCH AN ACCURATE CEREMONY HALL.
THE NOBLESSE SHOULDN'T HAVE THE KNOWLEDGE FOR THIS...
HRM?
AHH, I SEE...
YOU REALLY ARE JUST HERE HERE FOR A "FAVOR," EH?
WHAT'S THAT SUPPOSED TO MEEEAN ...?
KATSUN (CLANG)
IT'S OBVIOUS IF YOU THINK ABOUT IT.

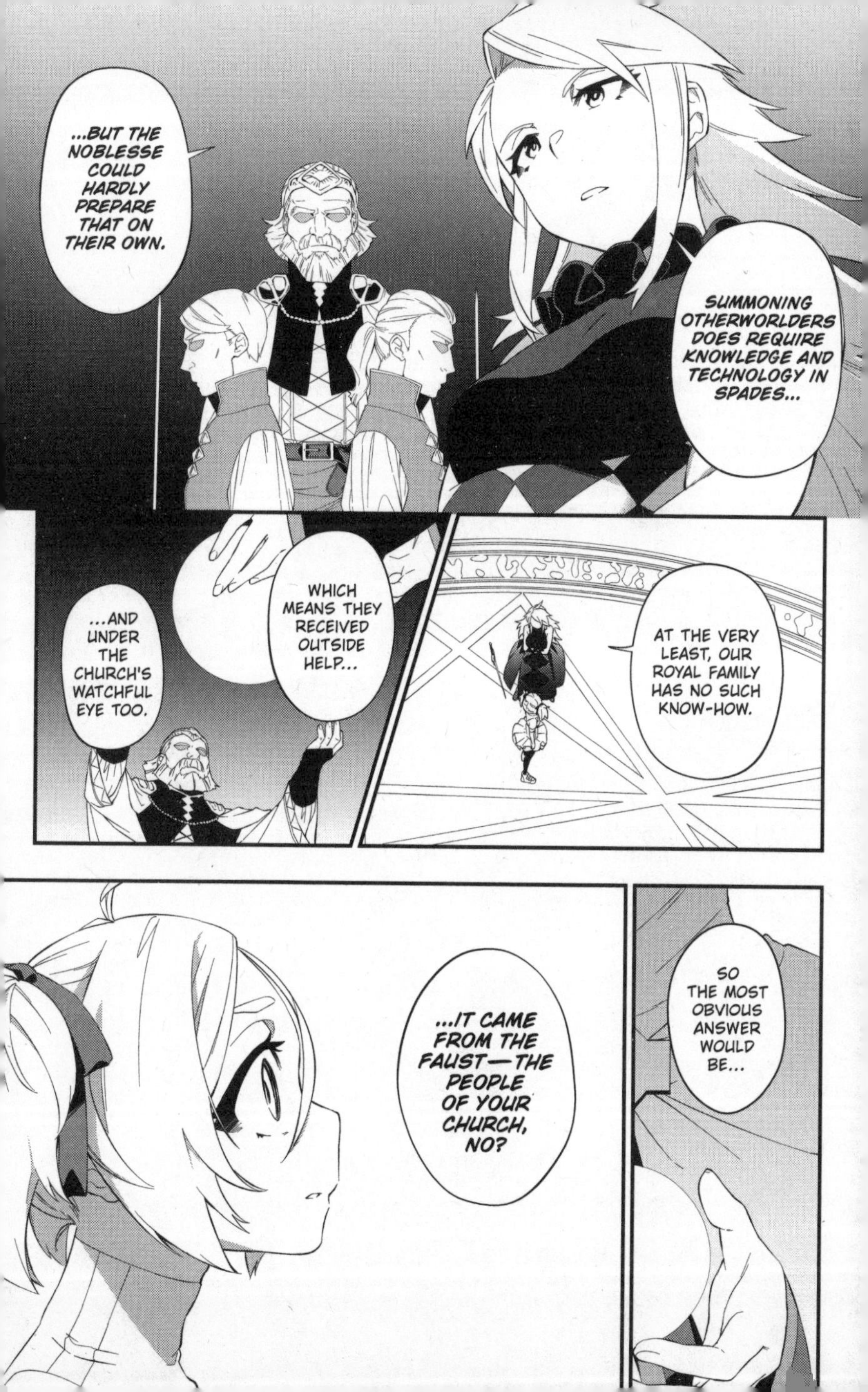
SUMMONING OTHERWORLDERS DOES REQUIRE KNOWLEDGE AND TECHNOLOGY IN SPADES...
...BUT THE NOBLESSE COULD HARDLY PREPARE THAT ON THEIR OWN.
AT THE VERY LEAST, OUR ROYAL FAMILY HAS NO SUCH KNOW-HOW.
WHICH MEANS THEY RECEIVED OUTSIDE HELP...
...AND UNDER THE CHURCH'S WATCHFUL EYE TOO.
SO THE MOST OBVIOUS ANSWER WOULD BE...
...IT CAME FROM THE FAUST—THE PEOPLE OF YOUR CHURCH, NO?

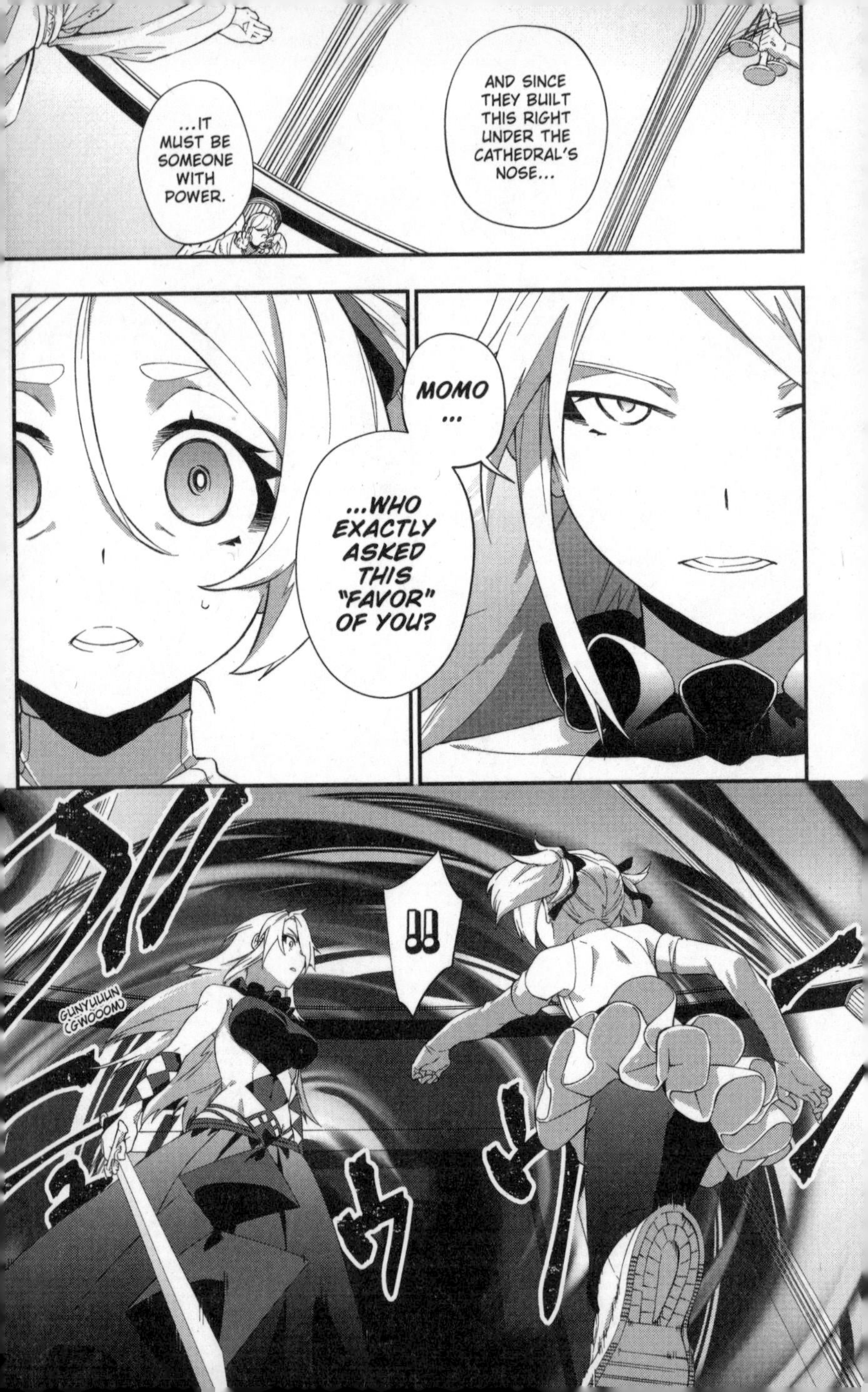
AND SINCE THEY BUILT THIS RIGHT UNDER THE CATHEDRAL'S NOSE...
...IT MUST BE SOMEONE WITH POWER.
MOMO...
...WHO EXACTLY ASKED THIS "FAVOR" OF YOU?
!!
GUNYUUUN (GWOOOM)

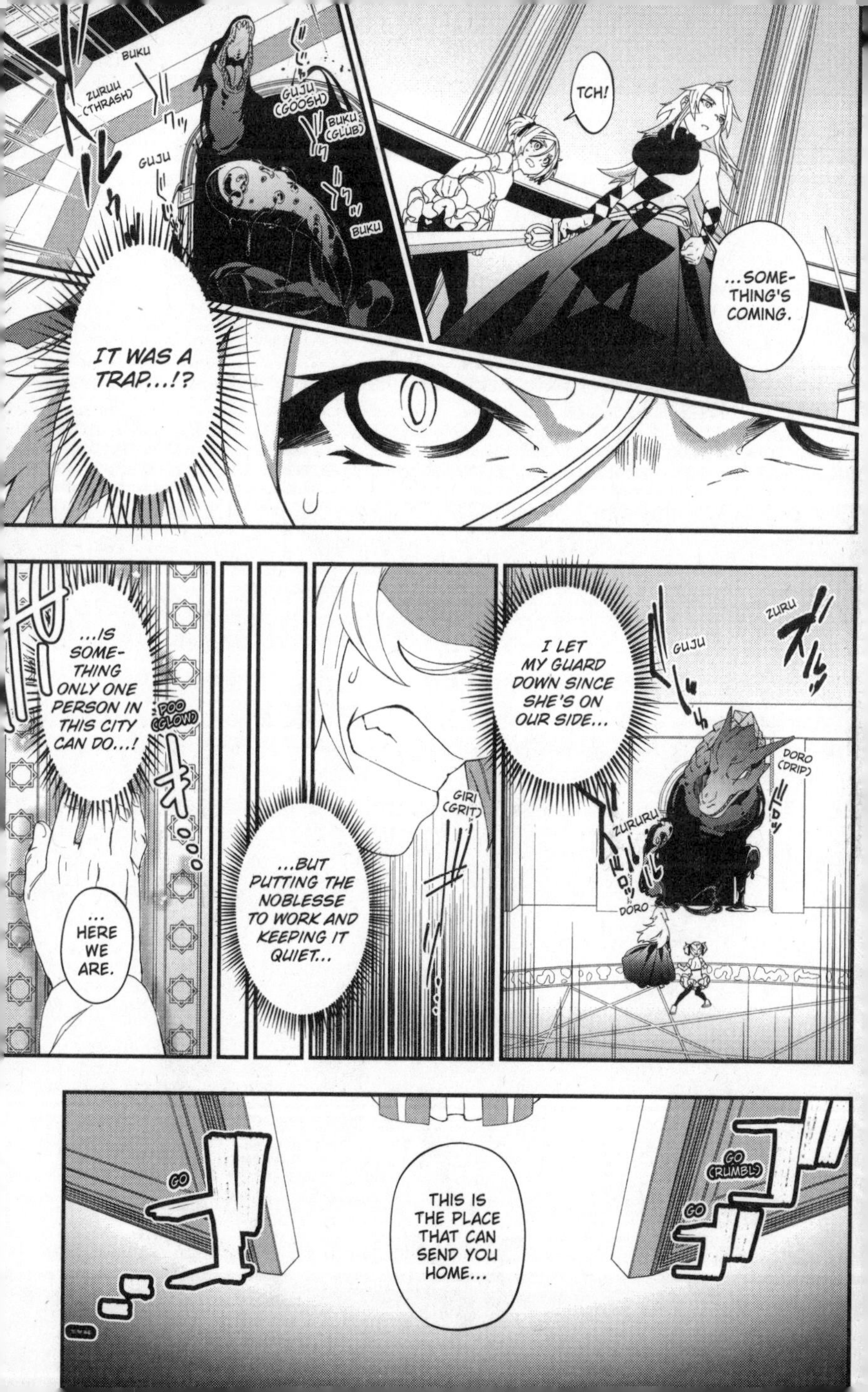

TCH!
...SOME-THING'S COMING.
GUJU (GOOSH)
BUKU (GLUB)
BUKU
BUKU
ZURUU (THRASH)
GUJU
IT WAS A TRAP...!?
ZURU
GUJU
I LET MY GUARD DOWN SINCE SHE'S ON OUR SIDE...
DORO (DRIP)
ZURURU
DORO
GIRI (GRIT)
...BUT PUTTING THE NOBLESSE TO WORK AND KEEPING IT QUIET...
...IS SOME-THING ONLY ONE PERSON IN THIS CITY CAN DO...!
POO (GLOW)
...HERE WE ARE.
GO (RUMBL)
GO
THIS IS THE PLACE THAT CAN SEND YOU HOME...
GO

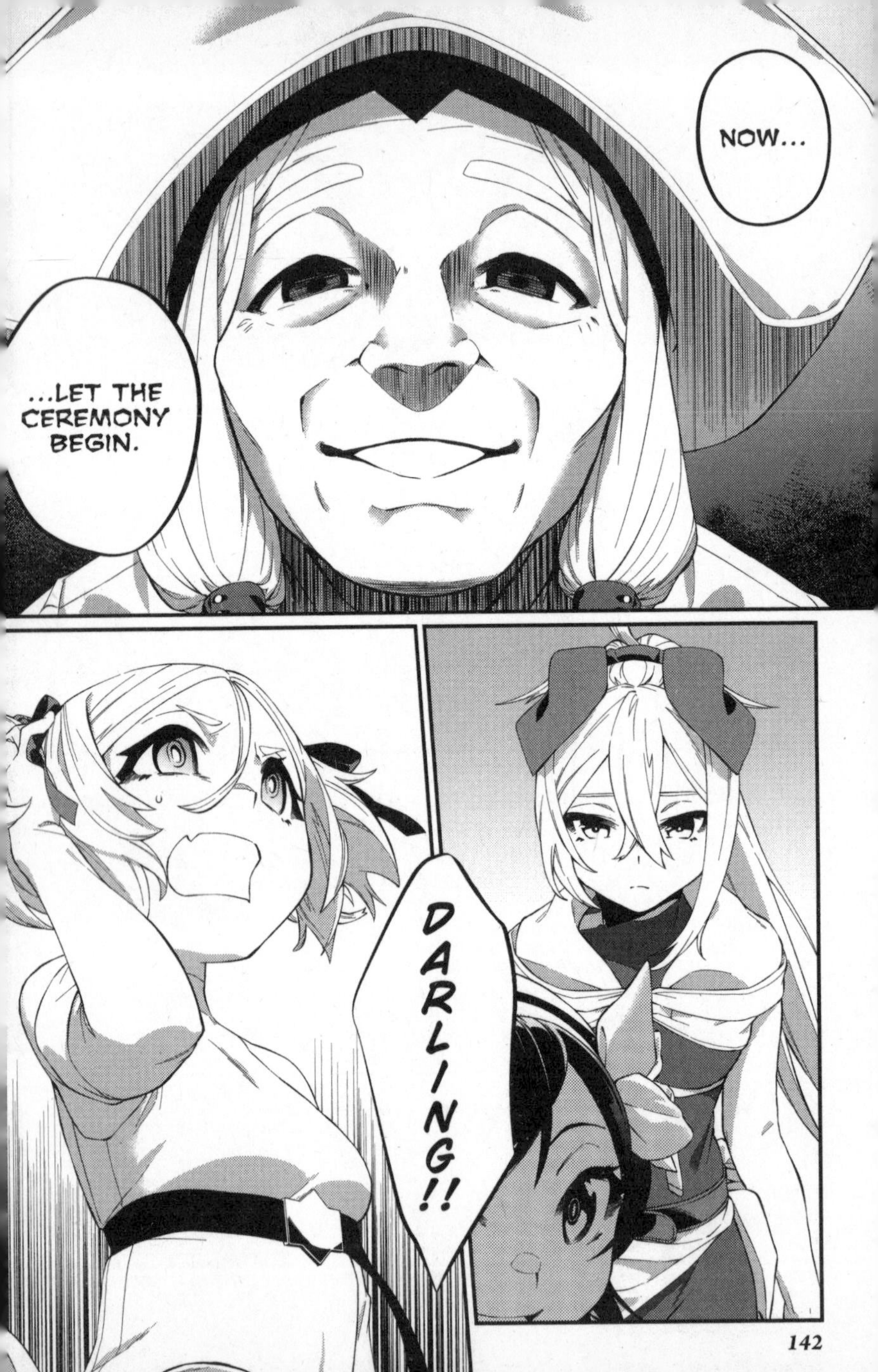
NOW...
...LET THE CEREMONY BEGIN.
DARLING!!

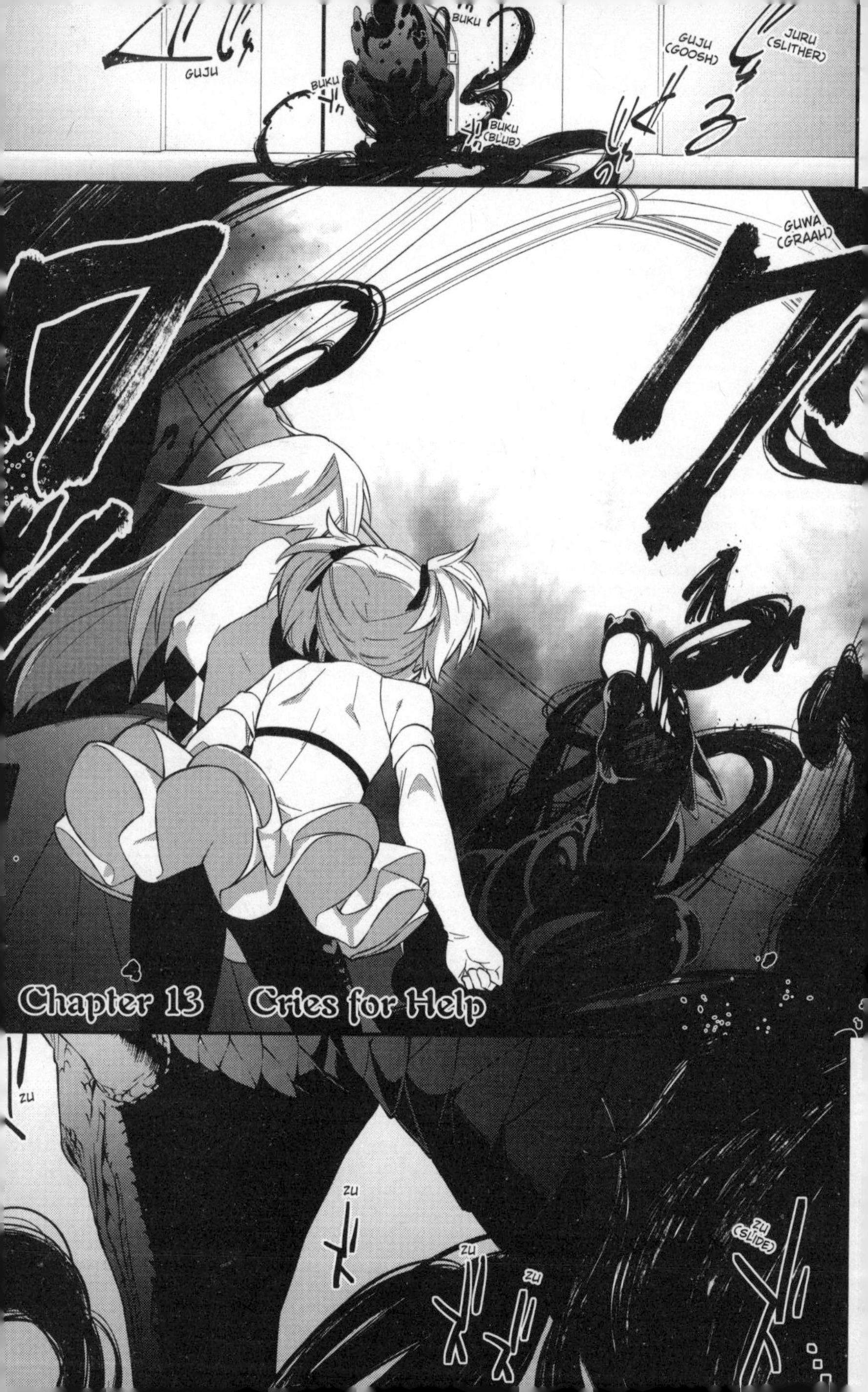
JURU (SLITHER)
GUJU (GOOSH)
BUKU
BUKU (BLUB)
BUKU
GUJU
GUWA (GRAAH)
Chapter 13 Cries for Help
ZU (SLIDE)
ZU
ZU
ZU
ZU

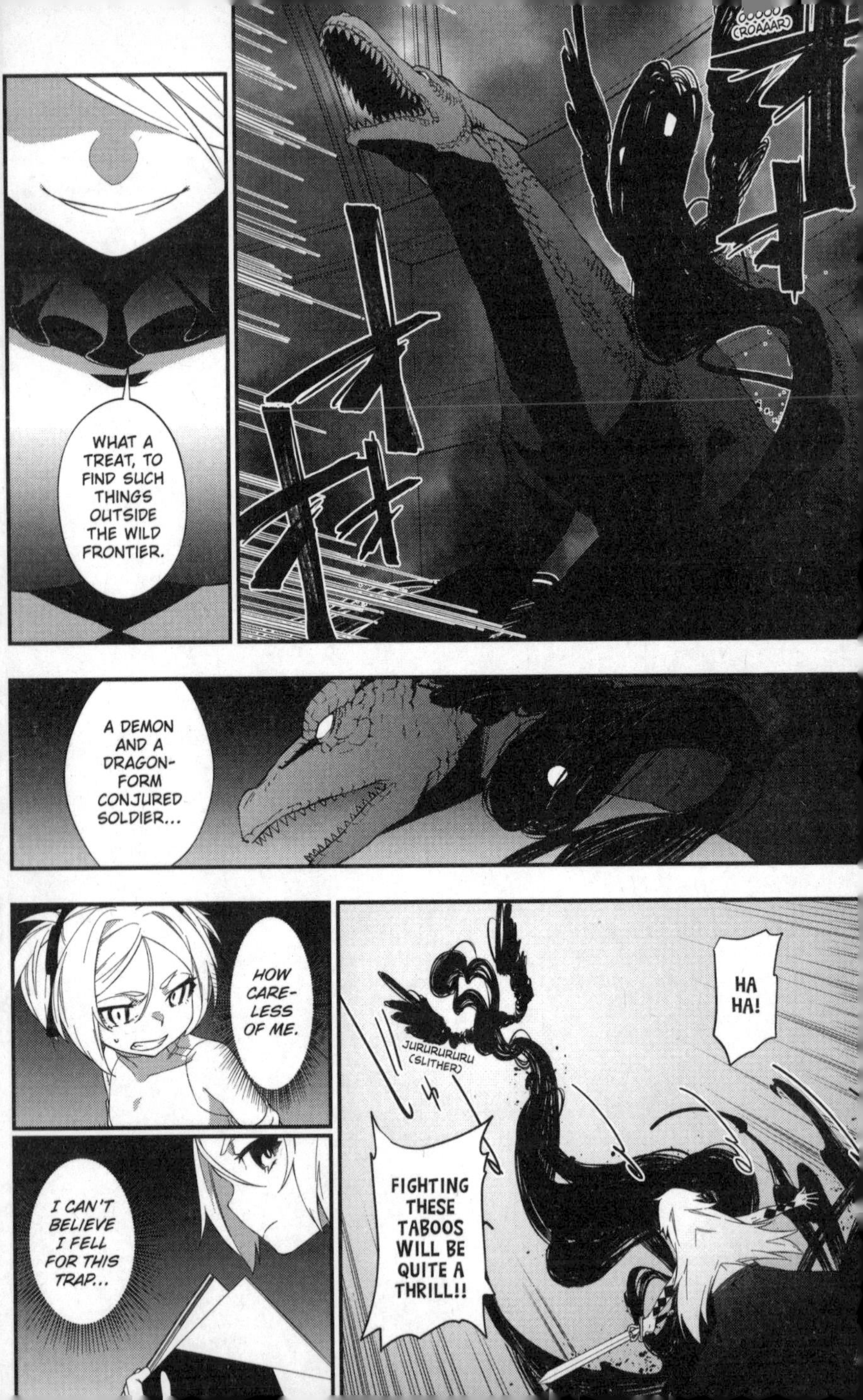
(ROAAAR)
WHAT A TREAT, TO FIND SUCH THINGS OUTSIDE THE WILD FRONTIER.
A DEMON AND A DRAGON-FORM CONJURED SOLDIER...
HA HA!
JURURURURU (SLITHER)
FIGHTING THESE TABOOS WILL BE QUITE A THRILL!!
HOW CARELESS OF ME.
I CAN'T BELIEVE I FELL FOR THIS TRAP...

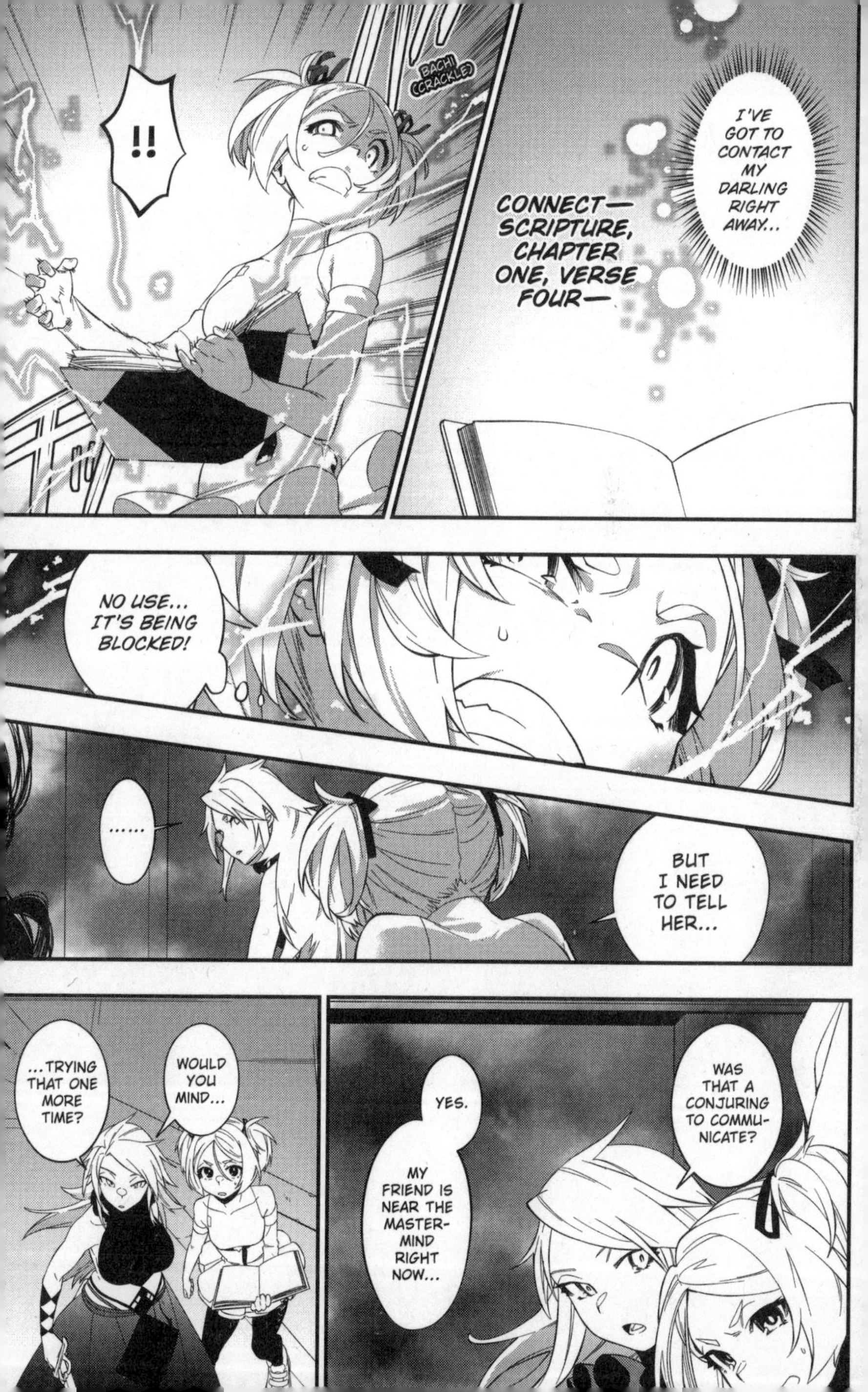
I'VE GOT TO CONTACT MY DARLING RIGHT AWAY...
CONNECT—SCRIPTURE, CHAPTER ONE, VERSE FOUR—
BACHI (CRACKLE)
!!
NO USE... IT'S BEING BLOCKED!
BUT I NEED TO TELL HER...
......
WAS THAT A CONJURING TO COMMUNICATE?
YES.
MY FRIEND IS NEAR THE MASTERMIND RIGHT NOW...
WOULD YOU MIND...
...TRYING THAT ONE MORE TIME?

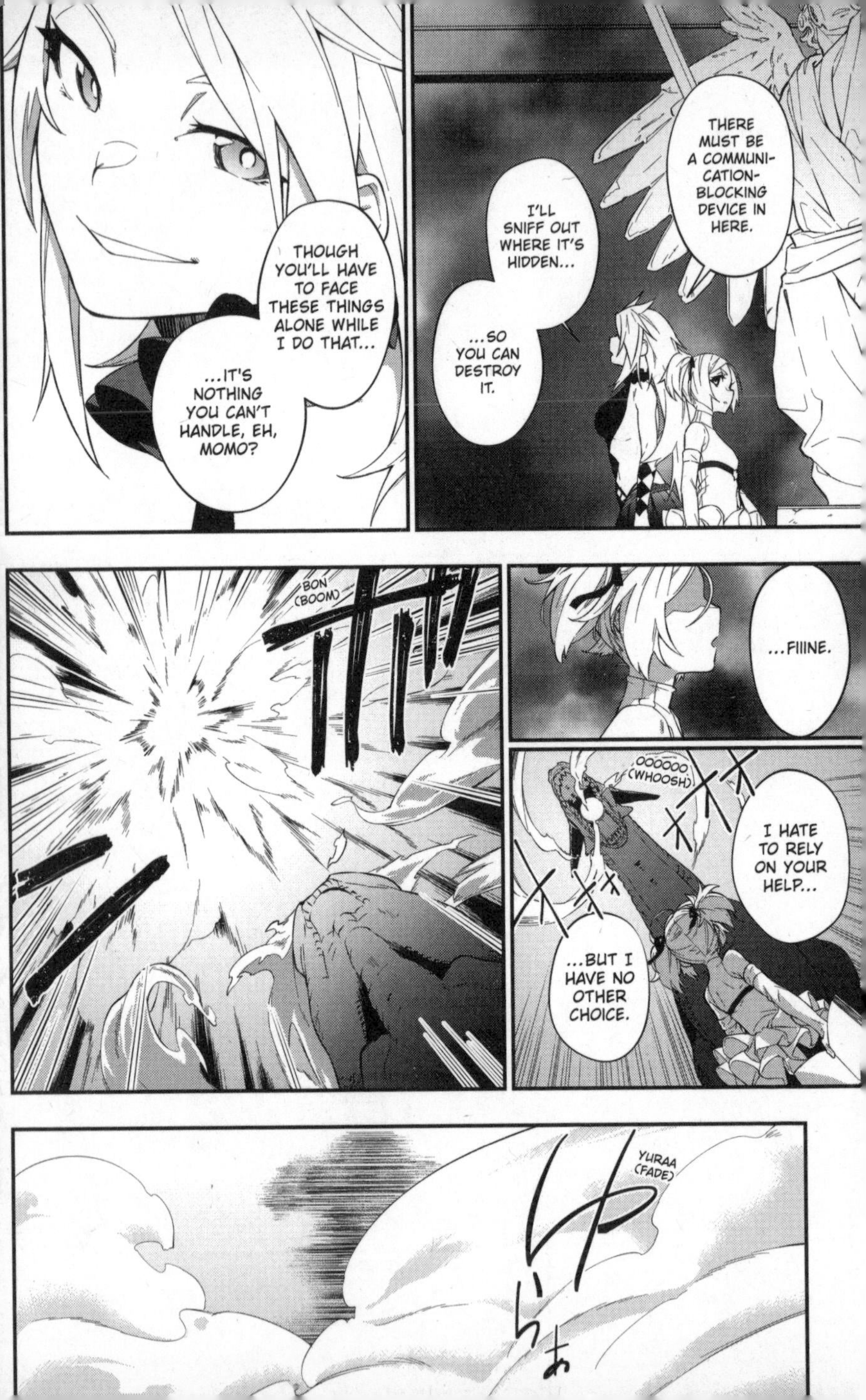
THERE MUST BE A COMMUNICATION-BLOCKING DEVICE IN HERE.
I'LL SNIFF OUT WHERE IT'S HIDDEN...
...SO YOU CAN DESTROY IT.
THOUGH YOU'LL HAVE TO FACE THESE THINGS ALONE WHILE I DO THAT...
...IT'S NOTHING YOU CAN'T HANDLE, EH, MOMO?
...FIIINE.
OOOOOO (WHOOSH)
I HATE TO RELY ON YOUR HELP...
...BUT I HAVE NO OTHER CHOICE.
BON (BOOM)
YURAA (FADE)

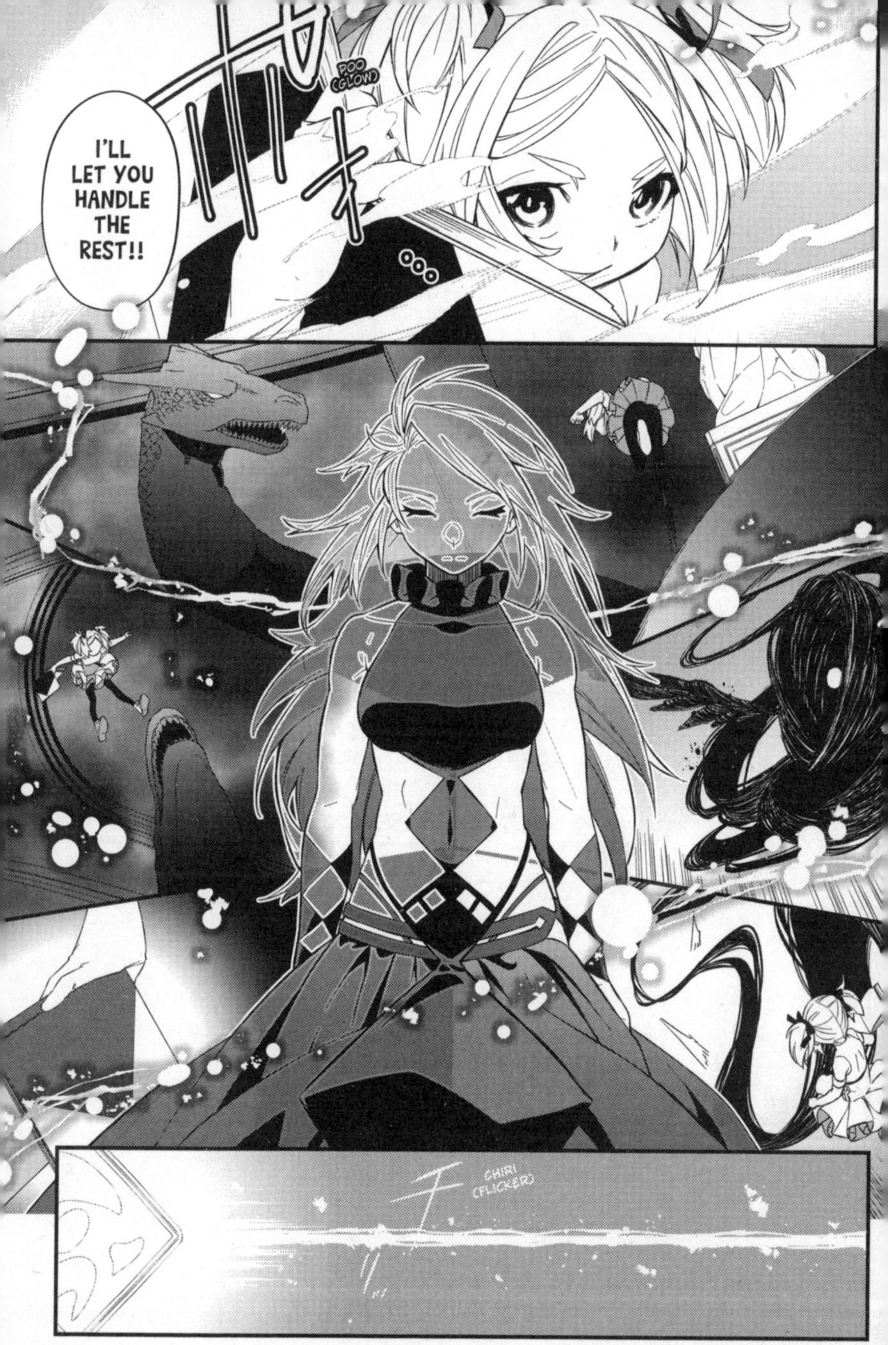
POO (GLOW)
I'LL LET YOU HANDLE THE REST!!
CHIRI (FLICKER)

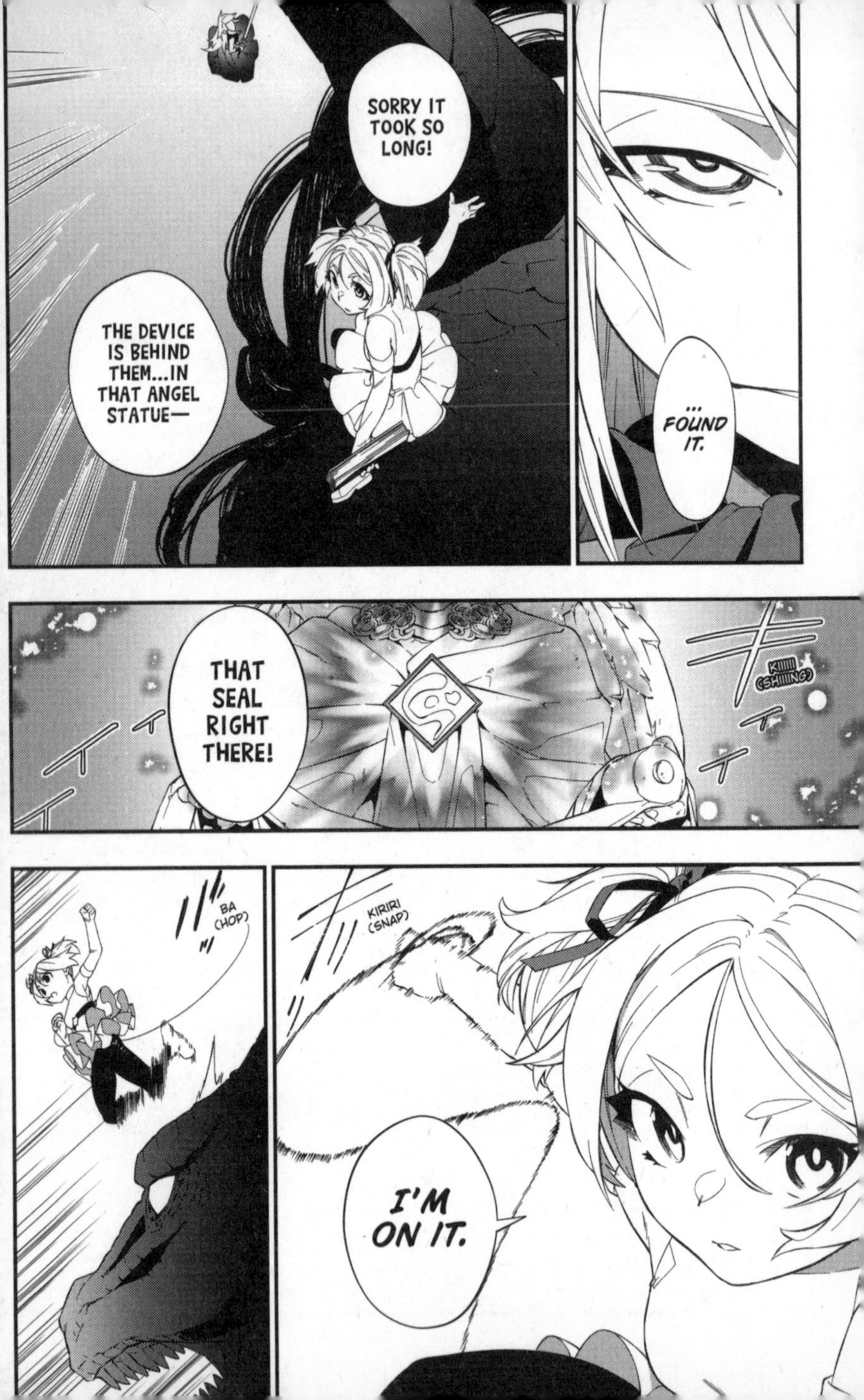
...FOUND IT.
SORRY IT TOOK SO LONG!
THE DEVICE IS BEHIND THEM...IN THAT ANGEL STATUE—
KIIIIII (SHIIIING)
THAT SEAL RIGHT THERE!
KIRIRI (SNAP)
I'M ON IT.
BA (HOP)

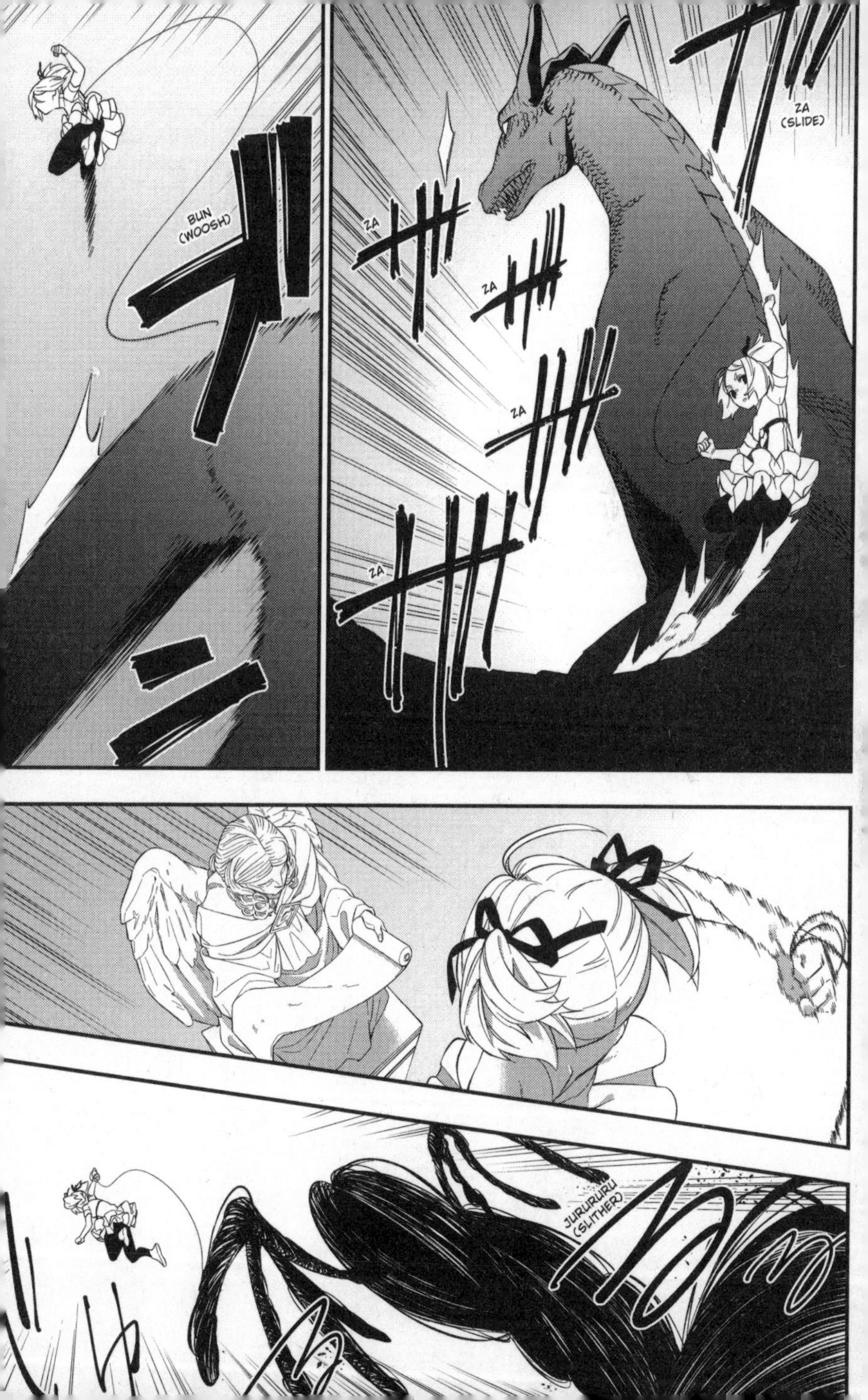
ZA
(SLIDE)
ZA
ZA
ZA
ZA
BUN
(WOOSH)
JURURURU
(SLITHER)

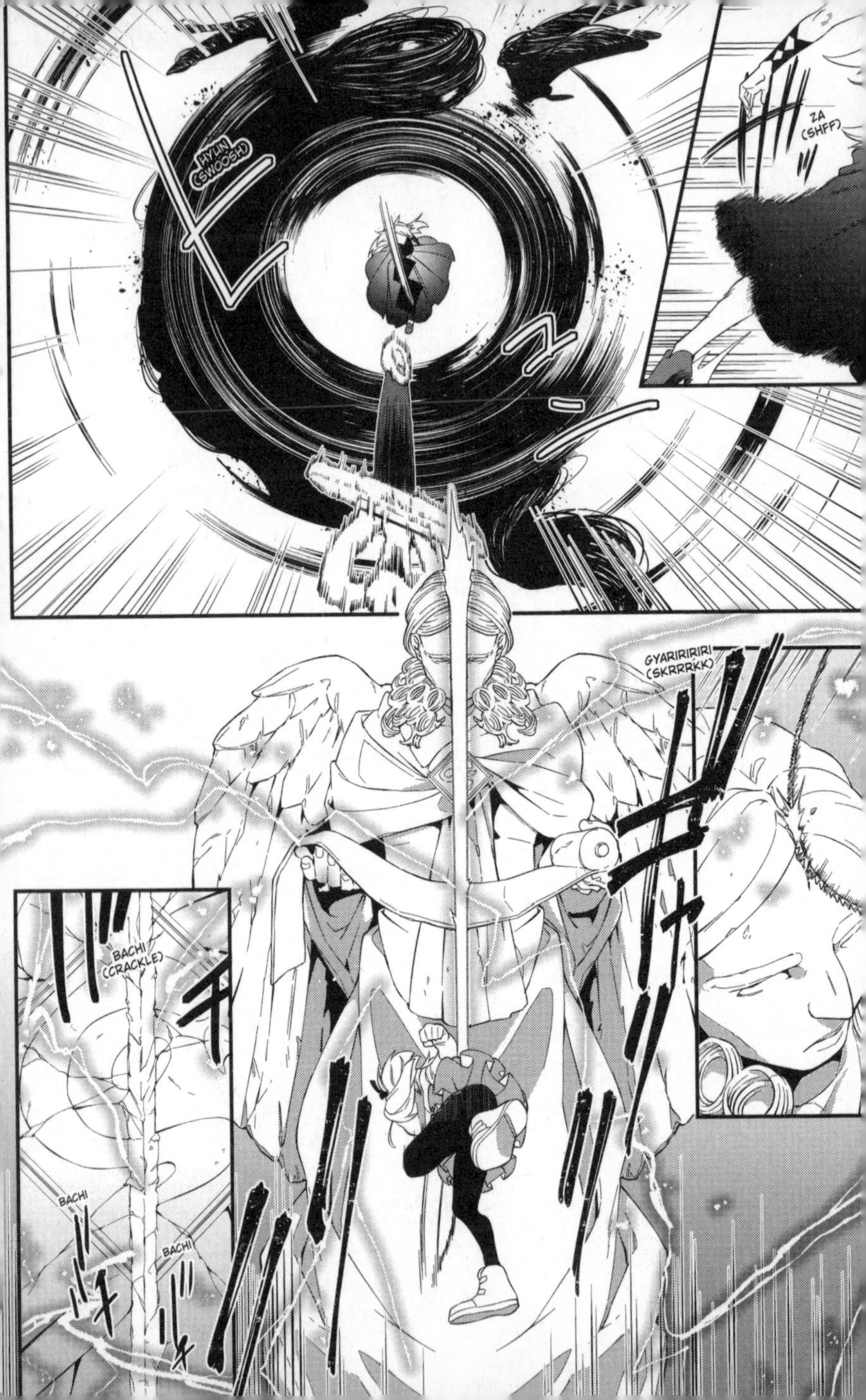
ZA (SHFF)
HYUN (SWOOSH)
GYARIRIRIRI (SKRRRKK)
BACHI (CRACKLE)
BACHI
BACHI

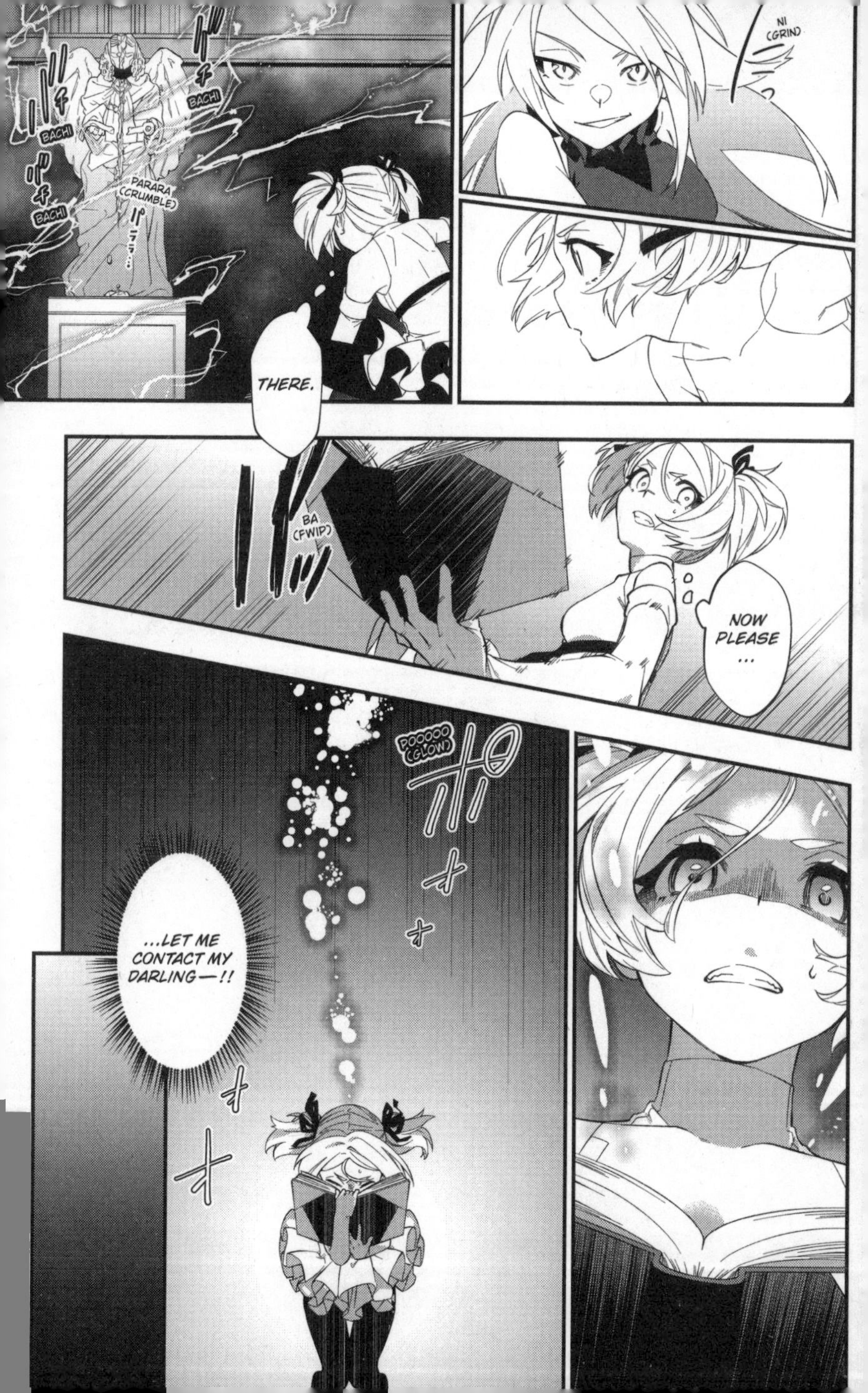
NI (GRIND)
BACHI
BACHI
PARARA (CRUMBLE)
BACHI
THERE.
BA (FWIP)
NOW PLEASE ...
POOOOO (GLOW)
...LET ME CONTACT MY DARLING—!!

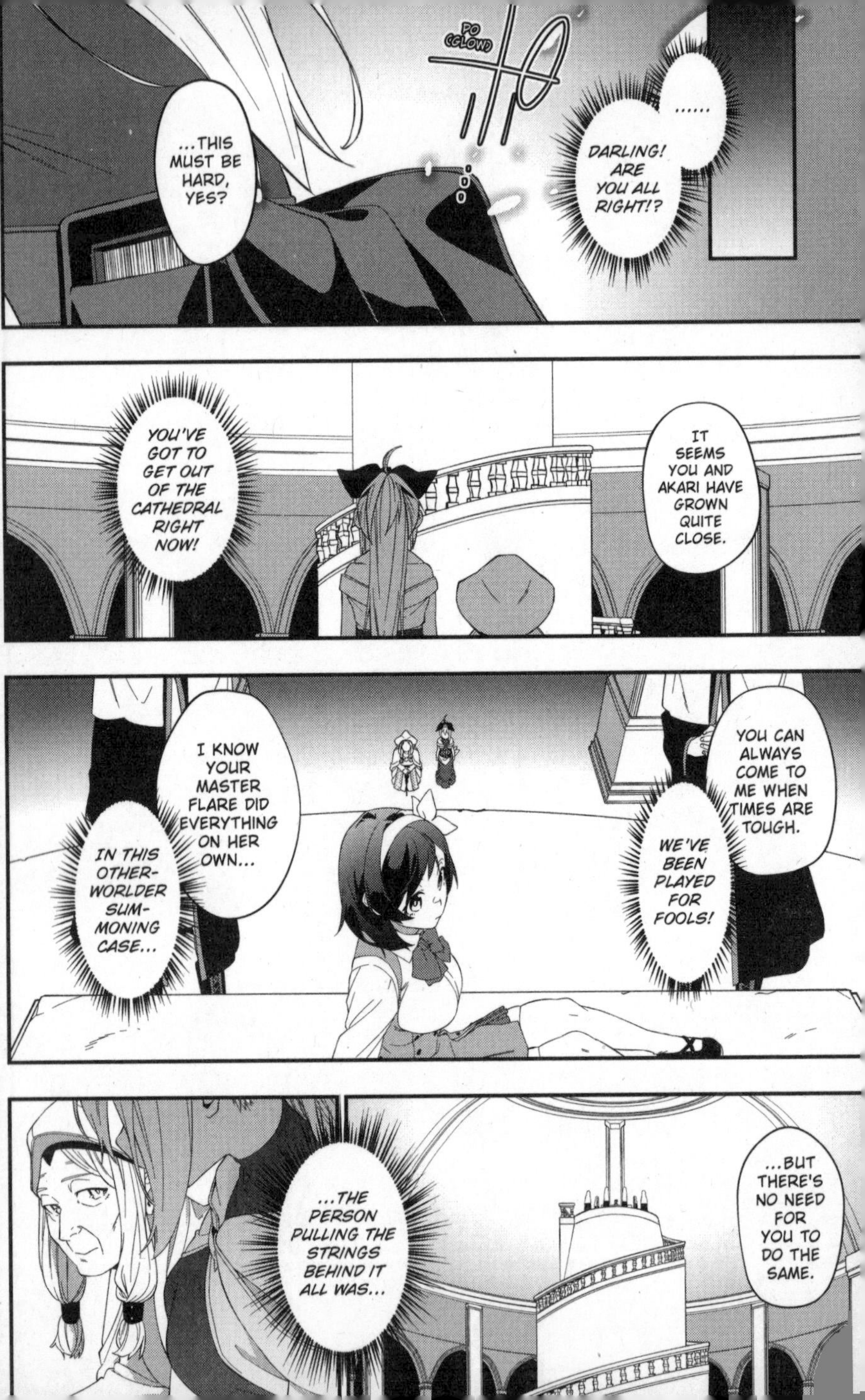
......
DARLING! ARE YOU ALL RIGHT!?
PO (GLOW)
...THIS MUST BE HARD, YES?
IT SEEMS YOU AND AKARI HAVE GROWN QUITE CLOSE.
YOU'VE GOT TO GET OUT OF THE CATHEDRAL RIGHT NOW!
YOU CAN ALWAYS COME TO ME WHEN TIMES ARE TOUGH.
WE'VE BEEN PLAYED FOR FOOLS!
I KNOW YOUR MASTER FLARE DID EVERYTHING ON HER OWN...
IN THIS OTHER-WORLDER SUMMONING CASE...
...BUT THERE'S NO NEED FOR YOU TO DO THE SAME.
...THE PERSON PULLING THE STRINGS BEHIND IT ALL WAS...

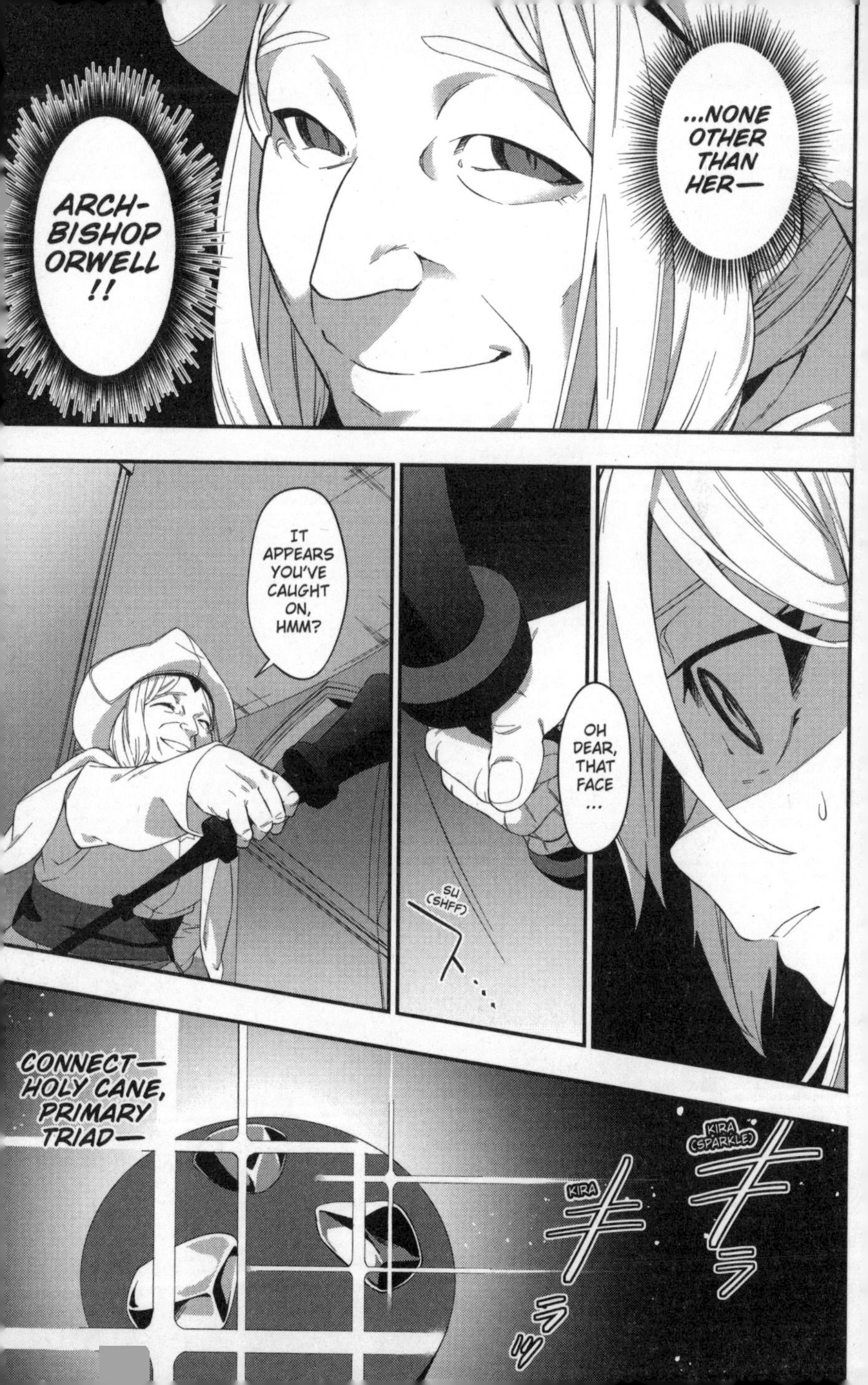
...NONE OTHER THAN HER—
ARCH-BISHOP ORWELL!!
OH DEAR, THAT FACE...
SU (SHFF)
IT APPEARS YOU'VE CAUGHT ON, HMM?
KIRA (SPARKLE)
KIRA
CONNECT— HOLY CANE, PRIMARY TRIAD—

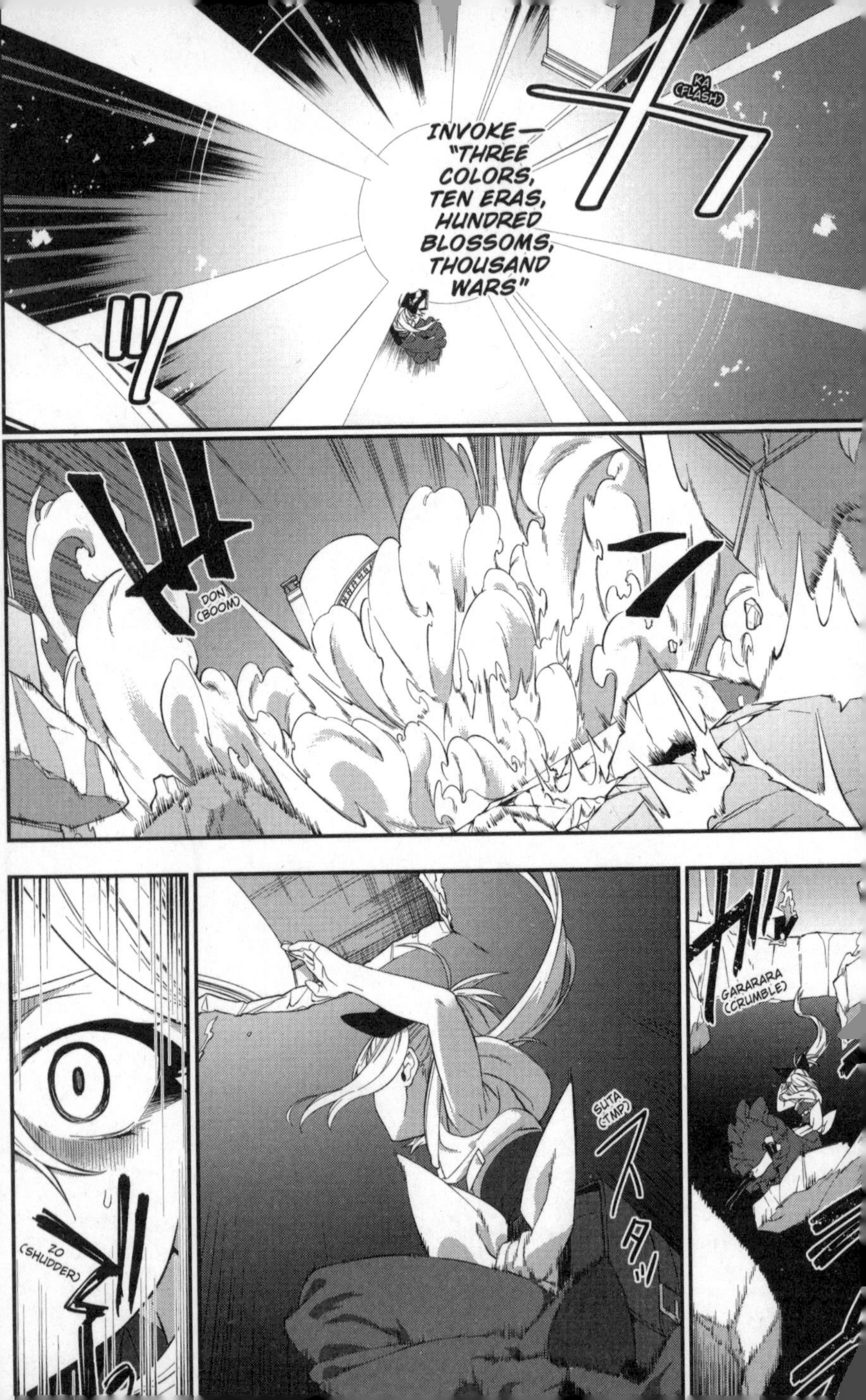
KA (FLASH)
INVOKE—"THREE COLORS, TEN ERAS, HUNDRED BLOSSOMS, THOUSAND WARS"
DON (BOOM)
GARARARA (CRUMBLE)
SUTA (TMP)
ZO (SHUDDER)

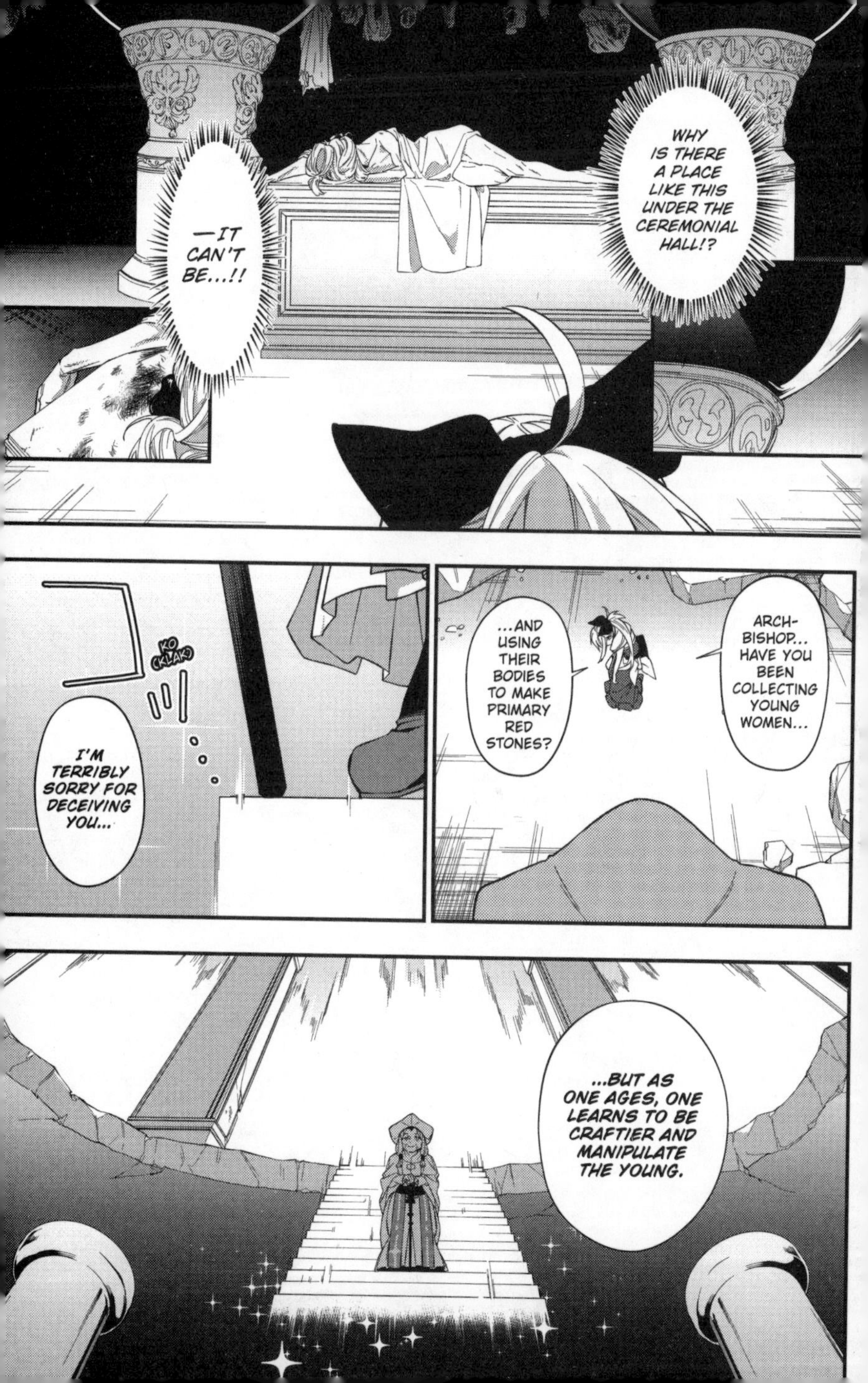
WHY IS THERE A PLACE LIKE THIS UNDER THE CEREMONIAL HALL!?
—IT CAN'T BE...!!
ARCH-BISHOP... HAVE YOU BEEN COLLECTING YOUNG WOMEN...
...AND USING THEIR BODIES TO MAKE PRIMARY RED STONES?
KO (KLAK)
I'M TERRIBLY SORRY FOR DECEIVING YOU...
...BUT AS ONE AGES, ONE LEARNS TO BE CRAFTIER AND MANIPULATE THE YOUNG.

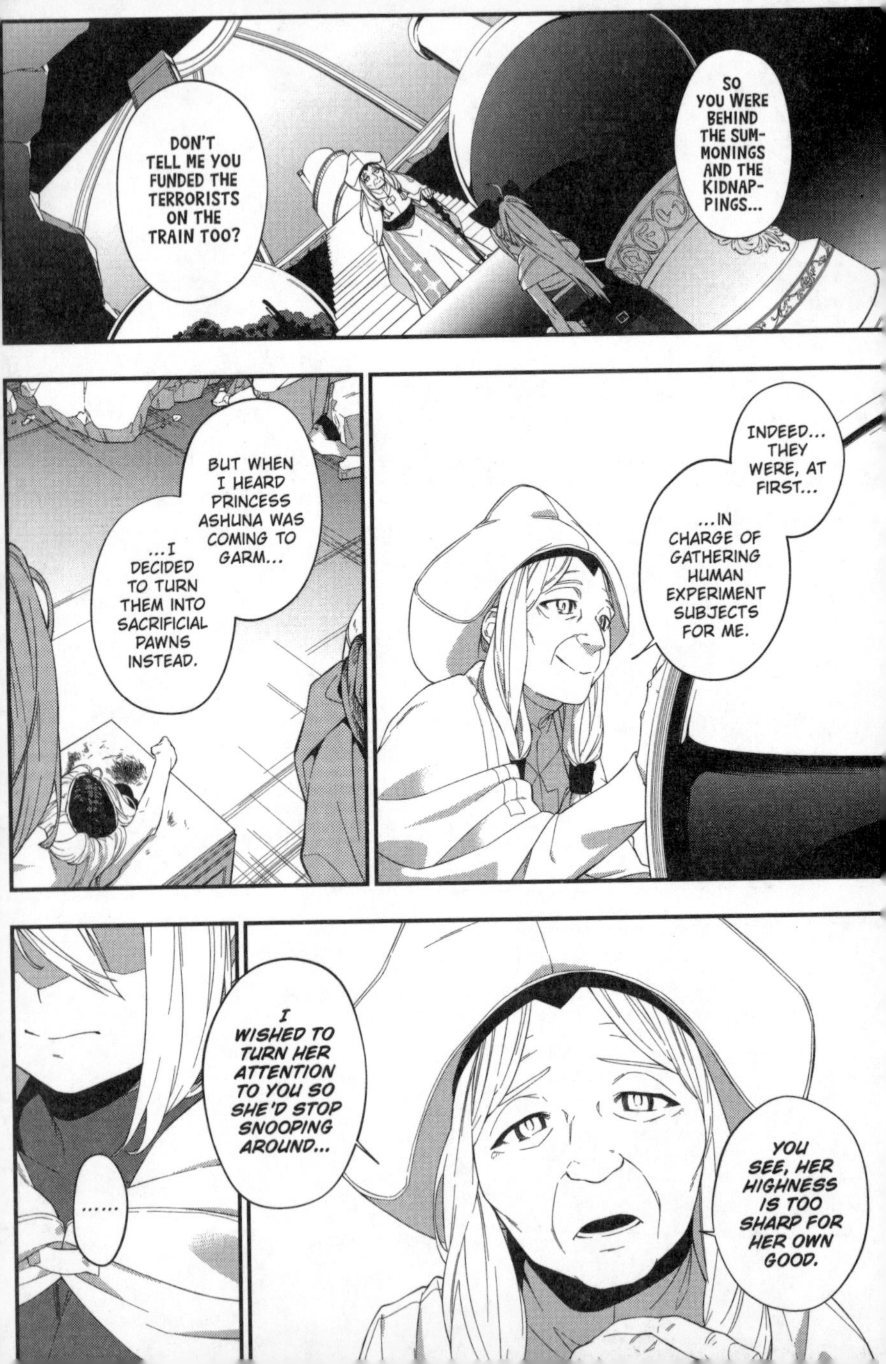
SO YOU WERE BEHIND THE SUM-MONINGS AND THE KIDNAP-PINGS...
DON'T TELL ME YOU FUNDED THE TERRORISTS ON THE TRAIN TOO?
INDEED... THEY WERE, AT FIRST...
...IN CHARGE OF GATHERING HUMAN EXPERIMENT SUBJECTS FOR ME.
BUT WHEN I HEARD PRINCESS ASHUNA WAS COMING TO GARM...
...I DECIDED TO TURN THEM INTO SACRIFICIAL PAWNS INSTEAD.
YOU SEE, HER HIGHNESS IS TOO SHARP FOR HER OWN GOOD.
I WISHED TO TURN HER ATTENTION TO YOU SO SHE'D STOP SNOOPING AROUND...
......

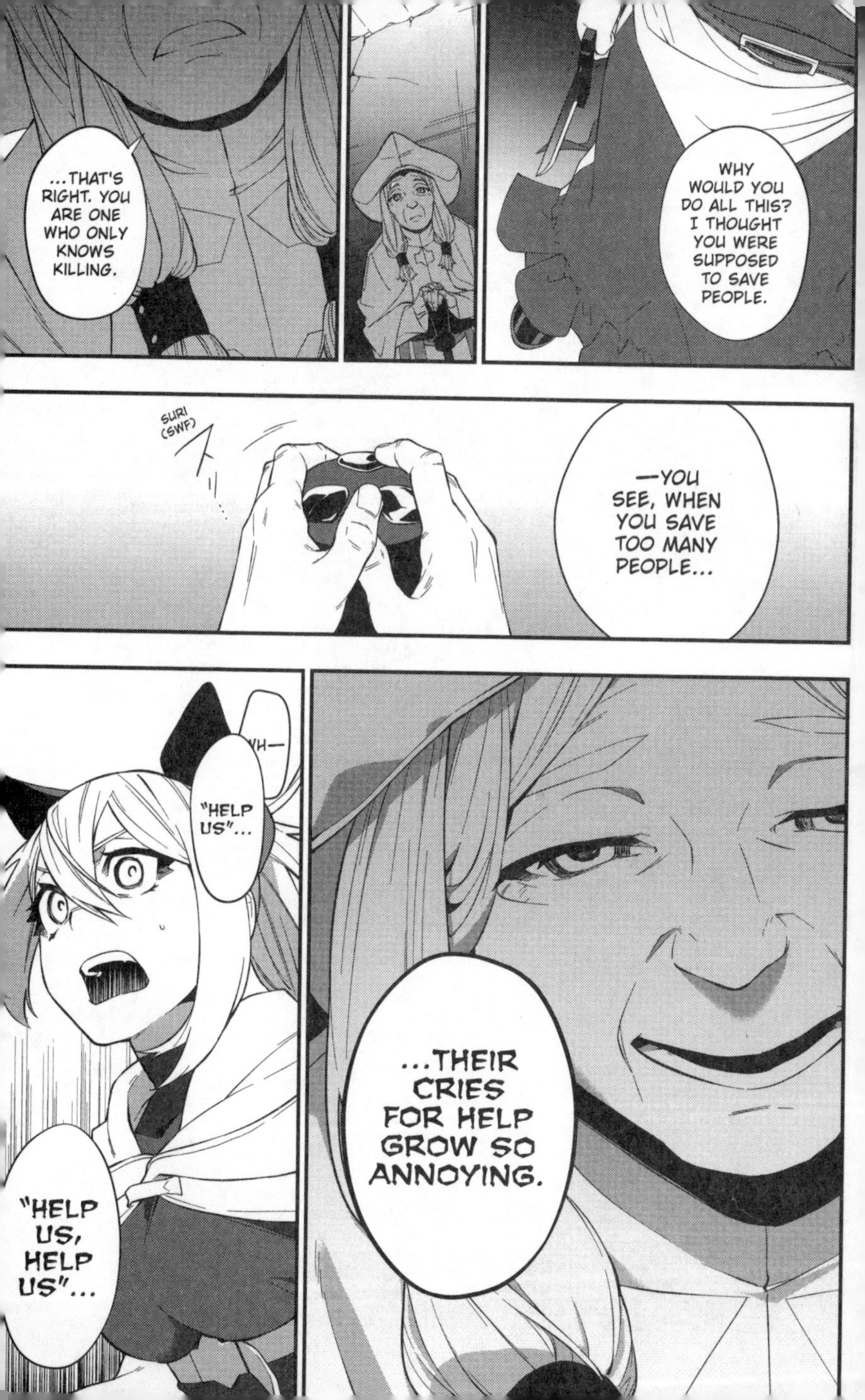
WHY WOULD YOU DO ALL THIS? I THOUGHT YOU WERE SUPPOSED TO SAVE PEOPLE.
...THAT'S RIGHT. YOU ARE ONE WHO ONLY KNOWS KILLING.
—YOU SEE, WHEN YOU SAVE TOO MANY PEOPLE...
SURI (SWF)
...THEIR CRIES FOR HELP GROW SO ANNOYING.
WH—
"HELP US"...
"HELP US, HELP US"...

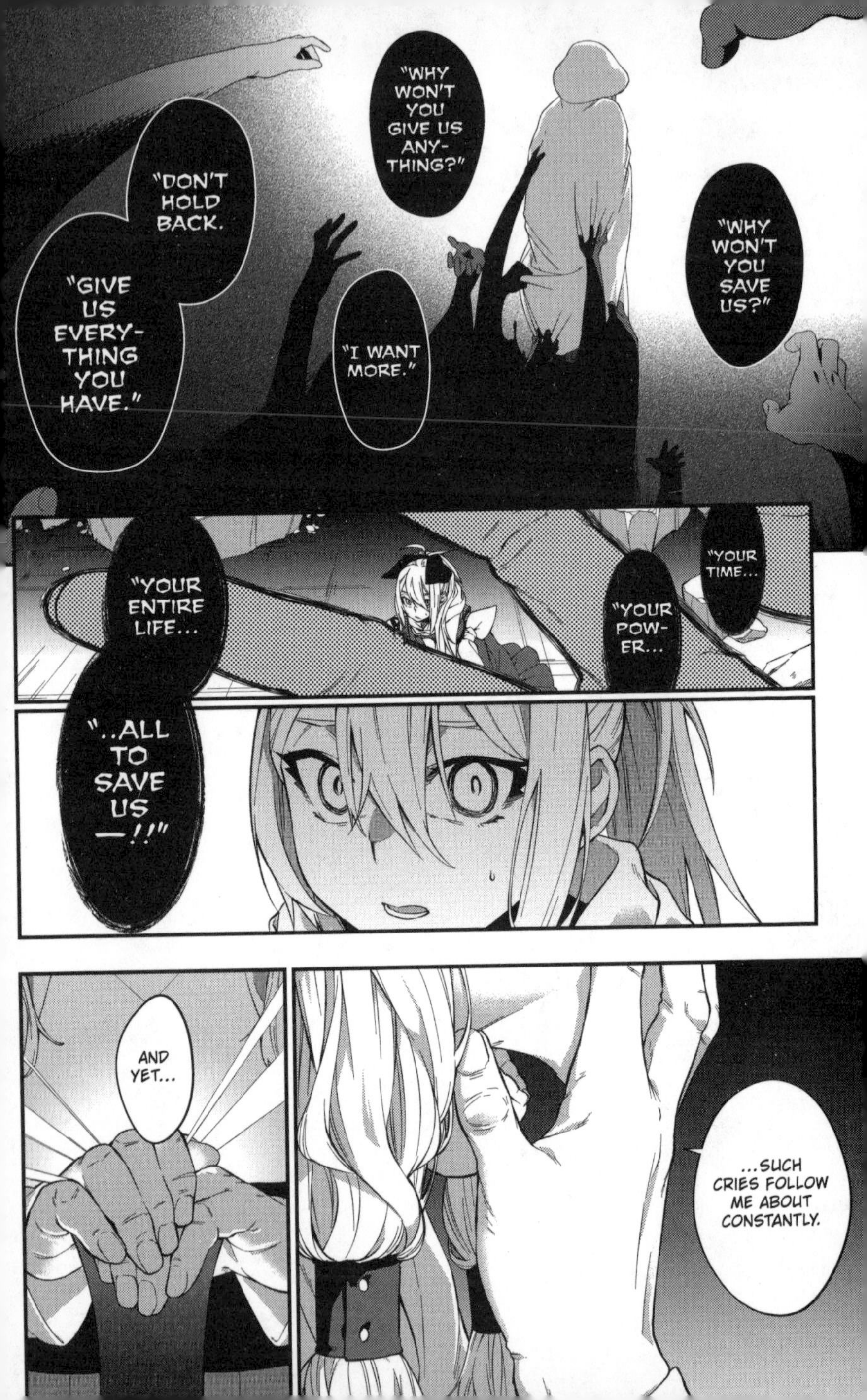
"WHY WON'T YOU GIVE US ANY-THING?"
"WHY WON'T YOU SAVE US?"
"DON'T HOLD BACK.
"I WANT MORE."
"GIVE US EVERY-THING YOU HAVE."
"YOUR TIME...
"YOUR POW-ER...
"YOUR ENTIRE LIFE...
"..ALL TO SAVE US —!!"
...SUCH CRIES FOLLOW ME ABOUT CONSTANTLY.
AND YET...

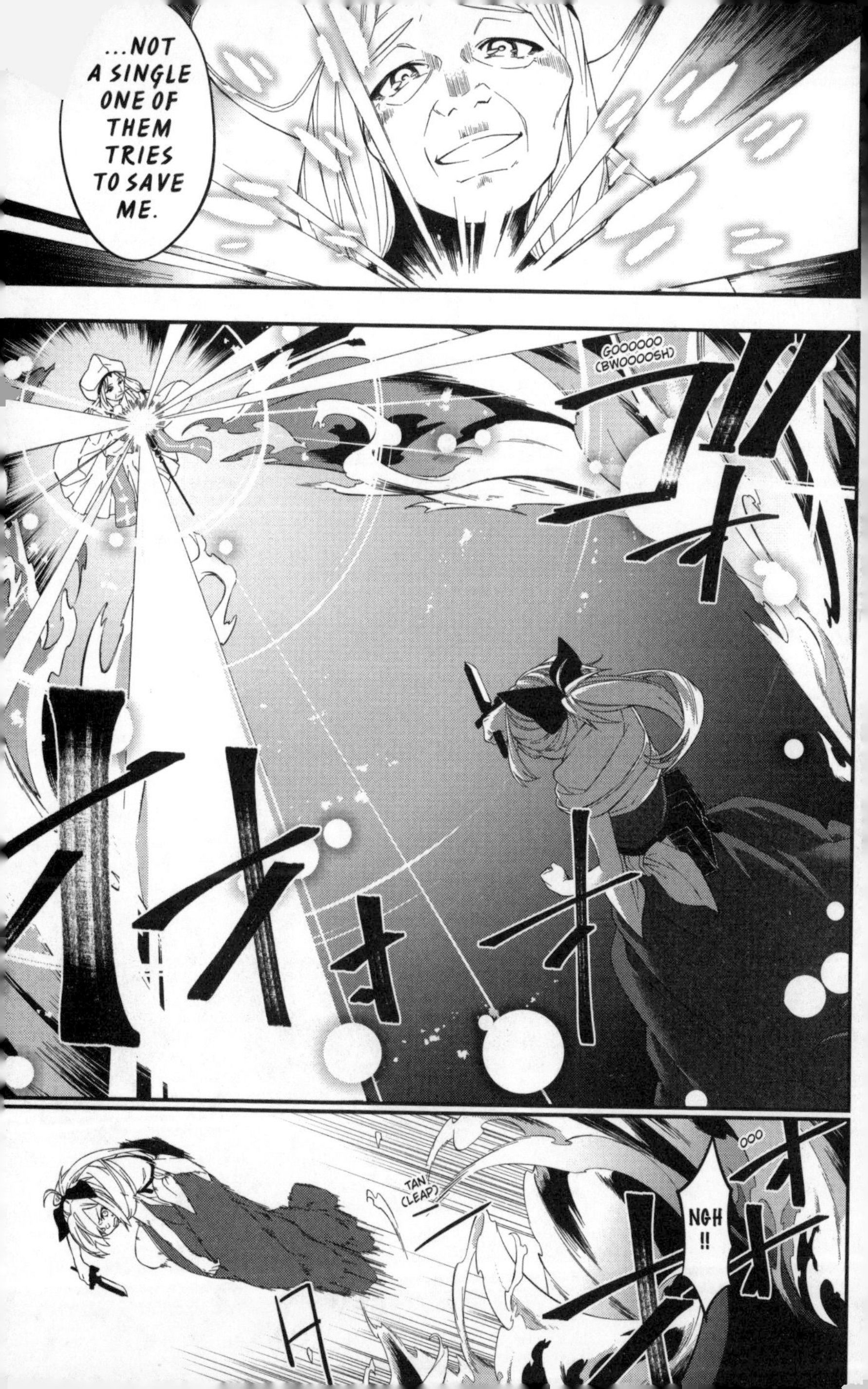
...NOT A SINGLE ONE OF THEM TRIES TO SAVE ME.
GOOOOOO (BWOOOOSH)
OOO
NGH !!
TAN (LEAP)

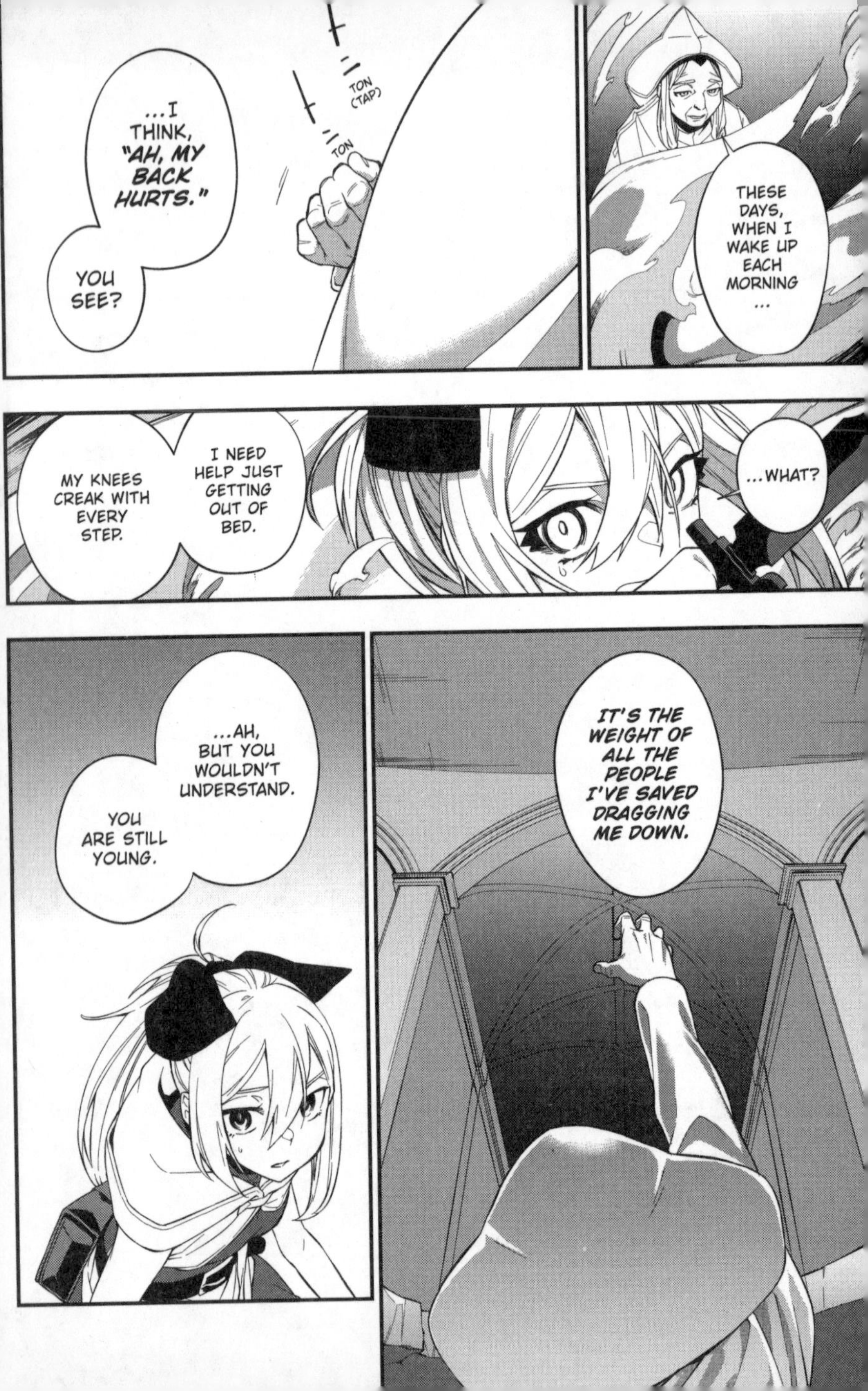
THESE DAYS, WHEN I WAKE UP EACH MORNING ...
TON (TAP)
TON
...I THINK, "AH, MY BACK HURTS."
YOU SEE?
...WHAT?
I NEED HELP JUST GETTING OUT OF BED.
MY KNEES CREAK WITH EVERY STEP.
IT'S THE WEIGHT OF ALL THE PEOPLE I'VE SAVED DRAGGING ME DOWN.
...AH, BUT YOU WOULDN'T UNDERSTAND.
YOU ARE STILL YOUNG.

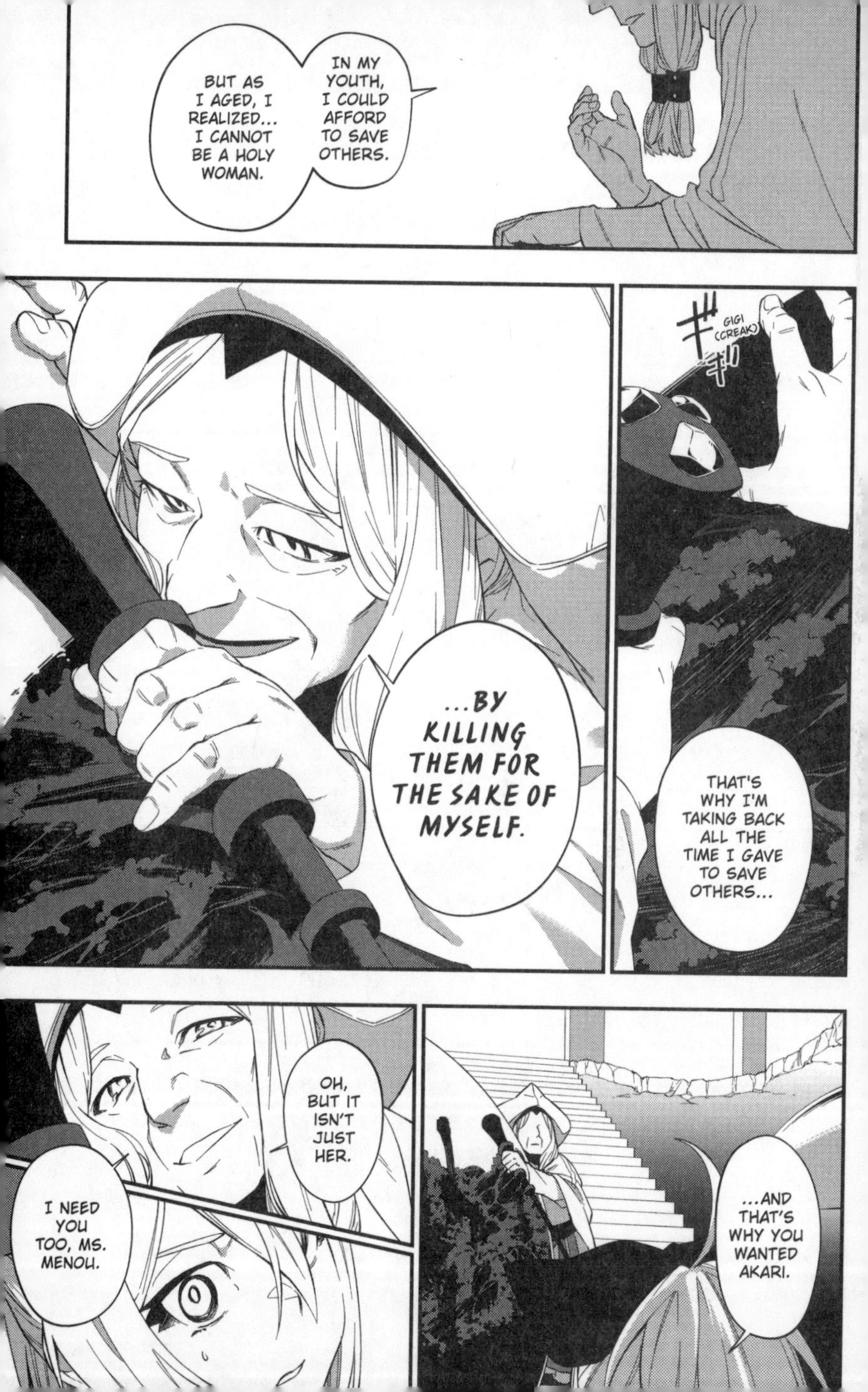
IN MY YOUTH, I COULD AFFORD TO SAVE OTHERS.
BUT AS I AGED, I REALIZED... I CANNOT BE A HOLY WOMAN.
GIGI (CREAK)
THAT'S WHY I'M TAKING BACK ALL THE TIME I GAVE TO SAVE OTHERS...
...BY KILLING THEM FOR THE SAKE OF MYSELF.
...AND THAT'S WHY YOU WANTED AKARI.
OH, BUT IT ISN'T JUST HER.
I NEED YOU TOO, MS. MENOU.

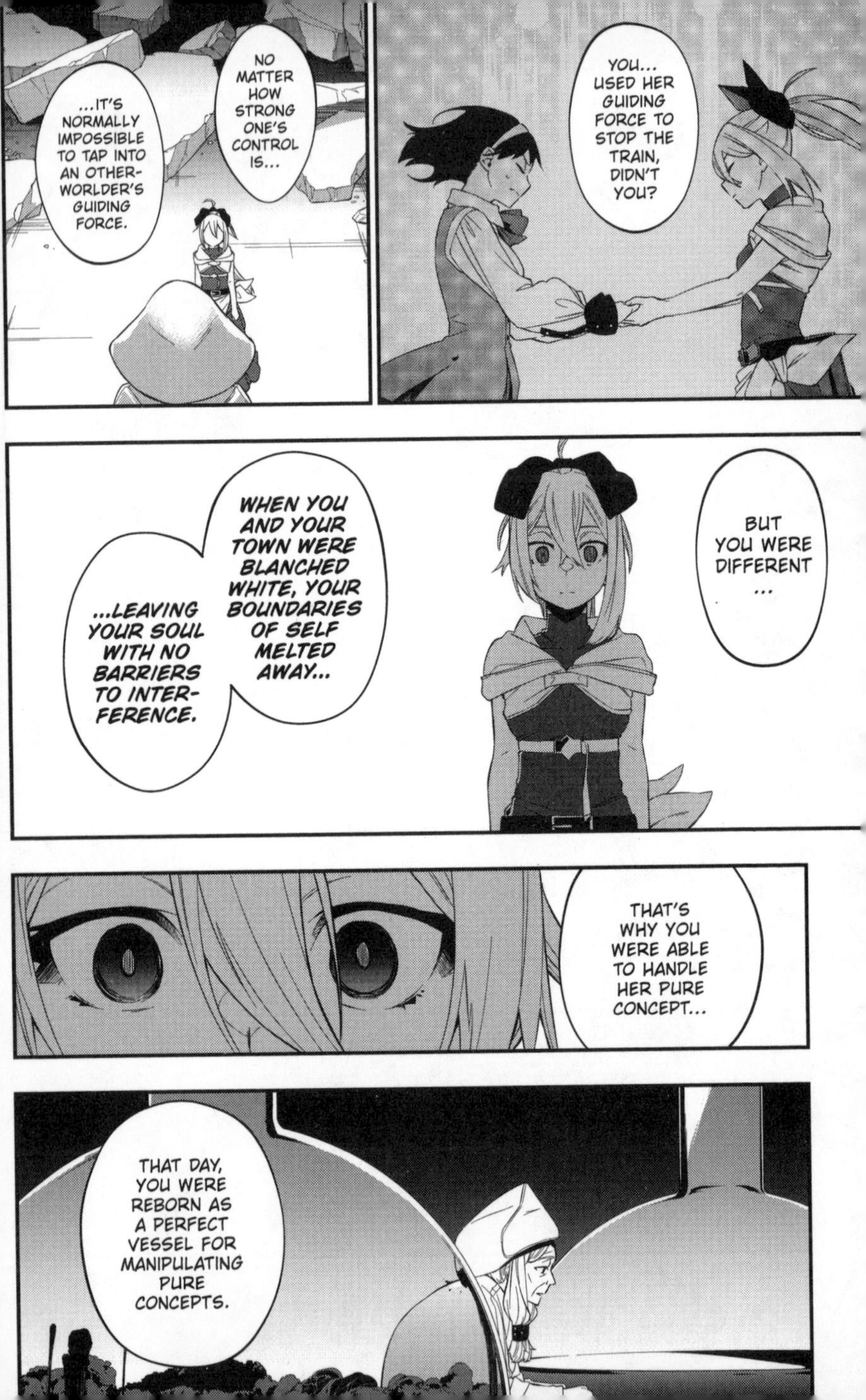
YOU... USED HER GUIDING FORCE TO STOP THE TRAIN, DIDN'T YOU?
NO MATTER HOW STRONG ONE'S CONTROL IS...
...IT'S NORMALLY IMPOSSIBLE TO TAP INTO AN OTHER-WORLDER'S GUIDING FORCE.
BUT YOU WERE DIFFERENT...
WHEN YOU AND YOUR TOWN WERE BLANCHED WHITE, YOUR BOUNDARIES OF SELF MELTED AWAY...
...LEAVING YOUR SOUL WITH NO BARRIERS TO INTERFERENCE.
THAT'S WHY YOU WERE ABLE TO HANDLE HER PURE CONCEPT...
THAT DAY, YOU WERE REBORN AS A PERFECT VESSEL FOR MANIPULATING PURE CONCEPTS.

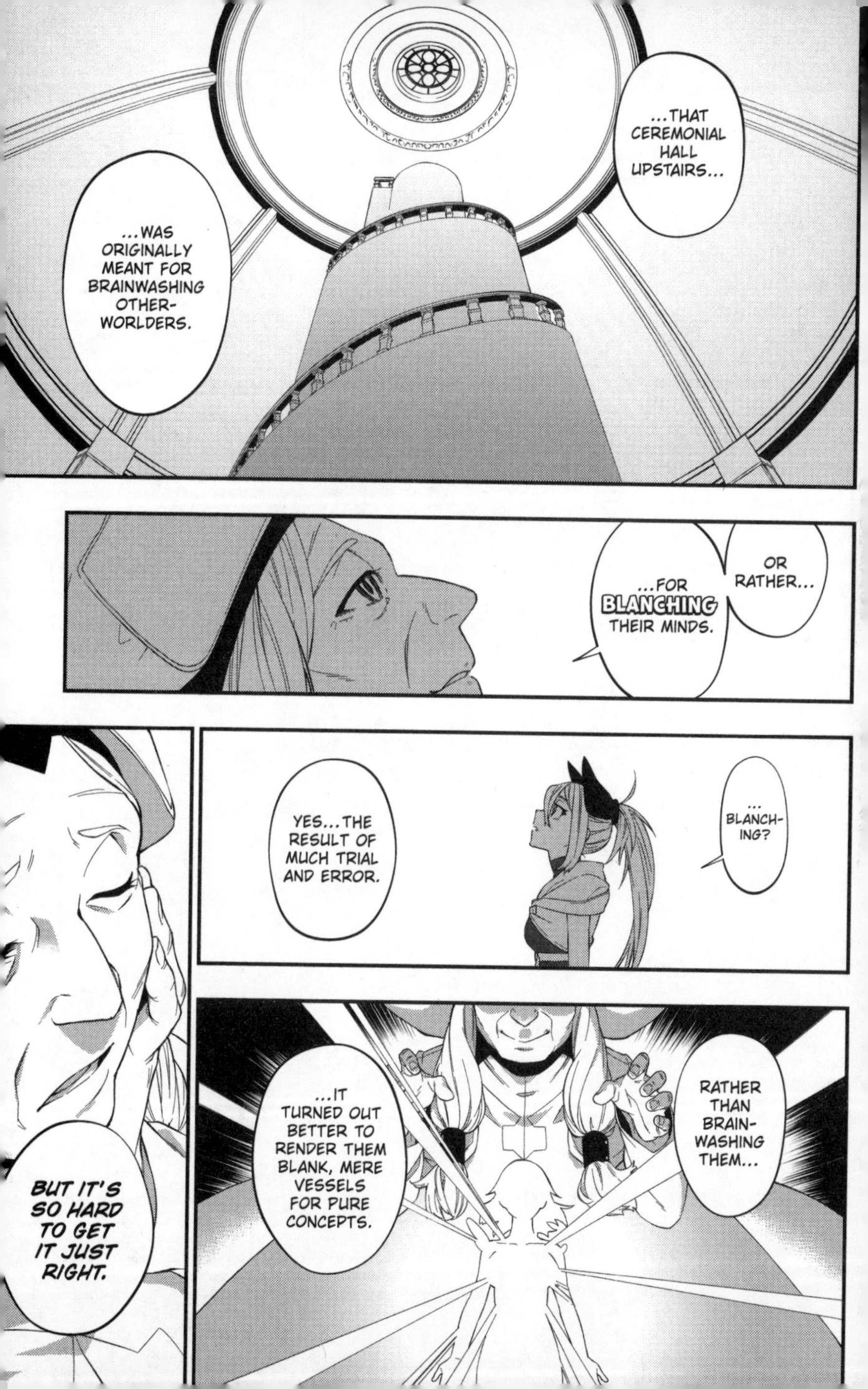
...THAT CEREMONIAL HALL UPSTAIRS...
...WAS ORIGINALLY MEANT FOR BRAINWASHING OTHER-WORLDERS.
OR RATHER...
...FOR BLANCHING THEIR MINDS.
...BLANCHING?
YES...THE RESULT OF MUCH TRIAL AND ERROR.
RATHER THAN BRAIN-WASHING THEM...
...IT TURNED OUT BETTER TO RENDER THEM BLANK, MERE VESSELS FOR PURE CONCEPTS.
BUT IT'S SO HARD TO GET IT JUST RIGHT.

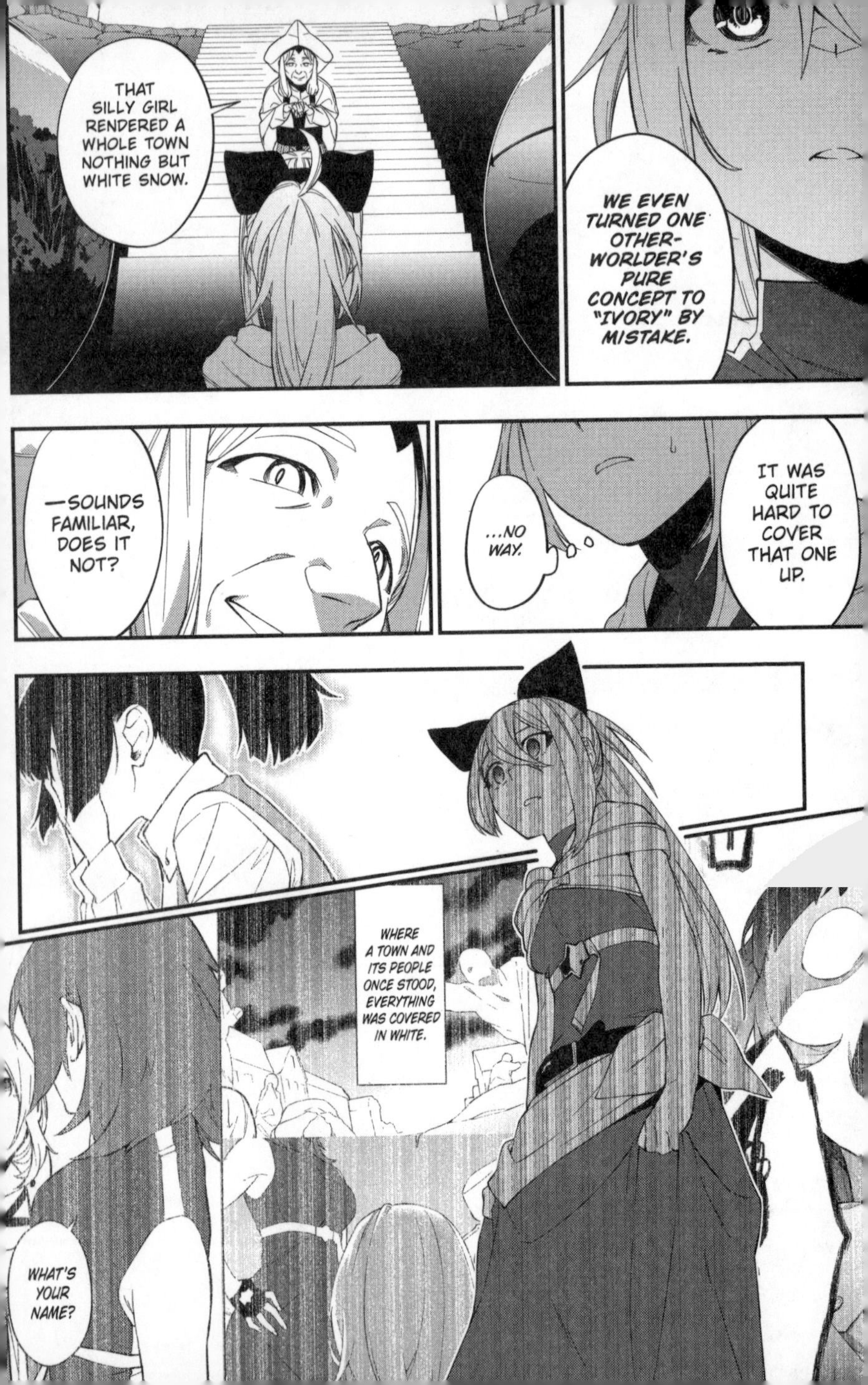
WE EVEN TURNED ONE OTHER-WORLDER'S PURE CONCEPT TO "IVORY" BY MISTAKE.
THAT SILLY GIRL RENDERED A WHOLE TOWN NOTHING BUT WHITE SNOW.
IT WAS QUITE HARD TO COVER THAT ONE UP.
...NO WAY.
—SOUNDS FAMILIAR, DOES IT NOT?
WHERE A TOWN AND ITS PEOPLE ONCE STOOD, EVERYTHING WAS COVERED IN WHITE.
WHAT'S YOUR NAME?

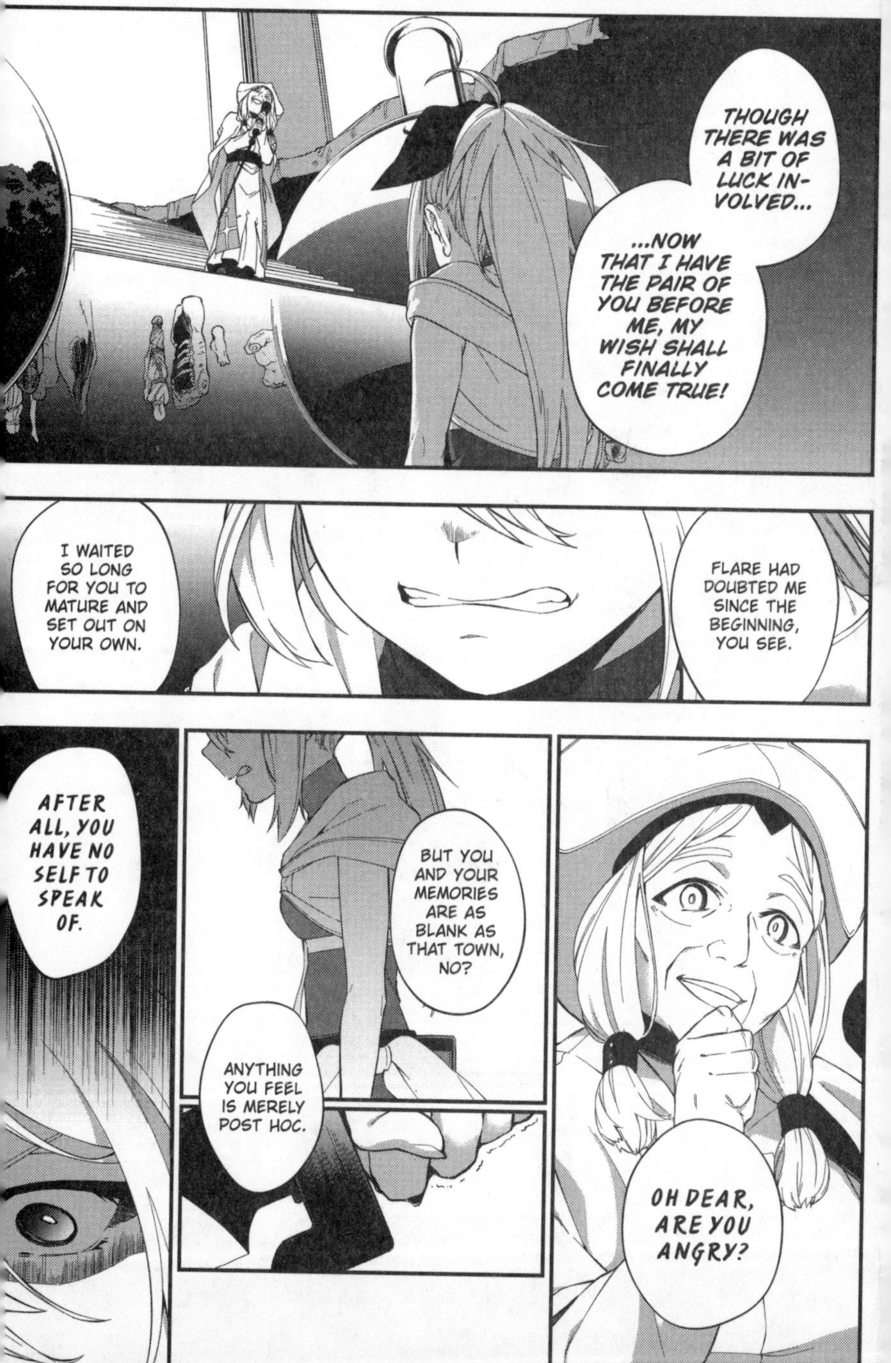
THOUGH THERE WAS A BIT OF LUCK IN-VOLVED...
...NOW THAT I HAVE THE PAIR OF YOU BEFORE ME, MY WISH SHALL FINALLY COME TRUE!
FLARE HAD DOUBTED ME SINCE THE BEGINNING, YOU SEE.
I WAITED SO LONG FOR YOU TO MATURE AND SET OUT ON YOUR OWN.
OH DEAR, ARE YOU ANGRY?
BUT YOU AND YOUR MEMORIES ARE AS BLANK AS THAT TOWN, NO?
ANYTHING YOU FEEL IS MERELY POST HOC.
AFTER ALL, YOU HAVE NO SELF TO SPEAK OF.

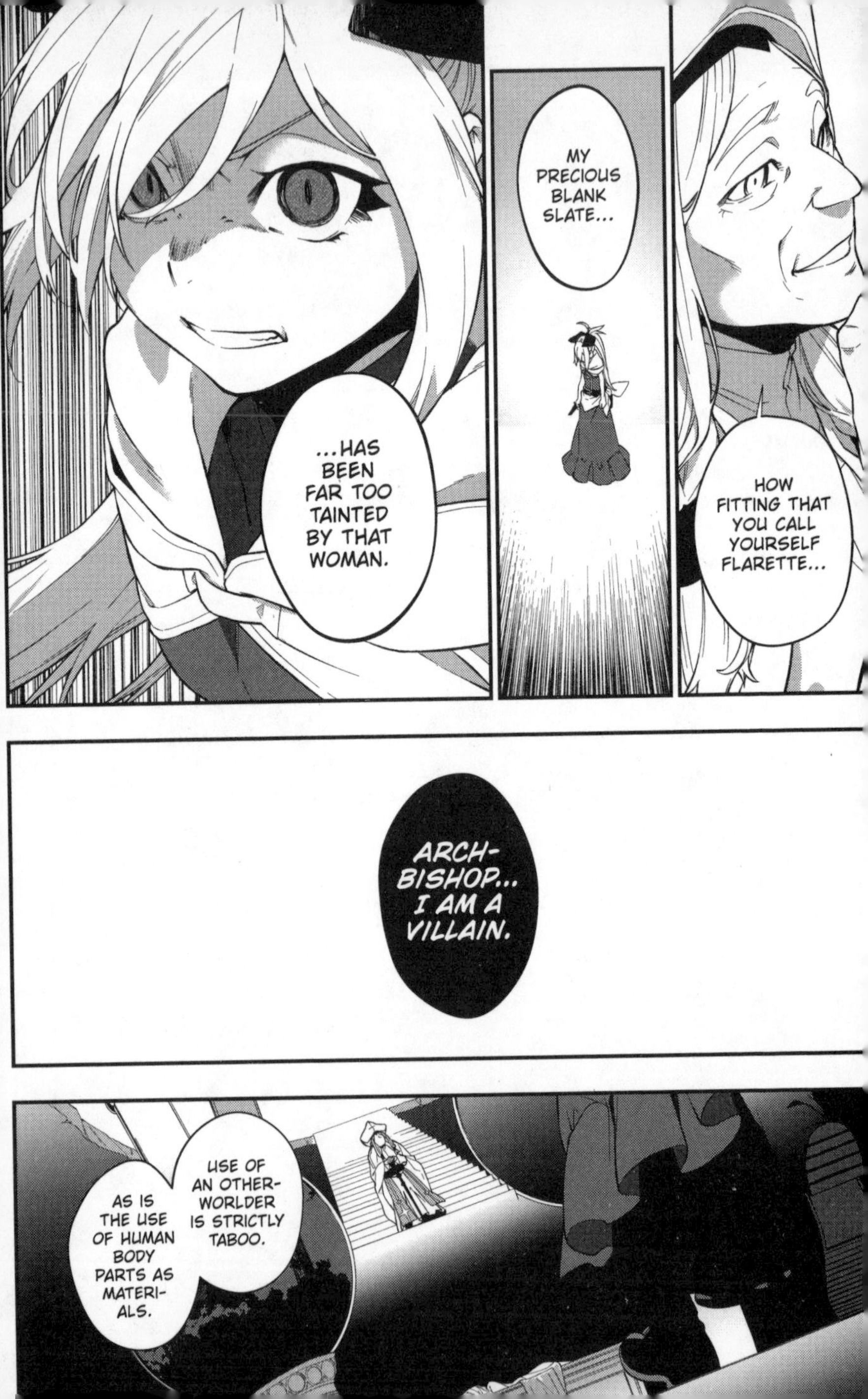
HOW FITTING THAT YOU CALL YOURSELF FLARETTE...
MY PRECIOUS BLANK SLATE...
...HAS BEEN FAR TOO TAINTED BY THAT WOMAN.
ARCH-BISHOP... I AM A VILLAIN.
USE OF AN OTHER-WORLDER IS STRICTLY TABOO.
AS IS THE USE OF HUMAN BODY PARTS AS MATERI-ALS.

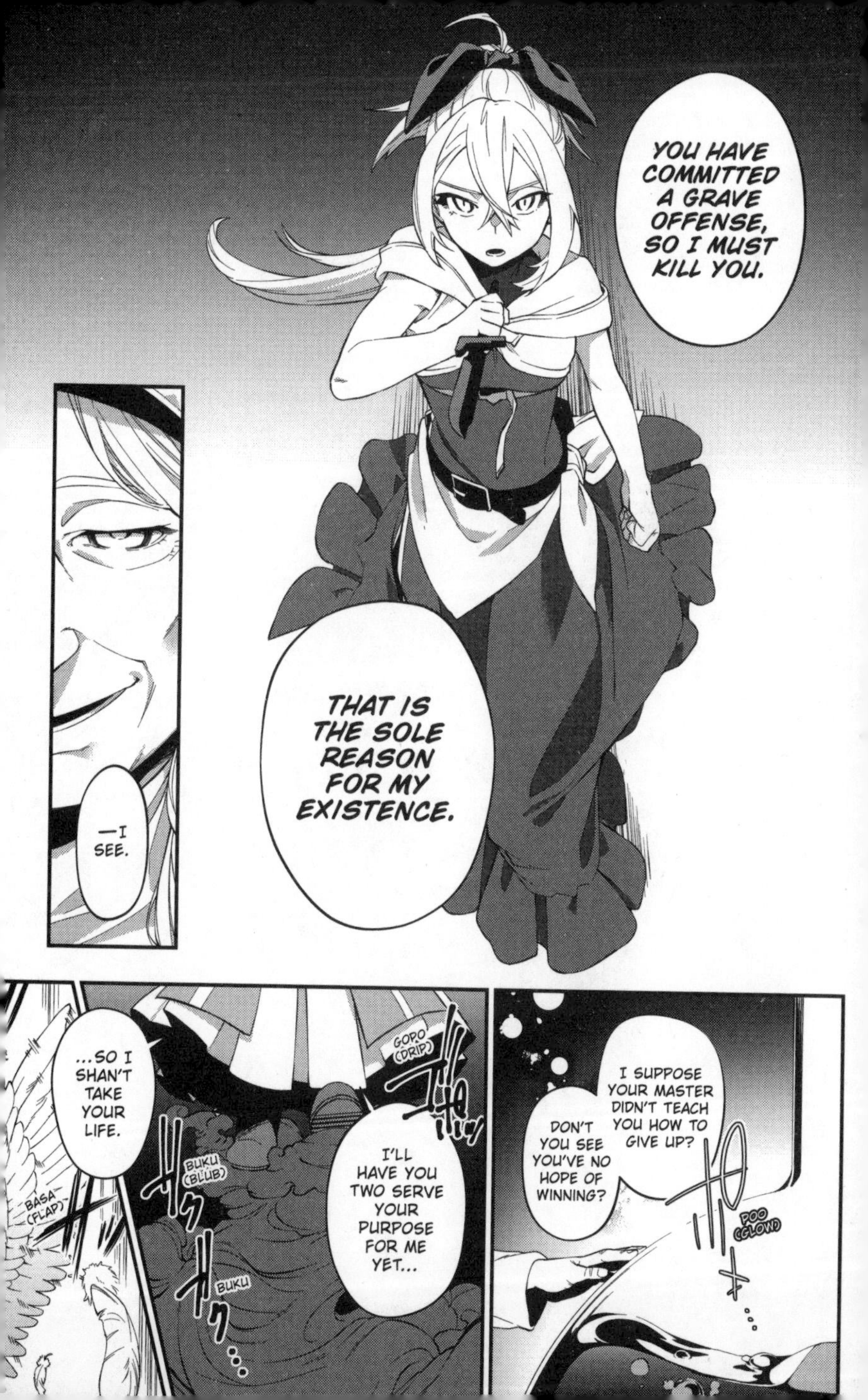
YOU HAVE COMMITTED A GRAVE OFFENSE, SO I MUST KILL YOU.
THAT IS THE SOLE REASON FOR MY EXISTENCE.
—I SEE.
I SUPPOSE YOUR MASTER DIDN'T TEACH YOU HOW TO GIVE UP?
DON'T YOU SEE YOU'VE NO HOPE OF WINNING?
POO (GLOW)
GOPO (DRIP)
...SO I SHAN'T TAKE YOUR LIFE.
I'LL HAVE YOU TWO SERVE YOUR PURPOSE FOR ME YET...
BUKU (BLUB)
BASA (FLAP)
BUKU

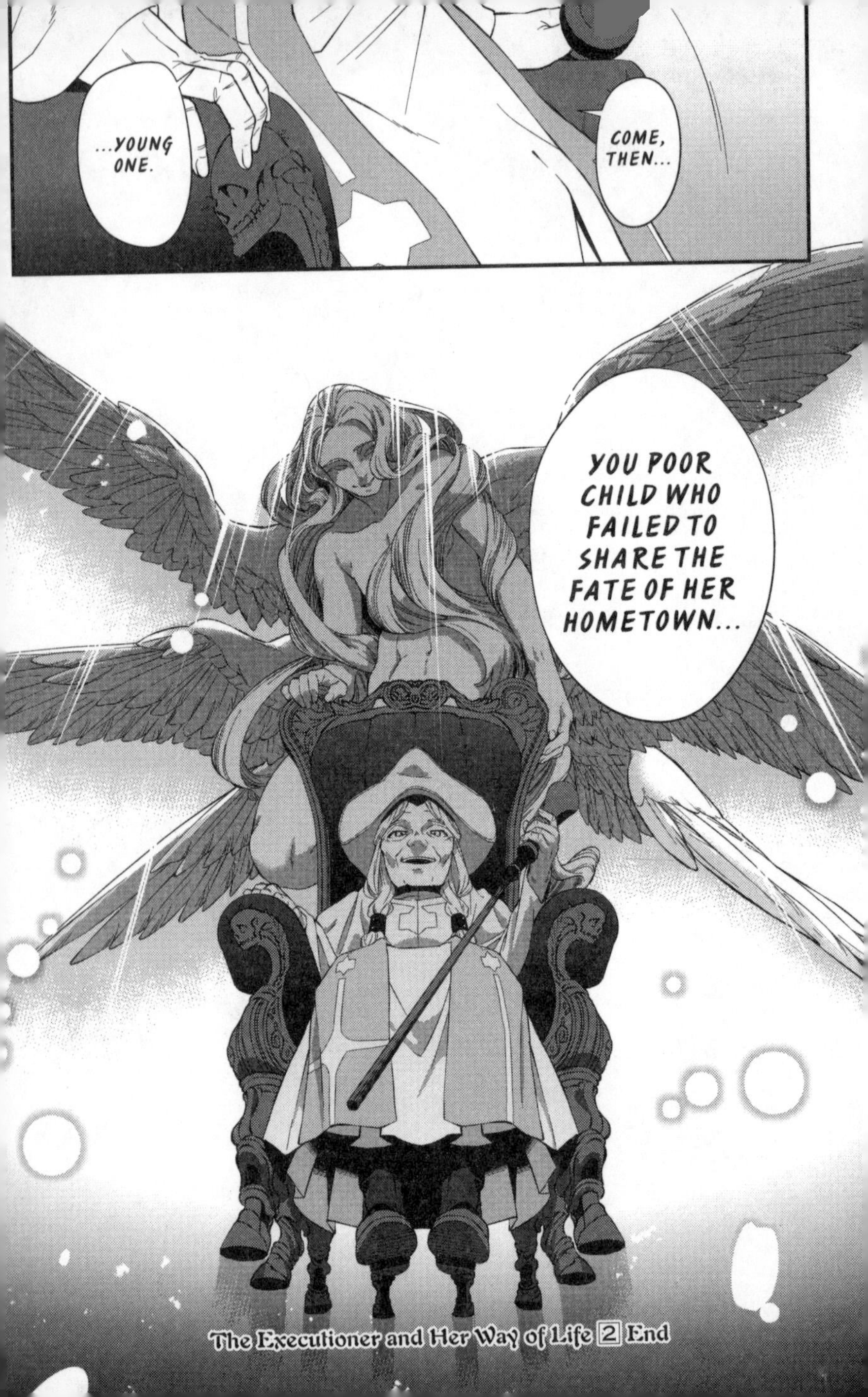
COME, THEN...
...YOUNG ONE.
YOU POOR CHILD WHO FAILED TO SHARE THE FATE OF HER HOMETOWN...
The Executioner and Her Way of Life 2 End

The Executioner and Her Way of Life

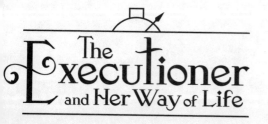

The Executioner and Her Way of Life

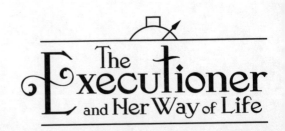

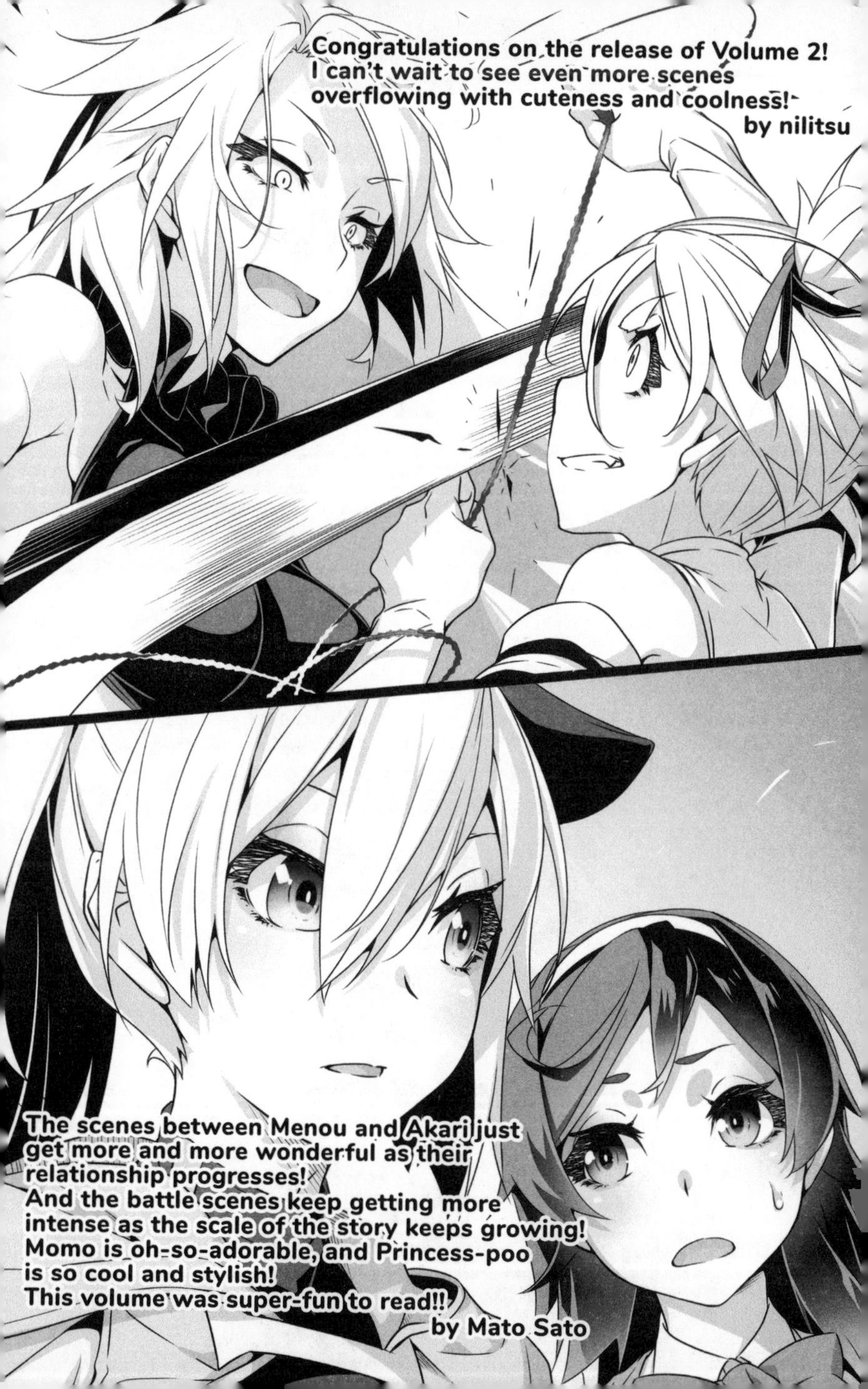
Congratulations on the release of Volume 2!
I can't wait to see even more scenes overflowing with cuteness and coolness!
by nilitsu
The scenes between Menou and Akari just get more and more wonderful as their relationship progresses!
And the battle scenes keep getting more intense as the scale of the story keeps growing!
Momo is oh-so-adorable, and Princess-poo is so cool and stylish!
This volume was super-fun to read!!
by Mato Sato

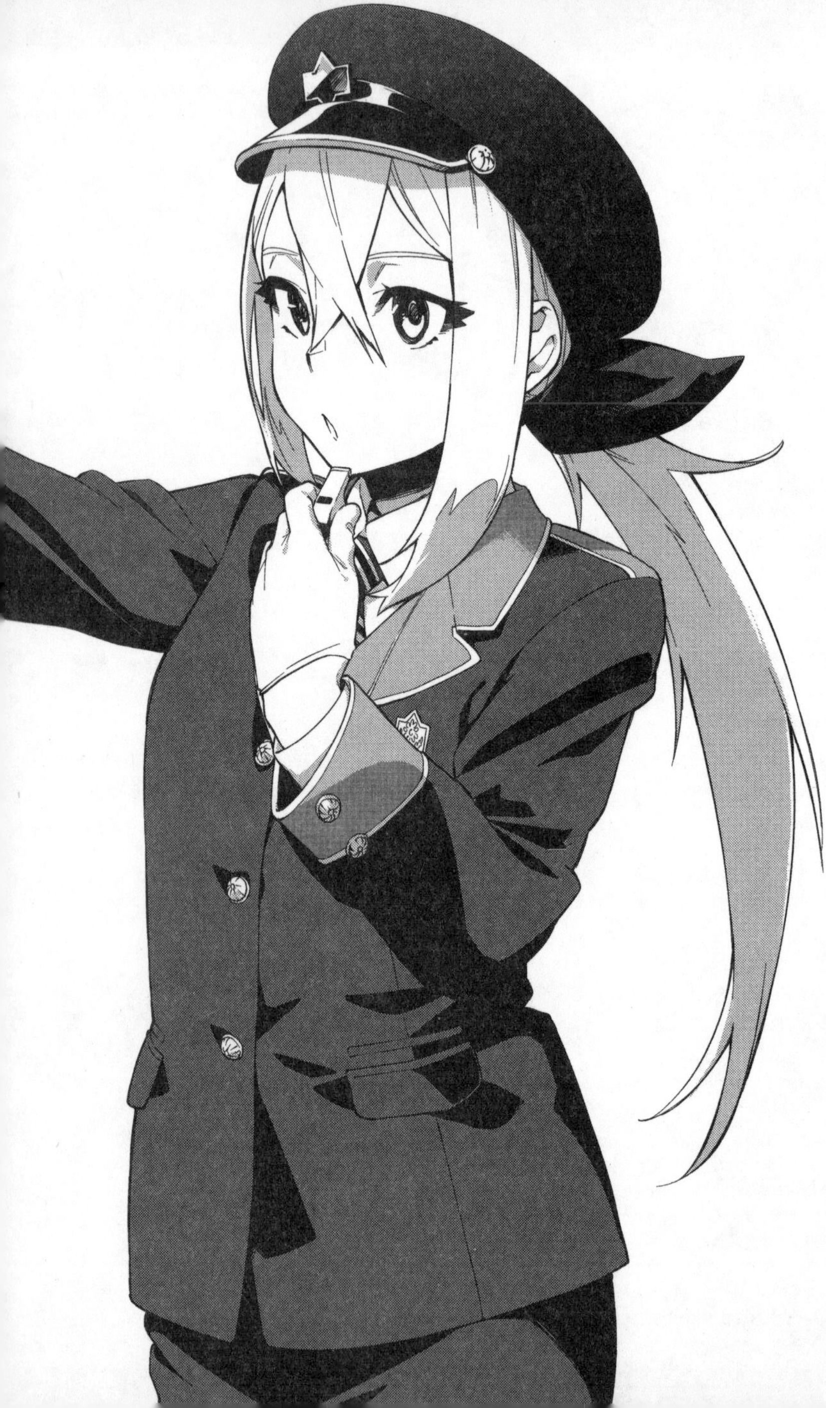

Volume 2!!

It still hasn't sunk in that I'm a real manga creator. When my editor said, "So, for Volume 2..." my first reaction was, "Huh!? What do you mean, Volume 2!?"

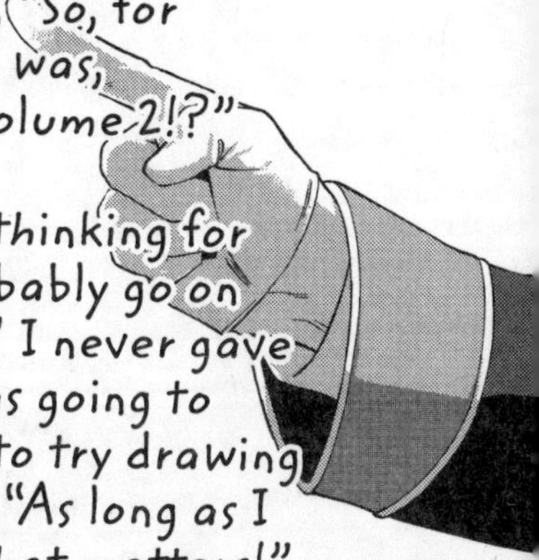

Ever since I was a kid, I kept thinking for no particular reason, "I'll probably go on drawing pictures all my life..." I never gave a second thought to how I was going to make a living until I decided to try drawing manga. Even now, I still think "As long as I can keep drawing, that's all that matters!" So maybe that's why it doesn't feel real...?

As I continue with this manga adaptation, all my days are spent thinking about how to draw and express the world of *Executioner*.

I'm sure there'll be a Volume 3 as well, so I hope I can continue to provide a little entertainment in all of your lives as the series goes on!

Ryo Mitsuya

SPECIAL THANKS

Kipoju

Namari's Brush

Kotarou Murakami

Toilet-bound Hanako-Kun

At Kamome Academy, rumors abound about the school's Seven Mysteries, one of which is Hanako-san. Said to occupy the third stall of the third floor girls' bathroom in the old school building, Hanako-san grants any wish when summoned. Nene Yashiro, an occult-loving high school girl who dreams of romance, ventures into this haunted bathroom...but the Hanako-san she meets there is nothing like she imagined! Kamome Academy's Hanako-san...is a boy!

I've Been Killing SLIMES for 300 Years and Maxed Out My Level

It's hard work taking it slow...

After living a painful life as an office worker, Azusa ended her short life by dying from overwork. So when she finds herself reincarnated as an undying, unaging witch in a new world, she vows to spend her days stress-free and as pleasantly as possible. She ekes out a living by hunting down the easiest targets—the slimes! But after centuries of doing this simple job, she's ended up with insane powers... how will she maintain her low-key life now?!

IN STORES NOW!

Light Novel Volumes 1–13

Manga Volumes 1–10

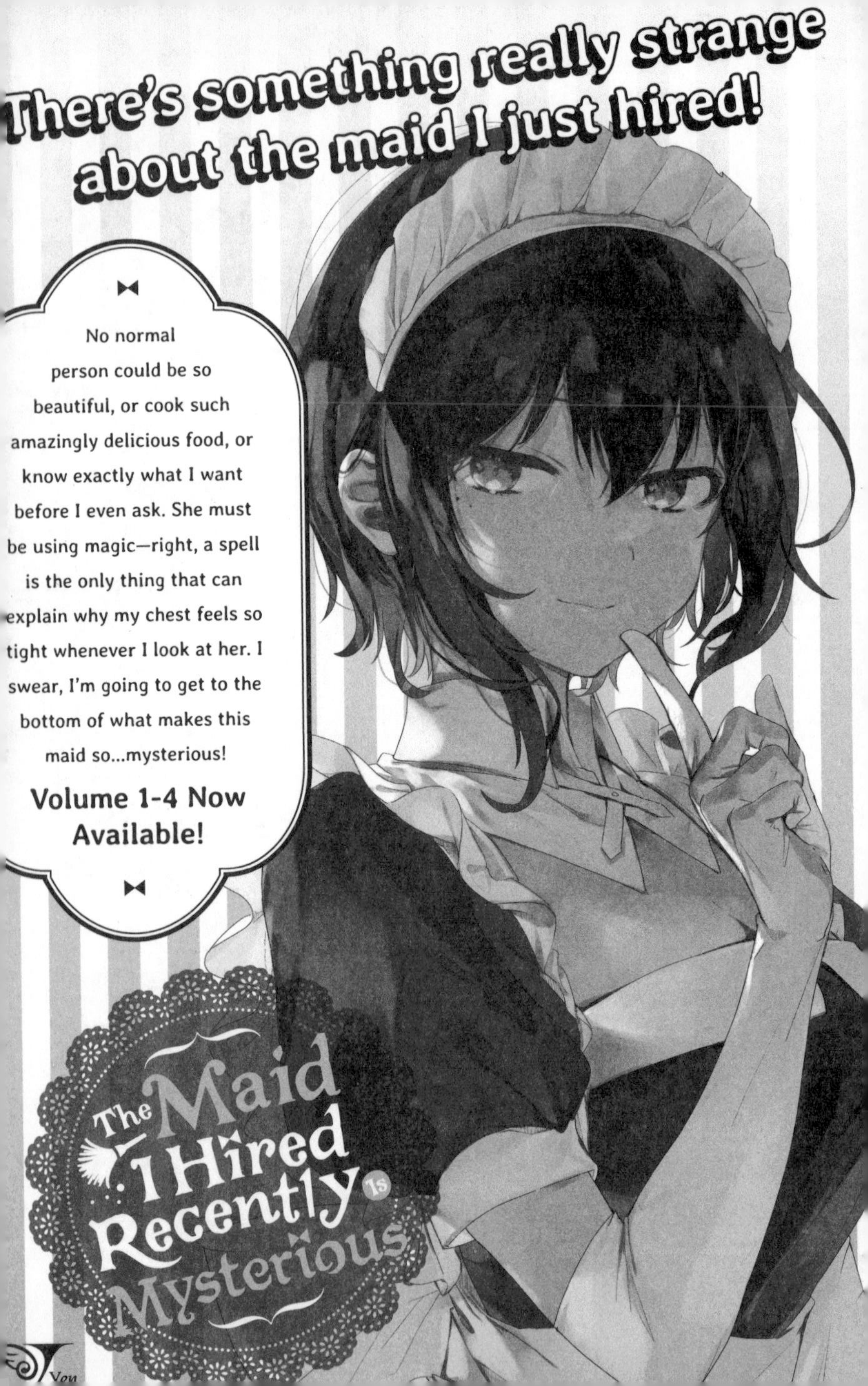
There's something really strange about the maid I just hired!
No normal person could be so beautiful, or cook such amazingly delicious food, or know exactly what I want before I even ask. She must be using magic—right, a spell is the only thing that can explain why my chest feels so tight whenever I look at her. I swear, I'm going to get to the bottom of what makes this maid so...mysterious!
Volume 1-4 Now Available!
The Maid I Hired Recently Is Mysterious

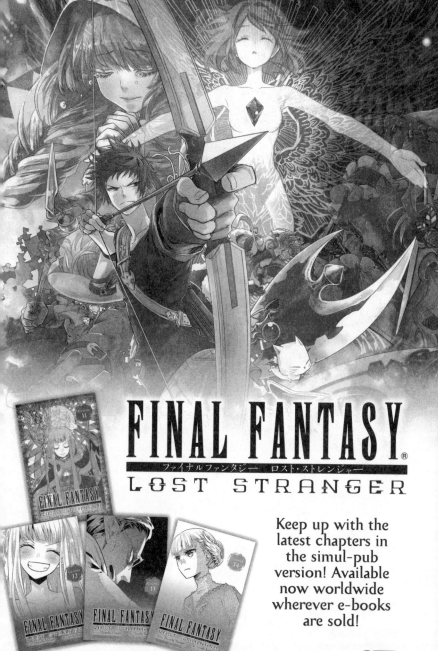

FINAL FANTASY

ファイナルファンタジー　ロスト・ストレンジャー

LOST STRANGER

Keep up with the latest chapters in the simul-pub version! Available now worldwide wherever e-books are sold!

For more information, visit www.yenpress.com

The Executioner and Her Way of Life

ORIGINAL STORY	ART	CHARACTER DESIGN
Mato Sato	Ryo Mitsuya	nilitsu

2

TRANSLATION		LETTERING
Jenny McKeon		Elena Pizarro Lanzas

SHOKEISHOUJO NO VIRGIN ROAD vol. 2
©Mato Sato/SB Creative Corp.
Original Character Designs: ©nilitsu/SB Creative Corp.
©2021 Ryo Mitsuya/SQUARE ENIX CO., LTD.
First published in Japan in 2021 by SQUARE ENIX CO., LTD. English translation rights arranged with SQUARE ENIX CO., LTD. And Yen Press, LLC through TUTTLE-MORI AGENCY, INC.

Yen Press
150 West 30th Street, 19th Floor
New York, NY 10001

Visit us at yenpress.com ◆ facebook.com/yenpress ◆ twitter.com/yenpress
yenpress.tumblr.com ◆ instagram.com/yenpress

First Yen Press Edition: March 2023
Edited by Yen Press Editorial: Jacquelyn Li, Carl Li
Designed by Yen Press Design: Liz Parlett

Yen Press is an imprint of Yen Press, LLC.
The Yen Press name and logo are trademarks of Yen Press, LLC.

Library of Congress Control Number: 2022940171

ISBNs: 978-1-9753-5229-5 (paperback)
978-1-9753-5230-1 (ebook)

1 3 5 7 9 10 8 6 4 2

WOR

Printed in the United States of America

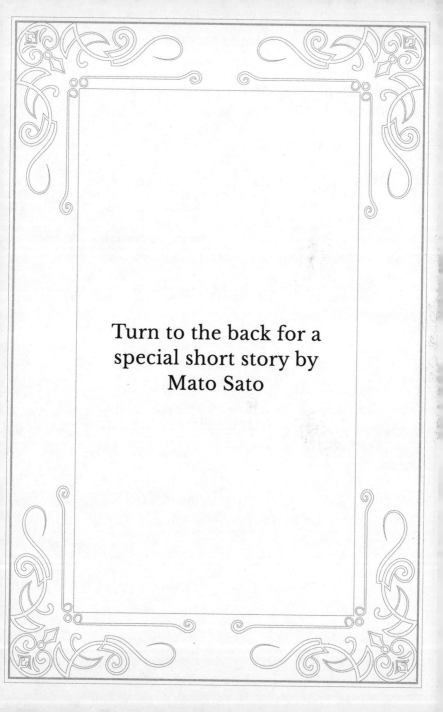

Turn to the back for a special short story by Mato Sato

broke through obstacles by using Guiding Enhancement to increase her natural strength, just as she did during the·combat exam. Since Momo possessed more raw force than most, the amount of time it took to invoke complicated scripture conjurings wasn't worth it to her.

"Hmph. That means you'll have no advantage against someone who has as much Guiding Force as you do. What do you plan to do then?"

"Nothing, really. I suppose I'll run away or ignore them."

"And what if they chase you down because of a grudge?"

"Well... Let's see."

A person with Guiding Force power to match Momo's... She could think of only one response if she was forced to battle such a foe.

"That would be incredibly annoying, I'm sure."

Momo wrinkled her nose with utter distaste, as though to suggest she never wished to meet that sort of person.

Faust—specifically, to don the white robes of a priestess's aide. Her natural skills and wits got her through the written test and interview, leaving the combat exam as her final trial.

Momo required only Guiding Enhancement to defeat the priestess. She handily outpaced her opponent's movements and crushed her attempts at scripture conjurings. It was an overwhelming victory via sheer Guiding Force strength, a talent that seemed to indicate that Momo was chosen by the heavens.

When she was little, such immense power in that petite frame made her emotionally unstable, but her wild behavior calmed when she found a trusted role model she called her "darling." Momo's natural talents were impressive even among the Faust. However, she had one fatal flaw.

"Your reliance on brute strength hasn't changed a bit, though."

"I don't need scripture conjurings to fight. And I've learned the most helpful support conjurings."

Momo responded quite indifferently to her master's observation.

She rarely used scripture conjurings, which required highly advanced Guiding Force manipulation. In most cases, she

The deciding blow sent a shock wave through the ground.

"Eeek...!"

The priestess who'd been called upon to serve as a test opponent tumbled to the ground with a shriek. Despite the embarrassing display, she was still a Faust priestess. She was strong enough to take on a similarly ranked knight, a Noblesse warrior, and win easily.

However, she'd been soundly defeated during a combat exam for Faust promotion by a girl young enough to be dubbed a child.

The little girl who'd shattered the priestess's pride with an overwhelming victory wore her pink hair in pigtails tied by two red ribbons. Her petite body clad in a nun's habit, she turned away from the crater her bare fist had created without even a backward glance.

"That's good enough, isn't it, Master?"

"I'd say so. No one could argue with those results. You pass, Momo."

The woman she called Master, also known as Flare, nodded magnanimously at the pupil from her monastery.

While Menou trained to become the youngest Executioner of all time, Momo was testing to become a member of the

The idea was merely a whim, yet it sounded surprisingly appealing.

Strong warriors in positions of power, especially the high-ranking priestesses of the Faust, were bound by many limitations. But what of those who dwelled in the dark underbelly of society? If a knight like Ashuna tried to bring evildoers back in line, she might just find a strong opponent where she least expected it.

"I suppose I'll start by traveling within our kingdom."

There was no time like the present for such ideas, so Ashuna prepared for her journey at once.

She saw no reason to remain within Grisarika's borders after roving the local areas. Perhaps, in her travels, she would encounter a stronger foe and get the chance to immerse herself in battle fully. Or she might discover a worthy opponent who would be her rival, crossing swords with her repeatedly.

If she could meet such a person...

"Why, that would be far more fun than falling in love."

Her heart danced with excitement over this yet-unseen adversary.

Lately, she was beginning to find the ease of all her triumphs a bit hollow.

How long had it been since she could truly unleash her full strength in practice? A princess of Grisarika Kingdom, Ashuna had qualified for knighthood and the right to carry a sword at fifteen. In only a few years, she had built up an impressive level of strength until there was virtually no one left on the royal grounds capable of matching her in battle.

Now that her battle prowess had grown so much, Ashuna was starved for a worthy opponent.

The Faust priestesses were seasoned warriors, but women of the cloth had no reason to cross blades with her. Surely the kingdom's strongest knight, who served Ashuna's elder sister, could easily parry Ashuna's deadliest attack. Unfortunately, he wouldn't do as an opponent for reasons wholly unrelated to strength.

Not only was Ashuna naturally blessed with immense Guiding Force, but she'd also forged herself into a wild and quick-witted warrior.

"Perhaps I should go on a journey..." Ashuna whispered the half-formed thought aloud. The day had ended, and she was back in her room.

The mock battle ended with the single strike of a sword.

"A grave miscalculation on my part... I yield."

The knight's blade had been knocked to the ground; his opponent's weapon hovered above his neck. He could hardly call himself a knight if he didn't acknowledge defeat here, so he raised both hands in surrender.

However, the knight showed no disappointment at his loss. If anything, his cheeks were flushed from admiration and respect.

"You never cease to amaze, Princess Ashuna. It's just as they say: You are peerless among knights and men."

"No need to flatter me. You fought well in your own right. Your swordsmanship was steadfast. The foundation that is your lengthy training is clear."

"Thank you very much! I'll continue working hard to be useful to the royal family!!"

Polite to the very end and still burning with passion, the knight left the training ground. Ashuna watched him go, maintaining the relaxed dignity of a victor and a royal, but her shoulders slumped with a sigh soon after.

"Peerless, eh...?"

The Executioner and
Her Way of Life
Special Short Story

Mato Sato

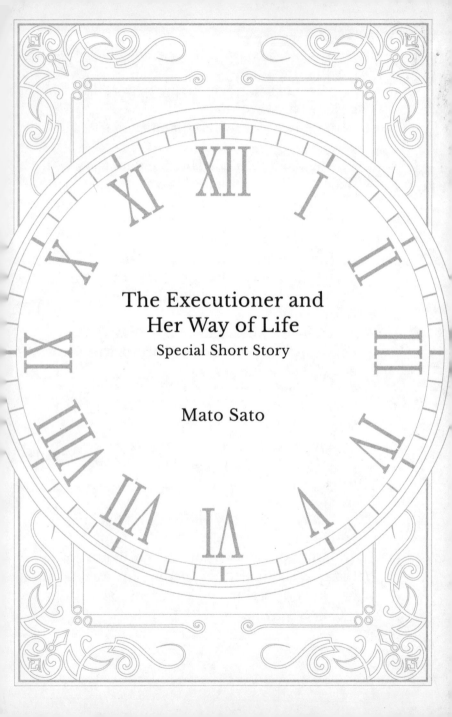